EMPEROR
OF
RUIN

Praise for *Ashes of the Sun*

"Wexler's post-apocalyptic world is rich with history and fascinating in its inventive combination of magic, alchemy, and technology. This standout series opener is a winner: intricate, immersive, and irresistible."
—*Booklist* (starred review)

"Wexler demonstrates a talent for worldbuilding... Familial tension, magic, and politics combine to kick this series off to a powerful start."
—*Publishers Weekly*

"*Ashes of the Sun* exists in the grey space between science fiction and fantasy, creating a world that felt fresh yet familiar at the same time... [It] evokes the expansive feel of some of my favorite sci-fi shows... I'll be eagerly waiting to see how it unfolds."   —*Fantasy Book Critic*

"*Ashes of the Sun* is an enormously fun, thought-provoking novel that is an outstanding launch novel for a series. Highly, highly recommended."
—*SFFWorld*

"There are monsters to fight and relics from a now-vanished, more advanced civilisation, which makes for some colourful world-building... The prose and pacing are strong, bolstered by impressively vivid action scenes."   —*SFX*

"Wexler's best work yet... *Ashes of the Sun* has scale and pace, and tension and batshit cool scenery, and I enjoyed it a hell of lot. (It's also queer as hell: that's always a nice bonus.) And I can't wait to see what comes next."

—*Tor.com*

"A real high-octane, dystopian fantasy thrill-ride... There are some extremely exciting showdowns, skirmishes, and fights against grotesque monstrosities... This novel acts as a complete standalone yet there is still so much to see and explore in Wexler's world."

—*Grimdark*

Praise for *Blood of the Chosen*

"An outstanding adventure with a swiftly paced narrative and fully developed characters who readers come to care about, *Blood of the Chosen* shows how the power of love can overcome political and racial differences. Wexler's many fans will rejoice, and science fantasy readers will be enthralled by this grand tale."

—*Booklist* (starred review)

"Burningblade & Silvereye is kind of a perfect blend of sci-fi and fantasy, and I wouldn't hesitate to recommend these books to fans of either genre. These books are fast-paced and fun, but also super gut-punchy and emotional... This book was just so badass and amazing, and I love everything about this world and these characters!"

—*Grimdark Dad*

"*Blood of the Chosen* is another excellent adventure in this fantasy/sci-fi hybrid world."

—*Fantasy Book Critic*

"A unique setting, an action-packed plot, and two opposed but simultaneously sympathetic narratives... This is a thrilling dream you can happily lose yourself in."

—*British Fantasy Society*

BY DJANGO WEXLER

BURNINGBLADE & SILVEREYE

Ashes of the Sun
Blood of the Chosen
Emperor of Ruin

THE SHADOW CAMPAIGNS

The Thousand Names
The Shadow Throne
The Price of Valor
The Guns of Empire
The Infernal Battalion

EMPEROR
OF
RUIN

Burningblade & Silvereye
Book 3

DJANGO WEXLER

An Ad Astra Book

First published in the UK in 2023 by Head of Zeus,
part of Bloomsbury Publishing Plc

9 7 5 3 1 2 4 6 8

A catalogue record for this book is available from the British Library.

Cover illustration by Scott Fischer
Map and chapter ornaments by Charis Loke

ISBN (HB): 9781801101424
ISBN (XTPB): 9781801101431
ISBN (E): 9781801101455

Printed and bound by CPI Group (UK) Ltd, Croydon, CR0 4YY

Head of Zeus Ltd
First Floor East
5–8 Hardwick Street
London EC1R 4RG
WWW.HEADOFZEUS.COM

For ZeraMax

THE ARCHIVE

SNOWSPEAR

LEVIATHAN'S WOMB

DEEPFIRE

Grœll

Meltrock

UQARIS

Drail

OBSTADT

LITNIN

River Gelu

Splinter Kingdoms

River Ghio

SPIRE KOTZED

Elven City

THE PURIFIER

Cliffedge

Khirkhaz

River Abrœm

100 KM

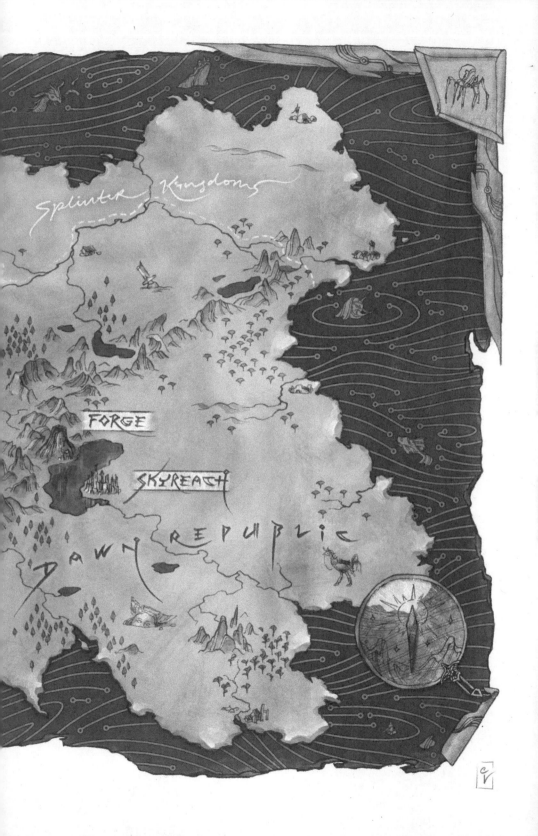

Cast of Characters

(as of the end of *Blood of the Chosen*)

Yora's crew in Deepfire

Yora—daughter of the famous failed revolutionary Kaidan Hidden-edge, and leader of a group of thieves and rebels opposed to the rule of **Dux Raskos Rottentooth**. Killed by **Tanax** in the centarchs' ambush of her group.

Gyre Silvereye—also known as Halfmask for the mask he wore to hide his missing eye. See the series recap.

Sarah—an arcanist and scavenger. Badly wounded by blaster fire in the centarchs' ambush, losing an arm, which was later replaced by a ghoul prosthetic. Traveled with **Gyre** to Khirkhaz and formed a relationship with **Elariel**. Escaped from the Purifier with Gyre and **Maya**.

Nevin—a thief and **Sarah**'s boyfriend. Disappeared after the centarchs' ambush.

Ibb—a scavenger. Abandoned the group for civilian life when **Kit**'s assignments proved too dangerous.

Harrow—a scavenger and animal handler. Tunnelborn, with a crush on **Yora**. Killed by a ghoul construct on one of **Kit**'s assignments.

Lynnia Sharptongue—an elderly alchemist and a close friend of **Yora**'s, with many connections to the underground.

Kitsraea Doomseeker ("Kit")—a famous scavenger, secretly working for the ghouls of Refuge. Ultimately traveled with **Gyre** and **Naumoriel** to Leviathan's Womb, and was mortally wounded in the confrontation atop the Leviathan. Gyre transferred her mind into the construct's analytica, and she currently inhabits its swarm of construct bodies.

Government of Deepfire

Dux Raskos Rottentooth—appointed governor of Deepfire for the Republic. Venal and corrupt. **Maya** exposed his involvement in a smuggling ring, and he fled Deepfire ahead of orders for his arrest.

Guria Fairshot—head of Deepfire's Auxiliaries, and **Raskos**' right-hand man. Arrested after **Maya** exposed Raskos.

Ghouls of Refuge

Naumoriel—Minister of the Exterior for the city of Refuge. Obsessed with restoring the Leviathan and using it to destroy the Order, he tasked **Kit** with finding the necessary arcana. Ultimately killed by **Gyre** to prevent the Leviathan from being unleashed on humanity.

Elariel—**Naumoriel**'s young assistant and **Kit**'s handler. Sentenced to death for **Naumoriel**'s failures. Her sentence was commuted to exile so she could help **Gyre** in Khirkhaz, and she was forcibly altered to appear human. In a relationship with **Sarah**. Escaped from the Purifier with Gyre and **Maya**.

Tyraves—new Minister of the Exterior after **Naumoriel**'s death. Helped **Gyre** set up the Khirkhaz expedition.

The Twilight Order

Maya Burningblade—agathios to **Jaedia**, later a full centarch. See the series recap.

Jaedia Suddenstorm—a centarch. Master to **Maya** and **Marn** and former agathios to **Basel**. Kept away from the Forge and Order politics. Ambushed and taken over by a "black spider," she traveled to Leviathan's Womb with **Nicomidi** before being confronted by Maya, **Tanax**, and **Beq**. Broke the black spider's control to save Maya and was saved by her in turn, but lapsed into a coma afterward.

Marn—agathios to **Jaedia**. Captured by *dhakim* and later rescued by **Maya**. Sent to the countryside to recover.

Baselanthus Coldflame—a Kyriliarch of the Council, leader of the Pragmatic faction. Master to **Jaedia**. Originally installed the Thing into **Maya**'s body.

Nicomidi Thunderclap—a Kyriliarch of the Council, leader of the Dogmatic faction. Master to **Tanax**. Revealed as a traitor to the Order, and allied to the spider-controlled **Jaedia**. Killed by her at Leviathan's Womb when he outlived his usefulness.

Prodominus Scatterbolt—a Kyriliarch of the Council, leader of the small Revivalist faction. Has a reputation for eccentricity. Followed **Maya** to the Purifier, confronted the **Corruptor**, and was killed helping everyone else escape.

Evinda Stonecutter—a centarch, well respected and politically neutral.

Va'aht Thousandcuts—a centarch, member of the Dogmatic faction. Originally took **Maya** from her home and destroyed **Gyre**'s eye. Defeated and wounded by Gyre at Spire Kotzed, but escaped.

Tanax Brokenedge—agathios to **Nicomidi**, later a full centarch. A rival to **Maya** on their first mission as agathia, but became an ally once his master's treachery was revealed. He and **Beq** are the only ones who know about the link between Maya and **Gyre**. Currently in Skyreach on assignment.

Varo Plagueluck—a scout and friend of **Maya**'s. Notorious for his disaster stories. Accompanied Maya to Khirkhaz and escaped with her and **Gyre** from the Purifier.

Bequaria ("Beq")—an arcanist and **Maya**'s lover. Went to Leviathan's Womb with Maya and knows about her link with **Gyre**. Accompanied Maya to Khirkhaz and escaped with her and Gyre from the Purifier.

Khirkhaz

Baron Apphia Kotzed—one of the Lightning Barons, driven from her ancestral seat for resisting Republic rule. Founder and tenuously in command of the Khirkhaz Commune. Became lovers with **Gyre** during the campaign to retake Spire Kotzed.
Nina Kotzed—**Apphia**'s teenage younger sister, also with the Commune.
Brennard—captain of **Apphia**'s guard, a tough professional soldier.
Vaela Racent Truestrike—elderly noblewoman of Khirkhaz and a leader in the Commune.

Empire of Ruin

Nial-Est-Ashok, the Corruptor—a Chosen warped into a monster with *dhaka*, creator of the black spiders and mastermind of the plot to get **Maya** to activate the Purifier.
The Eldest—one of the black spiders controlling a number of villages on the Forsaken Coast. Destroyed by **Maya**.

Series Recap

Gyre, accompanied by Kit's constructs, searches for a way back into Refuge. When he finally finds an entrance, he's captured and hauled before the Geraia, where Elariel is on trial for her life. Gyre convinces them to help him lead a rebellion against the Republic. They agree to let Elariel go into exile and assist him, but to protect Refuge's secret she's altered to look human.

Gyre and Elariel stop in Deepfire to meet Lynnia and Sarah. They buy a cargo of alchemical weapons and supplies with the funds provided by the ghouls. Gyre offers Sarah a ghoul-made replacement for her missing arm, and she agrees to accompany him. They begin the long journey south to Khirkhaz, where Gyre has rebel contacts.

In the Forge, Maya tends to the comatose Jaedia. Prodominus asks her to travel to the plaguespawn-haunted Forsaken Coast and visit the Archive to get information about a strange new arcana. Maya, Varo, and Beq undertake the journey, and when plaguespawn find them, they're forced to take shelter in a village. Soon the villagers are revealed to be servants of the Eldest, a black spider who controls the plaguespawn. Maya destroys him, at a brutal cost. At the Archive, they learn the mystery arcana is a "resonator," a communications device of unknown origin.

*   *   *

Gyre tries to avoid entanglements on the road, keeping to the Splinter Kingdoms to escape Republic forces. In the Kingdom of Ehrenvare, his goods are nearly seized, but he and the others manage to reclaim them and escape. They reach Cliffedge, on the border with Khirkhaz, and meet Nina Kotzed. She brings them to the rebel Khirkhaz Commune, in spite of the efforts of its warring factions. Her older sister, Apphia, is the Commune's leader, and she and Gyre form an accord. When the camp is attacked by a centarch and Gyre defeats her, the Commune unites behind them and makes plans to reclaim the fortress of Spire Kotzed.

After returning to the Forge and recovering from her ordeal, Maya learns that Prodominus is keeping information on the resonator from the Council. She resolves to break into his storehouse and investigate for herself, with help from Varo, Beq, and Tanax. They evade the alarms and retrieve the device. It activates, letting them speak to Ashok, the last of the Chosen. He gives them instructions for making their own resonator and says he needs Maya's help.

Beq assembles the new device, and Maya speaks to Ashok at greater length. He tells them that a machine called the Purifier exists in Khirkhaz, ready to destroy the Plague and allow the Chosen to return. Ashok insists that the enemy has infiltrated the Order and other centarchs can't be trusted. He tells Maya to join an expedition to Khirkhaz as cover.

In Khirkhaz, Gyre leads a sneak attack on Spire Kotzed, routing the garrison in a major victory for the Commune. The Republic forces, accompanied by Prodominus, Maya, Varo, Beq, and the centarch Va'aht—originally responsible for Gyre's mutilation—prepare a counterattack. Legionaries storm the gates, and the Commune forces, equipped with ghoul weapons, barely hold on. Gyre defeats Va'aht, but the cent-arch escapes.

Gyre confronts Maya, and his ghoul augmentations allow him to defeat her. She retreats with the rest of the Republic forces to their camp. Later, she sends Varo to ask Gyre for a meeting and explains to him her secret mission to the Purifier. To get Gyre's help, she lies and says the Purifier will eliminate the plaguespawn threat.

Gyre, Elariel, Sarah, and Kit join Maya, Varo, and Beq on the journey to the Purifier. They find the ancient machine hidden under a mountain, but the entrance is guarded by deadly traps. Only Elariel's knowledge allows them to escape, but she has to reveal herself as a ghoul to Maya. Maya confronts her, but Gyre steps in, and Maya's deception about the Purifier's purpose is revealed. Gyre refuses to allow Maya to bring the Chosen back to the world, and the siblings square off again. This time, when Gyre gets the upper hand, Maya disables the Thing—which the Archive identified as a power limiter—and unleashes her true strength to defeat him. Debilitated, she activates the Purifier, cleansing the world of the Plague.

Ashok emerges from a Gate, revealing himself as no longer Chosen but a twisted monstrosity—the Corruptor of ghoul legend. He wounds Maya, who falls unconscious, and easily defeats the others. Prodo-minus, who had followed the group undetected, arrives and fights a delaying action. He tells Gyre to get everyone through the Gate and to go back to the Forge and seek out Xalen. Kit sacrifices the last of her nearby construct bodies to distract the Corruptor, and the others escape through the Gate. Prodominus destroys the Gate behind them, killing himself in an explosion.

Afterward, Ashok recovers, irritated that he will have to make his way to the next nearest Gate but not terribly inconvenienced. He directs through his resonators that preparations in Skyreach begin at once.

Chapter One

Maya

Maya opened her eyes with a gasp, cradling her ruined hand against her chest.

For a moment she could see nothing at all, surrounded by total, inky darkness. Then something strobed in front of her, a jagged stroke of white-hot lightning, gone between blinks but leaving shimmering afterimages. A few heartbeats later there was another flash, farther off, and then still farther, twisting bolts marching into the distance.

Where am I?

Her head throbbed. She'd been in the Purifier's control room, trying to reason with Gyre. She'd used the ancient machine, and...

It destroyed the Plague. She'd *felt* it, the wave of energy that rippled out into the world as a self-sustaining chain reaction, tiny dark particles bursting into halos of brilliant light. *It worked.*

And then the Gate had opened, and Ashok had emerged. Or something had.

The Corruptor. Ashok's handsome form fused with a monstrous construct, a bloated, spider-legged thing of dark muscle and pulsing intestinal tubing. She'd tried to stop him, but he was a *Chosen.* His power was overwhelming. And then his resonator had exploded in her hand, shredding her flesh and spattering her with dark fluid. She'd felt the chill of the stuff through her agony.

But that was all she remembered.

Carefully, Maya sat up, finding a cold metal surface above her. She explored it with her good hand while lightning flashed again close by, bright and silent. She got a quick glimpse of a row of machines sitting on a long metal table. Crawling forward, she found she'd been sitting under a similar table. Lightning flashed in the next machine down, then the next, regular as a heartbeat. It was contained in crystalline spheres that sat atop complex assemblies of pipes and conduits.

It all looked like something that could be part of the Purifier, but they hadn't found any doors except to the control room. *Did Beq take me somewhere else in the complex?*

She cleared her throat. "H...hello?" Her voice quivered, and Maya gritted her teeth and steadied herself. "Hello? Beq? Varo? Gyre?"

There was no response except the silent flashes of lightning.

She touched her belt and was relieved to find her haken in its accustomed place. Laying a finger on it, she drew on *deiat* to summon a light. It was something she could do by reflex, which made it all the more unsettling when nothing appeared. Her heart double-thumped, and she forced herself to settle down.

My connection's burnt out from overuse. No wonder, given what she'd done in the Purifier. *It'll be fine in a few hours.* That was common enough, but this felt different somehow. Not like there was something wrong with her, but as though *deiat* itself were gone, the eternal fire of the sun snuffed out. *Which is ridiculous.*

With no better option, she started walking down the line of machines, navigating by the flashes. There were several more rows to either side, lightning trapped in the crystal spheres and thrashing like it wanted to escape. After a little while, she came to an archway opening onto a long corridor.

Here, at least, things were a little more familiar. The architecture wouldn't have looked out of place in the Forge, except that the walls and floor were iridescent gray unmetal instead of stone. Sunstones set in sconces at regular intervals threw a wan illumination. Both sides of the hall were lined with doorways, and though the rooms beyond were dark, Maya got glimpses of other strange machines. There were tanks of murky liquid, churning slowly in the faint light, and spiderwebs of tubing. The air was bone cold and smelled of metal.

Pausing a moment, Maya took a deep breath and uncurled her injured hand. It didn't hurt, but she couldn't feel much of anything from it, which seemed like a bad sign. To her surprise, the shredded flesh she remembered was gone. Her calloused brown skin was mottled with patches of pure darkness. She wiggled her fingers and watched them move as though they belonged to someone else.

If Ashok won, maybe he captured me? The thought brought a tightness to her chest—not for herself, since she seemed to be in one piece, but for the others. *If I'm alive, they must be too.* Maya refused to contemplate the alternative.

She kept walking, now with renewed purpose. Every room she passed was dark and silent, but ahead the corridor ended in another archway, and she made for that. It let onto a circular room ringed by several more archways, with a round console at its center studded with crystals and wire. Curved horns stuck up from the center, outlining the base of an invisible sphere. Maya guessed they were an image projector, like a larger version of the resonator.

A man stood at the controls, his back to Maya. He turned as she paused in the doorway.

"Hello, *sha'deia*," said Ashok. *The Corruptor.*

He looked fully human—or fully *Chosen*—without the monstrous grafts of metal and flesh. His face was sculpted and handsome, with high cheekbones and delicate features, and his slicked-back hair gleamed with the luster of true gold. He wore loose trousers and a cotton robe, all in white, open at the front to show off a well-muscled torso.

Maya's good hand had automatically drawn her haken. She tried to ignite it, but her effort of will produced only a frustrating silence. Ashok raised one eyebrow, and his lip quirked.

"Finding yourself a bit powerless?" he said. "Pity."

"Where are we?" Maya said. "What happened to the others?"

"I wouldn't worry about them." He ambled toward her, hands in his pockets. "We have bigger things to think about."

"Tell me what you've done with them," Maya grated.

"Honestly," Ashok said, "I'm just trying to have a quiet conversation—"

"*Tell me.*"

"I haven't *done* anything to them," he said, annoyed. "Nor do I have any idea where they are. Does that satisfy you?"

Maya stared at him for a moment. The Chosen's eyes glittered dangerously.

"So where am I?" she said.

"That's a complicated question. Where your *body* is, I couldn't tell you."

"My *body*?" Maya looked around. "This is some kind of dream?"

"In essence. But a dream we share." His smile grew wider, sharklike.

"If this is a dream, then I want to wake up."

"I'm afraid it's not that simple." He stepped forward, grabbing her wrist before she could back away, pulling up her injured hand. "We are linked now, you and I. Part of me is part of you, and always will be."

Maya stared at the dark splotches on her fingers. Her skin crawled and she yanked her hand away.

"So none of this is real."

Ashok made a so-so gesture. "As I said, it's complicated."

At least that explains why I can't touch deiat. Something deep in Maya shuddered in relief, but she did her best not to show it.

"Then why am I here?" she asked. "If you could have killed me with dreams, I assume you'd have done it already."

"Kill you?" His smile broadened again. "I'm not going to kill you,

Maya. In fact, I'm very eager to meet you in person. That's why I wanted to talk to you, in fact. I'm going to make you an offer."

"I'm not interested."

"I think you might be. If you truly care about your friends. Your brother. That arcanist girl." He smirked. "Yes, I thought so. The offer is this: find me, come to me, and I will forget they ever existed."

"Even if I thought that was a good idea, how could I possibly trust you? You *used* us."

"I did," Ashok said agreeably. "And would again, if I had to. But believe me when I say that while I require *your* assistance with certain projects, I have no interest in the others. If they stay out of the way, I will ignore them."

He leaned closer, eyes darkening. "If they do not, if you make things difficult, then I may become *irritated*. I *will* have you, *sha'deia*, one way or the other. But if I have to come and take you, then I promise I will kill everyone who helped you, everyone who sheltered you, everyone who so much as spared you a kind word, until you *beg* me to let you surrender. Understand?"

Maya set her jaw. "I understand that you're a monster."

"I never claimed otherwise." His smile returned. "Great things are coming, and you have a chance to be a part of them. I hope you make the right decision."

"I'll find you, all right," Maya promised. "I never should have listened to you, and I need to make up for that. I'm going to destroy you."

"So fierce," Ashok said. "But you cannot hide your doubts from me. Not here. Think on it, *sha'deia*. I will see you soon."

The world around Maya dissolved into darkness.

Gyre

Exhaustion pulled at Gyre like a pack full of stones, but he didn't dare close his eyes. Maya lay on the bedroll, her breathing fast and shallow, her crimson hair soaked with sweat. Every so often she coughed, flecking her lips with black and red sputum. Her left hand was bound in a ragged ball of cloth. Gyre had gotten only a glimpse of the injury as Varo had rapidly applied the makeshift bandage, but that had been enough to turn his stomach.

The sun had vanished entirely, leaving the abandoned cabin with only a single dim glowstone for illumination. Gyre had run out of energy even to pace, so he rocked back and forth on his heels, watching his sister's jerky breaths. When a rustle came from the other room, he froze, momentarily forgetting what he was supposed to do. Then he bounded to his feet as Elariel appeared in the doorway, rubbing her eyes blearily. Her clothes were scorched and sooty, and her red-brown hair was a filthy tangle.

"Oh, thank the fucking Chosen," Gyre muttered.

"Gyre?" Elariel said. "What happened? We made it through the Gate—"

"You collapsed," Gyre said. "Sarah carried you. We're in an old cabin Varo found, not far from Bastion."

Elariel shook her head. "Bastion?"

It was easy to forget that Elariel had spent her life in a cave. "A city in the northern Republic. It doesn't matter." Gyre took her by the arm and pulled her to the pallet. "You have to help Maya."

"I..." Elariel allowed herself to be moved a few steps, then pulled back. "What happened to Sarah and the others?"

"They went to the city to find supplies. We need food, bandages, quickheal."

"But..." Elariel chewed her lip.

"They'll be fine," Gyre said, though he had to admit it was more a hope than a certainty. "Sarah has Varo and Beq with her. But *please*—"

Elariel looked down at Maya, who coughed weakly and moaned in her sleep. The ghoul's fist clenched.

"She tried to kill me, Gyre," she said. "When she found out what I·was. She tried to kill *you*."

"I know. But—"

"She's a *centarch*. Like the one you killed at the Commune camp."

"I *know*." The word came out as a shout. Gyre took a few long breaths to calm himself. "She's my sister. I know you don't understand what that means." Ghouls were raised in group creches and didn't know their parents, let alone their siblings. "*Please*. It's...important."

Elariel studied his face for a long moment. She muttered something in her own language; Gyre guessed it was an obscenity.

"I'm keeping her haken," Elariel said, kneeling beside Maya and grabbing the bladeless sword from her belt.

"Fine." Gyre knelt too, and fought off a wave of dizziness.

Muttering another curse, Elariel laid her hands on Maya's side. Her eyes closed, eyelids twitching as she mumbled to herself. Gyre imagined the tendrils of *dhaka*, the life-magic that was everything Maya and the Twilight Order condemned, spreading out from the ghoul's touch to reach through Maya's body. He wasn't sure if Maya would have agreed to this or not. *But it's the only chance we have.*

"She's in bad shape," Elariel said quietly. "It's not just the hand. The Plague tore up her lungs, her throat—"

"Can you help her?" Gyre grated, his knuckles going white.

"I can," Elariel said. "But it's going to take time. She'll sleep for a while."

"Fine," Gyre said, breathing out. All the tension abruptly leaked out of him, leaving only the exhaustion. "That's fine."

"And there's something else." Elariel frowned, eyes still closed, and her fingers twitched. "Something in her blood. It's...strange."

"Is it hurting her?"

"Not that I can tell," Elariel said. "Which is good, because I can't get any kind of a grip on it. Her body won't acknowledge that it's there."

"We can deal with it later, then." Gyre sat back. "As long as she'll be okay."

"She will." Elariel opened her eyes, her expression softening. "Get some rest. I'll stay with her."

Gyre nodded dully. He dragged himself to the other room, where

Elariel had been lying on a second bedroll. There was no pillow, but it hardly mattered; he barely had time to lie flat before consciousness fled.

It seemed like no time at all had passed before his eyes opened, but by the lines of light clawing their way past rotting shutters, the sun was already rising. Birds twittered and squeaked outside. Gyre's throat felt like it was caked with soot, and his eyes like they had had their sockets packed with itchy straw, but it was still a considerable improvement on how he'd felt the night before. He rolled over and found his canteen, still a quarter full of tepid water. He drained it, hacked a blob of blue-black mucus onto the ancient floorboards, and slowly got to his feet.

Instinctively he found himself looking for Kit. She'd been his constant companion for months, her voice emerging from black spider-constructs linked to the arcana that contained her disembodied mind, back in the crippled Leviathan. But she'd sacrificed the last of her nearby bodies to buy them time to escape from the Corruptor. She could make more, given time, but thousands of kilometers separated Gyre from Leviathan's Womb. Gyre was surprised by how much he missed her sarcastic interjections. *Her conversation might have been filthy, but at least it was always upbeat.* Kit was firm in the conviction that the worst had already happened to her, so there was nowhere to go but up.

Groaning, Gyre shuffled to the door. Elariel sat against the wall in the other room, dozing beside Maya. The effects of the ghoul's ministrations were evident—Maya's color was much improved, her breathing was easier, and sweat no longer stood out on her forehead. Elariel stirred and yawned.

"It's about time to bring her back to waking," the ghoul said. "I thought it would be better if you were here."

"Thanks," Gyre said. "She's . . . all right?"

"I said she would be," Elariel said. "Her hand will require more healing, though, and fresh bandages. She'll need water, too."

"I'll get some." Gyre picked up a couple of extra canteens from among their scattered gear. "Give me a minute."

The woods, which had seemed claustrophobic in the pain and terror of the night before, were quite pleasant in the golden light of morning. The cabin was a log-walled single-story affair that might have been a shelter for hunters, but it had clearly gone unused for many years— the door hung by a single hinge and moss was slowly conquering the peaked roof. The remnants of a trail still led from the door down to a stream. Gyre drank until he'd cleared his throat, then filled the canteens and went back.

Elariel sat beside Maya, eyes closed. Gyre waited until she looked up, then offered her one of the canteens. She took it with a yawn.

"She'll wake up in a minute or two," the ghoul said. "When are the others getting back?"

"Soon, if everything went well."

"Wake me up when they get here."

"I will." Gyre hesitated. "Thank you, Elariel. I know this wasn't an easy choice."

"I just hope you're right about her." The ghoul frowned down at Maya. "If she wakes up and tries to kill us, forgive me if I say I told you so."

Gyre chuckled weakly. Elariel checked her belt for Maya's haken, then wandered into the other room. Gyre settled down beside the pallet as Maya began to shift restlessly. A few moments later, her eyes shot open, and she twitched as though she were trying to sit up. Gyre leaned forward and put a hand on her shoulder.

"Maya, hey. It's okay. Everything's okay."

"Gyre?" Maya blinked and managed to turn her head toward him.

"It's me. You're okay. Just relax."

"I can't...I can't move." Her good arm trembled at her side, lifting only a few centimeters from the mat.

"Elariel had you in a healing state. You're still coming out of it. Just wait for a minute."

"Elariel..." Maya's eyes widened. "With *dhaka*?"

"We didn't have a choice," Gyre said. "You would have died if she hadn't. I'm sorry, but I couldn't let that happen."

"I..." Maya concentrated for a moment and moved her arm enough to take Gyre's hand. "It's all right. I'm just a little out of it." Her expression tightened. "Where's Beq and the others?"

"They'll be here soon," Gyre said soothingly. "They went to find food."

"Good." She still looked haunted. "But... the Purifier..."

"Just rest. We'll talk about it when they get back."

"I let him *out*, Gyre." Maya strained and managed to sit up, panting with the effort. "He led me along by the nose and I was too plaguing blind to see it."

"It's not your fault—"

"Of course it is!"

"Not *just* your fault, at least," Gyre said. "We were all there."

"You tried to stop me."

"I tried," Gyre said with a wry smile.

"And Prodominus..." Maya stopped. "Is he here?"

Gyre shook his head. "He... stayed. I think he destroyed the Gate after we left, to keep the Corruptor from following."

"Chosen defend. I've never heard of a Gate being *destroyed*. The energy involved..." She shook her head. "At least he'd have died quickly."

"Maybe he destroyed the Corruptor, too."

Maya shook her head. "He's still alive. And he's coming after us. After *me*."

"You can't know that."

"I know, trust me." Her face was shadowed. "Though I suppose that may be too much to ask. I lied to you."

She had. Maya had convinced Gyre the Purifier would destroy the plaguespawn, rather than the Plague itself. Looking at her now, drawn and hollow-eyed, he had a hard time being angry about the betrayal.

"You did what you thought was best," he said carefully. "I can still trust in that."

"Ashok warned us you might be working with the ghouls to sabotage the Purifier."

Gyre gave a hollow laugh. "We had no idea the thing was there.

Although if we'd *known* you were trying to bring back a Chosen, we certainly would have tried to stop you."

"Chosen defend." Maya tipped her head back, fighting tears. "I thought... Well. I've made a plaguing mess."

"We're alive," Gyre said. "That's something."

"We are." Maya's lips tightened. "And I'm going to stop him. Whatever his plan is from here, I'm going to burn it down. I swear it."

Gyre had his own opinions on the practicality of that, but he held his tongue. Fortunately, at that moment there was a clatter of footsteps coming up the path. A party of three came inside, laden with heavy packs, and the air was suddenly full of excited shouting.

"Maya!" Beq dropped her burdens and ran to Maya's side, wrapping her arms around her. "Oh, thank the Chosen. I thought—I thought—"

"I'm okay," Maya said, pressing her face into Beq's long green braid. "I'm still here."

"I'm glad you're alive, too," Varo said, setting his pack down by the door. His light brown scalp, normally bald as an egg, was flecked with stubble after days in the wilderness. "I was hoping you wouldn't end up like my friend on our trek to Gubernin. He got bit by a snake on the first day, and he told us he was fine, but his foot kept swelling bigger and bigger. By the fifth day, he tried to walk on it and it just popped." He mimed an explosion with his hands. "Got all over *everything*, let me tell you."

"Thank you, Varo," Maya managed, still hugging Beq, her shoulders shaking with silent laughter. "I knew you'd have something appropriate to say."

"Where's Elariel?" Sarah said. She had a fresh cloak, and her left arm was wound in a sheet, concealing the ghoul-made prosthetic underneath.

"I'm here." Elariel appeared in the doorway, still yawning. "Just tired. Helping Maya took half the night."

"You healed her?" Beq said. "With *dhaka*?"

There was an abrupt silence. Maya drew herself up a little.

"Thank you," she said, bowing slightly to Elariel. "I owe you my life. I was... hasty, before. I'm glad you didn't hold that against me."

Elariel shrank in on herself under the combined gazes, her cheeks coloring.

"Thank Gyre," she muttered. "I wouldn't have, but he insisted."

Another awkward pause, which Varo broke by unbuckling his pack.

"We bought food," he said. "Or *I* bought food, anyway. Would you believe I'm the only one who had any money? One of the basic rules of being a scout—always have a few thalers tucked away. One time, my friend—"

"I'm starved," Maya interrupted.

There was a busy interval as the packs were broken open and supplies distributed. It was simple fare, fresh bread with butter and dried summerfruit, but it felt like a feast. Gyre wasn't sure how long it had been since his last meal—sometime before they'd reached the Purifier—but it felt like an eternity. Even Elariel settled down beside Sarah and tore into a round loaf with her teeth.

"Okay," Varo said, when everyone was satisfied. "Nobody wants to say it, so I will. What in the name of the Chosen do we do now?"

Elariel looked down at her hands. Beq looked to Maya, who had her eyes closed, her brow creased in thought. Gyre shifted uncomfortably. As he cleared his throat to speak, Maya came to a decision and leaned forward.

"I have made a terrible mistake," she said. Beq murmured something conciliatory, but Maya waved a hand. "Ashok lied to me, and I trusted him. You can blame me or not, whatever you prefer. The question is what we're going to do about it."

"The Order needs to be warned," Varo said.

"So does Apphia in Khirkhaz," Gyre said.

"My people, too," Elariel said. She got a look from Varo and bristled. "The Corruptor threatens everyone, not just humanity."

"Can we trust the Order?" Sarah said.

"Prodominus didn't think so," Gyre said. "He told me to take Maya to the Forge and find someone called Xalen. Said she was the only one we could trust."

"He's right," Maya said. "At least about not being able to trust everyone.

We know there were other resonators, other people taking Ashok's instructions. I've never heard of a Xalen, though. Have either of you?"

Beq and Varo both shook their heads.

"I need to get back to Deepfire," Elariel said. "As soon as possible."

"We're a long way from Deepfire," Sarah said. She carefully touched Elariel's stiff shoulder. "It'd take months to get there on foot, and we're in Republic territory."

"There's a Gate," Gyre said, "but—"

"It comes out in the Spike," Sarah finished. "The most heavily guarded place in the Auxie garrison."

"Then we go through the garrison," Elariel said. "Gyre can handle it, I'm sure. I'll recharge the energy bottles."

"I can't say I like the idea," Gyre said.

"And I'm not happy with the idea of opening a Gate so you can kill dozens of Auxiliaries on the other side," Varo said. "I realize needs must, but..."

"Gyre," Maya said. "Can we talk? In private?"

Gyre blinked. "Of course."

He offered his hand to help Maya up. They went out the front door, Maya's bare feet crunching amid the scatter of fallen leaves covering the forest floor. Inside, they could hear the argument continue.

"What's going on?" Gyre said.

"I want to make a deal," Maya said. "With Elariel. But I think it might work better if you help me sell it."

"What kind of a deal?"

"What she did for me..." She raised her injured hand, staring at its bandaged contours. "It doesn't hurt anymore. And my lungs feel... fine. I thought I was going to die."

"I know," Gyre said quietly.

"I have a mentor. Jaedia. My teacher. Almost my mother, after the Order took me. She... I love her very much." Maya's voice was unsteady. "I barely remember our real mother. I'm sorry if that makes me sound horrible to you."

"It's understandable. You were young."

"I was. And..." She shook her head. "It doesn't matter. The important thing is that Jaedia got hurt. One of the Corruptor's creatures took over her body. I saved her, but ever since then, she hasn't woken. I'm starting to think she never will. Unless..."

"Unless Elariel helps her," Gyre finished. "You're willing to do that? Use *dhaka*?"

Maya raised her bandaged hand. "I suppose I have to be. If it brings her back, I'd do anything."

"Elariel isn't going to want to help another centarch. And Jaedia's in the Forge, right? How are we going to get to her?"

"I'll figure that part out. Here's the deal: if Elariel will do what she can for Jaedia, I'll get you to Deepfire. I can use my authority as a centarch to get you past the garrison. I may get in trouble afterward, but..." She shrugged. "I'm not sure that matters much anymore."

"It's a plan, at least." Gyre pursed his lips. "I can talk to Elariel and Sarah. But no promises."

"I'll handle Varo and Beq," Maya said. "Thank you, Gyre."

"Don't thank me yet."

"Is she *mad*?" Elariel said, her color rising again. "This is obviously insane."

She paced up and down the little room. Maya had taken Varo and Beq outside, and Gyre could hear the quiet murmur of their conversation. Sarah stood by the door, trying to take Elariel's hand, but the ghoul kept stalking away from her.

"You have to admit," Sarah said, giving up, "it's a little crazy."

"A *little*?" Elariel rounded. "She wants us to go to the *Forge*. The headquarters of the Order that has *hunted* my people for four centuries."

"I realize it's not a great option," Gyre said. "But without her we don't have *any* great options. In case you haven't noticed, we're stuck in the middle of the Republic. Without her help, we're not going *anywhere*."

"Get her to open the Gate to Deepfire."

"There's a thousand armed soldiers on the other side."

"Better odds than we'd have at the Forge!"

"We're not going to *fight* our way in," Gyre said. "Maya and the others can cover for us. We just need to get in, find Jaedia and maybe this Xalen, and then get to a Gate."

"What do we care about Xalen?" Elariel said.

"Prodominus seemed to think she could help," Gyre said. "The more information we have about the Corruptor, the better."

Elariel looked back and forth between them, her eyes full of frustration. Turning to Sarah, she said, "And are you going along with this?"

"I..." Sarah hesitated. "It's dangerous. But I don't have any better ideas. I've been inside the Spike, El, and I don't like the thought of fighting our way out, even with Gyre's augmentations. It's the long way back to Deepfire, but it may be the fastest."

"If Maya and her friends decide to turn us in, it's the fastest way to an Order cell," Elariel said.

"Maya won't betray us," Gyre said.

"You trust her?" Elariel said. "Even after she brought us to the Purifier?"

Gyre nodded silently.

"Because you are the products of the same sexual union?"

"Because I *know* her. She's still the same Maya the Order dragged away, whatever they've done to her in the meantime."

Elariel stared at him, jaw working. Sarah put a hand gently on her shoulder.

"I trust *Gyre*," she said. "If he thinks this is the right plan..."

The ghoul sagged, tension going out of her like an expelled breath.

"I suppose," she muttered, "it's far from the first time that I've put my life in his hands. And Refuge *must* be warned of the Corruptor's coming. But I don't like this."

"I understand," Gyre said. "Honestly, I'm not excited about the idea myself."

Chapter Two

W e can't Gate directly to the Forge," Varo said. The six of them were gathered in a circle again, eating another meal of bread and fruit as the sun slid slowly toward afternoon. "The Gate chamber is always watched by a centarch and a squad of Legionaries, and the doors are sealed. There's no way past them."

"There must be another way in," Maya said. "What about the docks?"

Varo nodded. "That's our best bet. The scouts have a few tricks. I'm not supposed to share them with centarchs, so stay quiet about it." He grinned. "Though nobody ever said anything about rebels and secret ghouls. I guess the rest of you are in the clear."

Nobody laughed. *Nothing new there, I guess.*

"Where do we get a boat?" Beq said.

"In Skyreach," Varo said. He sketched a map on the dusty floor, an oval for the lake with the Forge on one side and Skyreach on the other. "The scouts always have a few on retainer to make quiet pickups."

"So now we're going to the capital of the Republic as well," Elariel muttered, arms pulled tight across her chest. "Wonderful."

"We can't take the Skyreach Gate," Beq said. "It lets out in the Senate building."

Varo nodded. "There's another Gate, about here"—he tapped the floor—"in the hills southeast of the city. It doesn't get used much, and it's not normally guarded. We can get into the city overland, blending in with the rest of the traffic."

Maya gave a slow nod. "That should work. And going through Skyreach has another advantage. We can get in touch with Tanax."

"Tanax?" Gyre frowned. "The centarch who was with you in Deepfire and at Leviathan's Womb?"

"He helped us get the resonator," Maya said. "We can trust him."

"He killed Yora," Sarah said conversationally. When everyone stopped to look at her, she shrugged. "I'm not saying it's a bad idea. Just thought it might be relevant."

"He did his best to kill me, too," Maya said. "When he discovered his mentor was a traitor to the Order, it...changed his thinking. He's been trying to make up for it."

"This plan gets better and better," Elariel growled.

"It's still a danger, talking to him," Gyre said. "Why risk it?"

"Because he'll know what's going on in the Forge. I have no idea how much they know or what we'll be walking into."

Gyre frowned, but nodded. Varo drew a line across the lake and continued.

"Once we meet Tanax and secure a boat, we cross the lake and enter the Forge from the bottom. If we put cloaks on all of you, you can pass for scouts; we don't usually go uniformed. Just let me and Maya do the talking. We find Jaedia in the hospital, take her to the Gate chamber, and get out of there."

"I thought the Gate chamber was under guard," Sarah said.

"As long as we have a centarch with us, they won't ask questions on the way out," Varo said. "Getting in is a lot harder. Maya would be expected to report to the Council."

"If anything goes wrong, we're plaguing fucked," Gyre said. "Stuck in a mountain full of angry centarchs with no way out. But I don't see a better way. When should we leave?"

"Tomorrow morning, I think," Varo said, glancing at the window. "It's a day's walk from the Gate to the city. If we leave at first light, we should have plenty of time."

"Okay," Gyre said, then hesitated and looked at Maya. "Tomorrow morning?"

She nodded. The group broke up, Elariel and Sarah retreating to the other room, Gyre and Varo going outside to make a fire and cook something for dinner. Maya, left alone with Beq, leaned against the wall with a sigh.

"Are you all right?" Beq said.

"Tired," Maya admitted. "Healing is hard work, I guess."

"It beats the alternative." Beq looked at Varo's diagram, then smudged it out with a foot. "When I saw you after we came through, I thought..."

"I know."

"It was the worst feeling I've ever had. Like someone reached inside me and pulled out my guts." She put a hand on her stomach, as though making sure no one had. "I went with the others to the city because they needed help finding bandages and medicine, and I knew it was your best chance. But the whole walk back, I kept thinking...if I get there and she's gone, then..."

"I'm okay, Beq." Maya reached out, and Beq shuffled closer, pressing against her side. Maya leaned against her, their foreheads touching. "I'll try not to scare you anymore."

"You will," Beq said softly. "Throwing yourself into danger is who you are."

"We'll just have to throw ourselves into danger together, then."

Beq nodded mutely. Maya kissed her, gently, and they sat for a long while, a small island of shared warmth against the growing chill of the afternoon. The crackle of a campfire came from outside, and the hiss of vulpi bacon in a pan. The smell drifted in a few moments later, reaching deep into Maya's mind and pulling memories from the depths of her childhood. For a moment she was sitting on her mother's lap, watching Gyre and her father lay the bacon over the fire, flickering light driving back the autumn darkness.

Gyre didn't say anything about Jaedia. It was hard to read him, the man her brother had grown into, with his scarred, silver eye and a killer's stillness. They'd talked only a little about what had happened to him between when she'd left and when he'd taken the role of Halfmask in Deepfire. Their parents were dead, though, he'd said that much. Maya felt guilty that she didn't feel more strongly about that.

After a few minutes, Gyre brought in a plate of hot bacon and grilled vegetables. Healing was apparently hungry work as well, and Maya's stomach was already rumbling. She fell on the food with a will. The smell lured Elariel and Sarah out, too, and they crunched through the crispy bacon in contemplative silence.

"I need to look at your hand," Elariel said, licking grease from her long fingers. "Wash it and redo the bandages."

"Of course."

Maya eyed another roast pepper, then regretfully decided against it. She followed Elariel out the door, past Gyre and the campfire and down to the little stream. The ghoul gestured for her to extend her hand. Maya did, and tried not to hold her breath as Elariel undid the rough bandage.

"Does it hurt?" the ghoul said.

"Not really. It feels...tender, maybe?"

"That's good. It's a lot of flesh to regrow. Have to get all the tendons and so on hooked up right. Don't look if you don't want to." The bandage was sticky with dried blood, and Elariel filled a bowl with water and trickled it onto the clots. When it soaked through, it was bitterly cold. Maya gritted her teeth as Elariel peeled the last few layers away.

She risked a glimpse. She'd expected—a wound, maybe, bloody and raw. Instead her hand was more or less whole, with no ragged edges of skin or bones showing, just unnaturally pink, unmarked flesh. Parts of her fingers and palm were *thinner* than they should be. As she watched, Elariel put a finger to one spot and the muscle *shifted*, as though there were something living under Maya's skin. She hastily shut her eyes.

"I'll keep it bandaged until tomorrow," the ghoul said, winding fresh linen. "You should probably wear a glove, too; it'll look strange to humans."

"Thank you," Maya said. "For this, and for agreeing to the plan."

"Don't." Elariel tied the bandage off and glared at her. "I'm not doing this for you. Your brother saved my life, and I owe him. That's all."

"I'm still grateful."

"Keep it to yourself," Elariel muttered, washing the bowl in the stream. "If I had the choice, I'd rid the world of your Order and everyone in it."

"I can understand that," Maya said. "I thought ghouls were..."

"Monsters. I know." Elariel straightened up. "Don't let me disabuse you."

In the morning, they gathered their packs, loaded with the remaining food and what supplies they'd found in Bastion. Varo had had the foresight to acquire hooded rain-cloaks for everyone, which he assured them would be inconspicuous when they got to Skyreach. When they left the cabin, Maya sent up a silent thanks to whatever forager had built it and left it there.

The last time Maya had used this Gate, she'd been with Jaedia and Marn, returning from the encounter with Hollis Plaguetouch. From that chance meeting, everything else had followed. Or so it had seemed at the time. Maya touched the Thing, still embedded in her flesh but now a dead lump of crystal and unmetal.

The Gate, at least, looked the same as ever. It was under a hollow hill, with a secret door that slid smoothly open at Maya's *deiat* command. Inside was a square unmetal room, big enough for a cart, with the twisted archway of the Gate at one end.

Maya had never been to the Gate in the hills near Skyreach, but Jaedia had made her memorize the codes for all seventy-nine Gates used by the Order. She woke the ancient arcana with a touch of *deiat*, and the surface of the arch clouded over with white mist. Elariel and Sarah regarded it with deep suspicion.

"What would happen," Sarah said, "if it stopped working when you were halfway through?"

"Funny you should say that," Varo said. "A friend of mine—"

"Varo," Maya said.

"—convinced his centarch to turn the Gate on and off to help him chop wood. Sliced it right through, smooth as glass." He looked around with mock innocence. "What?"

"This is how we got here," Gyre said, though he looked a little uneasy himself. "It'll be fine."

Maya sent a command to close the false hillside and stepped through the Gate, gesturing for the others to follow. As always, there was no more sensation than if she'd walked through fog. She emerged on a rocky hillside a few hundred kilometers to the southeast, with the sun a little bit higher in a blue sky broken only by wisps of cloud.

The Gate here was concealed by a cut in the rock, letting out onto a dry streambed. Scrub grass and spindly trees clung to the stone, turning into true woods farther down the flank of the hill. Where the ground flattened out, the woods ended abruptly, giving way to an endless patchwork quilt of fields.

The others came through, one by one. At Varo's instruction, they put on the travelers' cloaks, which did at least a passable job at concealing their weapons and the battle-worn state of their clothes. The scout led the way down the hill, following the streambed. After a brief walk through the woods—far airier and tamer than the forest they'd come from—they found a footpath between two fields that led to a dirt track rutted by cartwheels and speckled with bird shit.

There were people, here and there, but only in the distance. A cloud of dust marked a cart on a parallel road, and a small boy tending a herd of vulpi yearlings gave them a wave. Maya resisted the urge to wave back.

"Nobody's armed," Sarah said as they trudged along. "And the houses are just houses, not little forts."

"It's the heart of the Republic," Varo said. "The Legions keep the plaguespawn down, and there's nothing else to threaten people."

"But we have weapons," Elariel said. "We could kill that boy, take his vulpi, and his family could not stop us."

"If you did, the local magistrate would find out about it," Gyre said. "And they'd send the Auxies to arrest you and throw you in prison. So mostly people don't."

"Strange," the ghoul muttered. "Humans are so strange."

The day wore on. They stopped to eat lunch, and Maya had just finished her chunk of slightly stale bread when an old man with a two-bird cart pulled up close by. He tipped his hat and smiled toothlessly.

"Need a ride to the city?" he said. "There's room with the cabbages."

Maya eyed the back of the cart longingly, imagining the miles passing by without the weary effort of walking. But after a look from Gyre she shook her head and waved the old man on.

"Thanks," Varo said, "but we've got stops to make."

The carter shrugged and clicked his tongue, and his birds trotted away. Maya heaved herself to her feet and kept walking.

Skyreach was visible on the horizon long before they arrived, blued by distance into a monochrome mirage. The height of its towers was deceptive; it felt close by, until you walked for a while and realized that the spires were simply much taller than you'd imagined. Then you walked for a while longer and discovered they were taller still, as though the city were receding into the distance as you approached. The size of the buildings, so narrow that they looked like a tightly packed bundle of needles, defied the mind's intuition.

For good reason, I suppose. Like those of all the greatest of the old

Chosen cities, Skyreach's spires could support themselves against gravity only with a constant supply of *deiat*. If the Twilight Order were to vanish, the heart of the Republic would come crashing down, both figuratively and quite literally. The towers looked impossible because they were.

Maya had seen them before, of course—Skyreach was visible from the Forge on a clear day, and she'd visited with Varo and Beq to find Prodominus' resonator. But it felt different approaching on foot across the plains. The rest of the city, the sprawl of merely human buildings that clustered around the towers like grass at the base of a tree, didn't come up over the horizon until hours later. Gyre, Sarah, and Elariel, who'd never seen Skyreach, stared ahead with a strange mix of awe and apprehension.

There was no wall, no distinct outer boundary. Buildings appeared by the side of the road, inns and markets and stables, gradually jostling closer and closer together until they were cheek by jowl. Several roads converged, with cross streets between them, and without any real transition they were walking down a city street surrounded by an increasingly dense crowd. The spires seemed as distant as ever, their bases obscured by lesser buildings.

Maya called a halt, pulling the group aside in the shadow of a wagon unloading barrels of nyfa seeds. Elariel pressed close by Sarah's side, her eyes showing too much white. Even Sarah seemed a little overwhelmed. Deepfire was a city, of course, but it was a drop in the ocean compared to Skyreach.

"We'll find somewhere to stay the night," Maya said. "Varo, have you got enough cash left to cover rooms?"

Varo checked his pouch. "If we don't mind squeezing, but that and dinner will about wipe me out."

"When we get to Deepfire, I have plenty of money stashed," Gyre said.

"Don't worry, I've been keeping a tab." Varo grinned. "Let me try and find a place where we're not going to have to share with half the bedbugs in the city."

This far from the city center, the establishments did look distinctly on the run-down side. Varo led them off the main road, into a quieter back alley, and located a small building with a sign reading "Rooms" and a couple of children playing with sticks out front. The boys looked up at them in awe as they passed into a neat, if threadbare, front parlor, where a severely dressed woman looked them over and gave the impression that they were acceptable only by the barest of margins. She grudgingly took Varo's money and gave them the keys to a couple of rooms at the top of the stairs, each with one large—and clean—bed and little else.

"You all rest and eat something," Varo said, handing Maya a limp pouch with a few coins. "I'll get a message to Tanax."

"Thanks, Varo," Maya said quietly as the others moved past with a variety of sounds of relief.

"Only doing my job," Varo said with a sly smile.

"I shudder to think where we'd be without you."

"Probably better off," Varo said philosophically. "Most of my friends would've been."

Getting out of her boots, Maya had to admit, was a pleasure to rival any other. She lay back on the bed, calves throbbing as though angry to be relieved of their burden. Beq bent over and kissed her before hurrying downstairs in search of food, taking Sarah and Elariel with her. Maya knew she should follow, but for the moment all she wanted to do was close her eyes and ache.

"You okay?" Gyre said from the doorway.

"For someone who nearly died a couple of days ago, I'm fine," Maya said.

He gave a weak chuckle and sat down beside her. "I suppose the city is all old hat for you."

"It is and it isn't," Maya said. "I grew up in the country, mostly. Jaedia was always traveling, and that meant we spent a lot of time in little villages and towns. When we came back here, we stayed at the Forge." She rolled over so she could look up at him. "You can see the towers from there, but they seem…unreal, somehow. I always felt like Skyreach was more of an *idea* than an actual place. When I first got here and found out it was all crowds and streets full of bird shit, I was disappointed."

"Have you ever been up in the towers?"

Maya shook her head. "Tanax has. He was assigned to work with the Senate. It's the route to a Council seat, supposedly, but Jaedia never wanted that for me."

"I'd like to see what the world looks like from up there," Gyre said. "Just once."

"I used to imagine that," Maya said. "Picture myself in the towers, back in the world of the Chosen, with the air full of skyships and flitters."

"If we were in Elder days, you'd be a slave," Gyre said. "We all would. Humanity."

"The *Inheritance* says that people were happy."

"And the Chosen wrote the *Inheritance*, didn't they?"

Maya frowned, though not because of Gyre's jibes. She remembered the last vision she'd seen of the towers in the days of the Chosen. It wasn't a childhood fantasy, but the images Ashok had showed her in the secret projector under the Forge, watching the skyfortress *Pride in Power* celebrate its maiden voyage. Ashok had looked as he did in her dream, golden-haired and perfect, a parody of the hideous creature she'd seen in the flesh.

I should tell Gyre about the dream. But Maya wasn't sure she wanted to answer the questions that would follow. *It* might *have been just a dream.* She didn't believe that, not really. *If the Corruptor can reach into my mind like that... then what?*

"Maya?" Gyre said. "Are you falling asleep on me?"

"Sorry." Maya sat up with a groan. "Let's see if they've found anything for dinner."

Varo returned with Tanax not long after they'd finished eating. Tanax wore a cloak, too, and kept it pulled tight around himself until Gyre closed the door behind him. Only then did he relax, pulling his hood back to reveal aquiline features and deep brown skin, stereotypical of Republic nobility.

"Chosen defend, Maya," he said. "I was driving myself crazy worrying about you. When Varo found me I nearly jumped out of my skin. What did you *do* in Khirkhaz?"

"What do you mean, what did I do?" Maya said.

"I mean Council agents have questioned me twice in the past couple of days, trying to figure out where you've gone. All centarchs have orders to detain you on sight."

Maya's heart sank into her guts. She was speechless for a moment, and it was left to Gyre to ask, "Did they have a reason?"

"Officially, they want to question you about what happened in Khirkhaz. But I've heard a dozen rumors, and they keep getting crazier. People are saying that you killed Prodominus, or that you went over to the rebels. And—" He broke off, looking at Gyre. "This is him, isn't it? Your brother. Silvereye."

"The eye does sort of give it away," Gyre said mildly.

"Forgive me for asking, but isn't he on the other side? I know he helped you at Leviathan's Womb—after his girlfriend stabbed you—but are you sure this is the company we should be keeping? *He's* wanted by the Republic as well."

"It's a long story, and I'll catch you up later," Maya said. "The short version is that Ashok's a monster. Now he's loose and we have to stop him. If the Order is looking for me, that means we were right, and people on the Council are taking his instructions."

"Ashok? The—" Tanax stopped, looking at Gyre.

"He knows everything," Maya said. "And yes. He's not Chosen, not anymore."

"What happened in Khirkhaz after we left?" Gyre said. "Has there been any news?"

"Not a lot," Tanax said. "The Senate has proclaimed a great victory over the rebels, but they've been very quiet on the details."

"I certainly don't remember any great victory," Maya said.

"Unless they launched another attack after we left," Gyre said anxiously. "Have they said anything about Apphia—Baron Kotzed—"

Tanax shook his head. "Like I said, we've had no specifics."

"I can't see them launching another attack so soon," Maya said. "Not without Prodominus. I'm sure the Senate is just putting up a happy front for public consumption."

Gyre frowned, still anxious. Tanax looked at Maya like he had a hundred questions, but the one he asked was, "If you know they're after you, what in the name of the Chosen are you doing in *here*?"

"I don't plan to say," Maya said. "But there's things I need to do before I leave."

"What things? If you need supplies, I can probably—"

"Jaedia," Maya said. "I'm not leaving her behind."

Tanax fell silent for a long moment.

"Jaedia's in the Forge," he said.

"I know," Maya said. "That's why we're here. We're going in to get her."

"That's—"

"Crazy?" Maya said wearily.

"I was going to say 'bold,'" Tanax said. "But it's not actually as mad as it sounds. The Senate has announced a celebration of our victory starting tomorrow. There's going to be an address by the Council, and every centarch is expected to be in attendance. The Forge will be emptier than it's ever been. If you *have* to sneak in, you picked the right moment."

"Convenient," Gyre muttered. His expression suggested it was anything but.

"Varo thinks he has a way in," Maya said. "Scouts' tricks. But we need to get to the docks tomorrow."

"I can help with that," Tanax said. "You need to stay covered up, but I can flash my haken if we run into trouble."

"Thank you," Maya said. "I know I'm asking you to take a lot on faith."

"You certainly are, and you owe me a real explanation. But not right now." Tanax frowned. "I need to get back before I'm missed. I'll arrange some cover for myself tomorrow, and meet you here an hour after dawn."

He pulled his cloak back on, nodded to Gyre, and left.

"I told you he's come a long way," Maya said to Gyre.

"He trusts you, at least," Gyre said. "They all do."

Maya shrugged uncomfortably. "We've been through a lot."

"I imagine." He sighed. "I'll let the others know what the plan is."

He slipped out. Maya flopped heavily back on the bed, contemplating going to sleep like that and forcing Beq and Varo to wedge themselves in around her. Before she closed her eyes, the door opened again and Elariel came in, looking sour.

"I need to work on your hand," the ghoul said. "If it does well overnight, the bandage can come off tomorrow."

"Tomorrow." Maya sat up and held out her bandaged hand for Elariel to unwrap. "That's amazing."

"Depends on your perspective," Elariel said, undoing the knots.

"How so?"

"For us, this is normal. What you humans think of as caring for injuries, ghouls would call torture."

"Hmm." Maya looked away as Elariel went to work, poking and prodding the muscles under the fresh pink skin. The twisting sensation was difficult to ignore.

"This is what *dhaka* is *for*," Elariel muttered. Her voice was quiet but intense. "Healing. Creating constructs to take on the burdens of labor. Making things *better*. Your Order denies all of this to your own people in the name of keeping them 'safe.'"

"It's not the only thing *dhaka* can be used for, though," Maya said. "I've seen a *dhakim* twist himself into a monster. Bind plaguespawn to his will. Take people apart and use their flesh as weapons."

"*Zhei'dhaka*," Elariel spat.

"What?"

"It's..." She cocked her head. "'Self-*dhaka*'? 'Reflective *dhaka*'? Turning the power on the wielder. It's forbidden, and for good reason. No ghoul would do such a thing." Her lip twisted in irritation, and she took a calming breath before picking up a fresh bandage. "I'll wrap this for one more night, just to be safe."

There was a silent moment as the ghoul wound the bandage between Maya's fingers. Maya hesitated, cleared her throat, then said, "Can I ask you something about *dhaka*?"

"Not afraid your Order will declare you a heretic?" Elariel snapped.

"Apparently they're trying to arrest me regardless," Maya said. "So I think I can risk it."

Elariel snorted. "Ask, then."

"Is it possible use to *dhaka* to connect two people? So they can speak in one another's minds, over a distance."

Elariel gave her a strange look. "Why do you ask?"

"Just...curious."

"An odd thing to be curious about." The ghoul shrugged and went back to the bandage. "There is a way, but it's not commonly used. Only between married couples, and even then only between those who are truly dedicated to one another. Once established, the bond can never be broken, except by death. And some stories say not even then. There's a famous saga among my people, about two lovers who bond themselves and then become mortal enemies because they can no longer stand one another's thoughts."

"How is it done?"

"It's called a blood-bond. Each partner introduces some of their blood into the other. A tiny bit will do. The usual ritual is to cut your palms and press them together. It's fairly straightforward to set up a resonance between the two after that—essentially the same principle that lets constructs communicate at a distance—" She stopped and shrugged again. "The details would mean little to you, I fear."

"Probably," Maya said, staring at her bandaged hand. *Will he be in my dreams tonight?* "Thank you."

*   *   *

The room was just how she'd left it, a circular chamber centered on the dormant image projector and a ring-shaped control console. Other Chosen arcana lined the walls. Corridors led off, like the spokes of a wheel, lit only by the faint firefly lights of distant machines rumbling to themselves. Directly overhead, Maya noted, there was a shaft leading up, with a ladder bracketed to the wall.

But the room was empty, silent. There was no sign of Ashok. Maya looked around, frowning.

If he uses these dreams to communicate with me, and he's not here, then... what's going on?

Something moved. She spun on her heel, hand going to her haken, though she knew it would do no good here.

"Hello?" she said. "Ashok, are we playing games now?"

No answer. Maya's heart pounded.

"It seems beneath the dignity of the emperor to try for a cheap scare," Maya said.

Movement again. A shimmer in the air, a faint outline, like a pencil sketch long erased. Maya got a sense of a human shape, reaching toward her. She backed away, coming up against the console. It came after her, but slowly, as though the motion required great effort. The outstretched arm trembled. It suddenly seemed less as though the thing were trying to grab her and more like it was... beseeching? Beckoning?

"Hello?" Maya said. "Can you hear me? Who are you?"

"*...remember...*" The word was barely a breath of wind. "*...I... remember...*"

"What? What do you remember?"

"*...remember...please...*"

The hand, almost invisible, stretched toward her. Maya's arm came up automatically to push it away. Where they touched, there was a crackle, like the faintest spark of static electricity. Maya blinked, and—

—she was walking down a corridor in a crowd of people in strange clothing—

—she was kissing someone—

—a vulpi squealed in agony—

—a plaguespawn thrashing in a jar—

—a woman's face, screaming while it came apart—

—a light brighter than anything she'd ever seen—

—and a smiling face, with golden hair and red eyes. *Ashok.*

The images flashed through Maya's mind, too quick to understand, accompanied by flickers of emotion that were not her own. She jerked her hand back. The thing glided toward her and she stumbled away.

"Whatever you're doing, Ashok, it won't work!" Maya glanced around wildly, then back at the wavering figure. "Get *away* from me!"

To her surprise, it halted, shimmering in the air. Then, slowly, it began to dissolve, and the lab around her went with it.

"Wait." Maya shook her head in confusion. "What *are* you—"

Too late. With a sigh like a dying breath, the figure vanished into sparkling motes of dust, and Maya fell back into a more ordinary sort of dream.

Chapter Three

Sarah and Elariel were both still asleep when Gyre woke, the ghoul curled in a tight ball with Sarah wrapped protectively around her. He slipped quietly out of bed and took his pack out into the corridor. Maya was sitting on the floor, determinedly chewing her way through a twice-baked travel cake, and offered Gyre a limp wave as he sat beside her.

"The others still asleep?" Gyre said.

Maya nodded and swallowed. "We can wake them when Tanax gets here."

Gyre frowned. On close inspection, while Maya's color had returned, there were still bags under her eyes. "Is your hand still bothering you?"

"Not really." Maya flexed her bandaged fingers. "Just having a hard time sleeping."

"Understandable. If this goes wrong…"

"Yeah."

The door to her room opened and Varo emerged, yawning and rubbing his freshly shaved head. "What's for breakfast?"

"Travel rations," Gyre said grimly, opening his pack.

"Plague that," Varo muttered. "I'm going to find something edible."

"I thought you were out of coin?"

"A good scout is never *quite* broke," Varo said with a wink.

He returned a few minutes later with a platter piled with fresh bread and a crock of butter, and Gyre forced himself to leave some for the others. *It's not vulpi bacon, but it beats travel rations.* The three women came out shortly thereafter, lured by the smell, and by the time Tanax arrived, everyone was more or less awake.

"The 'victory celebration' is kicking off already," he said, voice low. "Lots of Auxies in the streets. We may be better off waiting."

"The crowds should help our chances," Gyre said. "The Auxies will have other things to worry about."

"It's your call," Tanax said, looking at Maya.

"I don't think we can afford to wait," Maya said. "Every day we stay here is dangerous too."

The other centarch gave a slow nod. "Then let's get moving. We may have to detour a bit."

They piled out of the inn, packs shouldered, cloaks drawn up around them. Traveling with such a large group made Gyre's skin prickle, but there was nothing for it. Splitting up would only have multiplied their difficulties. He took some comfort in the fact that the streets were indeed crowded, even at this relatively early hour. People were decorating as though for a harvest festival, draping colorful garlands across their doors and windows. The air buzzed with excitement.

From where they'd stayed on the outskirts of the city, Tanax led them north and west, toward the spires clustered by the edge of the lake. As they moved deeper into Skyreach, the character of the buildings changed, growing larger but more run-down. Four-story wooden tenements sagged against their neighbors, wrapped in rickety balconies and stairways. The streets, except for a few broad avenues, were smaller and full of obstacles. The locals, as far as Gyre could tell, didn't seem much better off than the tunnelborn back in Deepfire. *Not exactly what*

I imagined. To hear people in the mountains talk, all the streets in Sky-reach were supposed to be paved with gold.

"We're still outside the city proper," Varo said when Gyre mentioned it. "You need a permit to live inside the boundaries, and those are expensive, so all the servants and menials live out here."

"Not so different from Deepfire after all, then," Gyre muttered, feeling obscurely vindicated.

Now that he was looking for it, the official boundary was impossible to miss. A wide, curving street defined the sweep of an immense circle, and on the inner side the buildings flanking the road abruptly went from wood to stone, or even unmetal. Bright banners called attention to the shops and restaurants in each building. The crowd grew thicker still, and acquired a definite intention, shuffling along the streets in a packed mass. Gyre found himself pulled apart from his companions, hemmed in on all sides.

Plaguefire. Elariel. Gyre dug his elbows in and pushed over to the ghoul's side. She was pressed tight against Sarah's arm, breathing hard. Gyre caught the arcanist's eye, and between them they sought to create a clear space, stiff-arming annoyed pedestrians out of their path.

"Tanax," Gyre said. When the centarch didn't hear, he grabbed his sleeve and pulled him close. "We have to get out of the crowd."

"We just need to cross Second Avenue," Tanax said. "After that—" He trailed off, looking ahead. "Damn. Are those soldiers?"

Gyre raised himself on tiptoes to try to peer over the surrounding masses. There was indeed a cordon of spearpoints along the edge of a wide street ahead, with a matching rank of neatly uniformed Auxies on the other side. Their presence held back the crowds, keeping the avenue clear.

"We'll have to go around," he told Tanax. "They're not letting anyone through."

Tanax swore quietly, then nodded. "Stay close to me. There's a bridge a few blocks over."

Making sure everyone got the message took a few minutes, and cutting against the flow of the crowd was slow. Eventually they broke into the clear on a side street, and Gyre called a halt. Elariel sat down on the stone steps of a building, whimpering, with Sarah's arm around her shoulders.

"Fucking humans," she said quietly. "Too fucking many of you."

"Is she all right?" Tanax said to Gyre.

"She'll be okay in a minute." Gyre chose his words carefully, not certain if Maya had told her fellow centarch the truth about Elariel yet. "She has trouble with crowds."

Tanax nodded sympathetically. "I knew an agathios like that. After ten minutes at a party he had to go lie down."

"She's doing better than when we first traveled together," Gyre said. "I had to bribe her with bacon to get her to leave the wagon."

"I heard that," Elariel said, not looking up. "You're the one who keeps dragging me into these rats' nests."

Sarah touched her shoulder and clucked sympathetically. When the ghoul managed to regain her feet, they set out again, cutting across the flow of traffic. Around another corner, a larger cross street dipped under an arched unmetal bridge, providing a way to cut across the lines of Auxies. But here the soldiers were doing more than standing guard. A whole squad of them was working on a massive arcana, a thing on wheels the size of a cart with four upward-curving talons.

"What is that?" Gyre said, eyes narrowing. "Some kind of weapon?"

"It's an image projector," Beq said. "A big one." She touched the side of her spectacles, and the lenses shifted and flipped into place with a series of clicks.

"Maybe they're going to put on some kind of entertainment?" Sarah said.

"It's for the announcement," Varo said. "The Senate uses them when they want to talk to the whole city at once."

What exactly are they planning to announce? Gyre's thoughts went to Apphia again, and his stomach turned. He hadn't meant to abandon her when he'd gone to the Purifier with Maya, but here he was, a thousand kilometers away when she might be in danger. *Just like I was with Yora.* He shook his head, trying to banish the worries. "Come on. Let's keep moving."

Walking as nonchalantly as possible, they followed the road down into the cool shadows under the bridge. A few other people were taking the same route, but no one took any particular notice of their little group. Once they were past, climbing back up to street level, Gyre risked a look over his shoulder. Whatever the Auxies had been doing with the image projector, it was apparently finished, because they'd all stood back. An officer regarded the thing expectantly.

Maya was looking too, chewing her lip. "I think—"

There was a sound, a deep *thump*, like a vast drum in the far distance. Then, abruptly, a man stood astride the bridge, thirty meters high, his smile broad and friendly and his hair gleaming like gold.

Nial-Est-Ashok, the Corruptor, held up his hand and turned in a full circle. He had none of the monstrous appendages they'd seen in the Purifier, and looked every inch the noble Chosen.

"Tanax," Maya hissed. "What in the plaguing fuck is going on?"

"I have no idea," Tanax said. "Do you know this man?"

"That's *him*," Elariel said. "The Corruptor."

"He's—" Tanax began.

Ashok cut him off. His voice was as loud as thunder, with a basso rumble that made Gyre's teeth buzz.

"People of Skyreach and the Dawn Republic," he said. "I am Nial-Est-Ashok, of the Chosen. I have come before you today to say that you have my profound admiration."

Looking down the avenue, Gyre saw another image of Ashok a dozen blocks farther on, and another one beyond that, on and on. *He really can speak to the whole city.* The crowds up and down the avenue were staring in stunned silence at this figure from the Elder past.

"For four centuries," Ashok went on, "you have struggled alone, bereft of the leadership and protection that my kind has always provided you. You have been pressed on all sides, by plaguespawn and *dhakim*, by Splinter Kings who refuse our legacy, by rebels and trai-tors. And yet you have *endured*. In all that time, you have not allowed yourselves to slide into barbarism. I salute you. And I am here to bring you the best possible news. Your struggle"—he paused, drawing out the moment—"is *over!*"

For a second there was nothing but stillness. Then someone shouted approval, and a few more people joined in. Cheers rose, hesitantly, like wet kindling gradually taking fire. Ashok smiled, perfect teeth gleam-ing, and went on.

"For all this time, the centarchs of the Twilight Order and the wise men of the Senate have kept the flame of civilization burning, trusting in the plan handed down to them and confident of eventual deliver-ance. That day has arrived. I am here, the first of many, and I pledge to do as we Chosen have always done—to defend you, to guide you, to keep you safe and happy. I apologize, my friends, for our long absence. But no more! The Chosen have risen again!"

The cheering was in earnest now, a full-throated roar that rose and fell like distant waves. Ashok raised his arms, triumphant. His image shrank, the viewpoint pulling back to show more people standing behind him. Several ranks of old men and women in white robes, each with a single purple stripe, smiled with him. Gyre recognized the tra-ditional attire of the Republic Senate; the Senators, he thought, looked distinctly uncomfortable with the proceedings. Ashok looked over his shoulder at them, then back at the crowd.

"Today, in the chambers of the Senate, the Council of the Twilight Order and the government have conferred on me the responsibility for leading our great civilization to its glorious future. With their agree-ment, we have dissolved the Dawn Republic. It was created to help humanity through the dark times of the Plague, but the dark times are over. We are now, as we were for so many centuries, the Chosen Empire—limitless, beneficent, and invincible.

"The challenges before us remain formidable. But I can assure you, my friends, that they will be met. Plaguespawn will not harry your livestock and hunt your children. Rebels and traitors will no longer threaten your way of life. Lands lost to the wilds will be reclaimed. Because while I am the last of the Chosen, I am not alone."

A new sound joined the ecstatic cheering, a steady thump as regular as a trip-hammer. On the avenue behind them, threading between the lines of Auxies, came another kind of soldier. They wore armor like a Legionary's, overlapping plates and a blank-faced helmet, but where the Legions wore pure white, this armor was iridescent silver, hard-edged and jagged instead of smooth and curved. They walked in absolute unison, every movement the same, and the steady *thump* was the descent of thousands of feet at the same instant.

"I don't..." Tanax looked from Gyre to Maya and back. "He can't be serious. The Council would never—"

"No?" Maya looked haunted. "If the Chosen came to them and proclaimed their glorious return?" Her voice dropped. "It worked on me."

"He can't just... move in and take over," Beq said, fiddling nervously with her glasses. "Not just like that."

"Who's going to stop him?" Gyre said. "If he has the centarchs on his side, no one else can stand up to a Chosen."

"He was a lot gooier down in the caves," Varo said.

"I think he can change his appearance," Maya said. "At least over a projection."

"We have to get out of here," Elariel said. "Now."

"Agreed." Gyre struggled to tear his eyes from the lockstep marchers. "How much farther?"

"Not far," Tanax said. "Follow me."

It was easier going once they got away from the avenue, leaving the crowds and cheers behind. The normal business of the city had practically come to a halt, the cafés and shops empty. The deserted streets felt like the aftermath of a catastrophe.

And they are, even though no one knows it yet. Gyre found a flicker of frustrated rage growing inside him. He'd spent half his life trying to get people to recognize that the legacy of the Chosen was holding them back, a suit of armor that weighed down as much as it protected. *Now Daddy turns up again and says everything's going to be all right, and they're ready to hand him the world on a plate.*

Maybe the rest of the Republic won't go along with it. This was Skyreach, after all, where the influence of the Elder world was strongest. *But even if a place like Khirkhaz was willing to stand up for itself, what hope would they have against a* Chosen? Prodominus, a Kyriliarch of the Council, had barely been able to buy time against the Corruptor's power.

We have to get to Deepfire. That would give them a chance to rest and figure out what came next. *One step at a time.*

Passing a last line of buildings, they emerged onto the lakefront, where a vast landscape of docks, piers, and quays accommodated a bewildering variety of boats. Beyond them was water, flat and endless, stippled by waves and shrieking, diving gulls. Gyre, who'd never seen a body of water bigger than a river, was momentarily taken aback at the sight of it. The far shore was nearly invisible, with only the blued outlines of mountains rising in the misty distance.

"It's beautiful," Sarah said, eyes wide.

"We're going *out* on that?" Elariel said.

"It's perfectly safe," Tanax said. "The lake is calm this time of year."

"That's not as reassuring as you think," the ghoul muttered.

"There," Varo said abruptly. "Two piers down, with the blue-white pennant."

Gyre spotted the boat, which looked like any of a dozen others. A man and two women were aboard it, working on a net.

"You're sure?" Tanax said.

"I'm sure," Varo said. "Let me do the talking, but be ready to show your haken. Maya, keep your cloak tight."

They approached the pier in a tight group, with Varo and Tanax in the lead. One of the women, catching sight of them, jumped off the tail of the boat and came forward. She was tall, with curly blue-green hair, and chewed a wad of something black and unpleasant, tucking it into her cheek when she spoke.

"Can I help you lot?" she said.

"Hopefully," Varo said. "I'm looking for number 473."

"Huh." Her expression barely flickered. "Well, I guess you found it. But you picked a plague of a day. You've heard what's happening? Might be best to sit tight until—"

"We've heard," Tanax said. He pushed his cloak open wide enough to show the haken at his belt. "We need to return to the Forge, immediately and without notice."

"Ah. Of course, Centarch." The woman blinked, then turned to shout over her shoulder. "We're heading out! Get moving!"

The rest of the crew dropped what they were doing and started hurrying around the boat, untying ropes. The tall woman went to the back and checked a piece of crystalline arcana.

"I assume you'll want to go the fast way," she said. "We might have enough in the sunsplinter to make it, but, Centarch, if you wouldn't mind?"

"Certainly." Tanax stepped to the machine and touched his haken, drawing power to fill its reserves.

"The rest of you can sit down over here," she said. "We're not really set up for passengers, but the benches are all yours. Apologies for the smell."

The whole craft stank of fish, Gyre discovered, and the benches were low and splintery. The six of them sat facing each other, hoods drawn up, while the crew bustled and shouted back and forth. Once she was satisfied, the tall woman touched the crystalline controls on the face of the arcana engine, and the water at the back of the boat started churning into a froth. They eased forward, slowly at first but with increasing speed as they left the congestion of the shore behind.

Before long, the Skyreach shore had shrunk into the distance, the impossibly tall shadows of its spires mirroring the misty heights of the mountains on the other side. The engine rumbled and spat, and the water flowed past at a steady pace, but if not for the crash of waves against the bow, Gyre wouldn't have known they were moving at all.

Elariel, looking pained, was bent over with her palms on her forehead.

"How deep is it, do you think?" she muttered. "If this…contraption flipped over, how long would it take us to reach the bottom?"

"Technically," Varo said, "we wouldn't reach the bottom, because rotting bodies float. One time, my friend and I had to build a raft, right, and I thought—"

"There's plenty of traffic between the Forge and the city," Tanax said. "All the Order's supplies and so on. Someone would find you pretty quickly."

"Sure," Elariel said. "I mean, look at all the boats out here."

There was a moment while everyone looked around. No other boats were in sight.

"Normally, I mean," Tanax said. "Today may be an exception."

"Wonderful." Elariel sighed.

Gyre shifted on the bench, bending down beside Maya. She was hunched over, letting her hood fall around her face.

"You okay?" he said.

"Fine."

"Really."

Maya sighed. "Just…thinking. And wishing I wasn't." She tugged at the edge of her hood. "He really can just walk in, can't he? They're all so ready for a Chosen to turn up and fix everything. Like I said, I can't even blame them. I did the same thing, and that's why we're in this mess."

Gyre started to say something, but he bit it off. *It's hard to argue with that.* "Ashok is apparently pretty persuasive."

"He is. But it's more than that. He…fits. He knows what his role is supposed to be in the story we tell ourselves, and he just steps into it. For someone who's been hiding Chosen-know-where for four hundred years, he knows us pretty well."

"You think he has spies out here?"

"I know he does," Maya said darkly. "I've met some of them."

"That sounds unpleasant."

"You have no idea." Maya tugged on her hood again. "If we can just get Jaedia away from the Forge, and Elariel can help her…"

"What about this Xalen Prodominus told you about?"

"I have no idea. If she's a centarch, she might be in the city, and we don't dare look for her. But I've never heard of a Xalen, and I know all the centarchs. We could—"

She cut off abruptly as the tall woman came toward them from the bow, glancing briefly at the arcana engine. She gave Tanax a brisk nod.

"Not much more than another hour, I think. Shall I signal ahead?" She touched a hooded lantern mounted on the ship's rail.

"No," Tanax said, a little too quickly. "That won't be necessary."

"We're going to the green dock," Varo said.

The woman's eyebrows rose. "The green dock? With…" Her eyes flicked to Tanax, and Gyre recalled the scout's mention of secrets the centarchs weren't supposed to be privy to.

"Needs must," Varo said with a shrug.

"I suppose so," the woman said slowly. "But—"

The wind, calm so far, chose that moment to gust. The boat rocked as a wave struck it, making everyone clutch the benches for support. At the same time, Gyre felt the air tearing at his hood. He managed to grab it before it blew back, but not everyone was quick enough. Elariel was flailing at hers, and Maya—

Maya's long red hair was blowing in the wind. She stared at the tall woman, who was looking at her, astonished.

"It's *you*," the woman hissed, then her voice rose. "Burningblade!" She glanced from Maya to Tanax. "We have orders to take her into custody."

"I know," Tanax said, spreading his hands. "Listen—"

"And the green dock—" Gyre could see wheels turning behind the woman's eyes. Then, abruptly, she dove for the signal lantern.

Gyre concentrated, and something in his skull went *click*. The world slowed to a crawl, and every moving object telescoped into a chain of shadowy doubles that traced out possible paths. Gyre's ghoul-made silver sword whipped from its sheath, slashing cleanly through the wooden post so the lantern tumbled into the sea. Before the tall woman had done more than try to shout a warning, he had the blade at her throat, and he watched her go wide-eyed in comical slow motion.

Maya was on her feet, igniting her haken. She leveled the flaming weapon at the other two crew members, who held up their hands in surrender. Gyre turned his augmentations off, the world abruptly returning to real time.

"You won't get away with this, traitor," the tall woman said. Gyre had to give her points for bravery, spitting in the face of a centarch. "They're waiting for us back at the docks in Skyreach. If we don't show up or send a signal, they'll know something happened and warn the Forge."

Maya glanced uncertainly at Varo, who gave a resigned shrug.

"She's probably telling the truth," he said. "It's the sort of thing I would do."

"You call yourself a scout," the woman seethed. "Helping a renegade."

"It's a long story," Varo said. "And I don't think we have time. Should we tie them up with something?"

"Elariel?" Gyre said. "Can you—"

The ghoul gave a weary nod. The tall woman watched Elariel nervously as she came over and laid a hand on her arm. Then the sailor's eyes rolled up in her head and she collapsed, Gyre catching her before she hit the deck. The other two crew made startled noises but froze under Maya's glare as Elariel headed toward them.

"This makes things complicated," Tanax said, already crouching by the arcana engine. It sputtered to life, driving the boat forward. "Given how long it's taken us to cross—"

"I know." Gyre sheathed his sword. "We'll have to work fast."

Chapter Four

The vast shape of the Forge, half mountain and half fortress, loomed increasingly large as the little boat approached. Its massive bulk would once have been comforting, the physical incarnation of the solidity of the Order. Now every balcony and glowing window could hide a hostile pair of eyes, ready to raise the alarm.

No one will be watching. Servants took boats to and from the Forge docks all the time. There were guards there, and they handled the business of checking for intruders. As far as anyone on the upper levels was concerned, there was nothing unusual here.

The slope of the mountain descended directly into the water, without even the suggestion of a beach. A dozen piers protruded from the rock, each attached to the mouth of a tunnel that led to the Forge's massive storerooms and warehouses. Varo, now sitting at the engine to steer, avoided all of them and headed for a narrow inlet, a fold in the stone that ran halfway up the mountain. From a distance, it was just a natural wrinkle in the rock, but when they came close Maya could see it had been carved out to provide just enough space for a boat. At the far end was a small circular passage, barely big enough to walk with head bent. A large unmetal pipe ran down the bottom of it, curving over the lip of the rock and down into the inky water.

"Intake," Varo said. "It goes through a processing unit and then feeds the cisterns."

"It's blocked," Elariel said. It was true—a little ways beyond the entrance, an unmetal grille walled off the tunnel.

"As it should be. Point of weakness." Varo made his way to the front of the boat and clambered up into the passage. "But sometimes the pipe gets clogged, and the servants have to come out here and unjam it. They think they're the only ones who know the trick, but..."

His hands found two innocuous sections of the grille and twisted them. The unmetal rotated smoothly, first one way and then the other. There was a *clunk*, and Varo rolled the whole thing aside into a hidden slot in the stone.

"Let's just say the scouts are observant." He bowed slightly. "And we remember things other people have forgotten."

"The Council would be furious if they found out about this," Tanax said.

"Probably." Varo scratched his nose. "Are you planning on telling them?"

One by one, balancing carefully on the rocking bow of the boat, they climbed over the stone lip and into the tunnel. When they were all past, Varo rolled the grille back into place, locking it with a solid-sounding *chunk*. Sarah poked at the mechanism, clearly wanting to linger, but Gyre and Elariel pulled her onward.

The scout led the way deeper into the fortress. It grew dark as pitch, and Maya summoned a *deiat* light to guide them. Eventually it revealed a taller space the size of a closet, where the pipe joined up with several others and ran vertically into a hole in the ceiling. Varo found a latch on the wall and opened a narrow door, which let out into a more familiar-looking Forge corridor.

"And here we are. Bottom floor, not far from the quartermaster's desk." Varo grinned. "So what now?"

"The hospital is on the third level from the top," Maya said. "Just above the residences. We need to get there, then down to the fourth level and the Gate chamber. There'll be guards on the main stairs. But if we take the servants' passages…"

"I think that would draw more notice," Tanax said. "We should pretend we have nothing to hide for as long as we can. If you all stay cloaked, I can tell anyone who asks that you're scouts in my service."

"They'll remember you were with us," Gyre pointed out. "Even if we get away, won't they arrest you afterward?"

"I'm coming with you," Tanax said. "No helping that now. The boat crew would identify me anyway."

Maya expected Gyre to object, but he only glanced briefly at Sarah, then shrugged. "What about Xalen?"

Tanax frowned. "I don't think we have time to hunt all over the Forge for someone we don't even know is here."

"Prodominus thought it was important," Maya said. "He's been following the Corruptor longer than any of us. We have to at least try."

"How do you propose to find her, then?"

Beq raised a hand. "If she's not a centarch, then she must be a part of the support staff. The quartermaster's office has the personnel records. If a centarch were to come asking, I'm sure they'd find her for you."

"It's still a risk," Tanax said. "It costs us time."

"It's worth a shot," Maya decided.

"Then, let's move," Elariel said, looking around nervously. "The sooner we get out of this place, the better."

The quartermaster's desk was at the edge of a vast atrium, tiled like a checkerboard in black and white and set with tables and chairs. The library and storerooms let onto it as well. Maya had spent quite a bit of time here, planning her missions with Varo and Beq. It felt strange to be walking through the familiar space with her hood up, trying hard to avoid notice.

"Chosen defend," Gyre muttered beside her.

"Something wrong?"

"It's so *big*," he said quietly. "With this much stone carved out, it's a wonder the mountain is still standing."

"It reminds me of the ruins under Deepfire," Sarah said.

"Please." Elariel snorted. "Comparing our tunnels to this...monstrosity is an insult. Our constructions follow the flow of the rock, bringing out the shapes within it, not just slicing it into straight lines in accordance with some diagram."

"Quiet," Tanax said.

He led the group up to the polished wooden desk. A young woman wearing the quartermaster's insignia sat behind it, writing in a ledger. She looked up as they approached, then sat straighter at the sight of Tanax's haken.

"Centarch," she said. "How can I help you?"

"I'm looking for someone," Tanax said. "Xalen. Can you tell me where she works?"

"The name sounds familiar," the young woman said. "Xalen. One moment." She pulled out another ledger, ran her finger down it, and made a face. "Oh, of course. She works in the library, in the research group. But she can be difficult, I'm afraid. If you'd like, I can call one of the senior librarians to help you."

"That won't be necessary," Tanax said gruffly. "Thank you."

He turned and headed toward the library, boots clacking on the polished stone. Maya stepped up beside him once they were out of earshot.

"She's likely to be here, at any rate."

"Mmm," Tanax said. "Possibly. But our clock is ticking. If we can't make it to the Gate, all this is for nothing."

"We'll make it," Maya promised, then dropped back when they reached the library section. Tanax beckoned to a gray-robed servant, who was sweeping the floor without much energy. The man nearly jumped when he realized who was calling for him.

"—thought they were all on the other side of the plaguing lake," he muttered, then put on a false smile. "Hello, Centarch! How can I help you?"

"I'm looking for Xalen. Take me to her, please."

"I'm afraid I don't know a Xalen," he said. "Is she a librarian?"

"I'm told she's with the research group."

"Ah." His eyebrows rose. "If she's here, she'll be in the reading rooms. But most of our staff has the day off, so I'm not sure—"

"I'll look for her," Tanax said.

"Of course, Centarch." He hurried to one of the iron gates that blocked access to the depths of the library and unlocked it with a key from his belt. "Take a right turn at the end of the corridor." He eyed the rest of the group uncertainly. "Do your, ah, companions need to accompany you?"

"They do," Tanax said, putting an arrogant spin on the words.

"I see. Just be cautious around the books, please, all of you."

Tanax gave a curt nod and strode through the gate, the others following behind.

"Do most centarchs sound like that?" Sarah asked.

"Unfortunately," Beq said.

Tanax looked pained. "We usually keep to ourselves, and too many take the support staff for granted. Working with Maya has been... instructive."

"You're doing better," Varo said, slapping him on the shoulder. "Most of the time you sound almost human!"

"Thanks," Tanax drawled.

He stopped at the turn the librarian had indicated. There was a long line of doors on the right, each leading to a cell just big enough for a desk and chair. The first few were empty.

"I guess we check them all," Maya said uncertainly.

"Just follow the light." Varo pointed farther down the hall to the bright glow of a sunstone.

The room was much like the rest, except that the desk was piled high with books and scraps of paper, weighed down with broken bits of arcana. The woman who sat in the chair was surprisingly young, probably in her late teens like Maya herself. She was short and thin, with pale blue hair inexpertly cut short and sticking up in undisciplined tufts. Her left arm was pressed awkwardly to her chest and she used only her right, flipping rapidly through a heavy leather-bound book and making notes in startlingly tiny script.

"Xalen?" Tanax said.

"Set the food by the door," the woman said, not looking up. "I'm busy."

Tanax looked at Maya for a moment, then cleared his throat. "My name is *Centarch* Tanax Brokenedge," he said. "I'd like to speak with you."

"Centarch?" Her pen stopped scratching. "So you're not bringing my breakfast?"

"I'm afraid not," he said.

"Also it must be after noon by now," Sarah added.

"My lunch, then." Xalen's pen resumed its work. "As I said, I'm busy."

Tanax blinked, nonplussed. Maya could understand why; any member of the Order was supposed to obey the commands of a centarch, regardless of what their other duties entailed. Xalen, however, seemed intent on pretending that they didn't exist.

"I really would like a bit of your time," he tried again.

"Are you still here?" Xalen flipped pages in her book. "Do you not understand the word 'busy'?"

"But—"

"File a complaint with the Council if you'd like. People are always threatening to do that, Chosen know why."

"Does the Council discipline you?" Tanax asked.

"Not that I'm aware of. Prodominus is the only who comes down here anyway."

"It's Prodominus who sent us," Maya broke in. "He asked us to speak to you."

"Unlikely," Xalen said. Her pen still hadn't halted. "He never talks to anyone about me."

"How would we have known to look for you if he hadn't?" Maya said.

"Unclear. Either way, it can wait for his return. You can speak with him directly."

"Prodominus is dead," Gyre said impatiently. "So please—"

Xalen's pen stopped. "That's not possible."

"I'm afraid it's true," Maya said, glaring at Gyre. "We saw it happen."

"I see." Xalen set her pen down neatly and blew on her page, then put a broken piece of blaster on top to hold it in place. "That is... unfortunate."

"We're in a hurry," Tanax said, "so—"

The chair rotated abruptly. Xalen's lips were pressed into a tight line, and her big purple eyes shone with unshed tears.

"I must ask you to excuse me," she said. "I find myself with an urgent task. Good day."

She rose, bowed slightly to Tanax, and pushed past him out into the corridor.

"Wait," Gyre said. "We need to ask you—"

"Busy," Xalen sniffed. She turned and started walking down the corridor. "I'm... busy." Then, abruptly, she broke into a run.

Tanax swore and started to follow, but Maya held out a hand. "Let me talk to her."

"We don't have time for this," Gyre growled. Behind him, Elariel nodded emphatically.

"Just a few minutes," Maya said. "Stay here."

She hurried after Xalen without waiting for their approval. The researcher had already turned a corner up ahead, and Maya jogged to catch up. Another corridor let onto a number of small apartments, most of the doors standing open and the rooms within dusty and unoccupied. The one at the very end was closed, with light leaking out underneath. Maya tried the handle and found it unlocked.

The room was small but cozy, with a bed, a small stove, and a little pantry. Books, unsurprisingly, were everywhere, piled in neat stacks. Xalen stood at the foot of the bed, staring at nothing. Her hand clutched at her librarian's robe, twisting the fabric into tightening knots. Her breathing was fast and ragged.

"Xalen," Maya said quietly.

"Told you," Xalen mumbled. "Busy. Please."

"I'm sorry," Maya said. "We should have known you and Prodominus were close."

"Close." Xalen took a deep breath and let go of her robe, dabbing at her eyes with the back of her hand. "We...were, yes. He is... *was*... my father."

"Oh," Maya said, momentarily at a loss for words.

I'd never heard anything about Prodominus' daughter. It wasn't unusual for a centarch to have children—casual assignations weren't forbidden, and a few even married—but they would almost always live with their other parent, and Maya had never heard of any joining the Order. *Deiat* potential wasn't inheritable by blood, so children of centarchs were no more likely than any others to be able to become centarchs themselves.

"I apologize," Xalen said, while Maya collected her thoughts. "I have behaved... suboptimally."

"You don't have to apologize," Maya said. "I had no idea—"

"Grief is unproductive. Inefficient." Xalen turned around, her features under tight control. "You're Maya Burningblade, aren't you?"

For the second time in a few breaths, Maya was taken aback. She fought the urge to pull her hood a little tighter. "I'm not—"

"You don't need to hide from me," Xalen said. "Prodominus told me that if something happened to him, you might come to me, and I should trust you."

"Ah." Maya pulled her hood away gingerly. "The Council has declared me a traitor."

"The *Council.*" Xalen waved a hand dismissively, as though that were all that needed saying. "I assume my father was killed by the Corruptor?"

"Ah...yes," Maya said, fighting the feeling that she was half a step behind the conversation. "How do you know—"

"I helped him with his research. That was my purpose here. He's been trying to untangle the Corruptor's influence for years."

"Ashok—the Corruptor—is free," Maya said. "He just announced to all of Skyreach that the Council and the Senate have asked him to lead a new Chosen Empire."

"Unfortunate, but not surprising." Xalen took another deep breath and wiped at her eyes again. Her left arm, Maya noticed, was not merely held against her chest, but rested in a sort of sling sewn into the fabric of her robe. "And you've come to see me, as Prodominus instructed."

"That's right," Maya said, trying to regain control. "And we don't have much time. If someone raises the alarm—"

"Oh, time is of the essence. Come."

"Wait," Maya said as Xalen pushed past her. "Come *where*?"

"Prodominus' office," Xalen said. "He left instructions. I assume you have a plan to leave the Forge afterward?"

"Via Gate," Maya said, hurrying to keep up. "But—"

"I shall accompany you. I imagine the Corruptor would discover my efforts before long in any case. Do you trust these companions of yours?"

"I do," Maya said. They rounded the corner and found the others waiting for them. "Gyre—"

"About time," Gyre said. "The alert could come any minute."

"We should move quickly, then," Xalen said. "I apologize for my earlier infirmity."

"'We'?" Tanax said. "Maya, she's coming with us?"

"Apparently." Maya put a hand on Xalen's shoulder to slow her. To her surprise, the girl shrank away, taking a quick step backward.

"Do not touch me, please," Xalen said, taking deep breaths. "It is... a personal matter."

"Sorry," Maya said. "But slow down a minute. What exactly do we have to do in Prodominus' office?"

"He has a safe there, containing critical parts of his research on the Corruptor," Xalen said. "His instructions to me in the event of his death were that Maya Burningblade would ask for my help, and I was to make sure she retrieved those files."

"That's on the top level, with the rest of the Council offices," Tanax said. "We don't have *time*, not if we're going to grab Jaedia as well."

"Prodominus thought it was important enough to make me swear to pass the message to Maya," Gyre said.

"I do not know who Jaedia is, but she cannot be more important than the future of humanity," Xalen said.

"We're not leaving Jaedia," Maya said, shooting Xalen a hard look. "We'll have to split up. Tanax and Gyre can get the files while the rest of us find Jaedia."

Xalen shook her head. "The safe is keyed to you, Maya. Apart from Prodominus, only you can open it."

Maya glanced at Beq, who frowned. "I don't have my tools," she said. "And even if I did, I don't know how long it would take."

Plaguing fuck. Maya chewed her lip, excruciatingly aware of every passing heartbeat. *I can't leave Jaedia, not again—*

"You and Xalen find the files," Gyre said, "and the rest of us will get Jaedia."

Maya blinked. "But—"

"I know where she is," Beq said.

"And we'll need my authority to get her out," Tanax said slowly. "It might work."

But. For a moment, Maya's mind resisted. The only way to make sure Jaedia was really safe was to carry her with her own hands. *But*. Maya looked between her friends. She'd trusted them with her life— Beq, Tanax, Varo. *Even Gyre. And Elariel is the one I'm counting on to help Jaedia. But...*

"We'll get her out," Gyre said. "I promise."

"Okay." Maya took a deep breath. "I trust you."

"I could come up with you," Varo said.

"No." Maya's mind felt abruptly clear. "All you get Jaedia and head to the Gate. I'll meet you there as soon as Xalen and I find what we need." Her hand closed briefly around her haken. "And be ready to move fast."

Chapter Five

Gyre

They took the grand staircase up, spiraling around and around a massive open space at the center of the Forge, like a castle tower turned inside out. The *scale* of it all still amazed Gyre. He'd traversed many kilometers of ghoul tunnels buried under the Shattered Peaks, but they gave the impression of having been dug out one curving segment at a time, not as a single vast construction like this Chosen work.

That might explain the winces of aesthetic agony Elariel kept giving with each corner they rounded. Refuge, the last ghoul city, was larger than the Chosen fortress, but it looked much closer to a natural cave on a titanic scale. It's rooms and dwellings were embedded into monstrous stalactites and stalagmites, their surfaces mimicking native rock. This place was all smooth walls and right angles, treating the stone as nothing but a convenient medium.

The casual use of *deiat* was also breathtaking, in a way. Touches that would have signified immense wealth and status in Deepfire were a matter of course. Every wall was adorned with sunstones, for example, providing a clean white light instead of the dim greens and blues of glowstones or the flicker of lanterns. The pipes they'd passed, drawing in and purifying lake water, would have been impossible for anyone but an order of centarchs.

Unlike in Refuge, though, here there were human servants, scurrying along in shapeless gray robes with laundry or meals. *Deiat* could do wonders, but it couldn't animate constructs the way *dhaka* did. For all their power, the Chosen had been dependent on menials to perform the basic labor of life, and the Order was no different.

"This is it," Tanax said, breaking into Gyre's reverie. They were at a broad landing, with several corridors leading off. Gyre's legs were already aching, and Elariel was leaning against Sarah, puffing for breath. "Move quick, Maya. We'll see you at the Gate."

Maya, her hood once again drawn forward over her face, nodded and continued up the spiral steps with Xalen. Gyre suppressed a dark anxiety at the separation. *Maya will be fine. She can handle herself better than any of the rest of us.*

"Right," Tanax went on. "Follow me."

The corridors they passed through were all empty, though spotlessly free of dust. Through open doors, Gyre caught sight of neat, sparely furnished bedrooms, communal kitchens, and occasional baths. Sarah, following his gaze, raised her eyebrows.

"I have to say," she murmured, "I expected a little more luxury."

"Luxury isn't the way of the Order," Tanax said, pausing at an intersection. A gray-clad servant hurried past, paying them no mind.

"Tell that to Raskos," Gyre said.

"The duxes are part of the Republic, not the Order," Varo said. "If you want luxury, go look in the towers in Skyreach."

"Quiet," Elariel said. She stayed close to Sarah, looking at the floor as though hoping to lose herself in her hood.

"Indeed," Tanax said. "In here."

He pushed through a swinging door, and the others followed. The hospital was built on the same gargantuan scale as the rest of the complex, a huge, high-ceilinged room with space for a hundred beds. Most of it was used as storage, piled with crates, barrels, and smaller containers covered in a dense layer of dust. A dozen cots were in two neat rows, sectioned off from one another by canvas barriers.

"Over there," Beq said.

A lone woman lay in a bed piled high with blankets. She was in early middle age, with brilliant green hair clipped so short it was barely fuzz. Her cheeks were sunken and her eyes deep set, like her skull was pressing against the skin, trying to emerge.

It was strange that this person Gyre had never laid eyes on occupied such a central position in Maya's life. Beq made her way to the bed and clasped Jaedia's hand, and Gyre wondered if she'd known the older centarch too.

Elariel gave a surprised squeak, and Gyre turned to find an older man in a white robe pushing through the curtain, frowning at them. He stood straighter at the sight of Tanax and his haken, and his lips twitched into an unctuous smile.

"Centarch," he said. "I wasn't expecting anyone, with the celebration in the city."

"Important business," Tanax said. "I need a chair to move this woman. Quickly, please."

"Ah...to move her, Centarch?"

"Yes." Tanax stepped closer, glaring at the man. "Is there a problem?"

"I don't *think* so, Centarch, but..." The doctor squirmed like a mouse in a trap. "I'm afraid I will need to confirm your business with the Council."

"I'm *sorry?*"

"It's just that I have *specific* orders," the doctor said miserably. "And I can't allow you to move this *particular* patient until they are countermanded by someone in authority." He stepped backward. "If you'll excuse me for *just* a moment, I'll find someone to run upstairs—"

He froze, eyelids fluttering, then folded gently into a loose-limbed heap on the floor. Elariel stepped away from his unconscious form, shaking her head.

"I could see where that was going," she said. "Come on, we're wasting time. We need to get *out* of here."

"I..." Tanax set his jaw. "Right. Find a wheelchair; there should be a few around. There's a ramp down the hall that will keep us out of sight."

Gyre, Varo, and Beq pushed through the curtain and back into the larger hospital. Nothing moved, which Gyre hoped meant the doctor had been on duty alone. He headed for a desk near the back of the room, while Beq and Varo went to the piles of supplies.

There were no wheelchairs behind the desk, unfortunately, but something else caught Gyre's eye. One corner was a mess of stacked paperwork, but a single sheet of foolscap sat on the other end, and Gyre spotted Maya's name on it. He grabbed the note and read,

To All Hospital Staff,

Centarch Jaedia Suddenstorm is not to leave the hospital without my express orders, confirmed in person. If Centarch Maya Burningblade attempts to contact her, direct her to speak to me in my office. Do not sound a general alert. Do not disclose these orders to anyone but the Council.

Kyriliarch Baselanthus Coldflame

Gyre reread the note, stomach sinking, then hurried back to Tanax. Beq had found a wheelchair, an ancient-looking unmetal thing with frayed cushions, and she and Elariel were maneuvering the unconscious Jaedia into it. Without the blankets, the woman's frame was pitifully skinny under a thin hospital gown. When she slumped into the chair, Gyre had to watch for a long moment to make sure she was still breathing.

"Tanax," he said, turning away. "I think we have a problem. That doctor wasn't just acting on some general order."

He handed the centarch the note. Tanax read it quickly, frowning.

"This doesn't make sense," he said. "They can't have known we were coming. And if they did, why hasn't anyone sounded the alarm?"

"Because it's a trap," Varo said, reading over Tanax's shoulder. "Basel-anthus wants Maya to come to him."

"What?" Beq said, nearly dropping Jaedia.

"You think he's working for the Corruptor?" Gyre said.

"Maybe," Tanax said. "Basel served as Maya's mentor after Jaedia fell ill. He could just want an opportunity to talk her down before captur-ing her."

"Either way, they're not going to let her leave," Beq said. "We have to warn her!"

"Prodominus' office is near Basel's?" Gyre said.

"Just down the hall," Tanax said grimly.

Plaguing fuck. Gyre put a hand on his sword and checked his energy bottle. Half-full. He swapped it out with the last full one from his pack. *It'll have to be enough.*

"I'm going after her," he said. "Get Jaedia to the Gate. We'll be with you as soon as we can."

"I'll go with you," Tanax said immediately.

"No," Gyre snapped. "You need to talk us past the guards at the Gate, remember? And if it's centarchs she's up against, I'm the only other person who'll be much help."

"Fuck," Beq said softly.

"Take care of Jaedia. Maya will kill me herself if something happens to her."

Gyre pushed the door open, confirmed the corridor was still empty, and broke into a run.

Maya

The Kyriliarchs had their offices on the Forge's top floor, with the larger windows and broad balconies that elevated position afforded. Coming up the stairs, Maya had a sudden flash of memory, reporting to Basel's office to learn she'd been assigned her first mission away from Jaedia with Tanax, Beq, and Varo. Between nerves at the assignment, worry about Jaedia, and falling in love with Beq at first sight, it had been a busy day.

Now she had to stop herself from turning right, out of habit, and turned left instead. Prodominus' office was at the other end of the hall, the floor dusty with disuse. Maya had gotten the impression he didn't spend much time here, and he'd apparently forbidden the cleaners from disturbing anything. She stepped carefully, but puffs of dust still bloomed from her footsteps. Xalen, behind her, shuffled along in a waist-high gray cloud.

"Do you know where the safe is?" Maya said, looking over her shoulder. For a moment she tensed as someone moved at the other end of the corridor, but they quickly went out of sight. *Probably a servant.* Still, the place wasn't *completely* empty. *We need to be careful.*

"I have a description," Xalen said. "I've never been up here before."

"Never?"

"Prodominus was not public about our relationship. When he wanted to speak with me, he came down to the library."

"That seems...cruel," Maya said. "Was he ashamed of you?"

"I don't believe so," Xalen said, with no apparent concern. "He wanted to avoid complications, and I agreed. In any event, I only leave the library under extraordinary circumstances."

"Ah."

The door was unlocked, thankfully. The office beyond was just as Maya remembered it, a hopeless clutter of junk, martial trophies, and books. An ancient, tattered flag bearing the insignia of a kingdom Maya didn't recognize was draped over a suit of Legion armor on a stand. A blaster rifle lay on the desk, barrel removed and stock open to show its inner workings. Several piles of books, dangling paper-strip bookmarks like long tongues, sat in front of the only chair that wasn't buried.

"Interesting," Xalen said with a faint tinge of fascinated disgust in her voice. "I always suspected Prodominus had an untidy mind."

"Tell me the safe isn't buried under all this stuff."

"I don't believe so. It should be in the wall behind the desk. Look for a false panel."

Maya hurried around the desk, raising more clouds of dust. On the back wall, the polished rock of the Forge had been layered over with wood carved in a repeating pattern. She prodded the sections, one at a time, until she found a place that shifted under her fingers. It came away easily, revealing an unmetal door studded with arcana crystals. It was reminiscent of the safe that Beq had cracked in Prodominus' warehouse, where they'd found the resonator, but this time she had neither Beq nor her tool kit. *Let's hope this works.*

Touching her haken, Maya sent a narrow thread of *deiat* into the mechanism. Another safe might have required a code, even an image, to unlock—this one, apparently, was tuned to her identity itself. The crystal glowed briefly, and there was a deep *clunk*. The door swung silently open.

"That was straightforward," Xalen said. She leaned forward, her face alive with curiosity. "What has he left us?"

Inside the safe was a single leather case, thick with folded pages. Maya opened it and a dozen sheets of paper fell out, covered in a dense, hard-to-read hand. Xalen snatched them up, paging through so rapidly that Maya could only catch pieces over her shoulder.

—the last resort in the face of disaster—

—the Plague was unstoppable—

—sent to the Shattered Peaks—

"There is a great deal here," Xalen said. "I need more time."

"Good thing you're coming with us." Maya took the loose pages and crammed them back into the case, then handed the whole thing to Xalen, who stuck it inside her robe. "You'll have plenty of time to figure it out once we get out of here."

"Agreed," Xalen said, rising. "And—"

She stopped. Maya got up from behind the desk, brushing dust from her knees, and likewise froze. Baselanthus, Jaedia's mentor, stood in the doorway wearing a sad, weary smile.

"Hello, Maya," Basel said. He wore his robe of office, heavy and stitched through with silver, and carried a long unmetal staff topped with a cracked globe of crystalline arcana. Though he was bald as an egg, his beard was long and white, and his crimson eyes had lost none of their intelligent gleam.

"Kyriliarch." Maya stepped forward, between him and Xalen. "Whatever they've told you about me, you know it isn't true."

"I know." Basel beckoned. "Come. We don't have much time."

"Don't." Xalen's voice was a hiss. "He's one of them. The Corruptor's agents."

"What?" Maya glanced at her, then back to Basel. "Where are we going?"

"Away from here, for a start," Basel said. "We have matters to discuss, and there will be an alert any moment. Please, come."

Maya looked to Xalen. "He can't... He was Jaedia's mentor. He helped her *raise* me."

"Prodominus was certain," Xalen said, eyes narrowed.

"Prodominus is a traitor to the Order," Basel snapped. "We talked about my suspicions of him, Maya."

"We did." Maya looked up slowly, feeling something horrible churning at the back of her mind. Pieces fell into place, one by one. "But we were wrong. He only wanted to stop me from making a terrible mistake."

"I will be interested to hear your perspective," Basel said. "But *not here.*"

"I just need to ask you one question," Maya said. She felt sick, her gut full of acid. "The Thing."

The old man blinked. "What?"

"This device." She tapped the now-lifeless chunk of arcana in her chest. "You gave it to me."

"I did." Basel drew himself up. "It saved your life—"

"I know," Maya said. "I asked the Archive about it. It is—was—a power regulator, designed to keep me from drawing so much *deiat* that I would become vulnerable to the Plague."

Maya was certain Basel's eyes widened in surprise, just slightly, but he only stroked his beard and said, "Indeed."

"But *how*?" Maya's certainty was building by the moment. Her anger was right behind it. "The Archive *also* told me it would have required *dhaka*."

"We..." He looked pained a moment. "Yes. When we realized you would die for certain, we found a *dhakim*. In secret. We only wanted to help you, Maya."

"You're lying." Maya drew her haken, the blade igniting into a bar of white-hot fire. "Ashok told you what to do, didn't he? How long have you had one of his resonators?"

Baselanthus took a long step backward, holding his staff in front of him. "I don't know what you—"

"*How long?*"

Fire bloomed around Maya, almost of its own accord. A wind as hot as an oven's breath whipped toward the old man. Something changed in his eyes, a long-held mask falling away. His bushy eyebrows narrowed. Blue-white flames sprang up in a circle around him, so cold that crystals of ice webbed out along the stone walls. In the space between them, the air hissed and steamed.

"All your life, you stupid, ungrateful girl," Basel hissed. "He predicted your birth, told us where to find you and that you'd need protection from the Plague. Without him, you'd be dead a thousand times over."

Grief welled up from Maya's gut, and she set her jaw against it. *I have to ask.* "Did Jaedia know?"

"Of course not. She never could see the bigger picture. The greater good."

"You had me spy on Prodominus because you knew he was on to you. And then when we found the resonator—"

"Of course." A smile returned to Basel's lips. "Look what we have *accomplished*, Maya!"

"I let a monster out of its cage."

"You brought us a *savior*."

"Jaedia." More pieces unfolded in Maya's mind. "You sent her out to look for the black spider. Into an ambush."

Basel's smiled faded. "I did. It was the hardest thing I've ever done, Maya. You must believe me. Whatever her faults, Jaedia was like a daughter to me."

"So you sent her to die?" Maya said, voice rising. Sparks swirled wildly around her. "Worse than die. To be a puppet for exactly the *things* we swear an oath to destroy."

"I did what I had to do to bring the Chosen back," Basel said. "Whatever it cost me in pain and grief, it was worth every drop. You're young, Maya, and you don't understand. But I have *seen* the path humanity is on. Every year the Order is smaller, weaker. Every year the Republic loses ground to the Splinter Kings, and every year they in turn lose ground to the plaguespawn, chewing at us like vultures tearing at an open wound. Without the Chosen, humanity cannot stand."

"Ashok isn't a Chosen. Not anymore."

"He's the only chance we have left. The world will be *remade*. Shaped into something safe for us."

"I know what he wants the world to be." Maya's hand tightened on her haken as memories assailed her. "On the Forsaken Coast, I saw what one of his *children* had done to the people it was *protecting*."

"Irritating whelp," Basel snarled. He thumped his staff on the stone. "You don't need to understand, only obey."

"Get out of my way, Basel."

He gave her a pitying look. "Oh, Maya. Must we?"

Blue flame spun and flared. Lines of ice shot along the walls, a dozen at once, twisting in an ever-shifting pattern. Maya sensed the flow of *deiat*, threw out her own to counter, but Basel was *fast*, his flows weaving around hers like rabbits dodging a clumsy hound. She pulled back, and back again, finally withdrawing into a shield of roaring flame around her and Xalen. She crouched within it as the ice tendrils detonated, clawing at her defenses, sapping her power.

"When I move," Maya shouted, "find something to hide behind!"

Xalen, eyes wide, gave a furious nod. Maya concentrated, then blew her shield outward, a flare of power that shoved Basel's influence back. Before he could recover, she charged, haken raised. Out of the corner of her eye, she saw Xalen dive behind Prodominus' desk.

"Jaedia did not neglect your training, I see," Basel said. He backed up a step, and a blade of ice, razor sharp, sprouted from the wall to intercept Maya's swing. It shattered under the impact, but two more replaced it, and Maya had to fall back. "But you still have the folly of youth."

"And you're as arrogant as any old man," Maya said. She slashed through the ice, chunks shattering into glittering sprays of crystal. At a gesture, fire whirled around her, melting hoarfrost into billowing clouds of steam. She sent the flames rolling forward, where they were met by a wall of freezing mist. The stone underfoot groaned and split with a *crack*.

Basel's power spun wildly around him, lines of *deiat* twisting like a basket of snakes. He came at Maya again, and again her parries were too late and too slow, forcing her to retreat to a wild, inefficient defense. *Not good*. At this rate, she would tire long before he did, leaving her helpless, her connection to *deiat* burned out. *He's too fast*. Basel needed no clumsy gestures to control his flows, shifting them by will alone.

All right. I can't beat him on technique. And the old man knew better than to engage her blade to blade, keeping her back with *deiat* manifestations. *Let's see how he likes a little brute force, then.*

Maya burst out of her defensive crouch, another wild flare of energy shredding the icy tendrils for a few moments. In the brief respite, she extended her haken and sighted along it, concentrating her power in the blade. It swelled, growing so bright it left burning afterimages, a swelling ball of pure white plasma. Maya held it as long as she could, then let it pour outward in a torrent.

There was no technique here, no clever tricks or subtlety. Basel saw her coming a kilometer away, and wove his own power in a solid defense, her flames smashing into a shield of ice that regrew as fast as she wore it away. It was the correct countermove, instinct honed over a lifetime of dueling.

But this wasn't a duel, and Maya was no longer an ordinary cent-arch. She wrenched her connection to *deiat* open, drawing more power and still more. Flames haloed around her, torturing the air, twisting into a glowing nimbus. Her hair rose as though she was underwater, its brilliant red looking half like fire itself. The stones beneath her feet groaned, then cracked, then started to glow a sullen orange.

Her off hand went to the Thing, instinctively expecting it to be hot and angry against her skin. Whether she'd realized it or not, under its tutelage she'd always shied away from her true limits, like a child who learns not to touch the hot stove. But the arcana was dead and broken, and its restraints on Maya were gone.

And Basel fell back. Slowly, first one step, then another. He leaned toward her, both hands raised, like a man pushing into a hurricane wind. His ice sublimed, blowing apart in torrents of steam, flames creeping closer no matter how much he reinforced his defenses. However good his technique, his raw strength was still merely human, below the level where the Plague would have culled him. Maya's was not, not anymore.

Gritting her teeth, Maya stomped one foot, sending a pulse along the line of energy connecting them. The air detonated, shards of ice driven deep into the stone. Basel was picked up and tossed backward along the corridor, landing on his back and sliding several meters. His staff lay on the ground beside him, a melted ruin.

Maya lowered her haken. Flames guttered along the blackened walls, and the stone around her was spiderwebbed with fractures. She stalked forward.

Basel, struggling to rise, gave a low, hacking laugh.

"I always wondered," he said, "what you would be like when you reached your full strength. More fool me." He managed to reach his knees, and spat a glob of black phlegm on the ground. "Jaedia would be proud."

"Don't say her name," Maya growled. She stared down at him. "I should kill you."

"Probably." Basel gave a weary smile. "But that's the thing about old men. We may be arrogant, but we also like to have a backup plan. Evinda!"

The air in the corridor was abruptly alive with a storm of blaster fire.

Chapter Six

Gyre

Gyre crouched at the top of the stairs and wished he had better options.

Tanax's hurried instructions on how to find Prodominus' office had turned out to be unnecessary. At least two dozen Legionaries waited in the central atrium, their attention on one of the branching hallways. That, presumably, was where Maya was, and thus where Gyre needed to be. *But how to get there?*

His speed, *deiat* protection, and silver sword made him more than a match for a Legionary, but not for two whole squads' worth. *Some kind of distraction would go a long way.* He wished, again, that Kit was here. With her small, nimble construct bodies, well-timed distractions were a specialty of hers.

In the meantime, he kept his head behind the stone railing and waited for an opportunity. He thought it had come when thunderous noise started to echo out of the corridor, staccato blasts and flashes painting the walls with strobing shadows. But not one of the Legionaries so much as twitched, accustomed to working alongside centarchs and their spectacular manifestations. So Gyre waited and ground his teeth while the last rumble of thunder faded away to nothing.

Then, from down the corridor, a voice barked an order and the soldiers swung into action. The first squad charged, blasters spitting fire, while the second swung into covering positions.

Probably the best chance I'm going to get. Gyre charged, activating his augmentations as he sprinted up the last few stairs. The world slowed around him and his steps became long, floating glides.

The Legionaries heard him coming, and a decarch shouted a warning. Half the covering squad turned and fired, blaster rifles making their telltale *cracks*. *Deiat* bolts raced out, his silver eye extrapolating their trajectories. Gyre danced and spun, staying neatly out of their way. The bolts detonated with dull *booms* against the far wall.

He didn't *need* to dodge, strictly speaking. Thanks to the ghouls, he wore a harness that dissipated most emanations of *deiat*, including the sunsplinter-powered blaster bolts. *But the longer it takes them to realize that, the better.* He kept threading through their fire until he was scant meters away; then he abandoned subtlety and sprinted at his full augmented speed, drawing his silver sword. Blaster bolts faded into nothingness where they should have impacted him.

Even the ghoul weapon wouldn't penetrate the thickest unmetal of a Legionary's armor, but Gyre had plenty of practice finding the weak spots. He reached the first soldier, still clutching his rifle, and put the tip of the blade up through the bottom of his chin. The next had time to reach for her sword, but the motion exposed her unprotected armpit, and Gyre's weapon punched through and into her chest. She fell away as the next man swung at him, a swarm of shadow-swords indicating probable attacks. Gyre ducked, slashing the inside of the soldier's thigh and watching a spurt of blood lazily paint the stones.

Three down and far too many to go. Auxies would have run for it, but Legionaries, as usual, were made of sterner stuff. They all had their swords drawn now, unmetal blades a match for his, and they spread out in an arc to encircle him. Down the corridor, blaster fire continued, joined by the wild crackle and rush of flames. *Maya.*

No time to think. *I can't let them surround me.* He charged the man closest to the wall, made a slow feint until the soldier's blade came up to parry, then twisted abruptly to block the strike of the next Legionary over. Sparks flew, drifting lazily through the air in his enhanced perception. He rotated at the hip and kicked the first Legionary in the chestplate, sending him staggering into the wall, then slammed his elbow into the second soldier's throat. She stumbled backward as well, but by then a third man was closing, with more behind him. Gyre recovered from the kick, ducked under the Legionary's thrust, and killed him with a neat lunge of his own. His crumpling body fouled the two behind him for a moment, and Gyre danced away.

No good. There's too many. A pair of people emerged from the embattled hallway, an old man in scorched, smoking robes limping on the arm of a purple-haired woman with a haken in hand. The man seemed dazed, but the woman took in Gyre and the dead Legionaries in a single glance. She shoved her tottering companion toward one of the soldiers and raised her blade, a coruscating line of shimmering white energy.

"Get him out of here!" she shouted. "I'll handle Silvereye."

She knows my name. Gyre wondered if he should be flattered. Two of the Legionaries grabbed the old man and began a hurried retreat, while the others started to spread out around him again. The centarch came straight at him, sword coming up for a downward chop.

Typical. The centarch he'd fought at the Commune camp had been the same. Secure in the knowledge their panoplies would protect them from any conventional attack, they neglected defense, and his silver sword caught them off guard. *Let's end this quickly.*

He stepped forward and thrust, ready to foul the downward stroke with his shoulder and skewer the woman. Even as he moved, though, she *twisted* in a direction his shadow-projections had barely thought possible, fast enough that even in his slowed perception he didn't have time to adjust. His blade missed her side by centimeters, and at the same time she reversed her haken, ready to plunge it into his back. Only the speed of his augmentations let Gyre throw himself forward, landing inelegantly on his stomach and rolling to one side to avoid a Legionary sword coming down to skewer him like a fish.

Gyre swiveled, kicking the Legionary's legs out from under him and swarming to his feet as another soldier came in. This one swung high as well, but without the centarch's grace, and Gyre thrust into his armpit and spun away as he toppled. The centarch, though, was right behind the dying man, flicking a lightning-fast cut at Gyre's side. He parried, the energy blade *screeching* a protest, then parried again and again as she pressed the assault.

He was faster, he *had* to be faster, but somehow it wasn't quite enough. Her blows were so abrupt his silver eye didn't know what to make of them, spraying shadows unhelpfully in every direction. And when he attacked, she seemed to already know where his blows would land, fading away or deflecting with ease. Gyre gave ground, away from the corridor and into one of the atrium walls.

Just as he felt the rough stone against his back, the centarch paused, gesturing with her free hand. Arcs of white light, like scythe blades whipping through the air, slammed into the stone beside and above Gyre, cutting deep and raising a cloud of dust. Huge chunks of rock slid free, gathering speed and tumbling toward him.

It was a good trick, and an ordinary opponent would doubtless have been buried in falling stone. However, if Gyre's eye couldn't follow the centarch's swordplay, its projections were ideal for the mindless chunks of rock. He watched their trajectories, stepping adroitly into the gaps, and kicked out at a fist-sized stone as it passed to adjust its path just so. It hit the floor, bounced, and sprang directly into the centarch's face. She slashed at it, the rock detonating into a cloud of dust at the touch of her haken, but Gyre was right behind it to take advantage of her distraction. She twisted, leaping backward, but the tip of his sword drew a long cut down her side.

For a moment they stood, gazes locked. The centarch put her free hand to the cut and it came away bloody. She nodded to him, very slightly.

"*Basel!*"

The roar could only be Maya's. A Legionary flew from the corridor, trailing smoke, and landed in a clatter of armor. Flames billowed, and then Maya herself emerged, red hair haloed around her, her haken a line of burning white. The remaining Legionaries fell back, and Gyre's opponent retreated, getting between Maya and the soldiers carrying the old man. Surprise flitted across Maya's face when she saw Gyre, but she acknowledged him with only the briefest nod before returning her attention to the other centarch.

"Stonecutter," she said.

"Burningblade," the woman replied formally.

"You don't have to do this."

The centarch gave a regretful shrug. "Council's orders."

"Basel's orders, you mean," Maya said. "He's working for a monster."

"He is a Kyriliarch," the woman said, as though that ended the argument.

"You know this is wrong."

"Disobeying orders from the Council is wrong. Surrender, and if you've done nothing, you have nothing to fear."

"You can't believe that," Maya said. She raised her blade slowly. "I don't want to hurt you."

"I believe you."

The centarch glanced between her and Gyre. With an abrupt motion, she whipped her haken in a circle. Gyre braced for a wave of *deiat* power, but the energy was directed upward, carving deep into the stone of the ceiling. A massive wedge of rock fell in front of the centarch with a spectacular *crunch*, raising a billowing cloud of dust. More stones pattered down, and between their clattering Gyre could hear boots on stone rapidly retreating.

"She'll be back with reinforcements," Maya muttered. "Xalen! Come on!" Then, turning to Gyre: "What are you doing up here? Did you find Jaedia?"

"We found her," Gyre said. "The doctors were supposed to send you to Basel, so I figured it might be a trap." He looked ruefully at the devastated corridor. "Apparently you didn't need the help."

Maya shook her head. "I don't have enough left to take on Evinda. Not even close."

"Good thing she didn't know that."

"She's supposed to be the best swordswoman in the Order."

"I believe it." Gyre sheathed his blade and let his augmented perception fade. His energy bottle was mostly empty, and he switched to the half-full one. "I'm running low on power myself."

Xalen trotted through the clouds of smoke and ash that still wreathed the corridor, her hand covering her mouth. She gawked at the wreckage and the dead Legionaries, picking her way carefully to the pair of them.

"Have you still got everything?" Maya said.

Xalen patted her side. "Got it."

"Then let's get to the Gate before Evinda rounds up more of the garrison. Come on."

They pounded down the stairs, Gyre's knees screaming after only a few turns of the spiral. By the time they'd descended four levels, he was short of breath, and Xalen was stumbling weakly in their wake. A few servants jumped out of their way with shrieks of surprise, but no squads of Legionaries emerged to bar the path.

"There are always guards in the Gate chamber," Maya said as they turned a corner and jogged down a long corridor. "But Tanax will get rid of them."

"We can hope," Gyre muttered.

In this case, hope didn't last very long. Another turn brought them in sight of the Gate chamber, protected by a massive pair of unmetal doors. These stood thankfully half-open, but Tanax stood in front of them, arguing with a Legion decarch. A squad of Legionaries waited nervously behind her, blaster rifles at the ready.

"I told you to stand down," Tanax shouted. "I am under orders from the Council to see to the Gate chamber myself."

"Centarch, with respect, I need confirmation," the soldier said. From her frustration, this wasn't the first time they'd gone through this. "I can't leave the Gates without ensuring—" She caught sight of Maya. "Wait. Who are— Stop!"

Maya drew her haken and ignited it with a *snap-hiss*. She loped into a run and skidded to a halt at the end of the corridor, the tip of her glowing blade centimeters from the Legionary's throat. The other soldiers leveled their rifles.

"I'm Maya Burningblade, traitor to the Order," she snarled. "Anyone who doesn't want to die, get out of here now."

"I—I—"

Tanax sighed and drew his own haken, his blade an eye-twisting line of distorted space.

"I think it would be for the best, decarch, if you reported to the Council immediately."

The armored figure gave a nervous nod. She gestured to her soldiers, who parted to let Gyre and the others through. Maya came last, closing the doors behind her.

"Thank you," Tanax said. "They let us through easily enough, but I figured getting you past was going to be harder."

The room was almost entirely empty, a cylindrical cavity in the rock big enough to assemble a small army. At the far end, three Gates stood side by side, their twisted archways empty. Beq, Sarah, and Elariel stood beside them. Jaedia was slumped in a wheelchair, buried in blankets up to her shoulders. Maya ran to her side, then looked around.

"Varo. Where's Varo?" When Tanax looked pained, her eyes widened. "Did he—"

"He was with us when I left," Gyre said.

"Varo decided to stay behind," Beq said, circling the wheelchair to take Maya's hand. "He said he could be more use that way. He's going to try and find out what the Corruptor is planning and make his way to Deepfire overland."

"That's insane." Maya pulled away from Beq and strode back toward the doors. "We have to find him. He's going to get himself killed."

"We don't have *time*," Tanax hissed.

"You said yourself Evinda's coming," Gyre added. "And he might be right. If the Corruptor is going to come after us, we need all the warning we can get."

"But—"

As though the words had been a summoning, there was a *thump* at the doors. Evinda's shout cut through the babble.

"Burningblade! Last chance to surrender!"

"Plaguing *fuck*!" Maya's voice was ragged with frustration. She put her hand on her haken, and white-hot flame bloomed around the edges of the door. The unmetal drank it in, unscathed, but the stone of the doorway began to glow, first a dull red, then bright orange. It slumped, taffy-like, then returned to solidity as Maya pulled its heat away. The doors *thumped* again but couldn't open past the distorted doorframe.

Gyre stepped to his sister's side. She was breathing hard, shoulders shaking, and her eyes glittered with tears.

"He'll be okay," Gyre said.

"He'd better be," Maya whispered. "Or else I'll kill him."

"Open the sun-cursed Gate!" Elariel said.

In punctuation, there was a spatter of blaster fire from outside, and then the *crunch* of shattering stone. Faced with an unmetal barrier, Evinda had decided to simply cut it out of the wall.

"If we go through now, they'll be able to follow," Tanax said. "The Gates remember the last place they connected to. If I stay behind, lead them somewhere else—"

"No," Maya said. "We're not leaving anyone else behind, Chosen *fucking* damn it."

"Can we destroy the Gate on the other side, the way Prodominus did?" Gyre said.

Beq looked alarmed. "Not unless you want to blow us to pieces. But I have an idea. Maya, can you set a Gate to a null coordinate?"

"I think so," Maya said. "But—"

"Good enough," Beq said. "I'll explain once we're on the other side."

Maya hesitated a moment, then nodded. She touched her haken, and the center Gate came to life, a curtain of mist rolling up from the ground to fill the archway.

"Tanax, go. If there are guards on the other side, get them out of there. Beq, take Jaedia."

Tanax trotted through the cloud and vanished from sight. The others followed. Gyre waited with Maya, watching the stone around the doors crumbling.

"Maya!" The old man, Baselanthus, called out over the ongoing destruction. "This is not what Jaedia would have wanted!"

"If you think that, you never understood Jaedia," Maya shouted back. "Come on, Gyre."

Side by side, they stepped through the Gate.

Maya

The Gate chamber in the Spike was as bare and empty as the one on the other side, but considerably smaller and with only a single Gate. Tanax was in the process of closing the door, having been more successful in shooing out the guards on this side.

"Beq!" Maya said. "They're right behind us."

"Okay." Beq twisted the dial on her spectacles, lenses flipping back and forth. "Activate the Gate with a null destination, and give it as much power as it will take."

Maya touched her haken. Her power felt hesitant, twitchy like an overused muscle, but she coaxed a thread of *deiat* into the Gate, carrying the activation command with a blank where the target ought to be. The silvery mist churned.

Giving a Gate an nonexistent target was an easy enough mistake to make, and the consequences were nothing major—it simply didn't activate. This felt different, a shudder running through the thread connecting her to the ancient arcana. For an instant she was certain it was going to detonate, like the Gate Prodominus had destroyed, releasing all its intrinsic energy in a fireball that would blow them all to pieces. But the strange vibration died away, and the mist in the archway darkened, fading from silver to roiling black. When it didn't seem in danger of tearing itself apart, Maya fed it more power. The thing swallowed it into some internal reservoir. When she pulled her mental touch away, the dark mist remained.

Maya breathed out and glanced at Beq. "Did it work?"

"I think so." The arcanist adjusted her spectacles. "It's something I read about once. You can't open a Gate to a location where the Gate is in use, right? So if you want to *lock* a Gate, you just need to keep it open all the time. That would drain any centarch dry pretty quickly. But if you give the Gate a null destination, it doesn't actually *open*, so its power bleeds away very slowly. And if anyone else tries to open a Gate here, it still looks like it's in use—"

She cut off with a squeak as Maya wrapped her arms around her.

"You are a plaguing *genius*. You know that, right?"

Beq smiled shyly. "I have my suspicions, sometimes."

There was a long silence, tension draining away. Elariel slumped against the wall and slid down it, arms wrapped around her knees. Sarah went to comfort her. Xalen hovered awkwardly nearby, all her certainty suddenly gone. Tanax, by the door, looked equally lost, but it was Gyre who gave voice to the thought on everyone's mind.

"We made it," he said. "So now what?"

Chapter Seven

Tourmarch Ritabel, commander of the Deepfire garrison, had the sour look of someone who had already been having a hard time and was watching it get worse. She was a short, stocky woman in her thirties, blue-green hair clipped short to fit under an Auxiliary helmet. A thin scar cut across her chin, just below her lower lip, and went pale when she scowled, which was often.

Maya got the feeling she was swallowing a whole litany of choice comments, but what she actually *said*, eventually, was, "Welcome to Deepfire, Centarchs. How can I assist?"

They were in a conference room on the third floor of the Spike, as the palace complex in Deepfire was known. The center of it was Chosen work, from the Gate deep underground to the single tall spire that gave it its name, but it had accumulated a considerable human-built complex around it. This room was on the north side, looking out over a broad stretch of gardens and yards bounded by a tall stone wall. Beyond that Maya could see large, impressive houses, each set on its own estate screened by trees and hedges. Looming over them, like a mouthful of broken teeth, were the mountains that gave the Shattered Peaks their name, still jagged four hundred years after they'd been torn asunder.

She and Tanax sat at one end of the oval table, with Ritabel opposite, flanked by an assistant she hadn't introduced. The others were elsewhere in the palace, waiting while quarters were organized.

"First give me an update on the situation here," Tanax said, affecting the casual arrogance that people expected of centarchs.

"Of course. The city's been on edge since Dux Raskos went missing, and there's been an increase in crime and insurrectionary activity among the tunnelborn. My garrison is keeping on top of it, for the most part, but my people are being run ragged. As my reports have mentioned several times, we urgently need reinforcements. On the positive side, a group of citizens have formed a Merchant Council, and they've provided some welcome assistance. With Yora and Halfmask dead, the rebels have lost their focus, although we're keeping an eye on a number of potential leaders in the workers' organizations."

"When was the last time someone came through the Gate?" Tanax asked.

"Three weeks ago, Centarch, or a little more. A messenger with urgent dispatches. She stayed only an hour."

Maya breathed out, trying not to make her relief too obvious. Deepfire was an exclave, far to the north of the Republic's border. The next-nearest Gate was weeks away, and messages took a long time to come overland through the Splinter Kingdoms. If no one had come through the Gate in the time since the Corruptor had emerged, then his instructions couldn't have reached anyone in Deepfire.

Unless she's lying, of course, and this is a trap. With an effort, Maya set the thought aside. *If Ashok is that far ahead of us, we have bigger problems.* Certainly no one had called her out as a traitor to the Order—that information had only been distributed to centarchs, and there were none here in the city. Still, she'd agreed it was wiser to let Tanax take the lead.

"Understood," he said. "Tourmarch, I'm afraid things are going to become somewhat irregular for a time. As of this moment, I'm assuming command of the Deepfire garrison, on the orders of the Council."

"Assuming command, Centarch?" Ritabel's eyebrows drew together. "My chain of command runs through the dux to the Senate. While I'm happy to assist you as needed, I'm not sure—"

"Centarchs are empowered to assume control of any Republic military forces they deem necessary in a state of emergency," Tanax said brusquely.

"Can you elaborate on the nature of the emergency?"

"Not at the moment. With any luck, it won't reach us here, but the Council directs me to be prepared."

"I...understand." Maya could see the calculations running through Ritabel's mind. What Tanax was proposing *was* stretching his legal authority to its limit, and perhaps a bit beyond; ordinarily centarchs used their privileges to conscript local troops to help combat plaguespawn or bandits. At the same time, it wasn't as though you could *fake* being a centarch. *And, of course, there isn't much she can do to stop us if push really comes to shove.* Having chewed through all those contingencies, the tourmarch gave a slow nod. "I will place myself under your command, Centarch, but I must request that we send a messenger to bring confirmation of your orders as soon as possible. Ideally by Gate—"

"The Gate is unusable for the moment. But you're welcome to send your message overland."

"Thank you, Centarch," Ritabel said. Her eyes were still wary. "What are your orders?"

"For the moment, proceed as normal. Keep the Gate chamber under close guard, and no one is to be admitted apart from Maya and myself. We will keep you apprised as events warrant."

Maya could practically hear the Auxiliary's teeth grinding, but she gave another nod. "Understood."

"That's all."

Tanax stood, and Maya followed him out into the hall. They

stepped aside to let the tourmarch stalk past, trailing her aide. Tanax said, "That could have gone worse."

"Do we really need to assume command?"

"It seemed prudent. This way the garrison won't hinder us, and they won't ask too many questions."

"Until orders *do* manage to get here from the Republic."

"By then we'll need a new plan, whatever we end up doing," Tanax said. "Do you—"

"Tomorrow," Maya said, fighting not to show the panic that swept over her.

"Of course. It's been a long day."

She nodded. "I'm going to see Jaedia."

Tanax's expression softened. "I understand. I hope...Well. Good luck."

"Thank you."

What now? The words rang in Maya's head as he walked away. Gyre had spoken them, and everyone had looked at her. *Of course they did. You're the one who got them into this mess. Got the* world *into this mess.* It wasn't fair to blame them for looking to her for guidance, but...

Tomorrow. She shoved the thoughts down, feeling the bile building at the back of her throat.

The corridors of the Spike were a maze, and Maya had to flag down a servant to get directions. She finally found her way to a bedroom on the second floor, probably maids' quarters, small but well scrubbed. Jaedia lay under crisp white linen with blankets piled on top. Beq was in a chair in one corner, and Elariel stood beside the bed, eyes closed, hands on Jaedia's shoulder.

"Maya." Beq stood. "Is everything all right?"

"For the moment. The tourmarch is cooperating." Maya shut the door behind her and nodded at the silent ghoul. "Has she said anything?"

"Not yet."

Maya moved to Beq's side and felt her lover's fingers curl around hers. As she looked at Jaedia's features, bony and hollow-cheeked in place of her usual joyful smile, something in Maya's heart started to sink like a lead weight into mud.

Even if she does wake up, will she be the same? Whatever the black spider had done to her had been a violation at a basic level. Maya had burned it out of her, but... *What if she's not Jaedia anymore?* She found herself squeezing Beq's hand as though it were a lifeline.

Elariel shifted and opened her eyes. Maya's throat was suddenly too thick to speak.

"Ah, you're here," the ghoul said, shaking out her hands. "Good."

"What did you find?" Beq said, correctly guessing Maya wasn't in a position to speak.

"A lot of nerve damage," Elariel said, frowning a little. "She's healed somewhat, but the scarring is almost as bad. Without help, she'd never wake up."

"But you can help her," Beq said, glancing nervously at Maya.

"I can," Elariel said simply.

Maya let out a breath, slowly. Her heartbeat thumped in her ears, too fast.

"Thank you," she managed, very quietly.

"It's not going to be simple, though," the ghoul said.

"You mean there's a chance it might not... that she could..."

"If she was going to die, she'd have done it already," Elariel said. "I just mean it will take time."

"Oh." Maya deflated a little. "How long?"

"Hard to say. I need to go over her bit by bit and tease the scars out, regrow the tissue—"

"Days?" Maya said.

Elariel's eyebrows went up. "More like months. One, maybe two?"

"I...understand." Maya's mouth was dry. "And afterward she'll be...okay?"

"Hopefully." The ghoul sighed. "This isn't my area of expertise, you realize. I'm a construct designer. If we were back in Refuge, and Vodriel were here, Jaedia would be up and dancing by the weekend. Except Vodriel would never work on a human, of course. As it is, I can't promise there won't be a bit of tremor or a little memory loss. But she'll be awake and alive."

"That's all I could ask for." Maya bent her head. "Thank you. I know this isn't... natural for you, helping us like this."

Elariel colored slightly and coughed into her hand. "Well. We had a deal. And you haven't tried to kill me since that first time." At Maya's stricken expression, she hastily added, "That was a joke."

There was a long pause.

"Can... can you give me a moment?" Maya said.

"Of course." Elariel nodded and stepped away. Beq got up, moving to follow, but Maya grabbed her hand.

"Stay," Maya said. "Please."

Elariel shut the door. Maya sagged, and Beq maneuvered her carefully to sit on the floor, her back against Jaedia's bed. The arcanist took a seat beside her.

"It's good news, isn't it?" Beq said, a little timidly. "Jaedia will be okay."

"It is." Maya drew her knees in to her chest. "I'm just an awful person."

"What? Why?"

"Because I'm disappointed." Maya blew out a breath. "When Elariel said she could help, the first thing I thought was that if Jaedia's okay, if she wakes up, then she'll know what to do next. She'll tell me, and I'll do it, and I won't have to *decide*. I could apologize to her for what I did, and she'd make me go without dinner or something, and then it would be over." Maya pressed her face against her knees. "Stupid, I know. Stupid, stupid."

"Maya." Beq put an arm around her shoulders, pulling her close. "It's okay."

"It's not." Maya's voice was muffled. "I should be *happy*."

"You will. I promise. It's just hard. For all of us, but for you... I can't imagine."

"It's my fault."

"Maya..."

"It is. If the Corruptor takes over the world and makes us all into slaves like the Eldest did, it'll be my fault. And that means I have to stop him, somehow, but the whole Order is against me and Varo's gone and the way Gyre looks at me..." She pressed herself into Beq's side. "He blames me, and he's right. So what in the name of the Chosen am I supposed to do now?"

Maya's shoulders shook with quiet sobs. Beq held her quietly, running her fingers through long red hair grimed with sweat and blood.

"I don't know," the arcanist said after a while. "I don't have an answer. But I'll help you figure it out, and whatever it is, I'll be here with you. I know Tanax would say the same. And Varo said he'd be back, so he'll be back, and then he'll help too."

"It might not be enough," Maya whispered.

"It might not," Beq said. "But we'll be here anyway, whatever happens."

Another silence. Eventually Maya's body went calm, her heart slowing from its headlong race. The weariness of the past few hours caught up with her, and she felt like she could fall asleep where she sat, crick in her back or no. She turned her head to look at Beq.

"Thank you." Maya sniffed and wiped at her reddened eyes. "You're pretty good at this, you know?"

"I'm glad you say that," Beq said, "because I have no idea what I'm doing."

"I think I need to sleep." Maya leaned back against the bed. "Tomorrow..." She shook her head.

"Tomorrow?"

"Tomorrow," Maya said, trying to inject her voice with more confidence than she felt, "we figure out what comes next."

But that night, she dreamed.

Ashok stood in his strange facility, poking idly at the control console.

He looked as he'd appeared in the projections at Skyreach. The illusion seemed so real that Maya had to remind herself of his true, monstrous form.

"So," he said. "You have fled. Again."

"In spite of your best efforts," Maya said. "I hope I didn't hurt Basel too badly."

"He will live, I am told. And his companion Stonecutter said that your brother's skill with a sword is extraordinary."

"I'll pass along the compliment," Maya drawled.

"You understand, of course, that you can't run forever?" Ashok moved to stand in front of her, looking down with a fond smile. "The Republic is mine now. The Order."

"Really? Then why continue the trickery with projectors? Why not appear before them in person?"

"In due time." The Corruptor chuckled. "You really think to needle my vanity? I excised such useless feelings long ago. There are certain... prejudices, among humans, that mean I must conceal myself for the moment. In a generation or two, however, I have no doubt they will be ready to embrace me. It matters little. Unlike the rest of you, I have all the time in creation."

Maya looked up into his bright red eyes. "Then why bother?"

"Excuse me?"

"Why bother with any of this?" She spread her hands. "You've infiltrated the Order. You got Basel to protect me, raise me, all so I could get to the Purifier at the right moment and set you free." Maya paused, cocking her head. "Was it part of the plan when Hollis Plaguetouch ran into me? Or was that a mistake?"

"I believe it was an error, but I cannot be sure," Ashok said affably. "My children begin with as much of my mind as will fit in their limited bodies, but over time they diverge. When they return, I can learn what they have experienced, but that one was...lost." A smile played on his lips. "As you well know."

Interesting. Maya filed that away for future contemplation. "In any case. You've worked hard to get here. *Why?* If you have all the time in the world..."

"I see your error." The Corruptor shook his head. "You thought it was for my sake I planned all this. Believe me, I am entirely sincere when I assure you it was not. Were it left to me, I would be happy on my own, spending eternity unlocking the secrets of creation. It's not for my benefit I've returned to the world, Maya. It's for yours."

"Mine?"

"Humanity's, I should say." He turned away from Maya to pace around the console. "I meant what I said in Skyreach. Your people have the potential for greatness. But you *need* us, as you have always needed us, to protect and guide you. To shield you from your own worst impulses and from the monsters of the world."

"You Chosen failed once already."

"We did. And I bear the guilt for that, as the last of us. But I will not fail again."

"What makes you so sure?"

"In their pride, my people ignored the promise of *dhaka*. *Deiat* had always been enough, and it always would be. *Dhaka* was for little people, doing little things. But I learned." He stopped across from her, his hands on the edge of the console. "The rest of them couldn't even begin to imagine the possibilities of what I discovered. In the end, their empire was built on fear, on the grinding boot and fire from the sky. But *my* empire will be united by love, and so it will stand the test of time."

"Love?" Maya snorted. "You expect humanity to fall in love with you?"

"They will." Ashok's smile widened, and he spread his hands. "They won't have a choice. I will write love into their very flesh, into every piece of their being, to be passed on to all future generations." His red eyes drilled into her. "Struggle if you must, *sha'deia*. It matters not. For your children's children, love for their emperor will be all they ever know."

Maya closed her eyes, but it didn't matter. His laughter rang in her ears, and all she could see was Calla, lying in a pool of blood. Her village had *worshipped* one of the black spiders, the Eldest who kept them safe, giving over their bodies to become its host and plaguespawn. *My children begin with my mind*, Ashok had said. The Eldest had re-created his mad dream in miniature.

Dream. This is a dream. Her fists clenched at her sides. *Wake up, Maya. Wake up.*

When she opened her eyes, she was still in the darkened facility, but the Corruptor was gone. At the corner of her vision, something flickered, and Maya's breath caught.

"Hello?" she said. "Is someone there?"

Bit by bit, as if it were shy, the flickering, hazy outline took form in front of her. The fear Maya felt at its first appearance had been replaced by an intense curiosity.

The only person who should be able to get into my head is Ashok, if Elariel is right about the blood-bond. But this...creature, or whatever it was, didn't feel like Ashok at all. *It could be a trick.* But what would be the purpose?"

"...*remember*..." the thing breathed. "...*please*..."

"You want me to remember?" Maya said.

The faintest movement. It might have been a nod.

"When I touched you, I saw things. Those are your memories? And you want me to see them?"

Another nod. The wisp drifted closer.

Maya held out her hand, and the thing raised a faint arm to meet it. Where they nearly touched, there was a faint crackle and a soft spit of light. Just for a moment, Maya was walking down a hallway again, wearing strange clothes. Light came from sunstones overhead. She could see rooms with walls of smoked glass, and strange arcana, gleaming like new—

Like new. Maya's eyes widened. *This is a memory from* before *Elder times, before the Plague War.* It faded away as she lowered her hand, and the wisp jerked away.

"It's all right," Maya said. "Sorry. You just surprised me, that's all. Here." She extended her hand again. "I'm ready."

Slowly, the hazy thing reached out again. A hand, barely visible, pressed against Maya's own with a static sizzle. The vision took shape in Maya's mind, stronger now, another mind pressing in on her own. And Maya—

—*remembered*—

Chapter Eight

Zephkiel

"*I* heard he did something awful," Nia said. "So the Directorate decided to kick Suppli upstairs and bury this Ashok under the mountain."

"That does sound like the director," Zeph said.

"Right? Lucky us." Nia gestured with her fork. "Can I try that?"

"Oh, go ahead." Zeph wiped her lips with a napkin and pushed the bowl forward. "I'm full."

"Thanks." Nia speared a lump of leafy green stuff with reddish veins, studied it for a moment, and popped it in her mouth. "Mmm. Crunchy. What is it?"

"Some new cultivar the third floor is trying out. Lettuce-ish."

"Lettuce-ish." Nia snorted. "I like the dressing."

"Yeah, I think they got the kitchen to put their thumb on the scales. The actual plant doesn't really taste like much."

"And to think my mother was worried my diet wouldn't have enough variety up in the mountains."

Zeph laughed out loud. She'd had similar concerns when she'd first applied for a transfer to the lab here—the mountain facilities had a reputation as a hardship post, even if they were where some of the most exciting work on *dhaka* was being done. Fortunately, as she'd discovered, Stoneroot was different. In spite of the obvious disinterest of the Directorate, their results were useful enough that the facility merited its own Gate and a reasonably high network priority. Food from all over the Empire was, if not as available as it might have been in Skyreach, certainly not difficult to find.

And, of course, there was the produce of the labs themselves. Some of the things researchers ate as "experiments" were on the weird side for Zeph, but she was willing to risk taking what the horticultural labs offered. *They haven't poisoned me yet.*

The worst part of the job, honestly, was the lack of sunlight. The lighting in the labs was engineered to be a perfect replacement for natural illumination, and there were no physiological reasons why workers couldn't stay at their posts indefinitely. No matter how carefully the facility was designed, however, there was no escaping the knowledge that they were all buried under a million tons of rock, living in a honeycomb blasted out of the heart of a mountain. The small city on top of the lab, closer to the surface, at least had places where you could see the sky and taste the ice-cold air. In the lab itself, everything was filtered and textured and perfect.

She'd spent half a year's Gate allowance on a trip home a month before, just to be able to lie in the grass under the open air, and she already missed it. *No wonder they have a hard time finding any Chosen who wants to run the place.* Nial-Est-Ashok, the new arrival, would be her third boss in a year.

"Anyway," Nia said, munching on more of Zeph's salad. "You never finished the story from last night, about what's-his-name. The sled driver."

"Sidra." Zeph sighed. "It didn't work out."

"I gathered that," Nia said. "But I need details. Did you take him home?"

"No."

"Did he take *you* home?"

"*No.*" Zeph rolled her eyes. "There was no sex involved."

"Seems like a waste of a day off, if you ask me," Nia said. "You could have waited to dump him until afterward."

"I suppose *you* made good use of the time. How's Quin doing?"

"Badly, but only because I broke it off two weeks ago. I *told* you."

"Sorry."

"Don't be," Nia said. "I spent the day with Elin. He works in the supply corps. You think they're all frostbitten little trolls, but get that heavy coat and goggles off him, and—" She made a slightly obscene gesture, followed by an extremely obscene one. "So a good day," she concluded.

Zeph chuckled. "You never want to find someone that, you know, you actually like?"

"What's the point? They'd just leave. Everybody leaves eventually. It's not like people come to Stoneroot to settle down and start families. Someday I'll buy a place down in Grentia or something and have a few kids to make Mom happy. Until then..." She shrugged. "Have *you* ever considered loosening up a little and having some fun? *You* don't even need to take precautions."

Zeph accepted the jibe with good grace. Nia was solidly, even proudly baseline, with chestnut hair and brown eyes; she even had *periods*, which Zeph didn't envy one bit. She herself was a third-generation adjusted, with silver-white hair and orange-red eyes like her mother. Her father had been baseline, but the adjustment always bred true, and these days the old phenotypes were becoming uncommon.

"Well," Zeph said, spotting the clock on the wall behind Nia. "If we're done making fun of my love life, I need to go and meet our new lord and master. I drew the short straw on giving him the tour."

"Keep it short," Nia advised. "He won't care anyway."

"Believe me, I intend to."

"Cheer up. Maybe he's cute!"

Zeph snorted a laugh and got up from the table. The cafeteria was a large open space, occupying much of the center of the complex. Around it were the kitchens, the offices that housed the administrative staff, supply facilities, and the Gate itself. The lab administrator had his own suite of offices, including space for an assistant and a conference room. Zeph headed in that direction, stopping in the closest bathroom for a quick once-over in the mirror. *Never hurts to make a good impression on the boss, assuming he can be bothered to notice.*

The assistant's desk was still empty, but the door to the inner office stood open. Zeph knocked on it anyway and heard a thump from inside.

"Ow," someone said. "Come in."

She entered cautiously. During Suppli's tenure, she'd only been in here a few times, usually when she was being called on the carpet about budgetary overruns in her department. It had been decorated more like a throne room, with a flock of human assistants hovering around the Chosen administrator at all times. All that was gone now, shipped out with the old boss, and in its place was a utilitarian unmetal desk, a few chairs, and a broad worktable covered in books and papers. A map of the mountains around Stoneroot hung on the wall, annotated in pencil.

Emerging from under the desk, rubbing his head, was a Chosen.

Like all his race, Nial-Est-Ashok was devastatingly handsome, with sharp features, fine golden hair, and striking red eyes. But where the beauty of many Chosen was a cold thing, like the features of a heroic statue, there was something warmer in Ashok's face. A hint of human-ity, if seeing humanity in a Chosen wasn't a contradiction in terms. The fact that a being capable of leveling the entire complex had accidentally bumped his head on a desk was . . . unexpected, at least.

He wore a white wraparound robe over dark trousers, a researcher's outfit similar to her own. Another difference from Suppli, who'd gone to great lengths to keep up with the ever-changing fashions of the capi-tal, in spite of his exile.

"Hello," Ashok said. "Sorry about the mess."

Zeph bowed, raising her eyebrows. No Chosen had ever, to her knowledge, apologized to her for anything.

"Greetings, lord," she said, using the formal diction appropriate for addressing a Chosen. "I am Zephkiel Nimaria, Mammal Development Lead, and I am pleased to be in your service. Welcome to Stoneroot."

"Thanks." He gestured her up with a wave. "Don't bother with the 'lord.' Seems silly under the circumstances. Ashok is fine."

"As you wish." Zeph's eyebrows knit, but she smoothed her features. "Has your staff been delayed?"

"Haven't got a staff," he said cheerfully. "Before this I was living at Father's estate, and I wasn't going to drag any of the servants there into the mountains. I'll manage for myself. I usually do."

"I...see." Zeph did her best not to groan. *Manage for himself,* *that'll be the day. He's a Chosen. If he tries to treat my researchers like* *menials...* "If there's anything you require, please let me know. In the meantime, if you would like, I can offer you a tour of our facility."

Please say no, please say no. She had work to do in the afternoon. *The* *last thing I need is some Chosen poking at things he doesn't understand* *because he wants to seem diligent.*

"Absolutely," Ashok said, and Zeph suppressed another groan. "I've been reading up on your work here, and it's fascinating."

"You have?" Zeph said, startled.

"Of course. It was your team that pioneered the research on skeletal reabsorption in vulpi, wasn't it?"

"I..." Zeph blinked. "I mean, yes, it was. But..."

"Top-notch stuff," Ashok said. "I admit I found parts of your paper hard to follow, as an amateur, but I hope to get up to speed quickly."

"That's...excellent, lord. Ashok." Zeph hesitated, then said, "Would you like to begin with my lab, then?"

"Certainly. Lead the way!"

Showing off to the boss, she told herself as they descended the central stairway, was a perfectly ordinary thing to do. In the complicated web of office politics that was Stoneroot, having the administrator in her pocket would be the ultimate trump card. *Maybe I can finally get that lab space back from Biriend.* It was worth the odd looks she got on the stairs, with a Chosen trailing behind her like a lost puppy, gawking at everything.

They passed through the second floor, where the researchers and servants had their quarters, and the third, where *dhakim* poked and prodded plants of all varieties, searching out more productive—and tastier—crops to be distributed across the Empire. The fourth floor was divided between teams tasked with workbirds, reptiloid beasts, and her own mammalian unit. Below that, a portable barrier blocked the stairwell.

"I thought there were five levels," Ashok said, peering past it.

"The Directorate decided that the human adjustment unit needed its own facility," Zeph said. "The space is disused until we get the budget to reconfigure it."

"Zeph!" Nia popped out from a doorway leading into birdland, as the researchers called her domain. "How did it—oh!" Her face reddened, and she bent over in a deep bow. "Apologies, lord. I didn't see you."

"No offense taken," Ashok said. "Zephkiel was just showing me her work."

"This is Niatea Grinj, lo— Ashok," Zeph said. "Workbird Development Lead."

"A pleasure to meet you," the Chosen said, smiling. "I look forward to seeing your work as well."

"Ah... thank you, lord," Nia said, shooting Zeph a deeply curious look. "I'll leave you to your tour."

She bowed again and withdrew. Zeph pointed to the door to her lab, and Ashok followed her in. His eyes widened at the sight of it. The transparent specimen cases, full of vulpi at every stage of their life cycle; the dissection room, where a live animal was disassembled with *dhaka*, its organs neatly separating and sorting themselves under the supervision of a goggled researcher; banks of microscopes, lenses infused with *deiat* power, that let her team observe the effects of their *dhaka* on the tiniest parts of animals or examine their embryos. The Chosen ignored, or didn't notice, the startled looks and the waves of bows that followed him. Zeph winced at the processes interrupted and procedures left undone, but Ashok's apparent glee was infectious. By the end, when they reached the adjustment chamber itself, she was grinning.

"So this is where you do it?" He looked around the modest room, empty except for a steel platform in the center, topped with a glass cube.

"This is where we do fine adjustments," Zeph said. "The system can keep a sample in partial stasis for long periods, so we can do our work without worrying about the subject degrading. Typically that means an embryo, which we implant back into a host mother for development."

"Fascinating," Ashok said, touching the glass reverently. His fingers left dirty streaks. "It's strange to think that every vulpi I've ever eaten is descended from one created in a place like this."

"We *dhakim* are honored to contribute to the glory of the Empire," Zeph said, bowing her head.

"Sometimes I think *dhaka* is more important to the Empire than *deiat*," Ashok said wistfully. "It may not be able to blow up mountains, but this..."

Zeph reminded herself to tread carefully. Friendly as he was, Ashok was still a Chosen. "*Dhaka* has the advantage that anyone can learn to use it," she said. "It allows humans to bear some of the burden of improving everyone's lives."

"Anyone." Ashok's face fell. "And yet all the texts on the subject are lacking in detail. They explain *what* was done, but not *how*."

"It's difficult to convey in text," Zeph said carefully. "You need some experience, some reference points, before a description of technique makes any sense. *Dhakim* springs from *dhakim*."

It was an old aphorism, almost a cliché, but Ashok's eyes widened as though it had been a tremendous insight. He looked at her for a long moment, and if he hadn't been a Chosen, she would have thought he was embarrassed about something.

"If...I were to learn from one of your *dhakim*," he said slowly. "Learn these reference points. How long would it take to become a *dhakim* myself?"

"That...depends. It varies based on your natural talent and dedication to the work. Most of us take a few years, at least."

"Years." He muttered something to himself, then set his jaw. "Will you teach me?"

She wasn't sure what to think. Chosen didn't become *dhakim*—not that they *couldn't*, presumably, *dhaka* was a part of all living things, but they just...didn't. Born with command of *deiat*, the fire of creation, the power of the sun itself, they had never interested themselves in the grubby, messy world of living things. There wasn't a law to that effect, but it just...wasn't done.

Then again, Ashok hardly seems like a typical Chosen. And while training him would cut into her other work, it could only help her career prospects...

"If you desire it," Zeph said hesitantly.

"I do," Ashok said. "I want to understand *everything* that happens here. Otherwise, how can I possibly be in charge of it?"

Suppli had managed, and the administrators before him, just by barking a few orders and leaving the departments to manage themselves. Even the Directorate probably didn't understand much of the reports Zeph and the rest dutifully sent up the chain. *But it can't hurt, can it?*

"Then I'll teach you," Zeph said, and smiled.

Maya

Maya awoke, the dream shredding around her. She still felt Zeph's emotions, layered over her own. Cautious optimism, even a faint stir of attraction to this handsome Chosen who seemed to actually take an interest in her work. Maya felt like she was reading a horror story, and the protagonist was about to go into the basement with the monster.

But Ashok seems almost normal. Normal for a Chosen, anyway. *What happened to him? What happened to Zeph? And how in the plague am I seeing this?*

The darkness offered no answers. Beq lay in the bed beside her, still insensible, snoring with tiny adorable squeaks. Maya stared, trying to anchor herself on the familiar beauty of her lover. Her unbound hair, lying on the pillow like a river of green, the upward tilt of her nose, and her freckled cheeks. Smiling to herself, Maya settled back beside her and let her eyes close.

But sleep, alas, refused to come. Every time she felt herself drifting off, her thoughts turned to Ashok and Zeph, and whether she would find one or the other waiting in her dreams. That set her heart to racing again and made the rest seem far away. Eventually, Maya groaned and slipped out of bed, leaving Beq behind.

Her stomach rumbled, having had nothing since breakfast yesterday, and she set off to fill it. This wing of guest quarters had its own dining room, and she headed in that direction in hopes of a tray of rolls or leftover cheese. It was still well before dawn, and even the servants weren't yet awake, so it was a surprise to find a thin figure hunched over the dining room table. Xalen chewed absentmindedly on a heel of bread while staring intently at a mess of loose paper.

"No, I don't need assistance finding my room," she said without looking up as Maya entered. "Please leave me be."

"It's me," Maya said. "I don't mean to interrupt."

"Oh." Xalen frowned at her. "Apologies, I took you for a servant. The staff here are poorly trained, I think. At the Forge they know better than to intrude on a librarian's work."

"They probably don't get a lot of librarians in the guest quarters," Maya said. "Is there any more of that bread?"

Xalen slid a plate half-full of it in front of the seat beside her, and Maya settled down gratefully. The librarian glanced down at her work, sighed, and began stacking the papers one-handed. Her left arm, withered and immobile, hung in a sling pinned to her side.

"You don't have to stop on my account," Maya said, mouth full.

"My eyes are failing in any case," Xalen said. "I doubt I would make more progress tonight."

"Are those Prodominus' papers?"

Xalen nodded. "He considered them of the utmost importance. It's urgent that we discover why."

"To plan our next move?"

"Yes." Xalen finished stacking the papers. She stared down at them for a moment, her good hand flat on the tabletop. "There must be some way to destroy him."

Maya looked over at her, sitting quiet and still.

"Destroy the Corruptor," she said after a moment. "That's what's next, isn't it?"

"Of course." Xalen glanced at Maya, surprised. "Surely you knew that?"

"I...haven't had a lot of time to think." Maya looked down at her hand. It was whole now, the skin brown and unbroken, but she could still feel the ghost of pain. *And Ashok's blood, deep inside.* "But someone has to stop him."

"He has perverted the Order and the Republic," Xalen said. "What else can we do?"

"Run," Maya said. "Hide. Hope he leaves us alone." *The rest of you can, anyway. Ashok will be in* my *head until one of us is dead.* "The others may want to."

"But *you* will fight," Xalen said. She sounded anxious.

"I will."

"Then I'll help however I can." Xalen's hand closed into a fist. "Prodominus would have wanted that."

It was easy to forget, looking at Xalen's composed features, that she'd learned she lost her father only a day before. Maya could hear the emotion in her voice, but it was buried deep.

If anyone will understand what's happening to me, she will. And Xalen, Maya guessed, wasn't likely to panic. *Here goes nothing.*

"I have dreams," Maya said abruptly. "Not really dreams, I guess. More like visions. Ashok…talks to me."

There was a long silence. Xalen regarded her carefully, hand folded in her lap.

"I see," she said finally, as though Maya had announced her dinner preference. "You're certain they're not simply dreams?"

"I'm certain," Maya said. "He's told me things I couldn't possibly know otherwise." She explained what she'd seen, both Ashok in the strange facility and the even stranger trip into Zephkiel's memories. Xalen sat quietly, taking it in.

"I haven't told the others yet," Maya said when she was finished. "I thought they might react badly. Especially Gyre."

"Probably best to have waited until we escaped," Xalen agreed. "But you should share everything soon."

"Tomorrow," Maya said. "Though Chosen know what *else* I'm going to tell them."

"I'm not sure what you mean."

"What we do next. It's all very well to say we'll fight, but *how*? How do we stop Ashok when he has the whole Republic—excuse me, the *Empire*—behind him?"

"I hoped to find something in these pages," Xalen said. "But maybe your 'dreams' provide another potential resource. If Ashok is speaking to you, he may let slip more than he intended."

"I doubt it," Maya said. "He's pretty canny."

"With his words, perhaps. But from what I understand about the blood-bond, the connection is deeper than that. Emotions, images. Something may slip through."

Emotions. She certainly got those from Zephkiel. *And images…*

Something tickled at her mind. The *place* where she'd met the Corruptor, that room with the ring of consoles. *A place with no windows. And thinking about it now, it looks familiar…*

"The map," she said.

"I'm sorry?"

"I need to look at a map," Maya said. She glanced around wildly. "Can you help me find the palace library?"

Xalen grinned. "I would be more than happy to."

Chapter Nine

It was strange, for Gyre, to think that Raskos Rottentooth, the corrupt dux of Deepfire and his inveterate enemy for years, had sat at this same table with his henchmen. *He probably planned raids against us right here.* Taking the seat himself ought to have been a victory, but all Gyre felt was a passing amusement at the contrast.

The conference room was a large one, and even their expanded group didn't fill it. They took seats around the oval table as they filed in one by one. Elariel was sitting beside Gyre already, looking cleaner than she'd been on the road but just as dour. Sarah, now wearing short sleeves that showed off the burnished metal of her artificial arm, took the seat on his other side. Tanax, with the harried look of someone with too many responsibilities and too little time, took the chair opposite. Xalen slouched in not long after, her blue hair still a ragged mess, left arm resting in a cloth sling pinned to her shirt.

Maya and Beq were the last to arrive. Gyre's sister looked as though she'd barely slept, and Beq stayed close by her side, as though ready to grab her if she toppled over. There was no weakness in Maya's movements, however, and her expression was grimly determined.

Varo was still missing, of course, and Kit. Otherwise this represented the complete set of everyone who knew the truth about the Corruptor. *At least, the ones who are on* our *side.*

Without anyone saying anything out loud, all eyes had gone to Maya. She looked around, shrinking a little under the combined gazes, then visibly steeled herself.

"I'm glad you're all looking well," she said. "I know things have been hard."

There was a round of not-very-amused chuckles at the understatement.

"We need to decide . . . a lot of things," Maya went on. "And I have some, um, new information. First, though, Tanax—anything major going on in the city?"

"Not yet," Tanax said. "Tourmarch Ritabel and the garrison are following orders for now, but I don't know if it will last. A rider on a swift-bird could have gotten here from the next-closest Gate by now. We haven't spotted any official Republic messengers, but there are always caravans arriving from the Splinter Kingdoms. Rumors are going to start spreading of what's happened in the Republic, if they haven't already. What that's going to do to the situation in the streets, I have no idea."

"Do you think Ritabel would turn on us?"

"She seems a dedicated sort," Tanax said. "But that means if she gets an order from the appropriate authority, she'll follow it. That might mean an ambush, or just tipping off the Order that we're here and waiting for a few centarchs to ride over. Regardless, we're going to have to move soon. There are too many servants in the Spike to hope that people don't know we're here."

Maya's expression flickered, but she only nodded and looked around the table again. "We could keep moving, find somewhere to hide. Out west, maybe, or even up on the Forsaken Coast. But that wouldn't solve our problem. The Corruptor has taken the Republic and the Order, and he's coming for me." She glanced at Xalen and under the table took Beq's hand. "I intend to do something about it."

"Mad," Elariel said into the silence that followed. She slumped in her chair. "She's mad."

"I'm just not sure what exactly we *can* do," Sarah said hesitantly. "He's got the whole Republic military now, and the centarchs. And even if we can get past all of that, he's a Chosen. We're just not a match for him, are we?"

Another silence. Gyre took a deep breath.

"It's not a matter of whether we're a match for him," he said. "Either we kill him, or there's nothing left for any of us. That's all there is to it."

Elariel and Sarah both sat up a little straighter, looking at him. Maya's eyes were wide with surprise. Only Xalen was nodding approval, as though what he'd said was obvious.

It *was* obvious, really, but it had taken Gyre a long time to convince himself. The question had gnawed at him since the Corruptor's speech in Skyreach. Last night, as he lay in one of the palace's too-soft beds, the question had landed on him like a cart full of stones.

What now? Not for the world, or the Republic. *For* me.

What am I doing here?

He thought he'd answered that question for himself twelve years earlier, when Va'aht had carved out his eye and dragged Maya out of his life. In that moment, Gyre had solidified his purpose. The Order that did such things, and the Republic that let them happen, couldn't be allowed to continue. Everything he'd done since then—the long road to Deepfire, his years as Halfmask, his search for the Tomb and its unexpected conclusion—had been in service of that goal. He'd changed his approach after seeing the Leviathan; some things *were* too terrible to unleash, he'd discovered, even in the service of noble ends. The Khirkhaz Commune had provided an example of successful resistance, and he'd hoped to build on it. But—

Now there's the Corruptor. And he was sitting *beside* two centarchs, one of them his long-lost sister, in the seat of power of the dux of Deepfire. *So where does that leave me?*

He'd spent the evening tying himself into mental knots. The bare fact was this—ideals or no, he wasn't going to abandon Maya. *Not again.* And, gradually, he realized he didn't have to, because nothing had changed.

"I became Halfmask because I thought the Order had too much power," he said aloud. "If I believed that, then how much worse are things going to be with the Corruptor in charge?"

"The Order is not the same as that monster," Tanax said. "We *protect* people—"

"Tell that to Yora," Sarah said with unaccustomed vehemence. Tanax had the decency to look away.

"At the same time, it's an opportunity," Gyre said. "The Corruptor has rearranged the world. If we get rid of him, we may have the chance to rearrange it ourselves, for the better."

"Which still leaves the fact that all of this is *crazy*," Elariel said. "He's the *Corruptor*. A Chosen *and* a *dhakim*, who's modified himself with who-knows-what sun-cursed powers. We can't *stop* him. Even Prodominus barely slowed him down."

"I'm not saying it won't be difficult," Gyre said. "Maybe impossible. Probably I'll die in the attempt. But that was true when I decided to take on the Order, so I don't see why it should stop me now." He shrugged. "I can't speak for anyone else, of course."

"Gyre is right," Maya said. "Maybe it *is* impossible. But I'm going to try."

A pause. Beq pulled their clasped hands above the table.

"If it needs saying," she announced, "I'm with you. Till the end." She flushed a little, embarrassed at her own boldness. Maya gave her a look of deep gratitude.

Tanax cleared his throat. "I'm with you too, of course. I'm not going to leave the Order to Ashok. It isn't perfect"—he glanced at Sarah—"but I believe in its ideals. We just need to do better."

"I—" Sarah hesitated, looking between Gyre and Elariel. "I don't know."

"*I* do." The ghoul surged to her feet. To Gyre's surprise, her eyes were full of tears. "You're all going to *die*, and I..." Her lips pressed together tightly and she shook her head, then pushed angrily around the table toward the door. Sarah followed, exchanging a quick look with Gyre.

When they were gone, Gyre said, "I'll catch up with them later."

"If they want to leave, I won't stop them," Maya said. "Chosen know I understand the feeling. If I'm the one the Corruptor wants, I hope he'll leave them alone."

Xalen, who had vanished behind a sheaf of papers about halfway through the conversation, surfaced briefly.

"I have ample reason to want the Corruptor destroyed," she said. "As I told Maya, I will do what I can."

"Thank you," Maya said. "And there's something I need to tell the rest of you. I don't fully understand it, but...it may be useful." She squared her shoulders and took a breath. "The Corruptor speaks to me in my dreams."

There was a long, awkward silence. Gyre cleared his throat carefully.

"Are you sure..."

"That I'm not just going crazy?" Maya said. "Let's say I'm *reasonably* sure."

"But..." Tanax shook his head. "How?"

"I asked Elariel," Maya said. "There's a *dhaka* technique called a blood-bond, which connects two people's minds. To make it work, the two have to exchange blood. Beq, you remember the black stuff inside the resonator?"

"Ashok called it the resonating medium," Beq said, then her eyes went wide behind her spectacles. "You think—"

"Logical," Xalen said, without looking up from her notes. "Long-distance communication through *dhaka* involves separating two parts of a medium and relying on the continued ability of one part to affect the other."

"Wouldn't Ashok have needed some of *your* blood, then?" Beq said.

Maya grimaced. "Baselanthus had plenty of opportunities to get *that* for him."

"The important thing," Gyre said urgently, "is whether the Corruptor can *read your mind*. Because if he can, we're all *plagued*."

"He can't," Maya said. "That's what Elariel told me. It's only communication. He doesn't know anything I don't tell him."

"That's something," Gyre said, slumping back in his seat. "You said this could be useful. How?"

Maya exchanged a look with Xalen. "Because of what *he* tells *me*, even accidentally. In the dreams, we're always in a . . . facility, sort of a laboratory, with lots of arcana equipment and no windows. It's so consistent I think it has to be a real place. Maybe his base of operations."

"Or his childhood home," Tanax said. "It's a *dream*."

"We know he hid from the Plague for four centuries," Maya said. "He wasn't in stasis, because he was working with Basel and the black spiders to try and get someone to use the Purifier. He had to live *somewhere*, somewhere he could isolate himself completely. An underground laboratory sounds like a good spot."

"And if we could locate it," Xalen said, "there might be something there we could use. Information, or even something of his we could hold hostage."

"It's pretty thin," Tanax said doubtfully.

"Even if it is real," Beq said, "how could we possibly find it? If he comes and goes by Gate, it could be literally anywhere."

"That's what I was thinking," Maya said. "But last night I got another clue. There was a map—"

"—in your *dream*," Tanax put in.

"—in the dream I *shared* with Ashok. I *think* it showed the location of the lab, and it was *here*. In the mountains, maybe even near Deepfire. That narrows it down quite a bit, doesn't it?"

"Also logical," Xalen said. "One reason there was so much fighting here during the Plague War was that the mountains were a center of ghoul power. Ashok, though a Chosen, studied *dhaka*."

Gyre sat up straighter, suddenly energized, an idea crackling in his mind. *That could work.*

"This whole *city* is built on scavenging arcana from old tunnels," Tanax said. "There are hundreds of miles of them. We can't search for a lab while we keep running—"

"Then we don't run," Gyre said, one hand slamming excitedly on the table.

Everyone stared at him. Tanax said, "What do you mean?"

"Exactly that," Gyre said. "We stay here. We don't run."

"And what happens when the Corruptor comes after us?" Beq said.

"We fight, of course."

"The seven of us?" Tanax said. "Against the city garrison plus whatever centarchs and Legionaries and plague-knows-what creatures that monster sends?"

"Not *alone*," Gyre said. "Right now, you're as good as in charge of the city. We *keep* it that way. Keep the Gate closed, hold the walls, and the Corruptor can't get at us, can he?"

"Hold the city?" Tanax said, taken aback. His eyes narrowed. "It might work... but..."

"Deepfire is famously defensible," Xalen said. "The passes are narrow and supply lines are long."

"You said Ritabel would turn us in if she got orders," Beq said to Tanax.

"Then we do something about her," Gyre said. "Convince her, buy her, replace her. Doesn't matter."

"The garrison alone isn't going to be able to hold out, though," Tanax said. "Not against Legionaries."

"We take our case to the city," Gyre said. He could feel the plan solidifying in his mind. "The tunnelborn and the scavengers. I still have contacts here. If we can explain who Ashok really is, we can raise an army. Deepfire is full of arcana—alchemicals, blasters, everything we need. Elariel can ask the ghouls for help—surely they don't want to see the Corruptor take over any more than we do."

"If we do that," Maya said, breaking her thoughtful silence, "then people are going to get hurt. People who aren't involved in this yet."

"If you think that Ashok is going to be a kind, dutiful emperor who does well by his people, then we should run off to the Forsaken Coast and leave him to get on with it," Gyre said. "But he won't and we all know it. Whether they realize it or not, *everyone* is involved."

Another pause. Maya stared down at her hand, her lips moving slightly, eyes haunted and distant.

"*I will write love into their very flesh...*"

Before Gyre could ask what it meant, she looked up. "He's right. We may not have a better chance to make a stand."

"All based on some lab you think you saw in a *dream*?" Tanax said.

"The longer we wait, the stronger he gets," Maya said. "If not now, when?"

"I..." Tanax sat back, shaking his head. "I don't know."

"We can try, at least," Maya said. "We'll have a backup plan. But if we *can* get the city on our side..." She hesitated, looked at Gyre. "I don't even know where to start."

"I have some ideas." Gyre stood up from his chair. "Let me go and find Sarah and Elariel, and then I'll see about getting back in touch with some old friends."

It wasn't difficult to figure out where the ghoul and the arcanist had gone.

The street outside Lynnia's house hadn't changed much. It was lined with neat stone buildings, two or three stories high, pressed cheek by jowl, with only narrow alleys between them. Solid, respectable dwellings, neither the teeming tenements of the poor nor the palaces of the rich, housing the merchants, bankers, and tradesmen so essential to the commerce of the mountain-bound city.

Lynnia Sharptongue was officially an elderly spinster of reasonable means enjoying a comfortable retirement. Unofficially, there was an alchemist's lab to rival any in the city buried under her tidy little property, and her products were hailed as the best. And—for a time, at least—she had also dabbled in revolution.

For Gyre, merely being here set off a wave of nostalgia. This had been his home for more than a year, one of the rooms Lynnia rented on the second floor serving as his base of operations while he ran with Yora's crew of rebels and scavengers as the notorious Halfmask. It was here he'd first heard from Kit—Kitsraea Doomseeker—and agreed to help her in return for information on the last city of the ghouls.

But Lynnia, who had become nearly an adoptive mother to Yora, had taken her death hard and blamed Gyre. *Not unjustly.* He had… lost sight of things, for a time, ironically as part of the events that had given him his silver eye. Since then, his relationship with the alchemist had been rocky at best. Last time, Elariel had had to knock her out to keep her from kicking Gyre's ribs in.

Wincing preemptively at the memory, Gyre crossed the street and knocked at the door. It opened at once, revealing Lynnia's trademark scowl. As always, he was surprised by how small she was, short and bony, wrapped up against the chill. Her force of personality made her loom considerably larger in memory.

"Hello, Lynnia."

He braced for a kick to the shins or the blast of a stunner. Instead she only looked him up and down and gave a pained grunt.

"Figured you'd turn up," she said. "Can't seem to stop you."

"Is Sarah here?" Gyre said.

"Upstairs." The alchemist shot him a sidelong look. "At least this time you brought her back with one more arm instead of one less. Doesn't make up for everything, but it's a start. Found her a girl, too, from the look of it."

"I suppose I did," Gyre said.

Lynnia didn't move from the doorway. "And?"

"And what?"

"What is it you need from me this time? You only come by when you're dangling a sack of thalers in front of old Lynnia, get her to compromise her principles one more time, she's soft and everyone knows it. So out with it."

"Believe me," Gyre said, "if I ever thought you were *soft*, I've been cured of that impression. And I'm only here to see Sarah and Elariel, honestly." He reflected a moment. "There *might* be something we need your help with—"

"Ha! I knew it."

"But I don't think we're ready to get started." Lynnia could *probably* keep a secret, but he didn't want to risk showing their hand early. *Trying to get this city to defend itself will be hard enough.* "I have some new friends I need to introduce."

"If they're the *centarchs* you've been keeping company with at the palace, better not." The alchemist spat past Gyre onto the stoop. "Don't know what scheme you've got going, but I won't have their kind in the house."

"Fair enough." Gyre had frankly been surprised that Sarah was willing to work next to Tanax; asking Lynnia to look past Yora's death would be too much. "Can I come in?"

"I s'pose." She stepped aside grudgingly. "Did you get good use out of the load you took with you?"

"I promise they were all put to *excellent* use," Gyre said.

"Right up a Legionary's backside, I hope." Lynnia cackled. "Tell Sarah I've put a cold plate together for her and the girl. It's in the kitchen."

The nostalgia was even stronger upstairs. The first room on the left had been his own, and the one beside it had been Yora's, when she needed a place to stay in the upper city. Now the door to the latter stood open, and he could see Sarah's things inside. Sarah herself leaned against the wall, waiting for him.

"Hey," she said. "How'd it go?"

"We have...a plan. Kind of a plan." He explained, briefly, and she gave a low whistle.

"You two don't think small, do you?"

"It's never been my strong suit," Gyre said. "Will you help?"

"I'll do what I can here in the city." She glanced at the closed door to Gyre's old room. "But I'm not going to leave her alone. I have a hard time imagining what she's been through, and the thought of making it worse..." She shook her head.

"I understand," Gyre said. "Mostly I want you and Lynnia to try and get in touch with Yora's old contacts. Ibb, at least, and anyone else you can think of. See how many friends we have left."

"I can try. We burned a lot of bridges at the end."

"I know." He looked at the door. "Do you think she'll talk to me?"

"I haven't heard her throw anything for a few minutes," Sarah said. "You should be safe."

"She..." He hesitated, fighting embarrassment. "I'm glad she has you to look after her. I feel like I haven't done enough."

"She's not a child, Gyre." Sarah blew out a breath. "She's just scared, and in so far over her head she couldn't touch the surface with a ten-foot pole."

"Aren't we all," Gyre muttered. "You've talked to her, I hope, about... relationships? And expectations? We only had a brief conversation on the subject, but I got the impression the ghouls did things...differently."

"We've gone over it," Sarah said, smiling a little at his discomfiture. "To both our satisfaction, I think."

"Good." He was, he realized, putting off opening the door. He made himself thumb the latch. "Thanks, Sarah."

"Good luck."

His old room was warm and dark, the curtain pulled over the window. Gyre's silver eye showed him everything regardless. He was surprised to see things were just as he'd left them, a few of his old packs on top of a battered dresser, his pile of scavenger's rumors and sightings on the desk. *I thought Lynnia would have chucked everything into the street.* He'd never kept much here, a legacy of years on the road. *Though, I wonder...*

First things first. Elariel was lying on the bed, curled in on herself in a miserable ball. Gyre went and sat at a comfortable distance, then waited.

Eventually Elariel shifted slightly. "Have you come to tell me I'm being stupid?"

"No," Gyre said. "Because you aren't."

"Apparently I'm the only one who thinks that dying is scary. Everyone else is excited to dive into the maw of a rockcrusher."

"Didn't I actually do that, at one point?"

"You did. And if not for me you'd have been pulped." Elariel uncurled enough to raise her head. "Nobody's going to conveniently turn off the Corruptor, Gyre."

"I know."

"Then why aren't you *terrified*? Why am I the only one who's going out of her mind?"

"I honestly don't know," Gyre said. "Maybe I have a lot of experience being terrified."

"After traveling with you for a while, I believe it," Elariel said. She lowered her head again. "I never wanted this."

"You helped Naumoriel. You must have wanted *something*."

"I was stupid." Her voice was muffled. "He was *passionate*. It's not normal, for us. I was at a council meeting, and we'd spent hours on housing allocations, expansion planning, that sort of thing. A hundred hours of debate to be *certain* digging another dozen rooms wouldn't inconvenience anyone more than absolutely necessary. And then Naumoriel gets up and starts talking about reclaiming our destiny, and I thought... this is what I need." She dropped to a whisper. "Something to believe in."

"Did he tell you he wanted to destroy humanity?"

"No. It might not have mattered if he did, though. I didn't think much of humans in those days."

"You do now?"

"You're not vermin. You're just people. Like us. You have some weird ideas and your bodies are strange, but... still. People. I wish Naumoriel had come with me to see Deepfire. He might have understood."

Gyre sat for a moment in silence.

"I want to go home," Elariel said quietly. "I want to go back to my safe little room and my safe little life and debate housing allocations for the next hundred years. But I never will, will I?"

"I don't know," Gyre admitted. "Your people exiled you, and I'm not sure anything will change their minds. All I can say is that you'll always have a place with us."

"Up here. With the Corruptor."

"It's the only place I've got to offer. That's why we have to stop him." Gyre sighed. "If he restores the Empire, I'm not sure a few mountains are going to be enough to keep him out of Refuge, either."

"I know." Elariel unfolded, tentatively, and sat up. Her eyes were puffy and red from crying.

"You were going to send them a warning," Gyre said. "Can I help with that?"

Elariel sniffed. "I already did."

"How?"

"I cached some messenger-constructs in the city when I was working with Kit."

"Smart."

She shrugged. "I wish I believed it would help."

"You don't think they'll listen?"

"They'll listen. But all they'll do is close the doors even tighter and pretend the outside world doesn't exist. You met the Geraia."

"Briefly." The elder ghouls, ancient even by the standards of that long-lived race. Their fur patchy, carried everywhere on construct beds. "If they won't save themselves, then it's up to us, isn't it?"

"I suppose so." She looked up at him. "You really believe we can do it?"

"Maybe it helps that I wasn't raised on stories of the Corruptor. I only heard of him a couple of months ago; he's not my childhood bogeyman. And I've *seen* him. He's a monster, with a Chosen's power and a plaguespawn's body, but that hardly makes him invincible."

"He's got the Chosen's empire now too."

"So did the Chosen. Now they're all dead."

She chuckled weakly. "All we need is a new plague, then."

Gyre gave an encouraging nod. "Sarah's outside," he said. "Lynnia put out some food; go and eat something."

Elariel nodded. She got out of bed, a bit shaky, and stretched.

"This was your room, right?" she said.

"It was, for a while," Gyre said.

"You didn't do much decorating."

"No. I thought I had more important things to worry about."

"Do you regret what you did? Helping Naumoriel?"

"I...don't know." He closed his silver eye a moment, leaving him in darkness. "There were things I didn't understand back then. Maybe if I'd known everything, I wouldn't have done it. But if I hadn't found Maya, then maybe the Corruptor would have killed her when he got out and there would be nothing left to stop him. Or maybe he'd never have gotten out at all. You can drive yourself mad that way."

"Oh, I know." Elariel sighed. "You're right about one thing, though."

"What?"

"Food sounds good." She touched his shoulder as she passed. "Thanks."

"Anytime."

Gyre waited in the darkened room, lost in thought, as Elariel and Sarah descended the stairs. With a shake of his head he got up and pulled the curtain open, flooding the room with dingy light and raising a cloud of dust. Waving a hand, he opened the window as well, then turned to the wardrobe.

It was almost entirely empty. He'd never had many civilian clothes, and he'd taken most of them with him when he went south with Elariel. They were still with the much-abused wagons, which he'd last seen at Spire Kotzed. A single torn shirt, which he'd once hoped to mend, hung forlornly under a layer of dust.

Gyre was more interested in the base of the wardrobe. An inconspicuous hole near the back let him work a finger in and pry up the false bottom, revealing a few inches of space underneath. When he'd lived here, this had been his emergency stash, with a roll of thalers and a few choice alchemicals in case of emergency. He'd taken those when he'd left too. The mask, in its velvet bag, was all that was left.

Half a mask, to be exact, worked in silver with curving lines and a flat, dead eye to cover the empty socket underneath. He'd had two of the things made. One he'd lost in the burning warehouse where he'd first confronted Maya and he and Kit had barely escaped with their lives. This had been his backup, but he'd never needed it. The Half-mask identity was closed, behind him, replaced with Silvereye.

But there's still power in the legend, and I may need it. He slipped the mask back into its bag and put it in his pocket. *I'll have to bore an eye-hole, I suppose.*

"Brings back memories, doesn't it?" someone said behind him. "We never did fuck in here, though. Bed's a little small for it."

Gyre turned, hand dropping to his sword. There was no one in the room, no movement except for the curtain blowing in the draft from the window.

"Do you regret our bargain? You might think I would, under the circumstances, but I'm not so sure. I mean, if we hadn't done it, I'd definitely be dead, and not just half-dead or kind of dead or whatever I am now, so—"

Gyre's brow furrowed. "Kit?"

"Yes?"

"Where are you?"

"Here. Left. Down. There. See? Helloooo?"

At the foot of the bed, perched on one of the posts, was a tiny black creature the size of a mouse, or more accurately a large spider. It resembled the constructs he was familiar with, but it was smaller than even the dog-sized units, and its legs were longer and thinner. It waved at him with one minuscule claw.

"You like my new outfit?" Kit said. The spider gave an excited little shimmy. "I figured out how to tinker with the Leviathan's manufacturing prototypes. This should make it easier for me to ride on your shoulder."

"Very practical," Gyre managed, still getting over his shock.

"Also to sneak into your room at night," Kit said blithely. "Speaking of which, we need to hurry."

"Hurry? Where?"

"Khirkhaz. If we don't help Apphia, they're going to kill her for sure."

Chapter Ten

It was actually a lot more comfortable to carry Kit around in her tiny new body. More importantly, she could flatten herself under his collar and hide, which meant he could go out in public without people screaming about the plaguespawn on his shoulder.

"How many bodies did you bring with you?" Gyre muttered as they climbed out of the hired carriage at the Spike. *The hard part is going to be avoiding a reputation for talking to myself.*

"As many as I could round up. A few small ones hiding in the city, and a couple of dozen camped outside of town. The Leviathan is working on building more. Did you know it—I—can literally eat anything organic? Right now I have some bodies feeding it trees."

"I'll organize a wagon to get the rest of you to the palace without scaring anybody," Gyre said. "If we're going back to Khirkhaz, it'll have to be by Gate."

"Thank the Chosen," Kit said. "That trip was *so boring.*"

"What about escaping from Ehrenvare?"

"That was okay. Also watching Sarah and Elariel, until you made me stop."

"I *have* missed you," Gyre said, grinning.

"Of course you have," Kit said. "Who wouldn't miss me?"

"Stay hidden until I tell you. Tanax hasn't met you yet."

"Affirmative, sir!" He felt the spider give a tiny salute.

Maya was waiting at the main drive, and she escorted him inside, past the gaggle of uniformed servants and attentive guards. Gyre still wasn't used to strolling into the Spike like he owned the place, but Maya seemed utterly unbothered at receiving the bows of the Auxies. *Presumably she's used to it.* She seemed to have figured out the layout as well, taking him rapidly up several flights of stairs and down a corridor.

"What's going on?" she said when they were out of public view. "You said it was urgent."

"Wait till we're in private," Gyre said. "Is Tanax coming?"

She nodded and led him to a small drawing room, with several plump armchairs, a sideboard packed with bottles, and a bookshelf full of leather-bound volumes. Tanax was waiting for them with a frown, but he said nothing until Maya closed the door behind them.

"I thought we'd agreed on a plan this afternoon," he said. "At least in broad outline. Has something happened?"

"I heard from one of my companions," Gyre said. "We got separated, but she caught up with us and she has information."

"You should have brought her here, then."

"Well." Gyre looked at Maya. "It's a bit of a long story. Promise you won't hit anything with a haken, okay?"

"I—" Tanax cut off as Kit's spider emerged from Gyre's collar, waving its arms. "What . . . is that?"

"It's a ghoul construct," Gyre said as Maya also peered at the new, tiny body.

"Like the things we fought in Leviathan's Womb," Maya said.

"It looks like a plaguespawn," Tanax said darkly.

"That's because it's built with *dhaka*. Same basic principle, completely different results. Elariel could tell you more about it."

"And this tiny thing is your companion?"

"Kind of." He took a deep breath. "Due to a complicated set of circumstances, the mind of my friend Kit is currently inhabiting a swarm of these constructs. Kit, say hello."

"Hello," Kit said brightly. "You look a lot better than the last time I saw you."

"We've met?" Tanax said, eyebrows going up.

"I believe you were unconscious on the floor after losing a sword fight to Gyre," Kit said.

"Be nice," Gyre said.

"I'm just saying."

"If we're bringing up old times," Maya said, "I believe it was *you* who stabbed me from behind and left me for dead."

"Oh yeah!" Kit capered a little. "Then again, you seem not to have died, and *I* got disemboweled and turned into a swarm of self-assembling constructs, so really things worked out for everyone."

"*In any case*," Gyre said. "Kit accompanied me to Khirkhaz and came with us to the Purifier. But the last of the bodies she brought along was destroyed in the fight with the Corruptor, so I haven't heard from her until now."

"I'm glad you guys came back to Deepfire," Kit said. "I wasn't looking forward to trying to search the whole Republic."

"Okay," Tanax said. "I think I follow. So what information has she brought?"

"Strictly speaking," Kit said, "I still have one body left in Khirkhaz. In the fight for Spire Kotzed, one of them had most of its legs damaged, but it's otherwise still functional. Nina Kotzed picked me up after the battle while we were cleaning up the bodies."

"This is the baron's younger sister, correct?" Maya said. Gyre nodded.

"The baron was leading the rebellion, wasn't she?" Tanax said.

"And I was helping her," Gyre said, straightening up a little as if in challenge. Tanax met his eye but didn't comment. "We were . . . close."

"He means they were fucking," Kit said.

"Somehow I knew you would say that," Gyre said.

"I just like everyone to be on the same page."

"If the Republic forces are gone," Tanax said, "then your lover and her sister should be safe for the moment."

"They were, for a while," Kit said. "Then a whole new army marched through the Gate. That centarch Va'aht that Gyre fought at the Spire was in charge, and there were a whole bunch of new soldiers. Like Legionaries but with silver armor instead of white."

"We saw them in Skyreach," Maya said. "When the Corruptor made his triumphal entrance."

"Well, I can personally attest that they're bad news," Kit said. "A lot of the rebels had gone home, but there was still a reasonable force at the Spire. Those silver things went through them like an arrow through mist. They didn't bother with ladders, they just *climbed* over the walls like a bunch of monkeys, and they were *fast*. The rebels that tried to fight got butchered, even with ghoul swords and blasters. Apphia and a bunch of the others were captured, but Nina managed to hide until they moved on, and she kept my body with her."

Gyre felt a stab of guilt. He'd left the rebels behind—he hadn't intended to, but he had, and they'd been slaughtered. *Again.* His hand tightened at his side.

"Nina's holed up with some sympathetic villagers," Kit went on. "I told her I'd found you and that I'd ask for help. Apphia and the others are on their way to a prison camp, though, and Nina is certain this Va'aht will execute her. She said to beg you for help." The spider gave a multilegged shrug. "Do you actually want me to beg? I've never been good at it."

"No need," Gyre said. "I'm going after her."

"To Khirkhaz?" Tanax looked at Maya. "Is that possible?"

Maya nodded. "I've been talking to Beq. I can unlock the Gate and use it for transport, then lock it again afterward."

"Even so." Tanax shook his head. "The Khirkhaz Gate will be guarded, and with such a heavy presence of the Corruptor's troops, the risk is high. Can we afford to run it for such a limited objective?"

"Tanax—" Maya warned, but Gyre interrupted.

"Apphia's not worth it, you mean?" he said. "Because she's a rebel?"

"It has nothing to do with her being a rebel," the centarch snapped. "We're all rebels now. But you were the one who said we're working for the fate of humanity here. Do you really want to risk that for one person, lover or not?"

Gyre hesitated. Only for a moment, but it was long enough for something to twist in his gut. He gritted his teeth and bore down hard on the tiny seedling of doubt.

"I made promises that I intend to keep," he said.

"And having an experienced rebel like Apphia on our side might be useful," Maya said. "If Gyre and I move quickly—"

Tanax and Gyre both shook their heads.

"I need you here," Tanax said. "We're barely keeping the situation under control as it is, and someone has to search for this lab of yours."

"And I'll move faster alone," Gyre said. "If I'm going to meet up with Nina and what's left of the Commune, it'll be easier if I don't have a centarch to try and explain."

"How do you intend to get back?" Maya said. "One of us needs to open the Gate."

Gyre frowned, not having thought that far ahead. Tanax, to his surprise, said, "We can use a system like the Order messengers. Open the Gate for a short interval at a specific time every day."

Maya bit her lip. "I still don't like it."

"It's the best we're going to get," Gyre said. "Sarah and Lynnia will work on finding our old contacts. I'll go to Khirkhaz alone"—there was a pinch on his shoulder—"that is, I'll go to Khirkhaz with Kit and find Apphia, then get back here as soon as I can."

"I'll leave some of my bodies here to relay messages," Kit said. "I have a few more of the tiny ones; I can stay with you."

"Wonderful," Tanax said, with evident distaste. "All right. When are you planning to leave?"

"As soon as Kit's bodies get here," Gyre said. "I don't know how much time Apphia has."

"What about Va'aht?" Maya said.

"We've crossed swords once already," Gyre said grimly. "If he wants another try, I'm happy to oblige."

Gyre stood in front of the Gate in the stone chamber buried deep under the Spike, sword in hand, checking his gear one more time. On one hip he carried a blaster pistol and a sack with a selection of alchemicals; on the other was his energy bottle—full, thanks to Elariel. Another three were in his pack. That pack was strapped to one of Kit's medium-sized bodies, waist-high on a human, six limbs wrapped in thick striated muscle. Two more just like it stood at the ready, along with a dozen of the dog-sized versions.

"Ready?" Maya said, standing beside him. "Are you sure you don't want me to come through, just for—"

"I don't want anyone there to know where we came from," Gyre said. "Close the Gate just after we go through." He flashed her a cocky grin. "I'll be all right, I promise."

"You'd better. We need you, if we're going to have any chance at all." Maya touched her haken. "Here it goes."

Silvery mist filled the twisted archway. Gyre concentrated, activating his augmentations with a *click*, and ran forward through the suddenly somnolent world of drifting shadows. Something about the Gate made his eye go haywire, drawing wild streaks across his vision as it attempted to process his motion through the portal. He squeezed it shut and burst through, stepping from the gloom of the palace basement to bright afternoon sun.

The Khirkhaz Gate opened onto a flat, grassy stretch beside a river, with rocky hills rising in one direction and rolling fields stretching out in the other. The grass was somewhat the worse for wear, torn and trampled as if by the passage of an army. Of more urgent import were the four Legionaries on watch, blaster rifles in hand.

Fortunately for Gyre, they were watching the wrong way—against someone coming *toward* the Gate, rather than emerging from it. His sword thrust into the first sentry's side before she knew he was there, and he pivoted toward the next before the body had hit the ground. A few seconds later he was in the clear. He turned back to the Gate in time to see the silvery mist vanish behind the last of Kit's constructs.

"Neat work," Kit said. "Should we hide the bodies? When the next shift arrives they'll know we came through."

"Can't be helped," Gyre said, cleaning the blood from his blade. "It's not like a sentry detail would walk off the job. We'll just have to move fast." He shaded his eyes and looked across the plain, which was dotted with small villages. "Come on."

He stole a loadbird from the first farmstead they came to, clicking his tongue softly to calm the animal while he left a stack of thalers as payment. A swiftbird would be faster, but provincial farmers were unlikely to keep one, and in any event it would attract notice. He kept away from the roads until they'd gone far enough that no one was likely to recognize his mount, then guided the irritable bird back to the dirt track, deeply scored by wagon wheels. The loadbird settled down, placated by occasional breaks for nyfa seeds from his stolen saddlebags.

Kit's tiny body remained on his shoulder, while the rest of her swarm was only occasionally visible, scuttling through tall grass and unharvested crops alongside the road. Even the larger bodies were remarkably hard to see, moving in quick dashes.

"You're getting good at this," he said.

"Thanks," Kit said. "There's a lot of…instructions? Like the script of a play. And you can chain them together, or write new ones, or—it's hard to explain. The inside of the analytica is a weird place."

"I can imagine," Gyre said. "Or I can't, I guess. Whichever. How's Nina doing?"

"I'm not with her at the moment," Kit said. "She's hidden my body and gone out to meet the rebels in the village. I told her you're coming, though."

"I just hope we make it in time."

"We will," Kit said cheerfully. "Apphia knows a lot about the Commune. They'll torture her for information before they execute her."

"Very reassuring. Please don't say that to Nina."

The bird Gyre had stolen wasn't fast, but it was tireless in the way of loadbirds. It swept kilometers of dusty road underfoot with barely a squawk of complaint, and by the time evening began making itself felt, they had crossed out of the plains and into Khirkhaz's great central forest. Gyre kept riding, trusting his silver eye to navigate as the shadows of the trees grew around him. Kit's bodies ranged ahead and murmured warnings of riders or carters heading the other way.

"Something's wrong," Kit said in his ear. "Nina's not back, and I can hear fighting in the town."

"Plague it," Gyre growled. "Can your body there move at all?"

"Not enough legs left," Kit said. "I'll send some of the others ahead."

"How far out are we?"

"Half an hour."

"Hold on tight, then."

He made the low whistle that asked the bird for more speed, and the beast went from its usual lope into a flat-out run with its stubby vestigial wings extended. Even so, Kit's bodies outdistanced him, their black legs a blur. A loadbird, without the stamina of its warrior cousins, would exhaust itself quickly at this pace, but it covered a lot of ground. It was all Gyre could do to keep his mount on the road, steering with awkward jerks on the reins instead of clicks of the tongue.

"I hear blasters," Kit said, nearly lost in the slipstream. "And screams."

Plaguing fuck. *I'm so close.* He whistled again, asking for more speed, but the bird had none to give. Soon it began to wobble, footing becoming uncertain as its strength failed, and he had to call it back to a slower pace. Kit's bodies, not subject to such mortal restraints, ranged farther ahead.

"Fighting's stopped," she reported. "I don't hear anything."

After another quarter of an hour, the loadbird was wheezing. Gyre slid down, patting the thing's head and dumping it a small pile of nyfa seeds. He set off at a jog, silver eye turning twilight into day, alert for movement. Kit's larger bodies ran alongside him.

"I'm there," Kit said. "I don't see anyone moving. A few bodies."

"Look for Nina." *Hiding, or... otherwise.*

"Working on it."

The village seemed to appear in his path quite suddenly, the glow from its fires hidden by intervening trees. It occupied a clearing a few hundred meters across, where a couple of dozen buildings huddled together on a patch of bare earth dotted with massive stumps. Large earthen humps Gyre guessed were charcoal kilns occupied one side, with stacks of firewood lined up in front of them.

A few chimneys trickled smoke, and a small fire crackled at the corner of one building that had been partially demolished by a blaster bolt. Bodies were scattered across a central open space. A few had been armed, spears and axes lying among corpses torn and blackened by blaster fire. More had been cut down as they fled, bearing crimson sword strokes across their backs.

Worse, every building had its door torn from its hinges, and the modest furnishings inside were trampled and broken. Gyre slowed to a walk and peered at the ground, spotting the deep imprints of Legionary boots alongside the leather footwear of Auxies. *And a plaguing lot of them. Three squads at least.*

"The soldiers left a pretty clear trail," Kit said. "No sign that any of them stayed behind."

"Nina!" Gyre raised his voice. "If you're here, say something!"

Silence. The last light of the day was bleeding away, and stars began to peek through the trees.

Then there was a *thump*. Another. Gyre turned his head, trying to find the source, but Kit's bodies were already moving. They headed toward the damaged building, ignoring the low flames still licking at the rubble.

Someone had been firing from the downstairs window, and a blaster bolt had demolished that whole side of the wooden-walled structure. Gyre pushed through the wrecked front door and found the corpse of a woman lying amid the splintered furniture, half her face and upper body burned black from the blaster's impact. A broken crossbow lay nearby. The stairs to the second floor had collapsed, but there was a curtained doorway by the cookfire. It led to a storeroom, well stocked with sacks of flour and preserved meat. In one corner was a small barrel of salt, and as Gyre watched, it jumped and rattled. He moved it aside, and almost immediately part of the floor levered up, earth cascading away from the hidden trapdoor.

Nina emerged like some sort of spirit rising from the earth. Dirt grimed the teenager's face and coated her pink hair, which was fraying badly from its braid. Her eyes were bloodshot and she was breathing hard.

"G...Gyre?" She blinked, went to rub her face, and stopped herself. "You're really here? I'm not going crazy?"

"I'm here." Gyre extended a hand and she took it with both of hers. He leaned back and hauled her up, shedding a layer of soil. "Are you hurt?"

"I...I'm not. Bruised. Is— What happened to Keli and the others? Are they okay?"

She made a move to run past Gyre. He grabbed her shoulder to stop her, but not fast enough. She spotted the woman's corpse in the main room and fell to her knees, gasping.

"For me." Her voice was thick. "Plaguing fuck. They all died *for me*. I tried—Gyre, I tried—"

She turned to him, tears on her cheeks, her eyes frantic. Gyre grabbed her and pulled her against him, his arms around her shoulders. After a moment of struggle, she subsided, sobbing into his chest.

"You're okay," he said quietly. "It's okay."

It wasn't, by any stretch of the imagination, but it seemed like the words Nina needed to hear. She cried for a long while, and he waited until she was done. One of Kit's bodies peeked around the corner, and Gyre warned her off with a shake of his head.

"Fuck," Nina whispered very quietly.

"Can you walk?" Gyre said. "I'd like to get away from here."

She nodded, still pressed against him. Together they got up, and Gyre guided the girl outside. She went stiff at the sight of the bodies but said nothing, and he hurried her along until they reached the edge of town. Gyre found a sheltered spot by the base of a tree. He beckoned Kit over with his pack and dug for a canteen and some biscuit.

"Kit?" Nina said as the construct knelt beside her.

"Yup!" Kit said. "I told you I was fetching him."

"Thank you." Nina let out a long breath. "I didn't know if anyone could make it here."

"It's just the two of us," Gyre said. "Or at least one of me and a dozen of her. Can you tell me what happened?"

"I thought you were hiding out," Kit said. "You left me in the back of a wardrobe."

"Sorry," Nina said. "I didn't want anyone to raise a fuss about you." She looked up at Gyre. "Kit told you about what happened at the Spire?"

Gyre nodded.

"Brennard had some of his men smuggle me out when he was sure the battle was lost. They brought me here to stay with Keli and her husband, Mitik. They've been a part of the Commune's network for years. They agreed to hide me, but..."

"You were followed," Gyre said, wincing.

Nina nodded. "A column of troops found us. They started asking questions, and when the villagers wouldn't give me up, they declared the whole village guilty of treason and started shooting people. I was in the house, and Mitik got me hidden just before they kicked the door down. Keli tried to stop them." She sniffed and wiped her nose, smearing dirt.

"How many people in the village?" Gyre said.

"Not sure. A hundred or so?"

"There's not nearly enough bodies, then. They must have taken the rest captive."

"That's what they've been doing all through Khirkhaz. The new soldiers aren't bothering with arrests or evidence. They round people up, whole villages, and they just disappear. That's what happened to Apphia, Brennard, and the others after the battle. I was trying to find out where they were taken."

"This lot can't have gone far," Gyre said. "They can't march a bunch of prisoners through the dark. They must have a camp somewhere nearby."

"On it," Kit said, several of her smaller bodies skittering away.

"You can stay here with Kit," Gyre said. "I'll see what we're up against, and—"

"I'm coming with you," Nina said.

"Are you sure—"

"I'm *coming* with you." She shook her head. "I'm tired of hiding."

The camp occupied another clearing, about an hour's walk from the town. By the look of the bird shit on the ground, it had been there for several days. Gyre counted fifteen tents of the standard four-person variety used by Legionaries and Auxies, plus a larger one for officers.

Figure sixty soldiers. Mostly Auxies, but he saw at least one tent with Legionary kit. *Three squads and a Legionary detail, with a senior decarch in command.*

The villagers sat nearby in a dispirited group, watched by half a dozen Auxies. A few sported bandages, but the majority seemed unhurt. Their legs were hobbled with leather cords.

"I see Mitik," Nina said, pointing to one older man. "And Gharji, the mayor."

"We'll get them out," Gyre said. "And hopefully someone down there knows where they've taken your sister."

Nina nodded and hugged the blaster pistol Gyre had given her. "So what's the plan?"

They were hidden in the underbrush at the top of a slope some distance from the clearing. The sentries didn't seem particularly alert, but the camp wasn't large—there was no way they would be able to sneak fifty villagers away without raising an alarm. *That means we have to clear them out.* Sixty soldiers was a tall order for one man and a girl, even with a dozen constructs for backup. Kit's bodies weren't meant for head-on combat. *But they do* look *like plaguespawn...*

"Can you circle around to the other side?" he said to the spider on his shoulder.

"Already done," Kit said. "Wanted to make sure there were no surprises."

"Okay. When I say go, I want you to let them see a couple of your units, while the others make plenty of noise in the trees. Tear the tents down, spook the birds. Let them think a whole herd of plaguespawn is coming through."

"Sounds like a good time," Kit said, capering. "Just say the word."

"I'll head in and take out the Legionaries and the officers. Hopefully that'll break them."

"What do I do?" Nina said.

"When I reach the clearing, start shooting from here," Gyre said. "Hit the tents, start some fires. That should confuse them even more." *And keep you out of harm's way.* If—when—he found Apphia, he didn't want to have to tell her he'd gotten her little sister killed along the way.

"Okay." Nina checked the pistol. "I'm ready."

"Give me a few minutes to get in position."

Gyre eased forward through the brush. He picked a point midway between two bored-looking sentries, and neither caught the slight rustle as he slipped past. When he'd gotten as close as he dared, he crouched low and dug in his bag of alchemicals for a stunner.

"Ready?" he asked Kit.

"Always," she said.

He grinned and lobbed the stunner, immediately slapping one hand over his eyes. The little clay grenade landed among the tents and blossomed into a burst of white light and a *boom* that rattled Gyre's teeth. With a *click* at the base of his skull he engaged his augmentations, dropping into the slow-moving shadow-world. Screams were already rising across the camp.

Nina opened fire as he sprinted forward, blaster bolts crawling past his shoulder to detonate among the tents. The blasts flung dirt and burning canvas into the air, and the first sentry had foolishly turned to gawk, not even noticing Gyre's approach. Gyre swung his blade in a flat arc, the ghoul-made weapon cutting easily through flesh and bone to send the Auxie's head tumbling away. Jets of blood sprayed from severed arteries as the body collapsed.

Confused shouts came from several sides of the camp as the soldiers tried to coordinate a defense. Gyre heard "Plaguespawn!" and "Rebels!" as he sprinted between the tents at an impossible speed, ignoring Auxies not directly in his path. A tough-looking woman lost an arm and spun away shrieking, and a man who tried to level a spear was abruptly without half his weapon and both his hands. Terror was spreading, and terror was his friend. *It's only easy until they all come at me at once.*

In front of him was the officers' tent. The four Legionaries were there, two armored, two in underclothes but with blaster rifles in hand. An Auxie with a decarch's emblem was yelling orders, not very effectively. One of the Legionaries raised a rifle to her shoulder and fired, and Gyre saw one of Kit's bodies blow apart in slow motion. Another bolt from Nina raised a shower of scorched earth.

Gyre jumped a stack of firewood, hit the ground in a controlled roll, and popped up in the middle of the cluster of Legionaries. His blade licked out at one of the unarmored ones, carving a deep rent across his chest. The other gave ground hurriedly, trying to bring her blaster to bear, while her two armored companions drew their unmetal blades. The decarch collapsed backward into the tent, screaming.

As usual, while the Legionaries were well equipped and expertly trained, they were no match for Gyre's speed. He stabbed one in the throat while he was still raising his sword, then maneuvered him into the path of his companion to foul her attack. Behind him, the fourth Legionary fired, and Gyre saw projections of the blaster bolt spray past him. He ducked leisurely out of the way, letting the blast hit the soldier with the ruined throat. The woman behind him, startled, didn't have time to block when Gyre jammed his blade into her side. He whirled and went after the fourth soldier, ducking her blast and extending into a textbook lunge that put the tip of his blade through the center of her chest. She dropped her weapon, gurgling, then sagged. Gyre let the corpse slip off his sword, straightened up—

—and had barely a moment's warning as shadows filled the air around him. Too late to dodge the oncoming mass of metal, he swung his arm up to intercept a pair of hooked claws, keeping them away from his face at the expense of taking a couple of long cuts to his forearm. An instant later, something hit him in the stomach, hard enough to lift him off his feet and toss him into a nearby tent. Poles *cracked* as the fabric collapsed around him.

What the plaguing fuck—

No time to think. He grabbed another stunner and threw it directly toward his new opponent, closing his eyes and rolling away to buy time. The alchemical went off, deafeningly loud at this range, leaving no sound in the world but a sharp ringing. Afterimages blurred his vision, even through closed eyelids. *But he must be hurting worse.*

A swiping claw nearly ripped his face off. Gyre jerked backward, losing the tiniest chunk of the tip of his nose. He scrambled away, pawing through the dirt, blinking the colors from his eyes. The thing looked like a Legionary, a similar style of faceless armor. But it was gray, not white—*not gray, silver*—

The soldiers he'd seen in Skyreach, the ones Kit had told him were in Khirkhaz. *Nobody mentioned they were as fast as a plaguing viper!* The man held no sword, but two long, curved blades hooked down from each forearm past his hands, giving him a pair of wicked claws. The silver surface of his armor was marred by the blast of the stunner, but if the effects bothered him, it didn't show.

Gyre managed to scramble back to his feet, watching the shadows shift around his opponent. They warned him of the soldier's movements, but only barely, his speed stretching the limits of the silver eye's ability to keep up. Gyre dodged two horizontal swipes and countered with a cut to the head. The man raised an arm to block, a thick unmetal vambrace stopping the ghoul blade. He came on, oblivious to the chaos of the camp around them. Tents were burning and Auxies were fleeing for their lives.

Those claws are vicious, but I have better reach. Gyre feinted left, then right, drawing an attempted parry, then circling to aim a thrust at the base of the soldier's chestplate. Like a Legionary's, the silver armor was weak at the joints, and the ghoul sword broke through with a *crunch* and sank into the man's guts. Instead of falling, though, the silver-armored soldier stepped forward, driving Gyre's weapon farther into himself so that he could wrap his arms around Gyre. The deadly hug let the soldier slash his claws across Gyre's back, and he screamed in pain.

Something big hit them both, breaking the clinch and sending them toppling to the ground. One of Kit's larger bodies, which he'd left on the ridge with Nina, had apparently joined the fray. It skidded to a halt in the dirt, then jumped on top of the soldier, putting all its weight on his chest. The spider-construct wasn't *that* heavy—an ordinary man might have been able to wiggle out from under it—but this silver-armored soldier lifted the construct with one hand and hurled it aside like a paperweight. Gyre struggled up, in spite of the agony from his back, grabbing his blade as the man jumped to his feet like a jack-in-the-box.

A blaster *cracked* behind him, the bolt detonating against the soldier an instant later. At that range, even unmetal armor wasn't proof against the shock of a blaster bolt, and the man staggered backward. One side of his silver armor was charred, and his arm hung shredded and useless, but somehow he didn't fall. He didn't even waver, just leaned into a sprint, leading with his good arm and slashing for Gyre's eyes.

This time, Gyre had a moment to prepare, and he watched the shadows stretch out in front of his attacker. He sidestepped at the last instant, taking his sword in both hands for a powerful upward cut and catching the man under the armpit to sever his arm at the shoulder. It hung limp against his side, still attached by the armor plating, and the blood that pumped from the wound was black as pitch.

Oh, plaguing fuck. Gyre spun and kicked his disarmed opponent in the chest, sending him staggering backward to fall in the dirt. Kit didn't give him a chance to rise, two bodies hurrying to hold him down. Nina was just behind them, her blaster still smoking. Gyre shambled over to the furiously struggling soldier.

"I thought I told you to stay put," he croaked.

"You looked like you needed help," Nina said. "And I'm not that good a shot, so I had to get closer."

Gyre let the point drop. He knelt, one knee on the silver armor, and worked his sword through the straps holding the helmet in place. The featureless silver mask slid away, and underneath—

Of course. I ought to have known from the start.

The thing might be humanoid, but its features were anything but human. The face was all eyes, seven of them of varying sizes distributed across an oval of flesh. Black, skinless muscles bunched and twisted in its stocky neck.

Plaguespawn.

He'd fought humanoid plaguespawn beside the Corruptor in the Purifier. *They weren't as fast or as strong as this thing, though. Clearly he's made some improvements.*

"Oh, fucking Chosen defend," Nina breathed, looking down at the twitching, furious thing. "Is that—"

"Exactly what you think," Gyre said grimly.

"How do we kill it?"

"This *usually* works." He jammed his sword into the thing's exposed throat, pressing down until he heard a *crunch* of bone. To his great relief, the plaguespawn spasmed and stilled, though the mismatched eyes continued blinking for some time.

That's one. He thought of the parade in Skyreach, hundreds of the things marching in lockstep, and shuddered. *Chosen defend.*

"Are you all right?" Nina said after a moment. "You're bleeding."

"We'll deal with that in a minute," Gyre said. He pushed himself to his feet, feeling a fresh wave of pain from the slashes on his back. "Let's help these people first."

The camp was a shambles. Several fires were burning among the collapsed tents, and the packbirds had broken their ties and fled into the forest. The Auxies had followed them, apart from those sprawled motionless in the wreckage. The four Legionaries lay dead, but in the officer's tent—

Gyre heard a frightened intake of breath and smiled to himself.

"Go cut the villagers loose," he said to Nina. "Make sure no one ran off."

"Got it."

She headed for the huddle of frightened civilians, who'd sensibly thrown themselves flat for the duration of the fight. Two of Kit's bodies followed at her heels like loyal hounds. Gyre checked his energy bottle— low, but not empty yet—and pushed into the half-collapsed tent.

The Auxie decarch, an older man with gray in his dark purple hair and beard, was pressed into the back corner. He had a sword drawn, but the point wove figure eights in front of him. Gyre contemptuously whacked it out of the man's hands with the flat of his own blade.

"You...you..." The man swallowed, eyes wide. "You killed a Perfected. Who *are* you?"

"I'm the one who's going to ask you some questions," Gyre said. "If I like your answers, you can run off and round up your soldiers. Understood?"

"I...I can't." He looked away. "I can't—"

Gyre grabbed the man's foot and dragged him out through the tent flap, ignoring his terrified shrieks. He dropped the decarch between the plaguespawn's corpse and two of the dead Legionaries, and let him have a moment to take in the scene. Gyre cleared his throat.

"Please don't hurt me."

"I don't plan to. But those villagers you were holding captive? I'm the only thing standing between you and whatever they decide is justice. So if I were you, I'd stay on my good side."

The Auxie looked away, swallowing hard. "What do you want to know?"

"Start with where you were taking these people and why."

"Traitors are taken to the camp at Grayport," the decarch said. "I don't know what happens to them after that."

"Do you really think the whole village are traitors?"

"Orders direct from the Emperor. We're to round up everyone suspected of treason and leave it to higher authorities to sort out. I'm sure those who are innocent will be sent home."

"Oh, sure." Gyre kicked the dead plaguespawn. "With these guys on your side, that seems likely."

"I didn't—I don't know *what* that is. The Perfected never take their armor off. They're beyond human needs. The Emperor sends them to personally oversee our operations."

"I'll bet he does."

"Plaguing fucker!"

The woman Nina had identified as Gharji stormed over, backed by several more villagers. The others were huddled at the edge of the clearing, hesitant to approach the bodies, but Gharji stepped over the dead Auxies as though they were so many rocks. She grabbed the decarch by the collar and hauled him up. He looked desperately at Gyre.

"You said you would protect me!"

"I suppose I did." Gyre sighed and put a hand on Gharji's shoulder. "He's been very cooperative."

"Him and his bastard plaguepits killed Nori and Fern and Chosen know how many others!" Gharji growled. "What did any of them ever do to you?"

"Please," the officer squeaked. "I only followed my orders."

"*Fuck* your orders." Gharji raised a fist.

"Beating him to a pulp won't bring back those who died," Gyre said quietly. "And there's wounded among your people who need help."

"Fuck." Gharji let the officer drop and spat on him. "*Fuck.*"

"All right, clear out," Gyre said. "I'd disappear, if I were you. I doubt the *Emperor* will be forgiving."

The man gave him a wide-eyed stare for a few moments, then scrambled away, vanishing into the woods. Gharji seemed to deflate a little.

"You..." She looked around the clearing. "You did this? Alone?"

"Nina helped."

"Nina." Gharji looked over her shoulder. The girl was still freeing the last of the villagers from their hobbles. "Keli must have hidden her. When you were at the village, I don't suppose you found—"

"There was no one left alive there but Nina," Gyre said quietly.

"Fuck," Gharji muttered again. "What the *fuck* do we do now? What do I tell Emeri and Planne and—"

"I'm going to Grayport," Gyre said, trying to project a touch of authority. "That's where they were taking you, and there's some kind of camp there. I'm going to find Baron Kotzed and get her out."

"You'll..." The villager looked down at the dead plaguespawn and shuddered. "Plague, maybe you *can* do it. I should have known you were a Communard. They always had some good fighters. I never bought what Keli and Mitik were selling, but the baron always seemed like a good sort. I hope you find her."

"So do I," Gyre said.

Gharji let out a sigh, suddenly looking weary. "I'll...tell the others. Make sure they get home. Go on, and good luck to you. "

Gyre nodded. He waved to Nina, and she trotted back.

"Gharji will handle the villagers," he told her. "Let's get away from the scene and find somewhere to camp. Are you any good with a needle and thread?"

"Not really," Nina said.

"I'll show her," Kit said. "I sewed up a lot of wounds back when I had a body."

"Not the most comforting thing you could say," Gyre muttered. "In the morning we head south toward Grayport."

"Got it," Nina said. She knelt and grabbed a blaster rifle from one of the dead Legionaries, strapped it to her back, and took an unmetal sword as well. "Lead the way."

Chapter Eleven

Zephkiel

The passage of time was almost unnoticeable under the mountain. Spring slipped into summer into fall, and the only thing that changed was the character of the town above them, going from frenzied activity to a drowsy lethargy as the snows began and all but the most essential activity closed down for the year. The lab might as well have been in a different world, secure in its stony vaults, kept warm by *deiat* and supplied via Gate.

The other research leads were as surprised by Ashok as Zeph had been, but they adjusted. His casualness was welcome, but not everyone was happy with the attention he paid to their work. Or, as Nia put it one day over lunch, "He's always poking his nose into everything."

"He takes an interest," Zeph said, focusing on her plate. The meat today was roast vulpi, juicy and delicious, but she couldn't identify the thick, chewy grains underneath it. *Tasty, though.*

"It's annoying. I was getting ready to set up a sample today, and he happened to be walking by and stuck his head in. Next thing you know I have to give him an hour-long lecture on workbird flight adaptations and bone density."

"Would you rather have Suppli back? I don't miss *those* meetings."

"At least Suppli kept to himself." Nia smirked. "Though I can see why *you* prefer Ashok."

"What's *that* supposed to mean?"

"You spend an awful lot of time with him. He's always in your lab, and then after hours—"

"I told you, I'm teaching him the basics!" Zeph felt her cheeks burning. "You don't really think that...that we're..."

"Well, I do *now*," Nia said, leaning forward with a predatory grin. "Spill it."

"There's nothing to spill," Zeph said. "He's a *Chosen*."

"Who hasn't had *that* fantasy, right?"

"Me!"

"Oh, come on. It's like getting swept up by a god from the old stories. Beauty, wealth, unlimited power..."

"Everyone knows Chosen don't marry humans."

"Doesn't mean they don't fuck them," Nia said, eyebrows waggling.

That was true enough, of course. It was considered uncouth to mention it in polite circles, but it was common knowledge that it happened. How could it not? Rumor had it some Chosen kept whole stables of lovers in the hidden parts of their palaces. But it was difficult to think of *Ashok*, diffident, enthusiastic, and slightly awkward, as the master of some harem.

"It's *not* like that," Zeph insisted. "He's never shown any inclination to...that sort of thing."

"Bo-ring," Nia groaned. "Put the moves on him."

"I wouldn't even know where to start."

"He's probably too busy," Nia said, changing tack. "Do you know he has a secret lab?"

"He does not."

"He does, I swear. Vitar heard it from one of the servants. It's down on the fifth floor, in one of the old human-adjustment sectors. Nobody knows what he's doing down there, but it can't be aboveboard, can it?"

"He's the administrator. He's entitled to use the space however he likes."

"But why not tell us about it? *Something* strange is going on."

The conversation nagged at Zeph for the rest of the workday, running through her mind as she pulled a squealing vulpi into its component parts, coiling its intestines neatly in a dish for another researcher to examine. *He's never shown any interest in that direction...*

But... is that true? There were times, she was certain, when he looked at her...

Don't be stupid. He was a Chosen. Chosen didn't beat around the bush. If he...wanted her—Zeph's cheeks flushed again—he would just *say* so. Suppli certainly hadn't been shy about his requests, though as far as she knew he'd never taken a lover among the staff.

And if he asked... would I...

Damn it, Nia. She gritted her teeth and tried to concentrate.

After her shift, she was scheduled to meet some friends for cards, but she begged off and went up to the first floor, pacing around the half-full cafeteria. In each loop, she almost took the corridor that led to Ashok's office, but each time she stopped herself and stalked back to the stairs. Each time, though, she was unable to force herself to return to the quarters either.

Their next scheduled lesson wasn't until tomorrow night. She'd been looking forward to an evening off—teaching *dhaka* after working with it all day was exhausting—but now somehow she was impatient. It felt like Nia had ripped the scab off something that had been festering for a while, and the emotional pus was getting everywhere. *Wonderful metaphor, Zeph. Very attractive.*

Enough. She clenched her jaw so hard her teeth ached, and finally made the turn into the stairway. *Go downstairs, read that book on ocular development until you're bored enough to fall asleep, and—*

Ashok was ahead of her on the steps, oblivious to her presence. He trotted down, passing the second level. Without really making a conscious decision to do so, Zeph followed.

He's going somewhere, she rationalized. *He might need help, or...*

He didn't stop at the third level, or the fourth. The barrier to the fifth level had been shoved aside slightly, and the Chosen turned to slip through the gap. At a wave of his hand and an invisible application of *deiat,* the dormant lights came on, illuminating a pathway down and out of sight. Zeph halted, dithered briefly, and kept after him.

She found herself walking on tiptoe, and forced herself to stop. *What does it matter if he notices me? I'm not doing anything wrong.*

The fifth floor had been shut down in an orderly way, and it wasn't messy, but a thin layer of dust still covered everything. Ashok left clear footprints. He turned right at the first intersection, then opened a smoked-glass door leading into one of the old labs. There were lights on inside, and the faint hum of climate-control equipment.

Zeph went to the door, took the handle, and paused. *Am I really going to just walk in on him?* He was the administrator. He could have his own lab if he wanted, though it was possible that keeping it secret was against the rules.

And, in the back of her mind, ridiculous but impossible to ignore— he was a Chosen. If he was doing something bad in there, something she stumbled in and witnessed, then he could dispose of her with a flick of the fingers. It was against the laws of the Empire, but it happened, people whispered, more often than you might think.

It was that thought, oddly, that stiffened her spine. Ashok wasn't that kind of person, Chosen or not. He just *wasn't.* She took a long breath, opened the door, and went inside.

"Hello?" she said, in the half voice of someone who isn't sure if they really wanted to be heard. "Ashok?"

The lab had been gutted when it was closed down, leaving only unmetal tables and benches. Ashok had covered them with glass enclosures, each full of a few inches of soil and topped with a bright sunstone. *He must have gotten them from the third floor somehow.* Green shoots grew to varying heights or hung brown and wilted. *Experiments?*

There was a second room beyond the first, filled with more plants. Ashok, a watering can in hand, busied himself in the enclosures at the far end, humming a little tune. Zeph cleared her throat as she crossed the threshold, and he abruptly straightened up.

"Oh!" The look on his face was so profoundly *guilty* that for a moment Zeph was certain she really had walked in on something awful. He ran a hand through his golden hair. "Zephkiel. I...ah... wasn't expecting you."

"I didn't mean to intrude," Zeph lied. "I saw you on the stairs, and I thought..." She hesitated, then concluded lamely, "That you might need something."

"It's just as well. I was going to show you tomorrow, you just...startled me."

"What is this place? What are you doing here?" *And why are you keeping it secret?*

"Just somewhere for me to practice a little."

"Practice *dhaka*?" When he nodded, she looked around at the enclosures full of sprouts. "These are adjusted?"

"Most of them. Some are controls." He wore a guileless grin. "It took me quite a few tries. The first batch all died, and one from the second batch started eating its neighbors. But I'm getting better!"

Zeph blinked in astonishment. In their months of *dhaka* lessons, they'd covered the basics—the manipulation of living tissue and use of preexisting systems in the subject, vital for healing a wound or purging an infection. But she hadn't even begun discussing the minute manipulations that would allow for the adjustment of an organism's essence in the seed.

"You were right," Ashok said, seeing her surprise. "About *dhaka*, I mean. Obviously you were, since you're the expert. I'd done all this reading, but I didn't have the basic knowledge to understand it properly. After your instruction, though, things just started to click. Being able to use *deiat* helps as well, I think—you can *illuminate* what you're working on, expose it, and..." He shook his head, hand running through his hair. "It's hard to explain. I wish you could see it."

"What have you been trying to do?" Zeph said. "Are these plants from the third floor?"

"What? Oh no. These are special. I had a crate of bulbs brought through the Gate." He looked defensive. "It's part of my personal allowance, and it's a lot less than my predecessor used—"

"Bulbs?" Zeph knelt to examine one of the enclosures more carefully, and recognition struck. "These...Are these *bluehearts*?"

Ashok nodded. Zeph smiled, lost in memory for a moment.

"My mother used to plant bluehearts," she said quietly. "Back home they grow like crazy. There'd be beds of them around the house, and when spring came it'd be like waking up in the middle of the sky."

She remembered going outside as little girl, entranced by the overnight appearance of the pale blue flowers. Her mother taking her hand gently, to keep her from crushing the blossoms underfoot. Showing her how to water them, how to prune the dead leaves. Iraph, two years younger and still wild, tumbling through a bed at full speed in a storm of flying petals. Zeph had expected her mother to be angry, but she'd laughed and laughed.

"You talked about them a little," Ashok said. "And I looked in your file afterward. You used to order one every year."

She hadn't thought about that for a long time. *When did I stop?*

"I wanted to make you something," the Chosen went on. "As a gift, to thank you for everything you've done. Here, come see."

Zeph stepped forward, feeling half in a dream, still enmeshed in memories of the past. Farther on, the flowers had started to bloom, thick green buds unfolding into luxuriant bursts of soft blue petals tipped with white.

But they weren't all the bluehearts that she remembered. Some were obvious failures, with stunted, asymmetric flowers, or petals spotted with ugly tumorous growths. But others were flecked with spots of red, variegated in fascinating patterns, like ink mixing on a palette.

Finally, in front of Ashok, one specimen was perfect. Taller and larger than any of the others, it was a deep, beautiful purple, paling to pink at the very tips of the petals. Zeph bent close to stare at it. The top of the enclosure was open, and she could smell the subtle fragrance, bringing on another stab of memory.

"I was going to cut it and give it to you after our lesson tomorrow," Ashok said, just behind her.

"No!" Zeph was surprised by her own vehemence. "Don't cut it. Leave it to bloom. It's beautiful."

"Whatever you want," he said. "It's yours. And..."

He paused, and Zeph turned to face him. He was standing a bit too close, she realized.

"I wondered." The Chosen cleared his throat awkwardly. "If you would. That is. If you would be willing to..."

"To?" Zeph said. Her heart thundered.

"Have dinner with me sometime. Alone. There's quite a good kitchen in my suite."

His expression was so soft, so hopeful, that it tugged at Zeph's heart. There were a thousand reasons to say no, of course. He was her boss, and he was a *Chosen*. What was the most she could hope for? A quick fling before he moved on?

But...

"Yes," she said, before she could think better of it. "I'd like that."

Winter came early to the mountains. The doors to the surface iced over, and the town above Stoneroot slept, dreaming of spring. Work in the labs went on as ever. Experiments were conducted, samples analyzed, reports sent and received. The ever-present gossip mill churned, and for once there was something genuinely shocking to gossip about. Nial-Est-Ashok had taken a lover from among the staff. Not just a menial, but a research lead.

Zeph felt the looks every day and heard the whispers when they thought she wasn't paying attention. Scorn and disdain, jealousy and envy, even a few hints of sympathy. *Poor thing*, they said when she'd turned the corner. *How could she tell him no?*

They were right, as far as it went. How *could* she have said no, when Ashok was...Ashok, awkward and attentive and brilliant, his every emotion clearly painted on his face as though he were incapable of deceit?

She'd all but moved into his quarters after a while. The vast administrator suite was meant to accommodate a Chosen's full entourage, and since Ashok didn't have one there was plenty of room for both of them. And, guiltily, she'd come to enjoy the touches of luxury his position provided—his own kitchen, a private bath, a communications terminal.

On her day off, she awoke slowly in what her bedside clock told her was the late morning. Ashok's side of the big bed was empty, the sheets kicked back, and she heard him clattering about in the kitchen. Zeph rolled over and sat up, yawning.

"You let me sleep in," she said, vaguely accusatory.

"You looked like you needed it," Ashok said. "Tea?"

"Please."

He was probably right, she reflected. She'd been pushing hard at work lately. Her determination, if she was being honest, came as much from the looks her colleagues gave her as from anything else. *I deserve this position, whatever there is between me and Ashok.* Nia was still her best friend, thankfully, though she'd become much less curious about the details of Zeph's love life. But her other relationships, never strong, had withered.

And yet it didn't seem to matter. There was a warmth in her chest, like her own private sun. Love, and pride—she and Ashok worked together now, in his expanding lab on the fifth floor, pushing toward uses of *dhaka* no one had ever considered before. He was right that his ability to use *deiat* gave him definite advantages, the two forces complementing one another. *He can't be the first to discover that, can he?* Had no Chosen *ever* bothered to learn to use *dhaka* before?

Whatever the reason, the things he could do under her guidance were astounding. His adjusted plants could adapt to a wide variety of conditions, even cannibalizing other plants to get the nutrients they needed. With proper safeguards, they represented a breakthrough that would expand agriculture throughout the Empire, increasing yields and making previously worthless land bloom.

And that was only the beginning. Slowly, she was working toward introducing him to her own specialty. *If we can do this much with plants, just imagine . . .*

"Good morning," Ashok said, leaning in for a quick kiss before putting a mug of steaming tea in her hand.

"Mmph." She sipped the tea and sighed with pleasure. "Thank you."

"There was a message for you last night," he said, nodding at the communications terminal. "Long-routed."

"Mom, probably," Zeph said, drinking more tea. "Or Iraph." Though neither of them were the type to splurge on a Gated message when the slow post would do. Something coiled in Zeph's stomach, just for a moment. "I'd better take a look."

She took her mug and sat by the terminal. The image projector protruded from its top like a clawed hand. A few taps on the control crystals brought up the records. She verified her identity and unlocked her messages, highlighting those that hadn't come from inside the lab. There was only one, and it was indeed from her little sister. Zeph opened it, and her stomach fell.

Z—contact me immediately at the medical center. Anytime. Irie.

"I need to talk to someone," Zeph said, setting her tea down with a shaking hand. "Can I use this?"

"Go ahead," Ashok said. "Is everything all right?"

"I'm not sure yet." Zeph opened the connection. Going through the lab's primary communicator, it would have been a complex mess of negotiation, time allowances, and authorized expenditures. With Ashok's priority, everything simply *happened*, immediately. A hint of how life was for the Chosen.

The image projector flickered a few times, and then Iraph's face appeared above it. Zeph's little sister had the same silver-white hair, but short and in curls. There were circles under her eyes, and she'd been crying.

"Z, thank the sun," she said immediately. "It's Mom. She just...I turned around for a minute, and she was on the floor, blood from her nose everywhere—"

"Slow down," Zeph said, heart clenching like a fist. "Are you okay?"

"Me? I'm fine, but Mom—"

"You took her to the hospital?"

"We're at the medical facility now. Zeph, they're telling me it's primary CD."

"Oh no," Zeph gasped. *Fuck fuck* fuck. "They're sure?"

"Pretty sure." Iraph looked like she was drowning. "I just...I don't know what to *do*. They want me to take her home, but—"

"I'll come and help," Zeph said at once. "Just stay with her. It'll take me half a day by carriage from the Brattleford Gate."

"Thank you, Z." Iraph took a deep breath. "I can't talk long. I'll see you when you get here."

Iraph cut the connection. Zeph sat in silence for a few long moments, staring through the empty space where her sister's face had been.

"I'll make sure you have priority on the Gate," Ashok said behind her.

"Thank you." Zeph felt numb as the implications poured through her. Primary CD was a horrible disorder, eating away at the victim's brain function, but it took a year or more to kill. *There's no way Iraph can take care of Mom alone.* Her breath caught, and she voiced the thought out loud. "I'm going to have to stay."

"Stay at home, you mean?"

Zeph nodded dully. "Until Mom...until she..."

He put a hand on her shoulder. "I understand. I can arrange a leave of absence. The lab will be here when you get back."

"But...our work." She turned to him, blinking away tears.

"Your family is more important."

"I *know*." They'd been so close to a true breakthrough. *If I'm away for a year...*

"There's something I wanted to ask you," Ashok said. "And now I'm not sure when I'll next get the chance."

He squatted beside her chair, putting himself at her level. Zeph turned to face him, throat thick.

"I don't want to be apart from you for a year, or even a day," he said. "And I don't want to do the work without you."

"I know." Zeph felt guilt twist through her. "I'm *sorry*—"

"Please, don't be. What I mean is..." He paused, then blurted, "I think we should blood-bond. Before you leave."

"B...blood-bond?" Zeph sucked in a breath. "You can't be serious."

"I am."

"You're a *Chosen*. You can't..." She swallowed. "Not with me."

There was no rule or even tradition against it, per se, but only because she was fairly certain no one had ever contemplated such a thing. A blood-bond could only be established by a *dhakim*, and Ashok was the first Chosen she knew of who qualified.

And if a human *marrying* a Chosen was impossible, a blood-bond was doubly so. The connection it established was permanent and *irrevocable*, whatever might happen between them. Marriages could end, but blood-bonds never did, not until one or the other of them died.

"As a Chosen," Ashok said, "I can do what I like."

"If the Directorate found out, your family, they'd..." She licked her lips, realizing she had no idea what happened to Chosen who transgressed. Their society was above and apart from her world, by their own design.

"I wasn't planning on telling them. Were you?"

"No, but..." She swallowed. "What if, even years from now, you don't want to be with me anymore?"

"If I thought that was going to happen, I'd hardly make the offer, would I?" He leaned forward. "Please, Zeph. I need you. Now and forever. This way, you can do what you have to for your family and still be connected to me. I can stay here, continue the work, and still help you."

"I..." She gave a quick, jerky nod. "Yes. Let's do it. Quickly."

"I have everything we need. Sit at the table."

He hurried off, and Zeph shifted seats, pushing aside the remains of his breakfast. It was hard to comprehend how her life had upended itself in a quarter of an hour. *Mom...* Her eyes filled with tears, and she forced them down. *I have to keep it together. For Irie.*

Ashok returned with a clean towel and a curved blade in a leather sheath. He set the towel beside her and sat down.

"Put out your hand," he said, offering his own. Zeph extended her left hand, palm up on the towel.

Ashok drew the knife. It was unmetal, iridescent and gleaming, the edge sharper than sharp. Without any hesitation, he drew it across his palm, a quick motion that left a line of blood in its wake. Zeph gritted her teeth as he applied the knife to her, but there was no pain at first, the blade too sharp for that. Her skin parted easily, crimson filling the lines of her palm.

"There," Ashok said, setting the knife aside. "Now take my hand."

They pressed their palms together, blood squishing between them. Zeph fancied she could feel particles of him infiltrating her flesh, and hers seeping into his. The tiniest amount, but that was all it took. Ashok waited a second, two, three.

"I'll make the connection," he said. "Are you ready?"

She nodded. Her hand was beginning to sting, the promise of deeper pain to come. She could feel the touch of Ashok's *dhaka*, reaching out to her, tying their essences together. There was *resonance*, from blood to blood—no matter how far it was separated from the body, it would, however weakly, reflect the whole. The proper application of *dhaka* stabilized the channel, strengthened it.

It's done. Ashok's voice, exactly as if he'd spoken, but his lips didn't move. *I love you, Zeph. Forever.*

Forever, Zeph agreed.

She pulled her hand away. Ashok brushed it, and she felt the touch of his *dhaka* again, knitting the skin back together. When she wiped the blood away, her palm was whole. She sniffed back her tears and did the same for him, mending the cut with the efficiency she'd learned practicing on vulpi.

I have to go, she said. *Mom and Iraph are waiting for me.*

I know. Ashok smiled. *I'll be right beside you.*

Maya

Maya was still blinking the remnants of the dream away as she came downstairs. This time there had been no meeting with the Corruptor beforehand, no sign of the strange, half-formed spirit, just a long sequence of memories that weren't her own. She could still feel Zeph's excitement, and the plunge of her heart at the message from her sister.

And Ashok...At first she'd wondered if it were truly the same person. *He seems like he genuinely cares about her.* But there was an edge to him, a hint of obsession. The feeling of kissing him made Maya's gorge rise.

More importantly, I still have no idea where these dreams are coming from. There was no doubt they were Zephkiel's memories, but Zephkiel had to be long dead. *Even if she survived the Plague War, that was four centuries ago!* Elariel's knowledge of the blood-bond was purely theoretical, and Xalen didn't have anything to add. *I guess I'll have to figure this out on my own.*

Meanwhile, the city still needed to be administered, and that was increasingly up to her and Tanax. Maya turned up at the conference room, bleary-eyed and yawning, to find Tanax looking just as exhausted and Tourmarch Ritabel visibly annoyed. She smoothed her face and bowed respectfully to Maya, but her eyes remained narrowed.

"We should keep this as brief as we can," Tanax said. "I know we all have other places to be. But things are getting out of hand. Tourmarch?"

"Centarchs," Ritabel said. "There was a riot last night, out at the mouth of the western tunnels, just inside city limits. Four of my men were injured, and two tunnelborn were killed. That's the third night in a row there's been violence."

"What's causing the problems?" Maya said.

"There are rumors in the streets that the Chosen have returned," Ritabel said flatly. "That they proclaimed a new empire in Skyreach, abolished all debts, and declared all humans to have the rights of citizens. The Merchant Council is trying to suppress the talk, but the tunnelborn are organizing. There have been strikes and fighting at the big manufactories. The rioters say that the merchants are trying to cover up the truth."

"I see." Maya glanced at Tanax, who was keeping his face impassive.

"If this continues, I will not be able to maintain order," Ritabel said. "Already the security of the wealthier districts is effectively in the hands of the council and their mercenaries. If the tunnelborn move on the city in force, we could lose everything west of the Pit. And if the Gate remains closed, even the Spike would be vulnerable to a siege."

"What course do you recommend?" Tanax said.

"It's not a matter of recommendation," Ritabel said. "I need rein-forcements, immediately. At least another ten companies of Auxiliaries, and preferably a few squads of Legionaries." She paused, then added, "An update from Skyreach might calm the waters. We *must* open the Gate and contact the Senate."

"I hear you, Tourmarch," Tanax said wearily. "We'll do what we can. That'll be all for now."

"Yes, Centarch." She hesitated, then squared her shoulders. "Do you have any knowledge of what's happened in Skyreach? Are the rumors true?"

"All I have knowledge of," Tanax snapped, "are my orders. You should be content with the same."

"As you say, Centarch." Ritabel rose stiffly and bowed.

When she'd left the room, Tanax turned to Maya and sighed. "She's right, you know. We can't keep this up for long."

"Can we lock the city down to keep the rumors out?"

"No point in closing the stable door after the birds have escaped," Tanax said. "Besides, we need the caravans from the plains for food. Cut them off and the city would starve in a week. *Then* you'd see riots." He shrugged. "Besides, it's entirely possible the Corruptor's people are spreading the word deliberately. We haven't gotten any official messen-gers, but there could be any number of spies in the city by now. If the riots get bigger, we may need to leave in a hurry."

"We still don't know where Ashok's lab is." Her dream had been annoyingly free of information on Stoneroot's precise location, and none of the maps she'd looked up in the palace library showed it, even the oldest. "And Xalen's still working on finding some kind of last-ditch Chosen weapon. It might still function, like the Purifier."

"I know." Tanax ran his hand through his hair. "I'm buying you all the time I can. But Ritabel is losing confidence, and unless the two of us confront the rioters in person, her Auxiliaries aren't going to be able to hold the streets in any case."

The thought of confronting rioters made Maya shudder. Their ambush of the rebels had been bad enough—at least they'd been well armed. The idea of directing her fire against ordinary citizens turned her stomach. *That is not what* deiat *is meant for.* She didn't need the *Inheritance* to know it was wrong.

"Yeah," Tanax said at the look on her face. "But we're running out of options."

"I know." Maya leaned back in her chair. "I'm going to see Sarah this afternoon. She's been sounding out her old contacts about the possibility of raising the city against the Empire. Maybe she has good news."

"We need to start working on a backup plan."

Maya gave a tired nod. "I'll think about it."

The trouble was, there *was* no backup plan. Her dreams and Xalen's papers were the only leads they had on something—anything—that might give them a defense against the Corruptor. Abandon those, and it would just be a matter of fleeing until the Chosen's agents finally caught up with them.

Or else I could surrender and hope he spares the others. The image of Ashok's bright eyes as he grinned at Zeph ran through her mind. *He was mad* then, *and that was four hundred years ago.*

Her meeting with Sarah was at a tavern called the Smoking Wreckage, not far from the Spike and apparently a favorite hangout for off-duty Auxiliaries. Maya had decided to walk, hoping the fresh air would wake her up some, and gotten directions from a palace doorman. Until she arrived, though, she hadn't appreciated quite what those directions implied.

She'd seen the Pit, of course. It was hard to miss, a ragged-edged wound stretching north to south across the city, nearly bisecting the crater. Bridges spanned it near both ends where it was narrower, but in the center it yawned broad and unchallenged, big enough to swallow buildings whole, its depths forever shrouded in roiling, impenetrable mist.

Buildings were clustered along the edge, but not *too* close. The rock was pitted and worn by decades of acidic spume, and looked likely to crumble at the slightest touch. This made it all the more surprising when she arrived at the Smoking Wreckage, which was built not just *on* the edge but *past* it, atop a broad island of rock supported by a startlingly narrow column. A rope bridge connected it to the side of the Pit, and the tumbledown three-story building, elaborately propped and cantilevered, looked as though it was very close to deserving its name.

Maya wore her haken at the small of her back and dressed in civilian clothes she'd borrowed from the palace stores. No one looked at her twice in the street, but she did collect odd glances when she mounted the bridge. The few others she saw crossing all wore Auxiliary uniforms. No one said anything, though, and she did her best not to look down until she was on solid ground again. *Such as it is.*

A painted sign depicted the building as a burned-out ruin, with a blackened skeleton still standing at the bar. Maya went through the open double doors and found a large room centered on a circular bar and crammed with tables. Few of them were occupied tonight—there was a large party of Auxiliaries in one corner, and a few other solitary drinkers, but most of the seats were empty. She spotted Sarah, who waved her over.

"Do you want something to drink?" Sarah said.

"Coffee, if they have it. I'm short on sleep." Maya settled down as Sarah signaled the bartender. On Sarah's shoulder, one of Kit's tiny spider-constructs gave an elaborate multilegged bow.

"Always liked this place," Sarah said. "Drinks are cheap and there's always a fight about something or other."

Kit danced excitedly. "Plus upstairs there are girls who will—"

Maya cleared her throat.

"*Very* flexible, is all I'm saying," Kit said. "This is where Gyre and I first met."

"Down here or upstairs?" Sarah said, smiling.

"Sort of progressing from one to the other. I wanted to see how he performed." At Maya's flush, she cackled.

"In any case," Maya said. "How is he doing in Khirkhaz?"

"Still riding south," Kit said. "Very dull. We should be at Grayport in a day or two."

The fact that the construct intelligence was both here *and* there took some getting used to. *At least we can communicate without using the Gate. I wish Varo had one of those spiders with him.* They had still heard nothing from the scout.

"Tell him to hurry as much as he can," Maya said. "If things blow up here, it may not be safe to use the Gate."

Sarah nodded grimly. "It's getting bad. The tunnelborn are angry, and the Auxies are stretched thin. The 'Merchant Council' isn't helping either."

"They should at least be in favor of law and order," Maya said.

"Rich idiots think the best way to keep order is to crack skulls," Kit said, skittering back and forth in front of Sarah. "They hire other idiots to do it for them and it makes everything worse. What the fuck do they think is going to happen if the tunnelborn *really* rise up? That a few hundred rented psychopaths are going to defend their estates?"

"Maybe we can convince them to be a little more…constructive," Maya said. "I'll tell Tanax. Have you had any luck getting to your old tunnelborn contacts?"

"Not much," Sarah admitted. "Yora was the one who really knew everybody, and things change fast down in the tunnels. There's a new boss, Rikard Gemspotter, who seems to be the one people listen to. So far I haven't managed to get close to him." She shrugged. "I met with a few friends, but the scavengers aren't worried about the Empire one way or the other. And Rikard's people are *excited* about it. They're calling it the dawn of a new golden age."

"I can't even blame them," Maya said with a sigh. "If I hadn't been involved in all this, I probably would have thought the same. We've seen the Corruptor, but..."

"Just claiming he's a monster isn't going to get anyone to rise up and fight," Sarah said. "Especially if it's my word against Rikard's proclamations. If the Empire showed up tomorrow, the tunnelborn would welcome them with open arms."

Maya pressed her lips together. She knew Ashok better than anyone in four hundred years, especially if Zephkiel's dreams were to be believed. But that wasn't likely to sway many minds either.

"Keep trying," Maya said. It was the only thing she could think of, and she did her best to ignore the skeptical look in Sarah's eyes. "And maybe start looking into a hidden route out of the city. Just in case."

"*That* at least should be easy. If there's one thing this place has to spare, it's tunnels and bolt-holes." She leaned back in her chair. "Speaking of which. Any new ideas on how to track down the lab before—"

She stopped as someone burst in the front door, nearly colliding with one of the servers. It was Xalen, excited and out of breath, as though she'd just run all the way from the palace. She cast about wildly, spotted their table, and hurried over.

"I figured it out," she said, wild energy practically crackling from her fingertips.

"Wonderful," Maya said. "Figured what out?"

"The file. Prodominus didn't know what he had, but he knew he had something, and I figured it out. He'd dug up a lot of old reports, some mentions in later histories, and—" She ran out of breath and paused a moment to inhale. Sarah leaned across the table, almost equally excited.

"And? You found something?"

Xalen nodded, returning to something like her usual calm. "The

Chosen hid something in the mountains at the height of the Plague, around the same time they started building the Purifier. In the file they call it their last hope, or last resort, but it looks like no one ever got around to using it."

"Do you know what it is?" Sarah said.

"Not as such," Xalen said, shaking her head. "But I know *where* it is, which is almost as good."

"Another tunnel complex?" Sarah's brow furrowed. "It's hard to imagine something survived intact and hasn't been found. If there's another weapon buried somewhere—"

"That's just it. It's not buried." Xalen's eyes shone, and she pointed to the ceiling with her good hand. "The last skyfortress is still up *there*, after four hundred years, and the Chosen's last hope is on board."

"Here," Xalen said, when they'd all squeezed into the palace map room. Tanax had unfolded the biggest map of the mountains he could find, and Xalen hunched over the table to tap a spot north of Deepfire. "Mount Shroud."

In addition to Tanax, Maya had found Beq, who was nearly as excited at the news as Xalen had been. Her eagerness reminded Maya of their first sight of Grace, in the Splinter Kingdoms, a city named for the wreck of the skyfortress *Grace in Execution*. The hulk was embedded in the earth where it had crashed, a massive, curved expanse of unmetal and glass canted at a sharp angle and so large it literally overshadowed the city beneath it.

"That almost makes sense," Sarah said reflectively. "They call the mountain that because there's always cloud around the summit. You could probably hide a skyfortress in there."

"Which one is it?" Beq said. "Does it say?"

"*Pride in Power*," Xalen said. "The—"

"—the last skyfortress and the largest," Beq cut in, "equipped with the latest in flux-stabilized armor. Some scholars contend it was grounded after only a few flights and lost in one of the destroyed cities, but—"

"—but *Caethrim* says that we should interpret Brecht to mean all eight of the skyfortresses fought in the war, and that *Pride in Power* had to be the one mentioned by Jina, since it was—"

"—*the only one not otherwise accounted for,*" they finished together. The pair stared at one another, eyes shining, and Maya suspected a friendship had just been cemented. Grinning broadly, she wrapped her arms around Beq and glared at Xalen with mock suspicion.

"She's mine! You can't have her." When Beq turned, Maya kissed her, to an excited skitter from Kit and a polite cough from Tanax.

"I don't mean to pour cold water on the party," Sarah said. "But I'm assuming the idea is for us to *get* to this skyfortress? In which case, the fact that it's hovering above the top of a monstrously tall mountain is not exactly convenient."

"It's accessible by flitter," Xalen said. "There's supposed to be an old flitter base built into the mountain. All we need to do is find it."

"I thought flitters only worked in Skyreach," Maya said, trying not to think about her *last* experience with one of the little flyers. She'd ended up spinning wildly and nearly lost her lunch.

"They need a repulsion grid," Beq said with an eager nod. "But sky-fortresses after *Grace in Execution* were fitted with an inverted repulsion grid so they could be resupplied in the field. Any flitter can be config-ured to work with it." Seeing the slightly glazed look on Maya's face, she explained, "You just need to make it pull toward the grid instead of push off of it, since it's in the sky instead of under the ground."

"Right," Maya said. "Obviously." Tanax was trying and failing to suppress a chuckle. "How long will it take to get there?"

"A few days," Sarah said. "Plus whatever time it takes to locate the base."

"That means we'd have to hold the city at least that long." She looked at Tanax. "One of us would have to go, to operate the flitter."

"It can't be me," he said. "Unless we're ready to abandon Deepfire."

"Then I'll do it," Maya said. "Can you hold out that long?"

He sucked his teeth. "It'd be easier if Gyre got back. But I think we have to take the risk. The whole point of staying in Deepfire is finding something to use against the Corruptor. If we have a lead, we have to follow it."

"Beq, will you come with me?" Maya said.

"Is that a *joke*?" Beq was practically vibrating. "'Beq, do you want to come and do something you've dreamed of since you were four years old?' Why, yes, Maya, I think I can find the time."

Maya grinned again. "That's one. Sarah—"

"Much as I would love to go," Sarah said, "I think I need to keep working on the tunnelborn."

"Xalen?" Beq said.

"Fieldwork is not my specialty," she said. "I believe I will remain here, with the maps. Kit can pass a message if you need my assistance."

"Nobody asked if *I* want to go," Kit said, then laughed into the abrupt silence. "*Obviously* I want to go. I was a scavenger before my untimely demise, remember? What kind of Doomseeker would I be if I turned this down?"

"Are we certain it's still up there, though?" Beq said, with the look of someone who'd discovered an unexpected snag. "Even skyfortresses can't store enough *deiat* energy to operate for four hundred years. Without a living Chosen aboard, it must have shut down by now."

"If it had crashed in the mountains, someone would have heard about it," Sarah pointed out. "Something that big isn't exactly hard to find."

"I agree," Xalen said. "I don't know how, but it must still be aloft."

"Either way, we have to try," Maya said. The others nodded along with her. "If it really was the Chosen's last resort, it could be our best shot at finding something that can stop the Corruptor."

Chapter Twelve

Looking out from the hill above Grayport, Gyre could, for the first time in his life, see the ocean. It stretched on and on, rolling blue-gray water out to the horizon, where the boundary between sea and hazy sky became imperceptible. Boats crawled across it like insects, their miniature sails dwarfed by the vast expanses of water.

"Meh," said Kit, sitting on his shoulder. "I thought it'd be bigger."

"We should go," Nina said anxiously. She held the reins of two load-birds, their heads drooping after a long day's ride. "It'll be dark before we get there."

"Just a minute," Gyre said. He returned his attention to the town, trying to memorize the general layout.

Grayport had apparently been named for the color of its stones, but the moniker was apt for the city as a whole. The buildings seemed to reflect the gray skies and gray sea, with walls of damp plaster and roofs of thatch or gray slate. The river Vozt, curving lazily down from the hills, swung past the city in a wide arc before turning back to empty into a sweeping bay, protected from the sea by a line of rocky barrier islets. On the point where river and bay met there was a small wood-and-stone fortress, frowning out over the rows of docks and smoking-houses. A gray haze filled the air, reminding Gyre of the fogs belched from the Pit in Deepfire.

East and north of the river were larger houses, free of the stench of industry. But Gyre's gaze was drawn the other way, past the tight-packed slums where the fishermen and their families lived. On the outskirts of town, where the land rose into a promontory surrounded on three sides by water, a dozen large, low buildings now stood. The marks of their construction were still on the ground, and their walls were the light brown of unweathered timber. A fence four meters high ran across the neck of the peninsula, with a single Gate toward the western side, closest to the city.

"That has to be it," he said. "A camp, like the decarch said. And it looks like it was thrown up in the last couple of months."

Nina shaded her eyes, squinting—Gyre occasionally forgot that the precision his silver eye provided wasn't available to everyone—but finally she looked back at him and nodded.

"I don't remember anything being there last time I was in Grayport," she said. "So how do we get in?"

Gyre winced. Her hurry was understandable—every moment of delay was a moment that a horrible fate might befall her sister. *But if we're careless, we're just going to get ourselves caught as well.* Before coming to Khirkhaz, he might have been more confident in his ability to fight his way out of whatever happened. *But if they have more than one of those Perfected things down there, I definitely don't want to try my luck.*

"First we get a closer look. Kit, leave your bodies hiding here for now except this one"—he tapped the tiny spider—"but be ready to sneak into town. If something goes wrong, come find us."

"... What?" Kit's spider wobbled a little. "Yes. Right. Sneak into town."

"Are you okay?" Nina said.

"Sorry. Maya was talking. Still getting used to being in two places at once. The bodies move fine, but it's hard to carry on two conversations."

"At some point we're going to need your focus, Kit."

"I *know*," Kit said. "Incidentally, the things Maya yells at night are *not* what you would expect from a centarch—"

"*Kit*."

"Well, now *I* want to know," Nina said.

"Can we please go to the prison camp?" Gyre said.

"I'll tell you later," Kit stage-whispered to Nina.

Even the people of Grayport seemed afflicted by the town's general drabness, wearing dull grays and browns. What bright colors there were had faded pale in the sun and salt, or turned dark from the endless smoke. There was a steady stream of traffic down the road, Gyre was glad to see. *Nobody's likely to notice us.*

He boarded their exhausted birds at the first stable they passed, paying in advance for a week of food and lodging. From there, they walked through the maze-like alleys of the slums. There was none of the sense of danger here that Gyre sometimes felt in the nastier parts of Deepfire, the feeling of being watched by dozens of eyes. Everyone just seemed tired, trooping back from their boats after a day of hauling fish to fall asleep for a few hours before doing it all over again.

Another thing that stood out about the city, apart from its colorlessness, was how completely *human* it was. Most cities of the Republic and Splinter Kingdoms were built around Elder relics, whether it was Bastion's fortifications, Grace's crashed skyfortress, or the bottomless springs of Obstadt. Here every brick had been put in place by ordinary humans and animals, with no *deiat* to smooth the way. The Chosen skyships had no need of harbors or seas, so ports had sprung up only after the end of the Plague War.

The prison camp was on the far side of the slums, and Gyre stopped in the mouth of an alley to observe. A broad open space separated it from the last of the houses, with a tangle of charred debris hinting how it had been cleared. Beyond it was the fence, built of tall wooden poles sharpened into spikes and connected by long strips of riveted iron. There was no wall walk like a proper fortress, but a pair of guard towers had good views up and down either side.

Hasty construction, but not slipshod. Gyre guessed it was Legionary work. The long, low buildings he'd seen from the hilltop certainly had the look of Legionary barracks, the sort of thing they would build from local timber when they were deployed in the field for more than a few weeks. The gate was of similar construction, with slots carved through the wood for firing blasters. Two guards waited in front of it with cross-bows. They were Auxies, as were the silhouettes in the towers.

"It's getting darker," Nina whispered, crouching beside him. The sun had set, though no stars were visible through the haze. "If we wait a little longer, we can cross the open ground and get the drop on those soldiers. Take them out—"

"And kick the gate down?" Gyre said. "No. Who knows how many more they have inside? Besides, we need to get to Apphia before they catch on, if this is going to be a rescue mission."

"Okay." Nina bit her lip. "Can we climb the cliffs? Go around the wall?"

"Better, but I doubt it," Gyre said. "If there's Legionaries in there, they'll check the cliffs regularly. And we'd still need to get your sister out. I doubt she'd be in shape for a twenty-meter climb down slick rock."

"So *what* then?" Nina said. "*Don't* tell me it's impossible."

"Nothing's impossible with the right team," Gyre said. It had been a saying of Yora's, actually. "What we need is a distraction, something to draw everyone to the gate while we slip in another way."

"I could run around pretending to be plaguespawn," Kit said.

"I don't think your bodies are big enough to panic them," Gyre said. "What we need is a riot, or the threat of one. People around here can't be happy with the new empire rounding up prisoners."

"Organizing something like that takes too long," Nina said. "Believe me, we've done it a few times. You need to understand the town first, get the locals to trust you, convince them that whatever you're hoping to accomplish is worth the risk."

"Agreed. We need help, a local who has contacts here already. You and Apphia must know *someone*, right?"

"We never had a lot of friends in the coastal towns," Nina said. "And those we did have got rounded up or hunted down with Apphia." Her lips twisted into a frown. "Actually...I suppose..."

"Got an idea?"

"Maybe." Nina didn't look pleased. "Vaela Truestrike. You met her during the battle for the Spire. She and her family live in Grayport."

Gyre recalled the old woman, prickly and proud but steady in a pinch. She'd spent the battle tending the wounded with Elariel, unfazed by screams and gory wounds. "That's perfect."

"But I don't know if she'll help." Nina sighed. "She had an argument with my sister. She and her people had already pulled out when the Empire came for us. They didn't leave on good terms."

Chosen defend. Not exactly promising. Still, it was the best option in a field of one. "Do you know where she lives?"

"I think I can find out," Nina said. "But she's *definitely* not going to see us in the middle of the night."

"First thing in the morning, then." When Nina's face fell, he touched her shoulder. "Hey. Your sister's tough. She can make it one more day. And anyway, we'd need the time to put the distraction together." He looked back toward the camp. "This time tomorrow, we'll be on our way out of here."

They found rooms in a cheap inn along the riverfront. Gyre had trouble resting, even with Kit's sleepless spider standing watch. Nina, on the other hand, was out the moment her head hit the pillow, clearly exhausted. Gyre watched her slow breathing for a few moments, then pulled a blanket over her shoulders.

It was hard not to see a little of himself in the girl. Chased from her home at a young age, forced to learn the realities of life the hard way. To fight, to kill, to do what was necessary. *At least she had an older sister to look after her.*

Eventually he managed to doze a little. Kit woke him when sunlight infiltrated the ragged curtains, and after a hurried breakfast they found a boatman willing to take them to the far shore. The grandest homes were right on the bank, small compared to the palatial estates of the great merchants of Deepfire but still big enough to swallow a hundred of the shacks in the slums. There were guards and a few servants about, but most of the mansions seemed abandoned, their owners no doubt fled to the countryside until the political situation stabilized.

Behind the front rank there were the houses of the merely well-to-do, smaller and older. Nina took them down a street of these faded eminences until she found the one she was looking for. It was three stories, tall and boxy, with a slate roof showing considerable wear and stables on the verge of collapse. But there was a carriage parked outside, and lights burned in the windows.

"Follow my lead," Nina said. She smoothed the front of her shirt—not very effectively, after days in the wilderness—and knocked at the door. Gyre motioned for Kit to crouch further in the shadow of his collar.

The elderly man who answered wore a butler's uniform and a vacant expression. Tufts of white hair formed an archipelago on his otherwise bald pate. He blinked at Nina, trying to focus.

"Yes?" he said, and then after a few moments: "Miss?"

"I'd like to see Vaela Truestrike, please," Nina said. "Tell her it's urgent."

"May I. Ask. Your name?" the butler said, with long pauses for breath.

"I'd...rather not say. If you can ask her to come meet me..."

"Madam Racent. Is feeling. Poorly." The butler coughed with sudden, unexpected violence. "You'll have to. Return. Later."

"Please just let me see her for a moment," Nina said. "If—"

"Nina?" A young man's voice piped from the back of the hall. "Is that you?"

"I…" Nina was flustered until she spotted the speaker. "Fillow?"

"It is!" There was a squeak and a wheelchair emerged, propelled by a dark-haired boy in silk pajamas. "Let them in, Hetzer, it's all right. I'll take them to Great-Grandmother."

"Of course. Young master." Hetzer bowed, deep enough that Gyre seriously worried he would topple over, then shuffled away. Fillow rolled closer, then stopped when he saw Gyre.

"Silvereye." He sat up straighter. "I didn't know you were still in Khirkhaz."

"It's been a strange few weeks," Gyre said, shutting the door behind him. "But I'm back."

"Fillow, your leg!" Nina said. Following her gaze, Gyre saw that one of the boy's pajama legs hung loose and empty from the knee down. "What happened?"

"Ah yes." Fillow blushed and shifted uncomfortably. "Had to, ah, cut it off, I'm afraid. Great-Grandmother sent me home to recover from the wound, but it went bad. Quite bad, actually. No one's fault, just one of those things."

Details were coming back to Gyre. Fillow had fought in the battle at the Spire, and he had a vague memory of seeing him wounded during the fight against Va'aht and his Legionaries. He hadn't seen the boy around after that. *If his wound went bad, Elariel could have done something about it.* But Elariel had left with Gyre when he went to the Purifier.

"I've got a peg leg, very piratical, but I'm not terribly good with it yet," Fillow went on. "Fall over a lot, and so forth. So I'm using the chair most of the time. It's quite convenient once you get used to it."

"I'm so sorry," Nina said. "I never knew."

"I'm just glad to see you're all right!" he said. "After Great-Grandmother came home, she wouldn't tell me anything about what happened. There's been all kinds of rumors. People are saying the Commune was destroyed by the Legions."

"That's why we're here," Nina said. "We need to speak to Vaela."

"Of course. She's on the sunporch. I'm sure she'll be happy to see you."

Gyre was far from sure of that himself, but he followed Nina and Fillow through the house, across deep, musty carpets and past spindly tables crammed with dusty memorabilia. Paintings were everywhere, ancestors frowning down from every wall. The gazes seemed oppressive to Gyre, but Fillow wasn't bothered.

The sunporch was a glassed-in deck at the back of the house designed to catch the morning sun, of dubious utility in hazy Grayport. A few sprawling potted plants surrounded a sloping couch, on which Vaela Racent Truestrike lay bundled in blankets up to her chin.

Something had gone out of the old woman since Gyre had seen her last. He remembered her as aged but hardly frail, representing the Blacks—the traditional elites of Khirkhaz—with steely determination. Now she looked so fragile a stiff breeze might shatter her, gloved hands crossed in her lap, her eyes distant in her heavily lined face.

"Great-Grandmother?" Fillow said. "Look who's come to see us. It's Nina Kotzed!"

"Kotzed?" Vaela blinked, and some life returned to her features. She pulled herself up a little straighter to peer at them. "Nina. I thought…" She trailed off, chewing her lip. Then, with a sidelong glance at Fillow, she murmured, "Have you come here to kill me?"

"What?" Fillow said, shocked.

"Leave the boy out of it," Vaela said. "Please. He's a good lad, if a bit lacking in brains."

"I'm not here to hurt anyone," Nina said.

"Is he?" Vaela said, looking at Gyre. "Hello, Silvereye."

Gyre bowed slightly. "I'm just helping Nina."

"Great-Grandmother, why in the Chosen's name would she be here to kill you?" Fillow said.

"Because I left her," Vaela said, and coughed. "Her sister wouldn't budge, and we had words, and I left with everyone who would follow me. I only wanted the best for the Commune, but…"

"But then the Legionaries stormed the Spire," Gyre said.

Vaela nodded wearily. "I told Apphia it was foolish to stay where they could find us. We had our victory, but it didn't mean we could fight them head-on. The thing to do was split up again, I said, and use what we'd gained to improve our position with the people. But she had her home back, and she didn't want to leave it again." The old woman took a ragged breath. "I didn't mean to abandon her. I thought she'd come around before... what happened. But Nina still has every right to be angry."

"I'm not angry," Nina said. "Not about that, anyway. It wasn't the Legionaries that took the Spire, it was those new soldiers, the ones they call Perfected." She shuddered. "They're monsters. If you and your people had been there, it would just have been more bodies on the pyre."

Vaela nodded slowly. "I've heard about them. Skirmishes in the countryside. Everyone's lying low. Half my old supporters won't answer my letters anymore."

"Apphia's *here*," Nina said. "In the camp on the edge of town. We're going to break her out."

"A rescue!" Fillow breathed. "A swift strike, a daring escape. Rising from the ashes of defeat—"

"You're sure?" Vaela said. "You know she's alive?"

Nina hesitated. Gyre cut in, "They'll try to get information out of her. If I know Apphia, that'll take a while."

"Probably." Vaela snorted. "She was always a stubborn girl."

"We need your help," Nina said. "Please. I know you and Apphia fought, but you were always there when she needed you."

"Except at the very end," Vaela murmured.

"If you want to make amends," Gyre said, "this is your chance."

"We have to help them, Great-Grandmother," Fillow said. "Of course we do!"

"I think..." Vaela's voice trailed away again, then returned. "I think I would like a word with Silvereye. Alone. Fillow, why don't you show Nina the side garden?"

Nina looked questioningly at Gyre, who gave a quiet nod. Fillow stared at his great-grandmother for a moment but finally complied, wheeling himself ahead of Nina to a door at the end of the porch.

When they were gone, Vaela stared at Gyre, regaining something of the piercing gaze he remembered.

"What about you?" she said. "Are you also here to make amends? I wasn't the only one who abandoned Apphia."

Gyre had expected that, but it still stung. He took a deep breath and tried for calm.

"Apphia knew I was going, and gave me her blessing," he said. *It's not like it was with Yora. Not this time.*

"Of course she did. She's a silly little girl and you'd charmed your way into her bed with gifts and a pretty smile. You thought she would tell you no?"

"She's not a silly little girl. She's Baron Kotzed, and she knew exactly what she was doing. She'd been fighting the Republic practically her whole life."

"Pfah," Vaela spat. "Her whole life meaning 'a decade.' Spend as long as I have guiding a family through troubled waters, and you learn a thing or two. What did you think would happen after we took the Spire? The Republic would give up and go home?"

"I had planned to return sooner."

"We both know what plans are worth, boy."

Gyre wanted to explain the circumstances, that the rise of the Corruptor was more important than any revolution. *But what would be the point?*

"What do you want from me? An apology?"

"I know what that's worth, too." She closed her eyes, weariness descending. "You're right. I...owe Apphia something. But I want you to tell me that you're not going to abandon her again."

There was a long pause.

"I can't stay here," Gyre said slowly. "There are places I need to be, battles I need to fight. If Apphia wants to return to the Commune—"

"Then she's a fool. There's no Commune anymore, just a few idiots hiding in the woods."

"Nevertheless. If that's what she wants to do, I can't stop her. But I will...suggest...that she and Nina leave Khirkhaz with me, at least for a while. I hope that will keep her safe." *As safe as a known rebel can be in the new empire, at least.*

"I suppose that's all I can ask for." Vaela sighed and sucked her teeth. "I knew you were trouble. Too handsome by half. Should have put my plaguing foot down. But it's all piss in the river now. What is it you think I can do for you?"

"I need a distraction to get Apphia out, something to draw the guards' attention. I thought a protest at the front gate, a few rocks thrown, that sort of thing."

"Hmph." Vaela frowned. "Folks don't like the camp, that's certain. If I spread a few rumors...something could be arranged." Her face turned hard. "A protest is *all* it'll be, though. No one is going to storm that fence for you. I'm not getting my people hurt."

"That's all I'm asking for," Gyre said. "Starting around sundown, say, and lasting as long as possible."

"I'll do what I can." Vaela craned her neck and spat on the ground. "When you see Apphia, tell her I was right." She sighed again. "And tell her I'm sorry."

The old woman was true to her word. The sun was slipping below the horizon in the west, and torches were already flaring in front of the camp. A crowd was gathering, only a few dozen strong thus far but growing quickly. The two guards in front of the gate were looking distinctly nervous. Gyre could only hope that fear was communicated inside, pulling everyone's attention away.

He and Nina waited behind a hedgerow on the edge of the cleared zone in front of the fence. The eastern end of the log palisade was directly in front of them, joining a lower fence that lined the cliff where the peninsula fell off into the sea.

All six of Kit's larger bodies had joined them, infiltrating the city as it got dark enough. Gyre watched the protest and the waning sun and felt a rising nervousness. They were going in blind, which he never liked. *But we don't have much choice in the matter. As Nina says, we can't wait around forever.* Not to mention Kit reported things in Deepfire were rapidly coming to a boil.

"You're certain you can climb that?" Gyre said to Kit.

"Sure. The small bodies are the best climbers. Power-to-weight ratio and all that."

"And you can manage the dreamer?"

"I can manage."

The last thumb's worth of sun vanished, and the red glow of the clouds began to fade. He could hear shouts from the other end of the wall, angry yells from the crowd and bellows from the guards warning them back.

It's time.

"Go," he told Kit.

In a flash, one of her bodies scrambled over the hedge and scuttled across the clear space, pausing in the shadow of the wall. Gyre watched the guard tower that covered this section, but the man inside gave no indication he'd noticed. After a few moments, the spider-construct began climbing, its claws lodging in the wood. It made steady progress, a moving patch of shadow in the greater darkness. Moments later, it vanished onto the platform of the open-topped tower. A puff of white gas rose from the spot, drifting away on the breeze.

"Perfect," Kit said. "He's out cold."

Gyre exhaled a little of his tension. Dreamers were one of Lynnia's rarer creations, notoriously finicky and expensive. Anyone who breathed the fumes when the clay grenade burst was likely to end up taking an extended nap, which could make it as dangerous to the user as to the target. *It helps to have someone without lungs to deliver it.*

"Okay," he said aloud. "Nina, stay close, and don't use that thing unless you have to."

Nina hugged her blaster rifle to her chest and nodded.

"Kit, once we're through, spread out. Tell me if you find Apphia, but mostly I want to know where the guards are."

"Got it."

Gyre vaulted the hedgerow, running low and silent across the open space. There was a full energy bottle at his hip, but he didn't want to use it too soon. *Chosen know what'll happen once we're inside.* Fortunately, with the closest watchman asleep, the others didn't have a good angle to spot him. *And they've got bigger problems to worry about at the front gate.*

No cry of alarm had gone up by the time he reached the wall. Gyre drew his silver sword and rammed it into the wood where two of the logs met, the ghoul-made weapon punching through with only slight resistance. Slicing sideways was more difficult, like cutting hard cheese with a blunt knife, but with a little effort he'd cut a substantial chunk out of two logs, leaving a hole wide enough to squirm through. Kit's bodies swarmed in.

"You're clear for now," she said. "Go."

Gyre ducked his head and scrunched his shoulders to pass through the narrow space. Nina followed, considerably more easily.

He'd seen the camp from the hillside, so he had a rough idea of the layout. There were six buildings in two rows of three, plus a seventh farther out, at the tip of the little peninsula. The first six were all wooden, narrow windows covered with slats, roofed with fresh-cut shingles. The seventh building was stone walled and looked considerably better constructed.

Lanterns were everywhere, bobbing from the arms of guards making the rounds. As Gyre had hoped, the majority of them were converging on the front gate, where the shouting match was still in progress. A few dozen Auxies were gathered, loading their crossbows. *Let's hope they don't get trigger-happy.*

That left a few guards still patrolling, and one standing by the entrance to each of the buildings. *Plus possibly more inside.*

"Kit," he murmured, "tell me if you find any Legionaries or Perfected. All I can see from here is Auxies."

"On it." Kit's bodies skittered out into the dark. "Looks like all the prisoners are indoors. Windows are too narrow for me. No Legionaries I can see, but no Apphia either."

"She has to be here somewhere," Nina said.

"She is," Gyre assured her. "And she's the most infamous rebel in Khandar. Everyone will know where to find her. Wait here a moment and follow when I wave."

Nina gave a nervous nod. Gyre crept away from the wall, toward the closest of the camp buildings. The last of the patrolling guards had been drawn away to the gate, leaving only one light beside the door. Gyre carefully crept through the broad shadows it threw, flattening himself against the rough-hewn wood and working his way closer. When he reached the edge of the pool of brightness, he willed his aug-mentations into action.

Time telescoped, and the woman waiting at the door to the build-ing was suddenly frozen in mid-yawn. Gyre ran toward her, impossibly fast from her perspective. Before she had time to do more than widen her eyes in surprise, he drew his sword and thrust it through her throat. When she opened her mouth to scream, all that emerged was red foam. Gyre withdrew his sword and caught her collapsing body under the armpits, laying it quietly aside and letting time return to normal. Then he turned and waved his arm in front of the lantern.

Nina arrived a moment later, barely glancing at the dead guard. An iron padlock secured the door, but Gyre's sword bit through the hasp and it fell away. He opened the door just wide enough to slip through, and Nina soundlessly followed.

The building was just a long, narrow room, wide enough for two cots and a narrow aisle between them. Most of them were occupied by people in drab gray tunics sleeping under thin blankets. A small group had gathered at one end, trying to peer through the slit windows to see what was happening at the gate.

Gyre scanned the group, looking for Apphia's purple hair and scarred face. He didn't see anyone he recognized, but Nina did, darting forward into the darkness and grabbing the arm of a big man lying on his stomach.

"Fell!" She shook him. "Fell, it's Nina!"

The man pushed himself up on his elbows, bleary with sleep. "Little Nina?"

"Quiet," Gyre said, hurrying over to them. They were already getting glances from the other prisoners.

"It's me," Nina whispered.

"Thought you were dead," Fell rumbled. "Baron said you'd escaped, but..." He shook his head. "They catch you? Or..."

His eyes widened at the sight of the blaster rifle in Nina's arms. Gyre leaned in, voice low.

"This is a rescue," he said. "Can we rely on you to organize the rest of the prisoners?"

"I..." He came fully awake, sitting up in bed. "Yeah. How are we getting out?"

"There's a hole at the east end of the wall. Right now the guards are all over at the west end, where some of the locals are stirring them up. I need you to get everyone away as quietly as you can."

"Got it. They split us up, so I've got some friends in each bunk."

"Fell is one of Brennard's lieutenants," Nina explained. "Fell, where's my sister? Please tell me she's here."

"The baron's here. But..."

"But what?" Gyre said, heart dropping in his chest.

"They've been working on her, trying to get her to talk by threatening the rest of us," Fell said. "Then today they took her and the cap'n back into the stone building."

"What's in there?" Nina said.

"Don't know, but nobody that's gone in has come back. They take a few people each day."

Plaguing fuck. Nina's eyes were panicked. "We'll go and find her," Gyre said. "There's only one guard at each building. Can you handle that many?"

"Don't worry about it," Fell said. He raised a thick, scarred fist. "Go and get the baron and Cap'n Brennard."

Some of the other prisoners had awoken now, and there was a great deal of hushed whispering. Gyre hurried out, Nina close behind. Fell's voice rose above the clamor, telling them to keep quiet.

"If that keeps up," Gyre said to Kit, "the guards won't be able to miss it. Be ready."

"Standing by," Kit said. She sounded gleeful, as she always was when there was an opportunity for mayhem. "I've got two bodies waiting by the stone building. No guards I can see, but it's locked up tight."

"I figured."

Gyre put a hand in his sack of alchemicals, counting vials. After distributing supplies to Kit's bodies, he had fewer than a dozen of the little grenades left, but some of them packed a considerable punch. *Hopefully it's enough.*

Cutting between the prisoner barracks kept them out of sight of the guards until they reached the quiet of the seaward side of the camp. The stone building looked older, an L-shaped structure with a slate roof not far from the edge of the cliff. It had once had windows, but they'd been covered over with metal plates, and the door had been replaced as well. Gyre touched his sword, trying to decide on the best way in.

"They're onto us," Kit said. "Guards at the gate splitting up, a couple of squads heading to the barracks."

Plaguing fuck. "Blow it."

"*Fi*nally."

A few seconds later, a pair of massive *booms* echoed over the camp. Fountains of fire erupted into the night, not dying away but fizzing and sparking like living conflagrations, throwing white-hot sparks in all directions and bleeding thick, choking smoke.

That should slow them down, at least. But they were out of time for finesse. Gyre fished his last large bomb from the satchel and tossed the heavy, awkward grenade at the door, grabbing Nina and turning her away. There was a *crunch* and a muted roar, pebbles and dirt raining down all around them. When he looked back, the door was gone, along with a chunk of the surrounding wall. Broken slate from the roof pattered down like rain.

"Come on," he yelled at Nina, through the ringing in his ears. With a *click*, the world slowed, and his silver sword leapt into his hand. He'd expected guards inside—hopefully stunned by the blast—but to his surprise he found none, just an open foyer with several doors and no furnishings. One of the doors had scraped a wide semicircle in the dust, and he headed for it with long, floating strides.

Beyond was a corridor. More unused rooms on either side, desks and empty bookshelves. Wheel tracks in the dust led to the far end, where another door stood closed. Gyre hit it with his shoulder at a dead run, and the lock gave with a *crunch*, spraying bits of doorframe.

The first thing to hit him was the smell, the rancid sick-sweet stench of the offal pit behind a butcher shop. The room was large and square, with two rows of wooden tables. Crude manacles had been affixed to hold prisoners—they were empty, but at the near end of the room was a familiar scarred face.

"Apphia!" Nina screamed, skidding through the doorway. She ran to her sister, who was dressed in rags and covered in filth but seemed relatively intact.

The same could not be said for Brennard, who lay on the table at the far end of the room. He'd been tortured and flayed—

No. Not flayed, at least not by anything so crude as a knife. One of the old soldier's legs was gone, and the other lay…open, *disassembled*, as though human flesh could be taken apart as neatly as a clockwork mechanism. Skin was peeled and folded back, muscle unwoven in coiled threads, veins and nerves put aside. Beside the table, a gaunt figure in a dark gray smock liberally spattered with gore was picking the bones free as though from a fish he was preparing to cook. His gloved hands were bloody to the elbow.

And worst of all, Brennard was undoubtedly *alive*. Spittle dripped from the corner of his mouth, catching in his beard, and he gave a hoarse shriek at each new prod from the torturer.

"*Brennard!*" This scream was Apphia's, as she struggled against her bonds. She seemed oblivious to Nina's presence at her side. "Hurt *me*, you fucking plaguepit, leave him alone—" She dissolved into a coughing fit.

"I'm afraid not," the torturer said, straightening up. "My instructions are only to make you *pliable*. But"—he turned to Gyre—"it seems we have guests."

"Get away from him." Gyre skidded to a halt and leveled his sword. Out of the corner of his eye, he saw Nina fumbling with her blaster rifle.

"Gyre Silvereye." The bloody-handed man had a shock of white hair and nearly skeletal features. Gyre was certain he'd never seen him before. But there was, nonetheless, something *familiar* about his manner. "I was told you might be about."

"Back. Away." Gyre tensed, watching the shadow-images stretch around the torturer.

"So rude. And we're having such a lovely reunion."

He's mad. Not that there was any doubt about that. Gyre sprang forward, leaping the table in a single jump and slashing sideways, his stroke a silver blur that ought to have separated the lunatic's head from his body. But the torturer grabbed Brennard by the arm, and the cavalryman burst apart in welter of snapping bones and tearing flesh. Tentacles of muscle and cartilage shaped themselves out of the ruin, dripping crimson, whipping between Gyre and his opponent. The silver sword was deflected over the torturer's head and Gyre landed in a skid across the slippery floor.

Nina fired with a *crack*. The bolt detonated against the writhing meat, spattering charred pieces. Tentacles lashed out in response, reaching for her, and she screamed and dove for the floor. Gyre lunged, slicing the gory limbs apart, then spun into a furious attack. He hacked and cut, ghoul blade slashing through flesh and bone, tearing away the tendrils that got between him and the gaunt man.

"Impatient, too," the torturer said, skipping backward. "Always in a rush."

There was something on the back of his neck, something dark and bloated, legs twitching aimlessly. *The black spiders.* Maya had said they were *copies* of the Corruptor, his children. *No wonder he seems familiar.*

There was a heavy tread behind him and an unpleasant *squish.* Shadows reached out in the corner of his eye. Gyre spun, blade singing, only for it to bounce from thick unmetal armor with a fat spark. From the other tables, dark figures levered themselves up, silver-armored *things* with blank faceplates. They were all horribly *incomplete*, breastplates hanging open, trailing strings of muscle and long tubes leaking black pus. *Perfected. But not* finished. Gyre glanced at the empty tables and suddenly understood what had been happening here.

We need to go. There were muffled explosions from outside. Gyre sidestepped the closest Perfected's lunge and slashed through its shapeless viscera, taking advantage of its open chestplate. Black fluid torrented forth, and it fell twitching, but another stepped in behind it. Gyre had to duck to evade whipping tendrils from the black spider, and he rolled beneath one of the tables for a moment of calm. His free hand grabbed a pair of grenades from his satchel.

"Get Apphia out of here!" he shouted at Nina, who was just pushing herself up off the floor. "Kit, help her!"

One of Kit's small bodies scuttled through the door. Gyre emerged from the other side of the table, slashed a tendril apart, and hurled one grenade toward the spider. A thick tentacle whipped in to catch it, but the little bomb shattered on impact, splashing its contents all over the writhing mess that had once been Brennard. The liquid caught fire at once, burning with a hot white flame that filled the air with the stench of charred meat. The *dhakim* recoiled, beating at a drop that had gotten into his hair.

Gyre spun and found the first of the Perfected clambering over the table to get to him. It reached out, one-armed, but in its incomplete state it was too slow, and he evaded the grab and slashed it through its half-open breastplate. As it fell, he hurled the other grenade past it, catching one of the remaining Perfected in the faceplate and turning it into a roaring torch.

Nina had gotten Apphia out of the metal cuffs and helped her to her feet, though neither was moving quickly. Kit's body skittered along the table, dodging the flames, and leapt for the black spider and its host. The creature caught the little construct in both hands, holding Kit up as her legs wiggled furiously. But he was distracted, and Gyre didn't waste the opportunity. He lunged and speared the thing in the throat, his ghoul blade passing through the torturer's spine to skewer the spider clinging to the back of his neck. There was an insectile screech, and its legs spasmed and flailed. The host only bore a resigned expression, a sigh bubbling out through the tide of blood. Then both collapsed, and Gyre flicked the mix of red and black off his sword.

"Move fast, Gyre," Kit said on his shoulder. Her other body was struggling free of the black spider's corpse. "Things are getting exciting outside."

"Doing the best I can," Gyre muttered. The energy bottle at his side was hot from overuse and nearly empty, and he swapped it with a fresh one from his pack—one left—as he retreated. He caught up to Apphia and Nina in the corridor. Apphia was walking with a bit more purpose now, though she still leaned on her sister.

"Gyre," she breathed, as he rushed past. "Are you—"

"Later!" he said. "We're not out of this yet!"

The well-organized camp had been converted into something out of a nightmare. Four sparkers were still burning, sending out sprays of burning metal and gushing caustic smoke. With his silver eye, Gyre could just about make out a large crowd of people by the fence. Some of them had set up a makeshift barricade, built from the cots in the barracks. The boards were already riddled with crossbow bolts from the Auxies, and several bodies.

Fuck. He hadn't planned on having to evacuate the entire camp. The prisoners were slipping out through the hole he'd cut in the fence, but it was big enough for only one at a time, creating a bottleneck. It would be easiest to avoid the Auxies and cut another hole elsewhere, but...

"Kit, take all the bodies you have left and stay with Apphia and Nina," he said. "Have them head for the prisoners. I'll clear us a path."

She shouted an excited acknowledgment, and he put his head down and ran. He could see at least four squads of Auxies, far too many to take on in a straight-up fight. But they were facing away from him, toward the prisoners, and they didn't know he was coming. *Here goes nothing.*

He fingered the small bombs remaining in his satchel. *Stunner, sparker, smoker. Not much left.* Taking the first of these in hand, he hefted it as he approached the rear of the Auxie line, pitching it to land in the midst of them. The alchemical exploded with an earsplitting *bang* and a burst of blinding light, and Gyre arrived a moment later, his human eye dazzled but the silver one still clear. His blade whipped back and forth as he engaged the stunned soldiers, blood spraying in wide arcs. He'd cut down a half dozen before the rest began to recover. A few with spears turned in his direction, which was easy enough to avoid, dodging the shadow-projections of the tips and chopping away at the haft. But the line of crossbowmen was turning, too, and that was a different matter. *It's hard to dodge when there are two dozen bolts—*

"It's just one man!" a decarch screamed. "Shoot him! Shoot—"

Fell slammed into him full tilt. The man's considerable bulk bore the shrieking officer to the ground. More prisoners followed, abandoning their improvised shields to charge the Auxie line. A couple of crossbows snapped, and one woman at the head of the charge pitched backward, but the others came on, armed with nothing more than fists and desperate rage.

It was enough. Caught between Gyre's bloody onslaught and the prisoners they'd tormented, the Auxies broke, fleeing into the shadows and smoke. Gyre spared Fell a quick salute as he got up, knuckles bloody.

"Apphia's coming!" he shouted.

"Cap'n Brennard?" Fell said. Gyre shook his head, and the rebel spat on the ground.

"We need to take the gate!" Fell pointed to where another squad of

Auxies still held the main gate against the crowd outside. "We'll be all night getting out this way!"

"Follow me." Gyre leapt over bruised and broken bodies and ran to the wall. The parallel timbers were held in place by two iron strips—a quick slash of his ghoul blade and the metal parted, falling away. Gyre chopped downward a few times, hacking a short distance into the posts along the base.

He pointed with his sword, and Fell understood. He grabbed three other prisoners, all big, heavy men, and they crowded shoulder to shoulder and charged at the wall. All four of them slammed into it at once, and the weakened timbers gave way, the whole section Gyre had freed from the metal falling outward with a splintering crash. That left a gap in the fence two meters wide, and the rest of the prisoners immediately began to stream through. Fell and his companions had to roll aside to keep from being trampled.

Apphia and Nina had caught up by the time the way was clear for Gyre to step through. Fell pulled himself up, and a dozen others had gathered around him, tough-looking men and women Gyre assumed were former rebel fighters. The rest of the prisoners were still fleeing into the welcoming darkness.

"Baron," Fell said, attempting a clumsy bow. "I'm so glad you're safe."

"Fell." Apphia blinked. "I...I don't..."

"We can take her with us," Fell said to Gyre. "We'll head back to the forest, dig in deep."

"*No*," Nina said. "They'll come after her. We have to stay with Gyre."

"Apphia?" Gyre said. "Do you want to come with me?"

"I..." Apphia licked her lips and drew herself up with a visible effort of self-control. For a moment, she was Baron Kotzed. "I will remain with Gyre and my sister. The rest of you, stay out of the forest. Split up and lie low. But wait for my call. This isn't over."

"Of course." Fell gave another bow, more successfully. "We'll be ready, Baron."

Apphia nodded. The small group jogged away, Fell already barking orders. As soon as they were out of sight, she sagged, barely supporting herself on Nina's arm.

"I've got you," Nina said, catching her sister around the shoulders. "We're getting out of here."

Vaela had been as good as her word. She'd arranged one of the vacant mansions as a rendezvous, and her people had cut the locks on the stables. Three swiftbirds were waiting, harnessed and ready.

"She's not going to be able to ride," Nina said.

Gyre gave a weary grunt. He'd finally let his augmented perception fade, and the exhaustion of the fight was rolling over him. His sword arm ached, his human eye was red and itching from smoke, and his ears still rang from the blasts. There was nothing he wanted more than to collapse into one of the empty stalls and rest, but he forced himself to check the birds and lead them outside, one by one.

"You'll have to double up," he said. That would be a heavy load for a swiftbird, but it wouldn't be for long. "We'll ride out of town a ways, then find somewhere to hole up until morning."

Nina nodded. She looked as weary as Gyre felt, but together they helped Apphia into the swiftbird's saddle. Nina clambered up behind her, barely able to see over her taller sister's shoulder. Gyre mounted one of the other swiftbirds, with the spare's reins tied to his saddle.

Grayport was already boiling with soldiers, their lantern-bearing patrols crisscrossing the streets like a swarm of angry fireflies. Fortunately, they focused their attention on the east bank of the river, rather than among the looming, empty houses of the wealthy. Gyre led the way north, across lawns and through gardens, staying away from the main road.

The land soon rose to rolling hills, their slopes terraced into orchards. Following a little stream, they found their way into a copse of trees, dense enough to deter casual visitors. The birds didn't like it, high-stepping through the cluttered ground and giving rumbling chirps, but after they dismounted Gyre got them calmed and tied up, munching on nyfa seeds from their saddlebags.

Apphia had fallen asleep, and Nina needed Gyre's help to get her to the ground. They wrapped her in a thick blanket, and Nina curled up beside her.

"Get as much sleep as you can," Gyre told her. "In the morning we ride straight for the Gate."

Nina nodded, wrapping her arms around her sister. Gyre settled himself against a tree nearby, feeling his body creaking like a rusty machine.

"We've left the rest of my bodies behind," Kit said. "I'll try to catch up, just to have them on hand. This one can keep watch."

"Thanks," Gyre said. He felt sleep dragging at him already. "Everything okay with Maya and the others?"

"So far so good with Maya. Deepfire is going less well. It's good that you're in a hurry. Tanax needs your help."

"Wonderful." He watched the two sleeping girls for a moment. "We got her out. When we first found Nina, I was sure..."

"Yeah," Kit said. "I know the feeling."

"What the black spider was doing..." Gyre groped for the right words. "He was *building* the Perfected. Constructing them from... from *spare parts*."

"You'd think I would be less disgusted given that my current body was made in much the same way," Kit said. "But you'd be wrong. Not that I used *human* parts to make my bodies, obviously."

"It's the same thing plaguespawn have been doing for four hundred years. Tearing people to shreds and building more of themselves from the wreckage. This is just a little more orderly."

"Perfected."

"Exactly." He looked at the little construct. "Have you told Maya about this?"

"I will when we have a moment. She's a bit busy."

"She knows the most about those fucking spiders," Gyre said. "There must be more of them. The Corruptor had hundreds of Perfected in Skyreach. He must have camps like this all over the Republic."

"Fuck," Kit said. "I've seen an awful lot, but... *plaguing fuck.*"

Gyre nodded, exhausted, and leaned back against the tree. His eyes closed, almost of their own accord, and he slept. Time seemed to jerk forward, the opposite of when he used his silver eye, so that the hours until dawn passed in a flickering moment. He awoke with his mouth thick, his head throbbing, and his muscles in collective revolt.

"Gyre?"

He looked over to find Apphia awake, propped on one elbow. She was still filthy, her hair matted with dirt and gore, but her eyes had lost the stunned, hollow look. Nina was still sleeping beside her, nestled into the crook of her arm.

"Morning," Gyre grunted.

"It wasn't a dream, then," Apphia said. "I wasn't sure."

"Not unless I'm dreaming a killer headache."

She gave a small chuckle, then shook her head. "You came for me."

"I'm sorry I couldn't come sooner."

"How did you know to come at all? We hadn't heard anything from you for weeks."

"You can thank me for that," said Kit. "One of my damaged bodies was left at the Spire. Nina found it and asked me to contact Gyre. It took me a little while to find him."

Apphia started, noticing the tiny construct for the first time. "You had to... find him?"

"It's a long story," Gyre said. "I'll fill you in, but it'll have to be on the road."

"Where are we going?" Apphia said.

"The Gate."

"We can't activate the Gate, unless you have a centarch in your back pocket." Apphia's eyes narrowed. "You don't, right?"

"Next best thing," Gyre said. "I have one on the other side, and he's opening the Gate at noon."

"Why would a centarch be working with you? And *where* on the other side?"

"Like I said—"

"A long story." Apphia let out a breath. "Not like I have any alternative but to trust you."

"We can talk things over once we're safe. They'll still be searching for us, I'm certain."

"I know. Just…" A shadow flickered over Apphia's face. "One thing. Brennard."

Gyre winced. "I'm sorry. That thing…"

"He's dead?" Apphia leaned forward. "*Dead*, you're certain? Not trapped as some monster?"

"I burned what was left of him," Gyre said. "I'm certain."

"That's…something." Apphia let out a breath. "Thank you. For all of this."

"Thank me once we're out of it," Gyre said.

Chapter Thirteen

Maya

Maya found Beq waiting for her in the hall. Her hair was tied back in a fresh braid, and she'd changed into her worn travel clothes, much patched and mended after their violent excursions.

"I feel like I should be carrying more stuff," Beq said. "When we left the Forge the first time, I could barely walk with my pack on."

"You didn't complain," Maya said.

"I wasn't going to complain in front of the girl I had a crush on," Beq said.

Maya chuckled. "I think I spent half that trip trying to keep myself from staring at you."

"Sorry I couldn't be there," Kit said, her tiny spider clinging to Maya's shoulder. "Sounds like a good time."

Beq started, coloring. "Sorry. I didn't see you there."

"Don't apologize on my account. I need details."

"*Anyway,*" Maya said, "do we need to track anything down from the stores?"

"Sarah and I took care of it," Kit said. "Stuff from the palace wouldn't be any good anyway. We stocked up on decent scavenger gear. Just head up to the Gap and down the steps, and I'll meet up with you."

The hired carriage in front of the palace took them north and west, where the respectable brick and stone buildings gave way to warehouses and manufactories, vast blocks of industry with chimneys belching dark smoke. Armed guards waited outside most of them, hard-looking people in scavenged armor, carrying crossbows or blaster pistols. Broken windows gaped like lost teeth.

Eventually the industrial districts gave way to broken, rocky ground, the road switchbacking as it led up the wall of the crater. When they turned sideways, Maya could see Hunter's Gap, like a bite taken out of the bowl holding the city. The road ended just below it, and the driver halted his birds and opened the door. If he saw anything odd about two underequipped young women heading out into the mountains alone, he kept his opinions to himself.

They climbed the short distance to the Gap and paused for a moment on the high ground. Mountains stretched as far as the eye could see, peak after peak, each with its blanket of white. Ahead, the ground sloped steeply downward into a valley with a little river at the bottom. Scavengers had built a makeshift stair, which wandered back and forth down the rocky mountainside until it reached the flats far below.

"My knees ache just looking at it," Beq said after a moment of silence.

"Glad I don't have those anymore," Kit said. "It's not all this bad, I promise. We can stay in the valleys until we get close to Mount Shroud."

It took nearly an hour to descend, and in addition to her aching knees Maya tried not to think about how they would have to come back *up*, assuming everything went well. *Maybe there's a Gate in the skyfortress.* She didn't think Gates worked that way. Life was rarely so convenient.

It was cold, too, and getting colder. Though it was only midafternoon, the surrounding peaks cast huge shadows, blocking the sun from much of the valley. She was grateful to see five of Kit's larger bodies, each as big as a loadbird, sitting at the base of the steps with their legs folded under them. They carried large, ill-fitting canvas packs. A pair of smaller bodies were pulling one of these open, revealing lots of fur-lined leather.

"Gear up," Kit instructed. "You can leave the heaviest coats for when we get on the mountain, but take the rest."

Maya didn't need prompting. With a thick winter coat, a hat that covered her ears with fur flaps, and woolen mittens, the trip felt abruptly more doable. Kit distributed food and water as well, and Maya and Beq munched their way through the familiar bland twice-baked crackers and some dried spiced fruit.

"If Varo was here," Beq said, "he'd tell a story about a friend of his who went out once without her hat."

"When they found her in the morning," Maya volunteered, "they thought she was asleep, until someone grabbed her hand and it broke right off!"

"Actually," Kit said, "this one time, a guy I knew was taking a piss in a blizzard—"

"Please don't," Maya said, as Beq broke down laughing.

"*Right* off," Kit said. "Let's make a few more kilometers before it gets dark."

With proper clothes and relatively flat ground to walk on, the going was much more pleasant. They walked beside the river, which Kit said was called the Brink. Pine trees hunched over against the wind and bushes were already skeletal and bare in anticipation of winter. The shadows grew longer, and as the light began to fade from the sky, they reached a place where a smaller valley joined up. Maya picked a camp-site set against a large boulder, conscious that she was probably making a dozen basic mistakes that Varo would have quietly corrected. Kit's constructs pitched their tent with practiced efficiency, working in uni-son like a single creature's limbs.

"I feel a bit like I'm on a guided tour," Maya said. "One of those things where a gang of nobles goes out 'roughing it,' only there's a gaggle of servants doing all the work before they get there."

"You'll always have *one* important job," Beq said, glancing meaningfully at the small pyramid of wood and brush she'd prepared. Maya put her hand to her haken, and flame burst up through the center, crackling merrily.

Gotten pretty good at that. The first time she'd tried it, years ago, she'd detonated the campfire and spread sparks and debris for a dozen meters.

After a dinner of roasted potatoes and vulpi bacon, Maya and Beq retired to their tent. Kit's tiny spider, in spite of her objections, stayed outside.

"Fine," she said. "Shut me out in the cold!"

"I thought you didn't feel cold," Beq said, peering at the little thing through her spectacles.

"I don't. But it's the principle of the thing."

"Good *night*," Maya said firmly, closing the flap. She conjured a tiny will-o'-the-wisp in the sudden darkness, the soft light reflecting in Beq's glasses and throwing their shadows against the walls.

Maya shrugged out of her coat and hat—it was surprisingly warm inside, certainly better than the Order-issued tents she was used to. After a moment, Beq did likewise, folding them up in silence.

"Something the matter?"

"I realized I'm having fun," Beq said.

"That seems like a good thing."

"It feels wrong. We're being hunted by a plaguespawn Chosen four centuries old, who wants to capture you for who-knows-what horrible purpose. The Republic is gone and the world is crashing down around our ears. What business do I have having *fun*?"

When she put it that way, Maya understood the feeling. "You have to take your happiness where you find it, I suppose. If climbing down stairs and eating stale biscuit is your idea of happiness."

"As long as I can do it with you," Beq said. She hesitated, flushing, and looked like she wished she could take the line back.

"Hey." Maya reached out and took her hand. "It's the same for me. You know that, right?"

"I know." Beq's voice was quiet.

"Beq. What's going on?"

"What's going on is that I'm a terrible person," Beq said, flopping down on the bedroll.

"I thought that was *my* line." Maya knelt beside her, put a hand on the small of her back. "And we both know it's not true."

"What else do you call it? All that stuff is happening, *you* are working so hard to stop it, and meanwhile here *I* am moping because..." She hesitated, then said in one breath, "Because I don't get to spend enough time with my girlfriend. You have important things to do, I don't have any right to complain. But I spend all day with Sarah, or Xalen, or by myself, and it feels like there's this *ache* in the middle of my chest." She pressed her face into the bedroll, carefully pushing her spectacles out of the way. "This probably doesn't make any sense."

"It makes perfect sense." After a moment, Maya stretched out beside Beq, one arm curled around her. "I'm sorry."

"Don't apologize," Beq mumbled. "That makes it worse. Some future historian is going to write, 'Maya and her friends *would* have saved the world, but Beq was being weird and distracted her.'"

Maya snorted a laugh and squeezed Beq a little closer.

"I just..." Beq's voice was quiet. "I'm not good at...this. Being with someone. I didn't even know it was something I wanted until I met you. And now I feel...like this, and I don't know how to talk about it, and also I'm scared all the time that something terrible is going to happen—"

"Hey." Maya kissed Beq on the cheek. "You think *I* know what I'm doing? The sum of my romantic experience was a couple of longing looks and a lot of sweaty fantasies."

"I know. I'm sorry. I shouldn't put this on you—"

"*Listen*. Please. I'm scared too, all right? You know I am. But we're going to get through this, whatever happens. You and me, together.

We'll get rid of the Corruptor and Jaedia will wake up and we will...
figure things out. I promise. We'll have plenty of time."

"I'll hold you to that."

Beq's voice was thick. She raised her head from the bedroll, eyes
heavy with tears. Maya wiped them away with her thumb and kissed
her. Beq's mouth opened under hers, and Maya was surprised to find
Beq's hand running up the inside of her thigh. Her breath hitched, skin
pebbling under her leggings.

Beq paused. "You... I mean, we don't have to..."

"No! Or, yes. I do want to. I just thought... you were crying..."

"Sorry. Is it weird?"

"I have no idea." Maya pushed Beq over onto her back, then sat
straddling her, fingers fumbling at the laces of her shirt. "It's *you*. That's
all that matters."

"I've been having, um, 'sweaty fantasies,'" Beq said, leaning up on
her elbows to kiss Maya again. "It's your fault, you know. My dreams
never used to be so... frustrating."

Maya laughed and pressed Beq down into the bedroll.

Zephkiel

The mountains had a different feel from the air. The few times Zephkiel had been to the surface were rugged affairs, bundled up against the
wind and cold even at the height of summer, the peaks rising around
them like jagged teeth in some monstrous maw. From five thousand
meters up, those same mountains looked delicate, frosted with snow
and wound through with rivers of clouds, like the most perfect frosted
dessert topped with airy spun sugar. The howl and bite of the wind
were banished to the other side of the transparent canopy.

The skyship *Strive to Perfection* had made the long trip from the
south in three leisurely days, taking on new passengers and cargo at
half a dozen points along the way. Zeph had chosen this route because

she didn't have enough Gate credit for her luggage, swollen by two heavy trunks from her mother's house. Honestly, though, she found that she preferred it. The speed of the Gates was unnerving, moving from *here* to *there* so seamlessly that it hardly seemed like a trip at all. It felt like the world had rearranged itself around you instead in some cosmic prank. From the nose of the skyship, she'd watched the Empire roll out underneath her, underlining the reality of the distance she was traveling.

This is real. We're really going back. She kept her thoughts to herself, a reflex that was second nature. Still, she could feel Ashok's presence as always, like a background hum in her mind.

It had been more than a year now, since she'd left the lab. The reunion with Iraph had been even worse than she'd anticipated, her sister's relief quickly giving way to a storm of accusations and tears. Having patched that over the best she could, she'd visited her mother, which had been a different kind of horrible. There was already something gone from behind her eyes, and the knowledge that it would only get worse was haunting.

She'd leaned heavily on Ashok those first few weeks. Sometimes it seemed like their blood-bond was all that was keeping her afloat, the warmth of his presence always at her side. She'd helped him with his work, thinking through problems together, *feeling* his joy when she found a clever solution. It made the rest bearable.

Over time, though, the balance had shifted. She'd grown closer to Iraph, once the initial boil had been lanced and the pus of guilt and resentment drained away. Her sister had always felt like she lived her life in Zeph's shadow, staying behind in their modest hometown instead of vanishing into the research utopia of the mountains. They'd talked more and more, late nights with a bottle of wine in the kitchen of the house Zeph had grown up in.

She'd grown closer with her mother as well, the shock of seeing what she lost replaced with the joy in how much remained, even as her illness progressed. When she'd died, Iraph and Zeph had cried together, and

Zeph hadn't thought about telling Ashok until the following morning. His presence was always there, but they'd spoken less and less. When he asked for her help with his work, she often had nothing to say.

It had taken another few months to wind up her mother's affairs, empty and sell her house, and conclude all the other arrangements. The work had seemed as though it would never end, until it abruptly did, and it was time for Zeph to return to the lab she'd left behind. *To the lab, and to Ashok.* The months they'd spent together felt like a strange dream, and she had no idea what she would wake to when she landed.

For now, she left their mental link alone. *I'll send to him when we're a little closer.* It was hard to admit, even to herself, that she was eager to put off the reunion.

"It's a beautiful view."

Zeph blinked, drawn out of her reverie. The mountain ahead of them blazed with colored light, markers illuminating the entrances to dozens of tunnels. Through the wispy cloud that surrounded it, the lamps turned into soft-colored jewels, shifting in the wind.

"It is," Zeph said, and glanced at her interlocuter. She didn't recognize him, not a surprise since she hadn't gotten to know anyone on the ship except the cabin steward. He was an older man, in his fifties perhaps, with blue hair so dark it was almost black except where it was shot with gray. His long coat was gray as well, and his shirt, so the only hint of color was a pair of emerald green eyes. He nodded politely, and Zeph gave him an uncertain nod in return. "I'm sorry, should I recognize you? It's been a while since I was in the mountains."

"We've never met," he said. "But you're Zephkiel, of the Stoneroot lab, correct?"

"That's right." Zeph straightened up, increasingly alarmed. "Who are you?"

"My name is Spinakker. Directorate Intelligence. I'd like a few words with you, if you don't mind."

Now she was *definitely* alarmed. The Directorate's infamous Intelligence division reported directly to the top of the Chosen hierarchy.

Its agents went where they pleased and did what they liked, secure in the knowledge that their Chosen patrons outranked anyone else. Their mission was nothing less than the preservation of the Empire as a whole.

"Is there...Am I in trouble?" Zeph managed. She thought immediately of the blood-bond. *If someone found out...* It wasn't against the *law,* but that didn't matter much if some senior Chosen expressed their disapproval.

"No, not at all," Spinakker said, a hint of amusement in his eyes. "I'm just looking for information."

"What kind of information? You know I've been away from the lab for a year, I assume."

"I do, thank you. It's why I'm contacting you. You know Nial-Est-Ashok, I take it?"

"Yes," Zeph said carefully. "He's the administrator of the facility and my direct superior."

A faint smile crossed Spinakker's lips. "You know him a little better than that."

"I..." She swallowed. "I do. We were...lovers."

"Were? Or are?"

"I haven't seen him for a year," Zephkiel said. "I don't know if things have changed."

"You haven't been in contact with him during that time?"

"No. Not very much, anyway." There hadn't been any physical messages, which surely Spinakker already knew. *But if he knows about the bond, he'll know I'm lying.*

"I see." His face gave no hint as to what he thought about her answer. "Then you haven't participated in his research in some time."

"No." That, at least, was true. "Has he been working on something unusual?"

"We're not sure. Which is the problem, really." Spinakker examined his coat cuffs for a moment. "My department is not accustomed to being kept out of the loop. And Ashok's requisitions for equipment have been... excessive. There is some concern that he's gone haring off in an unauthorized direction."

"I don't know anything about that," Zeph said. There had been the lab on the fifth floor, which hadn't *exactly* been authorized, but surely *that* wasn't enough to require a visit from Directorate Intelligence. *They'd just send him a memo.* "I'm sorry I can't help you."

"No need to apologize. I came here to ask you a favor."

"A favor?"

"I'd like you to keep your eyes open. Ashok trusts you. Don't do anything out of the ordinary, but if he takes you into his confidence, pay attention. If something sounds... off, I hope you'll contact me about it."

He produced a card, which was blank except for his name and network address. She took it reluctantly.

"I know this is difficult to think about," he said. "Believe me when I say it may be the best thing for Ashok and everyone else involved. If he is barking up the wrong tree, so to speak, then the sooner it gets sorted out, the sooner we can get him back on track. Understand?"

"I understand." Zeph tucked the card into her pocket. "But you're looking in the wrong place, I'm sure of it."

"I certainly hope so." Spinakker smiled humorlessly and stepped away from the canopy. "Have a pleasant landing."

A flitter, descending the skyship's inverse repulsion grid, brought Zeph down to the surface. Most of the passengers took a larger shuttle to the town, but when she'd let Ashok know she was here, he'd immediately arranged for her to be taken to the lab's private dock. The little flyer touched down gently in a small cavern, protected by telescoping doors from the snow and wind outside. The air was dry and warm, the *deiat* climate system working overtime to keep the temperature stable.

Uniformed lab servants hurried to take her luggage. Behind them stood Ashok, wearing a quiet smile. His voice rang in her mind.

Welcome back. It's so good to see you.

"It's good to be back, Administrator," Zeph said aloud. They were in public, and she didn't want to get used to their private communication and tip someone off.

He raised one eyebrow but played along. "Welcome, Zeph. You have my condolences, of course."

That confused her for a moment. *Right. Mom.* Having lived with her mother's death for more than a year, it felt like the distant past, with the final conclusion just an inevitable coda. And the encounter with Spinakker had jumbled her thoughts. "Thank you. It's been…hard. But I'm looking forward to getting to work."

"I'm glad to hear it. We've got plenty for you to do."

He waved, and she walked to meet him. When she came near, he reached out and pulled her close, wrapping her in an embrace and kissing her thoroughly before she could raise an objection. The warmth and smell of him sent her falling back through time, as though the last year had never happened. But she retained enough presence of mind to think, *What are you* doing?

What I should have been doing last year, Ashok responded. *I love you, Zeph, and I'm not going to hide it.*

But—we agreed. You have your position to think of—

Once my family sees what I've done here, no one will give a decithaler who I'm sleeping with. He pulled away, smiling broadly. *Let me show you.*

Zeph blinked uncertainly, aware of the mute eyes of the servants on her back. She accepted his arm, and they walked from the dock to the central atrium. The first sight of the place, with its descending staircase and corridors radiating out like the petals of a flower, brought Zeph a palpable sense of nostalgia. This was as much home now as the house she'd so recently helped clean out. She couldn't help smiling.

Maybe I'm thinking too hard. There was a warm feeling in her chest, and Ashok's arm was twined through her own. *The last year would have thrown anyone off stride. But this is where I want to be.* She glanced sidelong at the Chosen beside her, with his perfect cheekbones and golden hair. *And this is who I want to be here with. Isn't it?*

Spinakker's card, nestled in her pocket, felt like a burr. She wished she had a private moment to fish it out and throw it away.

Not *everything* was the same as it had been. People still ate in the cafeteria, but there were fewer than there ought to have been, and the stairway seemed equally deserted. Above her, where the steps wound up into the town, a ring of unmetal surrounded the stairway. Safety doors, she guessed, capable of airtight closure in seconds. *But what would be the point of isolating the entire lab?*

She didn't send that thought to Ashok. Instead she asked him, *Is it a holiday? There aren't many people around.*

We've temporarily reduced staff, he sent back airily. *A few projects were moved elsewhere, and some people found other work. My budgetary allocations haven't been all that I would like.*

The lab had hit rough patches before, but the Directorate had never gone so far as to make substantial cuts to their budget. *Is Nia still around, do you know?*

Niatea? Yes, I believe so. He tugged her arm. *Come on. I have so much I want you to see.*

They hurried down the steps, hand in hand, Ashok eager as an excited child. The faces Zeph saw on the way down she mostly recognized, though the looks they gave her were unfamiliar, half-jealous and half-pitying. Most of the second floor was dark, with only a few of the labs still in operation. The third floor was in the same state. Her own lab on the fourth floor was still running, she was glad to see, but Ashok kept moving downward.

Here things were entirely unfamiliar. The whole fifth-floor landing had been remodeled, replaced with an unmetal air lock. Ashok activated it with a *deiat* ping and the doors parted, revealing a thicker, more substantial pair within. It looked odd, but it took Zeph a moment to place why. The wall had unmetal's telltale iridescence, but the shimmering colors *shifted*, as though the unmetal were subtly bulging and deforming.

"What *is* that?" she said aloud, pulling her hand away from Ashok to rub at her eyes. It was almost nauseating to look at.

"Safety precautions. Nothing but the best. The walls of the new lab are flux-stabilized." He rapped the door proudly. "You couldn't get through this with a hundred blasters. You get used to the colors, I promise."

Safety precautions? She kept her thoughts to herself as he opened the door. *What exactly is he worried about?*

The basic layout of the lab hadn't changed, but it seemed like every room had been gutted and rebuilt. The eye-twisting flux-stabilized lining was thankfully invisible from the inside, but brand-new unmetal-and-glass partitions were everywhere. The deep *thrum* of equipment filled the air, subtly rising and falling. A massive communications array occupied the center of the atrium, the curving spikes of its image projector big enough to hold a life-sized view.

"You built all this in a year?" she said.

"Less," Ashok said. "We finished months ago. I brought in experimental builder-constructs from the artificial-motion facility, the very latest thing. Have you seen them? Muscle force-grown over a metal skeleton, stronger than humans and just as nimble. Right now they need a *dhakim* to control them, but there's research—" He cut off, frowned. "Is something wrong?"

"I'm just…" Zeph looked around. "I didn't think things would have changed so much."

"I don't know that I could have imagined it, either! But we've come so far. Let me show you my breakthrough. In here."

He led the way down a corridor and into a large open lab. It looked like a descendent of his first secret room, glass cases lined up one after the next. Most were empty, but in the one Ashok led her to—

Zeph's breath caught. She was not, as a rule, squeamish. The nature of her job required the calm slaughter and disassembly of animal specimens—she'd probably killed hundreds of vulpi over the years, carefully separating their component parts for analysis. The gory innards of an animal, heart and lungs and intestines, held no terrors for her. But *this* was something else altogether.

The thing floated in the tank like the world's ugliest fish. It looked like a blob of muscle and organs about the size of a large melon, covered in patchy, rotting skin and tufts of hair. Bones stuck out of it at odd angles, all jumbled together, jaws and ribs and phalanges.

And it was *alive*. Muscles rippled, and a single eye blinked lazily, regarding the world outside the tank with an incurious gaze.

"Chosen *fucking* defend," Zeph swore, forgetting for a moment she was talking to one of them. "What *is* that thing?"

"I know it doesn't look like much," Ashok said. "We're still early in the process, lots of kinks to iron out. But it *works*, Zeph."

"*What* works?"

"I call it a memetically self-assembling composite organism. 'Comp,' for short. Watch."

He went to another bench and came back with a small glass cage containing a white mouse. The animal ran in circles, panicked, while Ashok slotted the cage into an opening on top of the tank. A lever opened the cage and sent the mouse into the brine.

The comp *pounced* immediately. Tendrils unfolded from its disordered body, grabbing the struggling rodent and drawing it close. But the mouse wasn't devoured as Zeph might have expected. Instead it came neatly apart in a way that was horribly familiar, skin sloughing off and muscles unraveling into strands, bones and guts and brain exposed in perfect detail. The organic debris drifted over to the larger mass, which shifted to incorporate it, piece by piece.

"It uses *dhaka*?" Zeph whispered. Her throat was dry. "On itself?"

Ashok nodded happily. "It can take apart any animal it encounters and use its substance to modify its own form. I define an ideal set of functions, but it decides on its own how best to achieve them. That's the 'memetic' part. It's not really a *creature*, you see? It's a *phenomenon* that uses flesh as a medium, like a wave that propagates through water but isn't really part of it—"

"That's impossible," Zeph said. "You can't use *dhaka* on your own body. It's the first thing everyone asks, in training, but it can't be done."

"That's what I read, too." Ashok frowned. "But the records are... incomplete. I've been scouring the library, and the best I can figure is that this kind of research—I call it *reflective dhaka*—has been deliberately suppressed. Anything relating to it, other than its impossibility, has been purged from the archives."

"Purged?" Zeph watched the thing in the tank winding its tentacles back into a ball. "Why?"

"I don't know. Maybe because the Chosen of the time thought it would threaten their power. In the old days they were very reluctant to allow work on *dhaka* at all."

"You're a Chosen, aren't you?"

"I'm a believer in the modern empire. We use *dhaka* and *deiat* to improve life for everyone. Can you imagine what this could do once we perfect it? Farm animals that assemble themselves from table scraps. Pest killers that breed from their victims, then vanish when their task is done. Maybe even bodies for all of us that can repair themselves! Imagine no one dying of old age—" He stopped abruptly and looked at her. "Your mother. Sorry. I hope I didn't—sorry."

"It's... all right." His contrition, the slight awkwardness of it, was the essence of the old Ashok, the one she'd fallen in love with. The burning desire to help, to be kind, but without knowing quite how. "I'm just... surprised, I guess. This is a lot to take in."

"I know. I probably should have worked up to it. I've just gotten so caught up, these last few months, and I wanted to show you." He shook his head. "Every time I find something new, my first instinct is to bring it to you. I've missed you a great deal, Zeph. I didn't want to intrude on your sister, even with the blood-bond, but..."

He came in to kiss her again, more tentatively, as though he feared she'd pull away. Zeph leaned into him, pressing her body against his, trying to feel the same certainty she had a year before.

It'll be all right, she thought to herself. *He's brilliant. And I can help him. We love each other. Everything will be all right.*

When she opened her eyes, though, the thing in the tank was staring at her.

Life spun toward normal, though it never quite reached it, like a wobbling top precessing in slow circles. Zeph moved back in with Ashok, dispensing with the fiction of keeping her own quarters. Her position in the facility had changed, become that of Ashok's chief deputy, in fact if not in name. In part this was because every project other than Ashok's comps had been pushed to the sidelines, either canceled or limping along on scraps. The other researchers looked at her with envy and scorn—not just because she was sleeping with the boss, but because her work with him had the best of everything.

Ashok had conscripted staff from the other research projects in addition to funds and equipment. At Zeph's suggestion, this included Nia, whose own work was languishing. She was grateful, and they still met in the cafeteria for lunch most days, but something about the relationship had changed. There was a guarded look in Nia's eyes now that hadn't been there before.

Only a few trusted staff got to work directly with the comps. Ashok was worried their appearance would prejudice people against them, which Zeph had to admit was a fair concern. She'd tried to overcome her own instinctive reaction to the twisted balls of guts and muscle, but they still turned her stomach on occasion, especially when "feeding." *It's no worse than tearing flesh into fragments with our teeth and then dissolving it in acid, right?* But human digestion, at least, happened on the *in*side.

One thing was certain. She'd started reading, following the path Ashok had laid out, and he was right about reflective *dhaka* and any experiments in that direction being removed from the literature. Once you knew what you were looking for, there were gaps, careers and laboratories that *should* have produced results that were nowhere to be found. *It's amazing no one has tried this before now. Of course, why investigate what everyone knows is impossible?*

Or, more darkly, *had* it been tried before? Had the same forces that had culled the libraries cut short the careers—or lives—of those who poked in the wrong places? Spinakker's card was still in her coat pocket. She thought about throwing it out a dozen times and had never quite been able to, though each time it felt like a betrayal of Ashok and his work. A tiny voice at the back of her mind, however, repeated what the Intelligence agent had said. *It may be the best thing for Ashok and everyone else involved.*

In the dark of the night, she saw the comp's slow-blinking eye and wondered, *What if the research was purged for a good reason?*

Zeph, I need you. Ashok's voice in her mind, breaking her out of a reverie. *Bring Nia downstairs for the next experiment?*

Be there soon, Zeph sent back.

She'd been in their quarters, zoning out instead of making her way through a ponderous two-hundred-year-old tome of experimental histories. Zeph shook her head, shrugged her coat on, and went to the door. Nia was in her office, now on the first floor near Zeph's.

"He needs us," Zeph said, poking her head through the door. "The third vulpi test. Are you ready?"

"Inasmuch as I can be ready for *that*," Nia said with a sigh. She grabbed her own coat from the back of her chair. "Honestly, I don't see how you hang on to your lunch."

"I've opened up a lot of vulpi," Zeph said. "We're hoping this time it'll stay close to the goal state. Ashok's made some adjustments."

"I'll bet he has," Nia muttered. "That last one got a little out of control."

That, in a nutshell, was the problem with Ashok's brilliant new project. In theory, his controlling plan—imprinted on the stuff he called "self-replicating reflective agent"—should suffuse every aspect of a comp's being. It shouldn't be *able* to develop other than along the lines the Chosen had ordained. In practice, the things were forever finding loopholes in their instructions, taking dangerous shortcuts and discovering solutions that technically worked but were unusable or unstable. One comp, for example, had been intended to develop legs—it had in fact developed hundreds of them, each only a few centimeters long, spread out all across its body to allow it a weird rolling motion across the floor.

They reached the fifth floor and the entrance to the new lab. The space for today's experiment had been cleared out, so the long table bore only the big tank containing the comp and a smaller unmetal cylinder for the reflective agent. On the floor, a yearling vulpi grunted contentedly to itself, face buried in a bowl of mash. It wore a leather harness connected to a pully on the ceiling so it could be lifted.

Ashok was already there, staring in at the comp and making hurried notes. He grinned at Zeph and nodded to Nia.

"We're nearly ready," he said. "Any questions?"

"I think we can handle it," Nia said, with a sidelong look at Zeph. She griped about being essentially manual labor on these tests, like they were lab servants fresh from training. Zeph gave a tiny shrug. *She's right, but what are we going to do about it?*

Ashok connected a hose from the tank of reflective agent to the comp's jar, and at his direction Zeph opened a valve and let the stuff flow through. What exactly the "agent" *was* was Ashok's most closely guarded secret, one he hadn't shared even with her. It looked like a fine slurry of black particles that dissipated quickly in liquid; Ashok handled it like concentrated acid, though he insisted this was just a precaution. In some way that Zeph didn't fully understand, it instructed the comps as to their ultimate objectives and set the parameters by which they would evolve.

It took only a few seconds to work, but Ashok waited a full minute to be certain the agent had been completely absorbed. Then Zeph unfastened the top of the comp's tank, stepping back quickly as the creature twitched and stirred. Ashok retreated to the corner of the room, notebook in hand, while Zeph and Nia knelt beside the vulpi and double-checked its harness.

"Seems like a shame," Nia said, tugging on the pulley line.

"If you start feeling sorry for the vulpi, you're in the wrong line of work."

"Not that. Just a waste of good bacon." She patted the animal. "You're such a delicious little thing, aren't you?"

Zeph chuckled. She gave Ashok the thumbs-up, and he gestured for them to proceed. Nia stepped back to work the pulley while Zeph steadied the vulpi.

Most yearlings were trusting enough that they took being lifted off the ground in stride. They'd been adjusted to be docile at this stage in their life cycle, to make herding and culling easy on the farmers. Only in their breeder stage did they become ornery, before turning sessile as terminals, ready for their final harvest. But in a wild population, behavioral traits were hard to breed completely true.

The vulpi began to struggle, legs milling wildly so it swung about on the line. She grabbed its front legs to calm it, but it spun about with a squeal, powerful hind legs kicking. They caught Zeph low in the chest, sending her stumbling backward with an *oof* and pushing the vulpi the other way. The animal, swinging on the rope like a pendulum on a line, rammed its bristly flank into Nia's face as she turned.

Time seemed to slow. Nia let go of the line and the vulpi plummeted back into its pen. Nia herself staggered backward toward the table. Ashok was shouting something, but Zeph was still fighting for breath, and she couldn't move fast enough—

Nia's shoulder bumped the comp's jar. It rocked on its base, liquid sloshing.

Oh, fuck.

Nia grabbed the table to steady herself. The jar rocked back, then settled. Zeph managed to get some air in her lungs and straightened up.

Lucky—

A black tendril whipped out of the open jar, fast as a pouncing cat. It slapped wetly across Nia's face, curling below her chin to grip her throat. Her mouth opened in the start of a scream, and then—

She came apart. Her clothes tore to shreds as her bones splayed outward, skin splitting neatly into strips. For a moment she hung there, roughly humanoid in shape, limbs fastidiously rearranged into tubes of muscle, coils of nerves, long bones and small. Her eyes were wide and twitching as her facial muscles peeled away to reveal the skull beneath. Behind her, the comp began to heave itself out of the jar, more tendrils stretching toward its waiting meal.

Zeph was screaming, a high, sustained note she hadn't know she could hit, the terrified squeal of the vulpi a discordant counterpoint. She backed away until she was up against the door, hand fumbling blindly for the handle. There was nothing in her mind but the need to get *away*, to flee from the nightmare—

White light filled her vision. The fire of the sun blasted up from the floor, a pyre that consumed table, jar, vulpi, and comp, along with the twitching mess of organic parts that had once been Zeph's best friend. It blinked out a few moments later, leaving slumped unmetal and ashes. Ashok, in the other corner of the room, lowered his hand and met Zeph's horrified eyes.

Are you all right? he sent her. *My love—*

Zeph finally found the handle. She shoved the door open and ran.

She was still moving.

How long could you live like that? Would you feel yourself coming apart? Would it hurt?

When she disassembled a vulpi, she conscientiously killed it first, a simple twist to still its heart and a short wait until it stopped twitching. But the comp had no reason to do that. They'd never instructed it to. *Only to grow, to use whatever it could grab and build itself toward a perfection we defined...*

In her mind, bones twisted outward, ripping through cloth, over and over. The air in the bathroom stank of vomit.

Zeph, please. Ashok's mental voice, followed by a knock at the door. "Zeph? Can you please just tell me you're not hurt?"

Zeph couldn't make her voice work, even if she'd wanted to. She huddled against the counter, pressed beside the toilet, her mouth rank and acid with bile.

"It was awful. I know. I'm so sorry. We should have...It doesn't matter. It won't happen again, I promise you. I was cutting corners I shouldn't have. We'll get a proper apparatus for testing, so no one is even close to the comp. You can help me design it. Zeph?"

She curled up even tighter. *Go away.*

Zeph wasn't sure if she'd meant to send him that thought, but after a few moments his reply came back.

Okay. I'm going to go clean up. I'll leave you alone for a while. When you're ready to talk, please let me know.

More footsteps outside. Then silence.

Zeph stayed where she was for a long time. The aches and pains of her body felt distant, as though they were happening to someone else, a character in a story she was reading.

Eventually she came back to herself, a little. She got up from where she'd been wedged, coughed over the toilet a little more, washed her mouth out. She opened the bathroom door and staggered through the administrator's quarters, looking for Ashok. He wasn't there, and the door was closed. She locked it and went to her drawers.

A few minutes later, sitting in front of the communications desk, she punched the appropriate code and took a depth breath. The image projector remained empty, but a bored-sounding voice said, "Who are you looking for?"

"This is Zephkiel, of the Stoneroot lab," Zeph said, in the calmest voice she could manage. "I'd like to speak to Spinakker, please."

Maya

The morning air was a cold shock against Maya's face. She stared unseeing at the jagged peaks around them, her mind full of images from her dream.

Plaguespawn. Ashok had been making *plaguespawn*, before the Plague War had even begun. *We always thought it was the ghouls who released them. But...*

"Well," Kit said from the ground, "it's good that *some* of us are getting laid."

Maya blinked and shook herself, emerging from her reverie. Kit's little spider scuttled up her body, tiny claws pricking, and settled on her shoulder. With an effort, Maya focused on the here and now, and her brow creased in a frown.

"Are you sneaking into my tent?" she said. The tiny construct contrived to look innocent.

"No, more's the pity. Gyre kept yelling at me about that. But my hearing's pretty good."

"Oh." Maya thought back to last night and felt her face grow warm. In the...heat of the moment, she'd forgotten there was someone else nearby. *Not that I was the only one.* "Um. Sorry."

"Why would you apologize?" Kit said. "These mountain treks are the perfect opportunity. It's cold out there, warm in the tent, you're close together..." She gave a wistful sigh. "For the first few days, anyway. After that everyone smells so bad it can be hard to work up the courage."

"That's an attractive image. Hopefully we won't be out that long."

"You never know," Kit said contemplatively. "This is about where Gyre and I fucked for the first time. We got stuck in a cave during a blizzard, we had to huddle together for warmth, that sort of thing."

Maya, who'd been taking a drink from her canteen, coughed violently. "*Thank* you for that image of my *brother.*"

"Honestly, I wasn't sure he would go for it. He can be kind of uptight sometimes."

"Really." Maya glanced at Kit again, then looked away. "How so?"

"Curious after all?"

"Not about *that*," Maya snapped, then softened. "About Gyre. He's my brother, but I hardly know him."

"Do you remember him from when you were kids?"

"Only a little. He was...responsible. I remember him always making sure his work was done before we would play. But he was always good to me. I got sick a lot, and he used to sit up nights."

"He told me you were bossy and wild."

Maya laughed. "He was probably right."

They walked in silence for a few moments. Beq was up ahead, leading the column of constructs beside the little river. They'd turned out of the valley of the Brink, following a smaller tributary that Kit said would lead them directly to Mount Shroud. Apart from the steady footfall of Kit's many bodies and the rustle of the wind, it was quiet, as though they were the only living things for kilometers.

"When I met Gyre," Kit said, "I was desperate. Did he tell you my story?"

Maya shook her head. Kit's little spider shifted, claws pricking.

"Let's just say I deserved my cognomen. Doomseeker. And he'd spent so long looking for the Tomb, the ghoul city, that he was feeling pretty desperate too. We combined our forces to make some extremely poor decisions."

"Was stabbing me one of them?" Maya said.

"Maybe. In retrospect. Did I say I'm sorry for that?"

"Not so far."

"I'm sorry, I guess. I thought I had a...a way to escape." She gestured to herself with a limb. "You can see how well that worked out for me."

Maya hesitated a moment. Kit's tone was flippant as usual, but there was something more underneath it. It was hard to remember, having known her only as a sarcastic spider-construct, that she'd once been a living woman.

"Anyway," Kit said into the silence. "I guess Gyre figured out he'd gotten it wrong in time."

"I guess he did."

"Hey!" Beq shouted, waving back at them. "Hurry up!"

Maya picked up the pace to catch up with her. They were turning a bend in the riverbed, and from where Beq was standing they were finally clear of a shoulder of rock that kinked the wall of the valley. Ahead loomed a massive mountain peak, which stretched upward until it abruptly vanished into a wall of thick, dark cloud. Maya saw a bright streak flicker through it and heard the distant rumble of thunder.

"That's Mount Shroud?" she said.

"That's it," Kit confirmed.

"Please tell me we don't have to climb it," Beq said.

"Fortunately no," Kit said. "At least not on the outside. The place is full of tunnels, and they've been pretty well explored by scavengers. Sarah got me in to see Lynnia's maps. There's a spot with an unmetal door nobody's ever been able to open, about halfway up the mountain. If we're right, that's the flitter base."

"And I should be able to open it if it's a *deiat* lock," Maya said. "Or burn through, if worse comes to worst."

"Exactly. But keep your eyes open. The reports don't say anything about lots of plaguespawn, but there are always some around."

They'd been remarkably unbothered by plaguespawn so far, but their luck couldn't hold forever. Maya nodded grimly and took Beq's hand.

The walk to the base of the mountain took the rest of the day, and they camped again in the lee of the mighty peak, close enough that the rolls of thunder made the tent shudder. Neither the racket nor the long day's march deterred Beq at all, however, and while Maya did her best to remember that Kit was waiting outside, when Beq's hands were on her, her best didn't amount to much. The little spider made no comment the following morning, but Maya could almost *feel* her smirking.

Kit led them to the tunnel entrance, a crack in the rock widened into a tunnel big enough to slip through with only a slight crouch. Detritus around the base indicated that they weren't the first party to come this way, but there was nothing fresh, only the remains of campfires and bits of broken equipment. A row of graves, marked by rusting swords stuck point-first in the ground, was a bit more ominous.

"Makes sense," Kit said. "People die out here, and nobody wants to haul them back to town."

"A lonely place to die," Beq said, fiddling with her spectacles.

"That's the mountains in a nutshell," Kit said. "Come on."

Gyre

They made better time once they swung out of the hills, the swiftbirds settling in to the fast, ground-devouring trot they could keep up for kilometer after kilometer. Gyre worried they were too visible, but speed was a better defense now than secrecy. Give the Corruptor too long to work out what had happened, and there would be a regiment of Perfected camped around the Gate.

As they rode, Gyre summarized what he knew. Maya's offer, the Purifier, the Corruptor, the flight to Deepfire. To Gyre's surprise, the news of the emergence of an ancient Chosen seemed to bother Apphia less than the fact that he'd allied himself with a pair of centarchs.

"You really trust her?" she said, voice raised over the *whip-whap-whip* sound of the running birds.

"Maya? I do."

"She tried to kill you. Several times, from the sound of it."

"I did the same to her. Anyway, Maya's...straightforward. If she's against you, she'll tell you she's against you and why. If she says she's with you, you can count on her."

"I'm not sure I believe any centarch would turn on the Order."

"If you asked her, she'd tell you the Order has turned on *her*. Working with the Corruptor and against their ideals."

"Do you believe that?"

"I believe that *she* believes it," Gyre said carefully. "She's always been like that. Idealistic."

Apphia snorted. "I had to grow out of *that* early."

"You weren't born with the power to burn cities."

"Once we're in Deepfire—" Apphia began, but Kit interrupted.

"South! Riders!"

Gyre turned. They were crossing a broad plain, heading up toward the next line of hills where the Gate was tucked away. It wasn't much more than ten or twenty kilometers to go. But about an equal distance away, to the south, a cloud of dust was rising. *Riders, and more than a few of them.* Even his silver eye couldn't yet make out the details.

Estimating speeds and distances, he scowled. They'd made good time, and it was still at least an hour to noon. They'd get there well before the Gate opened, but their pursuers would arrive not long after.

"Kit," Gyre said. "Do you have a body with Tanax?"

"No, but I'll find him," Kit said. "He's out of the palace, though. It'll take time to get back."

"Tell him to hurry," Gyre said. "We're going to have company when we get there."

The swiftbirds ran, their steady pace eating away the distance, but the dust cloud grew ever larger. If their opponents had been on swift-birds as well, they might have been able to cut the fugitives off; fortunately, they rode warbirds, which could manage a short sprint for a charge but not over a longer distance. Whoever was in command knew where their quarry was headed, though, and led their men toward the Gate rather than trying to give chase. Their two parallel courses converged, growing nearer and nearer as the morning wore on.

By the time they splashed through a ford to cross the small river that ran by the Gate, Gyre's silver eye could make out a dozen birds and their armored riders. His swiftbird covered the last few hundred meters to the Gate in a mad dash, Nina and Apphia close behind him. The slender archway was right where he'd left it, as were the bodies of the Legionaries he'd killed on his way in. *Apparently no one has been through since then.* They stank after days in the sun, baking in their armor. Flies buzzed furiously.

"Urgh," Apphia said, holding her nose. "Now what?"

It was still at least a quarter of an hour to noon. "Kit?" Gyre said.

"Found Tanax. We're heading back to the palace."

"You may have noticed we're a little short on time." The oncoming birds pounded along the riverbank, dust billowing behind them.

"Oh really? Because I was encouraging him to dawdle and take in the sights!"

"How close are the rest of your bodies?"

"Not close enough," Kit said. "They can't keep up with swiftbirds."

Plaguing fuck. Gyre stared at the approaching cavalry. He could make out white unmetal armor. *A squad of Legionaries on warbirds. I've faced worse, right?* He checked the satchel of alchemicals, but it hadn't filled itself since last time—there was a smoker and a sparker left, and that was all.

"Nina, take your sister and find cover," Gyre said.

"I can take myself," Apphia said, swinging out of the saddle. She still walked with a limp, but her eyes were determined. Venturing close to one of the stinking corpses, she picked up the soldier's blaster rifle and checked its sunsplinter. "Over by those rocks, behind the Gate."

Nina nodded grimly, unslinging her own weapon. They took the birds with them, out of the line of fire. Gyre stood alone in front of the Gate, sparker in hand, and waited.

As they closed, the lead riders raised blasters of their own and opened fire. A spatter of bolts sprayed the ground around Gyre, detonating with a shower of earth, but the few that hit him directly simply vanished into his *deiat* shield. That spooked the Legionaries enough to slow their advance. But they didn't stop, drawing swords as they came on. When they were close enough, Gyre hurled the sparker in a low arc, pitched to land just ahead of the leaders.

His second-to-last alchemical detonated with a roar, erupting in a continuous shower of white-hot flecks of burning metal and a fountain of evil-smelling smoke. Even the warbirds shied away, and a couple of them panicked, squawking wildly and flapping their vestigial wings. The group broke up, spreading out, some of the soldiers dismounting while others fought to control their frantic animals.

One white-armored figure came on, bringing his warbird expertly through the smoke and ignoring the hissing sparks. Unlike the rest, this bird was armored, and the style—

Oh, plaguefire.

More *cracks*, this time from behind him. Apphia and Nina opened fire together, concentrating on the leading figure. One bolt slammed into his warbird, detonating against unmetal armor and sending the creature staggering. The other would have caught the rider, but he drew a bladeless sword, a blue-white line of raw *deiat* power springing into existence to intercept the bolt. He jumped from the saddle, a quick whistle sending his mount limping away to the rear.

"Va'aht," Gyre said. *Keep his attention.* Neither Nina nor Apphia had *deiat* shields, but the centarch didn't know that. Fortunately, Va'aht seemed as eager for a confrontation as Gyre was.

"Silvereye."

Gyre drew his sword and forced a grin. "How's the leg?"

The centarch pulled his helmet back so Gyre could see his sneer. His face was hollow and bony, and his purple-black hair whipped in the wind.

"Very funny," Va'aht said. "How's the eye?"

"It itches sometimes," Gyre said. "And aches a bit when it rains."

"If only I'd had the courtesy to slit your throat instead."

"If only I'd had the strength to slit yours," Gyre said. "But that mistake can be rectified."

"Indeed it can." Va'aht stalked back and forth, a meter beyond striking distance.

The more he wants to talk, the better. Gyre had to work hard not to look over his shoulder at the Gate.

"Tell me when Tanax is close," he murmured, and Kit pinched his shoulder in response. Louder, he said, "I thought you might have had enough last time."

"Last time you surprised me," the centarch said. "Or, rather, the weapons you scavenged from Chosen-know-where did."

"Would you like to know where?" Gyre said, improvising. "It doesn't matter now."

"Not particularly. Once I cut off your arms and legs, I'll deliver you to His Radiance, and you'll tell him everything he wants to know."

"Is that your new emperor? You do know he's a monster."

"He is *Chosen*." For a moment, the iron faith of a true believer showed in Va'aht's features. "Whatever else he may be is irrelevant. Our purpose is to serve."

"Excuse me if I think a little more highly of humanity than that."

"It doesn't matter what you think." Va'aht pulled his helmet back into place and brought up his haken. "Not anymore."

Gyre activated his augments. Va'aht came straight at him, not bothering with *deiat* manifestations that Gyre's shield would shrug off. His form was tight, too, with none of the casual reliance on his panoply he'd shown the first time. *He* has *learned something.*

But Gyre was still faster, and his ghoul eye showed him the shadowy paths of the centarch's strike. He stepped away from the first thrust, parried the second—

Va'aht changed his line of attack at the last minute, his blue-white blade slipping over to reach for Gyre's side. Gyre had to throw himself backward, the crackling buzz of the energy weapon missing him by centimeters. Va'aht followed up quickly, another simple thrust that turned into a complex disengage at the last possible moment. It was all Gyre could do to parry and parry again, giving ground.

He knows me. Somehow, the centarch had intuited how Gyre's eye functioned. His attacks changed unpredictably at the last moment, thwarting the shadow-world predictions. *Impressive, given that we only fought for a minute or so.* Gyre had to consciously ignore the projections, focus on the reality, his speed barely enough to counter the centarch's greater skill.

More armored figures were filtering forward. The Legionaries, dismounted and swords drawn, edged around the still-roaring sparker and moved to surround him.

"This would be a *really* good time for a way out, Kit," Gyre managed, parrying another determined onslaught with a spray of sparks.

"Nearly there!" Kit said. "We're running down the steps."

Nearly wasn't going to cut it. The Legionaries were surrounding him—Gyre danced away from Va'aht and tried to engage one, but she simply backed off and let the centarch catch up. The Gate was only a few meters away, but they were going to cut him off before he got there.

"Go to Apphia and get them running for the Gate," Gyre said.

"But—"

"Now!"

The little spider leapt from his shoulder, scuttling between the legs of a Legionary toward where Apphia and her sister had taken cover. Gyre parried, dodged away from Va'aht, parried another strike from a Legionary behind him, and dodged again. He grabbed for his satchel with his free hand, yanked the smoker out, then ripped the empty bag free from its strap.

"Stop!" he shouted, grenade and sack held up together. "You know what *this* is full of, don't you?"

"Self-immolation, Silvereye?" Va'aht said, voice metallic in the confines of his helmet. "You don't strike me as the type."

But he halted, just for a moment. The Legionaries stopped advancing, spreading out a little, braced against the coming explosion.

"He won't," Va'aht ordered. "It's a bluff. Take him!"

Gyre smiled savagely and hurled the sack to the ground. Va'aht jerked backward, blue-white energy blooming around him in a protective barrier, while his Legionaries crouched or threw themselves flat in anticipation of the blast.

The smoker burst with a *pop*, a thick white cloud hissing out all around Gyre. The rest of the satchel was empty, of course, and he guessed he had perhaps three seconds before they figured that out. But with his augmentations, three seconds could get him a long way.

One, and he was past the line of Legionaries, outpacing the spreading smoke cloud, leaping over the rotting bodies and running for the Gate.

Two, and the most beautiful sight in the world, a curtain of silver-gray descending to fill the archway. Apphia and Nina were already running for it, throwing themselves through.

Three, and Gyre skidded to a halt, sword raised in salute, unable to resist a parting shot.

"Give the Emperor my regards!"

He stepped backward, bright daylight turning instantly to the gloom under the Spike. Tanax stood facing the Gate, one of Kit's bodies on his shoulder, his face flushed and out of breath from a long run.

"Close it!" Gyre shouted, as soon as he spotted Apphia and Nina on the floor nearby. "Close it and lock it!"

The Gate's misty curtain went black. Gyre collapsed to his knees, struggling for breath—half from the exertion, and half from imagining the look on Va'aht's face when the smoke cleared.

"I apologize for anything I said earlier," he managed. "That was *excellent* timing."

"It's good to see you." Tanax shook his head wearily. "We need your help. The city is about to explode."

Gyre couldn't contain it. He leaned back, elbows on the stone floor, and broke down laughing.

Chapter Fourteen

The plaguespawn tensed, exposed muscles coiling, mismatched teeth bared. Then it leapt, fast as a snake, jaws open wide—

And Kit's foot came down hard, crushing the thing into paste against the smooth stone floor.

"Thanks," Maya said, fastidiously stepping around the little black spot.

"No problem," Kit said. "Quick little plaguepits, aren't they?"

They'd run into a few plaguespawn since entering the tunnels, but they'd all been like this one, little bigger than the rats and bats that were their normal prey. Their presence, Kit said, was a sure sign that no one had traversed these routes for some time.

"Plaguespawn look for light and heat, right? And humans have both. So a tunnel that sees a lot of traffic is going to attract all the plaguespawn in the area, and these little ones will get thinned out pretty quickly. They're nastier than rats, but not nearly as smart."

Maya was also beginning to see what Elariel meant about the difference between ghoul architecture and Chosen. The ghoul tunnels were perfectly circular, with no right angles in sight. They also had a regular texture to them, as though they'd been chewed out by some monstrous worm, rather than the melted, glass-like finish she was used to from the Forge. To build something like this *without* using *deiat* was an impressive accomplishment. *And Kit says there are tunnels like this all over the mountains...*

She shook her head, concentrating on the map. They'd copied it from one of Lynnia's—the alchemist collected sketches and reports from scavengers and sold the maps to outbound expeditions. The dates on this one were old, none from the previous decade, which matched Kit's assertion that no one had explored here in some time.

Maya could find no logic in the spaghetti-tangle of tunnels and branches, with intermittent dead ends and sharp turns. *Either the ghouls used it for something I don't understand, or else they made it confusing on purpose.* The latter, actually, seemed plausible. All these tunnels had been dug during the Plague War, after the ghouls had rebelled against the Chosen and been pushed underground.

Generations of scavengers had carefully charted the twists and drop-offs as they systematically stripped out anything of value. The spot they were headed to, deep within the mountain, bore the annotation *A panel of unmetal, four meters by four, deeply embedded within the surrounding rock. No apparent means of access.* Under that, in another hand, was scrawled, *Wartime barricade? Accessible via another entrance?*

None had ever been found, evidently, and with the plunder exhausted the scavengers had moved on. *But none of them ever had a centarch along.*

Kit's small bodies were in the vanguard, with the larger ones bearing their packs bringing up the rear. Maya kept a small *deiat* light hovering over their heads, while Beq peered around in fascinated excitement, clicking her lenses to zoom in on some interesting detail. After a while, though, she gave an irritated sigh.

"What's wrong?" Maya asked.

"It's like walking through a museum where someone burned all the paintings to keep warm." She glared at Kit's nearest body. "We could have learned so much from a place like this, but your people were more interested in grinding it up to make bombs."

"And quick-heal, and bone-break potion, and a hundred other things," Kit said. "Besides, don't blame me. Most of this was scavenged before I was born. *And* it's not exactly like your Order was out here conducting scientific inquiries."

"We should have been," Beq grumbled, looking to Maya for support.

"No argument from me," Maya said.

In fact, she mused, how much had the Order's mission gotten twisted over the years? *We tracked down Hollis Plaguetouch because he was a* dhakim. *But that was one of the Corruptor's spiders. How many other* dhakim *were his creatures?* The Order had always been surprised at how knowledge of *dhaka* would spread, no matter how thoroughly it was stamped out. *Dogmatics like Nicomidi blamed the ghouls. But I wonder whether it was the Corruptor all along.*

"Here," Kit said, breaking her reverie. Maya turned the corner and found a patch of iridescent silver in the wall. It broke into the smooth roundness of the corridor like an intrusion from another world, surrounded by a scatter of tumbled boulders. Kit's bodies spread out to either side of it, and Beq rapped it with one hand.

"Definitely unmetal," she said. "Which is weird, here in a ghoul warren. That's promising."

"I'll try to open it," Maya said. If she had to, she could cut through, but if this was a door, it might still function. *Hopefully one that doesn't require a particular code or command.* She touched her haken and directed a stream of *deiat* power toward the blank surface.

To her relief, something inside took hold immediately, drinking in energy. More energy than she expected, actually, for a simple door—it reminded her of activating the Archive. The panel split down the center, the sections retracting smoothly into the walls. Lights came on, revealing a corridor beyond—a more "normal" corridor, in Maya's view, square walled and painted off-white.

There was a grinding sound, rock on rock. Maya thought it came from the door as well, some bit of broken machinery, until Kit shouted a warning.

"Constructs!" The boulders were unfolding, stony skins breaking apart in a horribly familiar fashion. Underneath their rocky exterior the constructs were humanoid, black muscles stretched over steel frames equipped with long, curved blades. One of them slashed at Kit's closest body, which skittered out of the way.

"Ghoul trap," Beq said. "They couldn't get in, but they didn't want anyone else to—"

"Or else they want to destroy whatever's inside," Maya said. Her haken ignited with a *snap-hiss*. "Get behind me. Kit, get inside and see if there's anything waiting for us."

"Got it!" Kit chirped. Her bodies, faster than the bulky ghoul constructs, scurried past Maya on either side. Beq followed, drawing her pistol and sighting over Maya's shoulder. A blaster bolt *cracked*, then vanished just before impact.

A deiat shield. Maya gave ground, letting the ponderous rock-things bunch up in the doorway. Her haken burned in front of her, but taking the monsters on up close wasn't appealing. It had taken her and Gyre both to bring one down under the Purifier. *On the other hand...*

She raised her palm. A line of fire lanced out, vanishing where it touched the first construct, the *deiat* energy swirling into nothingness like water disappearing down a bathtub drain. Maya narrowed her gaze.

Everything has a limit. She pulled harder. The fire went from orange to yellow to white, so bright it hurt the eye. The construct kept coming, but slower, leaning forward. Streamers of fire wrapped it, dancing wildly around the flickering globe of protection.

Harder. As she had against Baselanthus. *The fire of creation. The sun itself.* The air *throbbed*. Rock around the entrance was melting, white-hot and dripping like a candle in a forge. Hot air rushed around Maya, her hair whipping wildly. The shield was a wound in the luminous world.

Then, abruptly, it was gone. Between one moment and the next, the barrier collapsed, and Maya's full power hit the unprotected construct. It came apart like a pile of dry leaves in a windstorm, body shredded, skeleton turned to metal droplets. The one behind it lasted only a second longer before it, too, was overwhelmed. Then the next, and the next, the beam punching through them in turn until it hit the opposite wall of the tunnel in a great blast of molten rock.

Maya closed her fingers, and the blaze vanished. Instinctively, her hand went to the Thing, expecting to find it white-hot, but the little arcana was cold and dead beneath her shirt. The limits it had placed on her power were gone.

"*After all this time.*" The voice was faint, nearly inaudible amid the swirling hot wind and the ping of cooling metal. "*The one I have been waiting for.*"

"Who's there?" Maya raised her haken, looking around for the source. *I have had a lifetime's worth of voices in my head already.* "Where are you?"

No one answered.

"You heard that, right?" Maya said to Kit's little spider.

"The last bit," Kit said. "Something about waiting for someone?"

Maya breathed out, a little relieved. *At least there isn't someone* else *with direct access to my mind.*

"Which means," Kit went on, "that somebody knows we're here."

Maya looked over the molten doorway and shrugged.

"At this point," she said, "I think we've abandoned subtlety."

The facility beyond the door was exactly what Xalen had predicted. The corridor split, one way leading to a set of rooms with low tables that looked like an office or cafeteria. The other direction ended in a huge, high-ceilinged room facing a massive pair of doors. A variety of arcana, none of which Maya understood, were mounted on carts or projecting out of the ground. The three vehicles that stood among it, at least, were comprehensible enough.

"Flitters," Beq confirmed, barely restraining her delight as she rushed forward. Maya hesitated, a warning coming to her lips, but she bit it back. *Beq knows what she's doing.* And Kit's bodies were already spread around the room—if there was anything obviously dangerous, she'd have said something.

While recognizable as the same kind of vehicle they'd flown in Sky-reach, these flitters were clearly more sophisticated. The ones in the city had been, essentially, a big bathtub or rowboat with an arcana engine mounted on the back, about as aerodynamic as a sack of bricks. These had four seats inside a snub-nosed, streamlined canopy, unmetal on the bottom and transparent above. Beq descended on them like a starving man on a banquet, pulling a heavy leather wallet of tools out of her pack.

"Anything else here?" Maya asked Kit.

"Not that I can find. No exits other than the big doors. Hear any more voices?"

Maya scowled. "No."

"This thing is going to need some work," Beq announced, struggling to pull a curved unmetal plate off the flitter. Maya stepped forward to help, but one of Kit's bodies was already there, grabbing the piece with its forelimbs. Others clustered around.

"But you can fix it?" Maya said.

"I think so." Beq peered at the revealed arcana, a labyrinth of crystals and sparkling wire. "I may have to steal parts from the other two."

"As long as it will get us there and back." Maya grinned, but Beq gave a serious nod.

"It's a matter of stress on the side-load boards. The couplings are unmetal, but there's dust all through the gyro—I can probably clean it—" Her monologue devolved into muttering as she adjusted her spectacles, leaning forward into the guts of the machine. Kit's bodies stood at the ready beside her.

"Well." Maya cleared her throat. "I'll just leave you to it, then."

Since just lurking behind Beq felt vaguely off-putting—though

Maya was certain that Beq herself was completely unaware of it—she decided to give the rest of the facility a closer look. Going back to the room with the tables, she poked in the corners and examined a few scraps of graying, moldy paper.

"Is this the sort of place you'd find, when you were scavenging?" she asked Kit.

"Not really. It was usually more...weapons and armor, military stuff from the war." The little spider gripped her collar. "Sorry, I can't talk at the moment. Helping Beq with some tight work."

"Ah. Go ahead."

Maya lifted a shred of paper, which crumbled between her fingers. Before it vanished entirely, she made out some kind of drawing—a crude one, stick figures. *Hmm.* Experimentally, she sat at one of the tables. Even without a cushion, it was so low she couldn't get her knees underneath.

At the back of the room was a doorway leading to another chamber of similar size, empty except for heaps of splintered wood and fungus that might have once been furniture. Another door led onward, this one closed but unlocked. The third chamber featured unmetal gantries, like the skeletons of buildings in miniature. They were only as high as Maya's chin, but each one had a tiny ladder, meant for small hands—

Perspective shifted, recontextualizing what she saw. *Bunk beds. These are bunk beds.* The frames, anyway, with mattresses and bedding long since rotted to shreds. There were a couple dozen of them, none long enough for Maya herself.

"It's a nursery," she told Kit.

She'd never imagined the Chosen having nurseries. In fact, she'd never pictured the Chosen having children—in her mind's eye they were always fully grown, mantled in terrible power. But of course they must have had children, and places to take care of them. *But why here?*

"Hmm?" Kit said. "What is?"

"This." Maya gestured. "It's all for children. Beds, a playroom, a dining room."

"Oh." The little spider skittered forward and looked around. "Odd."

"Nobody's found one before?"

"Not that I know of. The Chosen mostly didn't live in the mountains if they could help it. They came here to kill ghouls."

And they wouldn't bring their kids for that. There was one more door, but it led only to a small chamber Maya assumed was a toilet, overgrown with ropy fungus. *So not much of a nursery, then.* She wouldn't have wanted to try to take care of a few dozen kids in this tiny space.

"Maybe it was for humans," she wondered aloud. "They brought servants into the mountains, surely."

"I assume. Mostly soldiers, though."

Maybe... There was the wisp of an idea in her mind, but Kit interrupted before it gelled.

"Beq says she's ready."

Maya turned and jogged back to the main chamber. Beq was replacing a large panel, two of Kit's spiders assisting. She wiped her hands on her trousers, leaving gray stripes, and gave Maya a thumbs-up.

"Didn't have to replace the whole board," she said. "Or the gyro. So we shouldn't end up like last time."

"Last time?" Kit said.

"Maya had to run the flitter without the controls and guidance," Beq said. "It didn't go well."

"I'd like to see *you* try it," Maya said, grinning. "We got there in the end, didn't we?"

"And you only almost tipped us over the side in two or three spots."

"Well, let me know if you want to walk next time." Maya paused in front of the sleek flitter. "So what do I do?"

"Just feed it power. The engine should take care of the rest."

Maya touched her haken and directed a tendril of *deiat* at the arcana. It grabbed hold eagerly, sucking energy into its internal reserves. The flitter began to hum, and then, without fuss, it rose several inches into the air, shedding a layer of dust.

"Yes!" Beq grabbed Maya excitedly, smearing her with dust as well. "Told you it would work."

She tapped on the glass, and a panel swung outward, allowing them to enter. Beq took a seat in the front, behind a set of arcana controls. Maya took the chair beside her, and four of Kit's small bodies piled into the back.

"The rest will have to stay here," Kit said, one of her larger bodies settling beside the hovering craft. "I'll keep a watch."

"You're sure you can fly this?" Maya said.

"Reasonably sure," Beq said, examining the crystals, levers, and dials. "There can't be that much to it, right?" Her eyes were aglow with excitement. "You need to open the doors."

"Right." Maya sent another thread of *deiat* upward. There was a *crunch* as the double doors pulled apart, sliding along the wall to reveal an upward-sloping passage. More lights came on to illuminate it.

A new sound filled the chamber, a distant shriek that it took Maya a moment to identify as the wind. Eddies gusted around the flitter, raising swirling dust devils.

"Hold on tight," Beq muttered. She edged one of the levers forward.

The little craft rose, very slowly. Beq tilted the lever farther and their speed increased. Another tweak and they started forward as well, heading smoothly for the shaft. Beside them, Kit waved.

Beq's control was, Maya had to admit, considerably steadier than her own attempt had been. *She gets to use the* levers, *though.* The shaft was wide enough that an occasional sideways lurch didn't put them in danger of colliding with the walls. Meter by meter they rose, lights crawling past at steady intervals, the muffled sound of the wind growing louder. Flickering stark-white illumination began to war with the stones. Then, at last, they reached the surface.

The shaft was open at this end, concealed in a deep fold in the craggy surface of Mount Shroud. Rising past it, they were instantly engulfed in a driving rain, which sent rivulets of black grime running along the flitter's windscreen. The wind raged and screamed, and the flitter lurched as it caught the brunt of it, doing unpleasant things to Maya's stomach.

Thick dark cloud surrounded them completely, concealing the flank of the mountain after only a few dozen meters. They were within Mount Shroud's permanent thunderstorm, Maya realized, and to underscore the point lightning flickered overhead, its brilliance throwing stark shadows. The *boom* that followed a moment later resonated in her bones.

"This. Is. *Amazing.*" Kit's tiny spider jumped off Maya's shoulder, skittering past the control board and pressing itself against the glass. Another lightning bolt tore past with a ripping *crack*, and Kit jumped in delight. "Can you make it go fast? We need to go *fast.*"

"We absolutely do not," Maya said. Her stomach roiled. Somehow *not* being at the controls was worse than being at them and not knowing what she was doing. "Beq, do not go fast."

"Oh, come on," Kit said. "Do a loop, at least. Just a little loop."

"Please be quiet," Beq said, her tongue poking out from between her teeth as she concentrated. "Or I'll end up doing a loop right into the side of the mountain."

"That would be fine too," Kit said.

"Speaking for those of us *without* backup bodies, it would not," Maya said.

The flitter rose clear of the mountain. Its speed became nearly impossible to judge, with identical blackness in every direction. Shifting winds made the craft lurch and judder, spraying the rain across its canopy. A bead of sweat ran down from Beq's hairline and hung from the tip of her nose. Maya thought about brushing it away but decided against it.

Lightning *cracked* around them, a snaking, twisting bolt that left Maya's eyes full of burning afterimages.

"The flitter's protected from those," she muttered. "Right?"

The drop of sweat fell from Beq's nose and splashed on the control lever. "I'm really hoping we don't have to find out."

And then, abruptly, there was light.

Not daylight. There were still black clouds in every direction, but they were farther away, as though they'd flown into a giant cavity on the inside of the thunderstorm. Lightning flashed and crackled across the inner edge of a vast oval space, but didn't cross the invisible boundary. Actinic blue-white light stabbed out from the center to match the storm's fury, enormous beams sweeping over the roiling face of the clouds in a long, slow circuit. One of them caught the flitter for a moment, throwing Maya and Beq into sharp relief.

When it passed, and Maya blinked away the dazzle, she could see softer lights illuminating the surface of...something. At first her mind refused to parse it as a single object, insisting that each patch of brilliance must be a separate island hovering in the center of the cloud. As they continued to rise, though, parallax resolved it into one gargantuan shape, like a whale to the flitter's minnow, a mountain of unmetal hanging impossibly in the air.

The skyfortress *Pride in Power* had the classic flattened-teardrop shape, thickest at the rounded front edge and narrowing to a long, thin "tail" at the rear. Its surface was smooth, almost featureless, scored with barely visible crisscrossing lines. Maya had seen it before, in the projected image Ashok had shown them at the Forge, but then the skyfortress had been a distant thing, like a cloud on the horizon. Having it actually hovering just above her was a very different experience.

"Oh, plaguing *fuck*," Kit said. Her voice was thick. "Oh, by all the Chosen's perfect titties. I don't fucking believe it. If I still had hands I'd be sticking them into my pants right now."

"I thought you agreed with Xalen," Beq said, her eyes fixed on the slowly approaching behemoth. "That this thing had to be here."

"There's agreeing with a theory, and there's seeing it in person," Kit said. "Chosen defend. If I'd found this place as a scavenger, I would have ruled the fucking world."

"Isn't ruling the world how you ended up trying to steal the Leviathan?" Maya said. "And ended up like...you know. Not to mention stabbing me."

"You're really never going to let that go, are you?"

"No." Maya pressed Beq's shoulder. "You are fucking amazing. You know that, right?"

"I have an inkling," Beq said.

For a moment, they all just stared at the silent dreadnought.

"So, not to bring us down to earth," Kit said, "*so to speak*, but, uh, what do we do now? I don't see a way in."

Another, more thoughtful silence.

"I could bring us around to the top," Beq said. "If we land the flitter there, we might be able to..."

"Cut a way in?" Maya said. "That seems...unwise. That ship is still..." The word she wanted to use was *alive*, because in some difficult-to-define way it so clearly was. But it seemed unnecessarily alarming, so she settled on, "...operating. It might not like it."

"There has to be *some* way to get the flitter on board," Beq said. "That's what the base was for, right? Flying up to the ship?"

"If you get closer I can try contacting it with *deiat*," Maya said.

"It's worth a try," Kit opined. Beq nodded.

"The trick," she said, as the skyfortress grew and grew above them, "is not running into it. It's hard to tell how far away we—"

The flitter lurched. Beq grabbed for the controls, wrenching the levers with increasing desperation, but every movement only caused their craft to wobble and shudder more alarmingly. Finally she took her hands off, sitting back, and the flitter evened out, accelerating upward.

"It's taken control," she said. "The ship. Which should be impossible without someone up there to activate it."

"This whole thing is impossible," Maya said. "It's been four hundred years. No matter how big its sunsplinters are, it should have run out of energy by now."

"Maybe there are still Chosen up there," Kit said.

"Then what have they been plaguing doing all this time?" Beq said.

"Ignoring us, I guess?" Kit ventured. "Like the ghouls of Refuge."

"That bodes poorly for knocking on their door," Maya muttered.

In the implacable grip of the skyfortress's control system, the flitter rose toward *Pride in Power*'s midsection, where it narrowed to meet its tail. There was something *odd* about the skyfortress's skin. Looking at it gave Maya a sense of motion even though it was clearly stationary, as though it were subtly flexing back and forth. It tickled her memory, almost familiar. A bright line appeared, widening into a rectangular opening. The flitter headed straight for it, slowing as it approached and coming to a halt in a cavernous hangar. The big doors closed beneath them, and the flitter drifted forward and settled down on a solid unmetal deck, occupying one of several large rectangles painted side by side. Some of the others already contained similar vehicles.

"I think we're here," Beq said. Her voice shook slightly. "The last skyfortress."

"Rule the *fucking* world," Kit said, her little spider pressed up against the glass again.

Maya touched the door. When it opened, chilly air flooded in, smelling faintly of metal. With a look at Beq, Maya clambered out, muscles protesting after being tensed for so long. Her boots clattered on the floor, shockingly loud in the vast, echoing space.

"Seems okay," she said.

Beq came down after her, followed by Kit's four small bodies. The tiny spider hurried to catch up, its claws pricking as it climbed Maya to regain its place on her shoulder.

The hangar was like a larger version of the space they'd left behind in the mountain. The flitter landing spots were surrounded by bulky arcana, and more strange machines lined the walls. There were two much larger rectangles, empty now, which Maya guessed were spaces for small skyships to land. In the middle distance was a pair of big double doors.

"Okay," Beq said, struggling to contain herself. "Okay okay okay. We made it."

"Again, now what?" Kit said. "There doesn't seem to be a welcoming committee."

"All the skyfortresses have similar layouts," Beq said. "I've studied them. The primary control chamber is at the front, just under the upper skin. The easiest way to get there is to go through the primary habitation space."

"Do you know the way?" Maya said.

"I...think so. But there will probably be signs, too." She pointed to the double doors. "Let's start over there."

It was going to be a long walk, Maya realized. Just reaching the edge of the hangar took a few minutes, and the double doors—which opened automatically as they approached, vanishing into the walls without even a *whoosh*—led to a wide, high-ceilinged corridor, straight and utterly empty. Equally large doorways led off to either side at regular intervals.

"Did the Chosen build this place for giants?" Kit said. Her spider-constructs' footfalls were a series of soft *tings* on the unmetal deck.

"This is for bulky cargo, I think," Beq said. "There's a repulsion grid—that's why the flitter works—so they probably used cargo autos to move things around."

"It'd be nice if we could find one," Maya said. "We've got a long way to go."

Beq nodded. Unfortunately, no cargo autos were in evidence, and Maya didn't want to risk leaving their path to search for one. Instead they walked, until they came to a strange little siding—a rectangular stretch bulging out from one wall of the corridor, surrounded by a low railing. Beq rushed toward it excitedly.

"This is what we want, if it works," she said.

"And this is?" Maya couldn't help but smile at her girlfriend's obvious excitement.

"Cargo lifter. Like the lifters in the towers in Skyreach. It'll take us up there."

She pointed at the ceiling, where a wide hatch stood closed. There was a small podium on the lifter with arcana controls, and once Maya and Kit were aboard, Beq prodded it. The floor beneath them started to ascend, smooth and powerful, while the hatch above opened wide.

They emerged into a city. Maya stared, blinking, certain for a moment they'd somehow passed through a Gate to the streets of Sky-reach. Buildings rose on both sides of an empty street, not as tall as the capital's towers but with the same unmetal-and-glass facades twisting into interesting shapes, upper floors balanced on pointed obelisks or impossibly thin stilts in defiance of gravity. Overhead was the roiling cloud outside, split by lightning, as though the entire top skin of the skyfortress was transparent.

"Forget the world," Kit whispered. "I'd just rule *here*, and let every-one else come to me."

"I thought the skyfortresses were warships," Maya said. "Why would they build something like this inside?"

"They were used in the Plague War, but that wasn't their original purpose," Beq said. "Eventually they were supposed to explore the world beyond the Empire. Find out what's past the oceans. To be... sort of an ambassador of civilization."

"What a waste," Kit said. "All this *stuff* hanging up here for four hundred years. If they'd landed it somewhere..."

Maya shook her head. "We have to keep moving. If there's some-thing here that can help us against the Corruptor, we need to find it and get back to Deepfire before someone burns the city down."

"This way," Beq said. She pointed down a long avenue. "There should be an atrium at the other end leading to the control section."

They walked through the city streets beneath the endless churn of the storm, and Maya hunched her shoulders, fighting off an uneasy feeling. The place was empty, but it was more than that. This wasn't a city that had been *abandoned*, its residents fleeing and leaving evidence of their lives behind. Everything was pristine. There were no nicks or bumps in the road, no scuffs or stains on the unmetal or smudges on the glass. It had the feel of a new-forged tool, still polished and oiled from the smithy, just unwrapped from a velvet cloth. No one had *ever* lived here.

And yet there was... something. Out of the corner of her eye, Maya kept seeing flashes of movement. Color reflected in a window, gone as

soon as she turned her head. It had to be the lightning, throwing strobing reflections, or else one of Kit's bodies skittering curiously to examine some bit of architecture, but Maya couldn't shake the feeling that
something was following them. Her hand dropped to her haken and
stayed there.

At the other end of the city, steps climbed up to a vast archway.
Beyond it was a wide circular space, lined with more arches leading
outward. Six transparent tubes climbed up into the ceiling, each with
a cylindrical thing at the bottom, like a cork in the neck of a bottle.
Maya took a guess.

"More lifters?"

Beq nodded. "We need to get up to the control area, on the top
deck."

"Great." Maya's gut, still unhappy about the flitter ride over, wasn't
fond of the weird heavy sensation the lifters gave her. She forced a smile
anyway. "Lead the way."

They got inside one of the things, a small circular room wrapped
in mirrors with glass doors. Beq touched the controls, and it ascended
smoothly, the atrium below them shrinking away with stomach-
churning rapidity. Maya was glad when they passed through the ceiling, continuing their ascent in darkness for half a minute or so. Then
light returned, the lifter coming gently to a halt in another circular
atrium, this one smaller and with a ceiling only a few meters overhead.

The door opened. As below, corridors led off in several directions,
like spokes on a wheel. Beq pointed straight ahead, where an archway
was labeled in Chosen glyphs Maya couldn't read.

"That should be the control room," Beq said.

"Any idea if it'll be locked?" Kit said. "Are we going to have to—"

"*I don't understand.*"

The new voice seemed to come from everywhere at once. It sounded
like the whisper Maya had heard in the base below, now at full volume
with a deep bass rumble. She came to a halt, grabbing her haken and
threading power to her panoply.

Ahead of them, under the arch Beq had pointed to, bright motes of energy coalesced out of thin air. They glowed in a rainbow of colors, fusing into a pure white light as they multiplied, filling out a shape like pouring hot glass into a mold. The form was humanoid, but a good three meters high, broad-shouldered and long-legged. There was a suggestion of robes and heavy bracelets on the forearms. The head was bald, and the glow became so bright around the face that any features were invisible.

"*I felt you,*" the apparition boomed. "*You must be of the Chosen. You destroyed the creatures of the ghouls. But now you bear one of their constructs on your shoulder, and you have brought a* human *here, into this final bastion. Who are you?*"

Maya looked at Beq, who raised her eyebrows emphatically. *I guess it's on me to answer this one.* Maya took a half step forward.

"My name is Maya Burningblade," she said. Her voice sounded reedy and weak after the apparition's bone-rattling growl. "Centarch of the Twilight Order. This is Bequaria, an arcanist of the Order, and… um…Kitsraea Doomseeker, currently inhabiting a swarm of ghoul constructs for reasons that are not entirely her own fault."

"Thanks," Kit hissed.

"*Centarch?*" The huge thing seemed taken aback. "*No. No human could wield* deiat *with such strength.*"

"Until recently, I would have agreed with that," Maya said. "It's a long story."

"*But if you are human…*" The apparition went silent. "*What have I done? You are not the one I await.*"

"We were hoping—" Maya began, but the thing cut her off, its voice rising to a shout.

"*You have doomed us all. Human! How could I have known?*"

"I just—"

"*One mistake, at least, I can correct. The ark will be cleansed before it is too late.*"

Oh, I don't like the sound of that. Maya drew her haken, blade igniting with a *snap-hiss*. The apparition raised a hand, and the energy that made up its substance lashed out in a beam of searing light. Maya wove a defense, a shield of flame wide enough to spread around her and Beq, but the impact still felt like a physical blow. Brilliant energy splashed around them, pitting the unmetal floor. It was all she could do to grit her teeth and hold on.

When the pressure relented, she didn't hesitate. The creature lowered its hand, puzzled, and Maya bounded forward across the blackened line where her shield had been. She covered the distance to the huge thing and slashed her haken through its knees, the flaming blade passing through with no difficulty at all. The apparition *shattered*, crazing like a mirror before dissolving into jagged fragments.

"*Oh, time has robbed me of my strength*," the voice boomed. "*That a human could withstand me. A sad state of affairs.*"

Motes converged behind Maya, halfway across the atrium, solidifying in moments into the apparition's glowing body. Maya raised a hand and sent a flaming lance through its chest. The thing shattered again, like she'd heaved a rock through a stained-glass window. Heartbeats later, the lights reconverged. The apparition raised both hands, sending a dozen glowing darts across the room on wide, looping paths. Maya lashed out with her haken as they came close, blotting the missiles out of the air with soundless explosions of brilliance.

"Beq!" she shouted. "We need cover!"

"Get to the doors!" Kit said in Maya's ears. One of her bodies was barreling down the corridor to the control room, stopping at a pair of unmetal doors. "I'll distract him!"

Beq started running. The rest of Kit's bodies, which had been waiting beside her, suddenly split up and skittered away from the apparition, for all the world like enormous cockroaches fleeing a giant. They seemed to provoke a similar level of disgust from the glowing creature, and a beam slashed a dark line across the floor until it caught up. Kit's body blew apart, leaving not even a bloodstain behind.

Plaguing fuck. Maya waved Beq past her, then retreated, haken raised. The corridor was a little lower, barely taller than the apparition. The doors at the other end didn't open at their approach, and Beq hurried to the control arcana. There was another shattering blast from the atrium.

"One body left out there," Kit said conversationally.

"Quickly, Beq!" Maya said.

"I'm working, I'm working!" She had already popped one of the control crystals out, messing with the wires beneath. "Give it a minute!"

"We haven't got a minute!" Maya said. "Kit, what *is* that thing?"

"Search me," Kit said. "At a guess, whatever's powering the ship." Another *boom*, shaking the floor. "That was the last one."

"Beq!"

"Got it!" Beq twisted something, and the double doors slid open a half meter, then stopped.

Good enough. Beq turned sideways and squirmed through. Maya felt *deiat* flare and spun to find another wave of twisting darts closing in. She gave herself over to the moment, following the currents of power, and her haken blurred in a complex arc that surrounded her with blasts of brilliant light. Her panoply flared under the residual energy, the power drain like an ice cube in her guts.

"Maya!" Beq said. "Come through!"

Maya sent a wave of flame licking out, shattering the apparition for a moment. She wedged herself through the narrow gap. Beside her, Beq did something to another control console, and the doors slammed closed.

"Will that keep him out?" Beq said.

"How should I know?" Maya backed away from the doors, haken raised. There was a thump, then another, like huge fists pounding. "Apparently it will."

"But not for long," Kit said.

A spot in the center of the door had begun to glow cherry red. As Maya watched, it spread outward, center brightening to orange. Not even unmetal would stand up to an application of *deiat* on that scale. *Fuck fuck plaguing* fuck—

She turned to look around their sanctum. It was a large octagonal space set with bank after bank of control consoles, full of blinking colored lights and tiny crystals. Two curved consoles flanked a large image projector in the center. Everything looked fantastically complex, and none of it made any sense whatsoever to Maya.

More importantly, for their immediate purposes, there were no other exits. *So we're trapped on the wrong side of a rapidly disintegrating door, and nothing I do bothers that ghost-thing for more than a second.*

"Maya?" Beq was staring at the glowing spot as though entranced. She tweaked her spectacles, darkened lenses clicking into place. "What now?"

"I'm thinking," Maya muttered. Her *deiat* connection already felt frayed. *Whatever that thing is, it throws around a lot of power.* Defending against it would exhaust her quickly. *So we can't run, we can't attack, and we can't defend. What does that leave?* "But I'm open to suggestions."

"We could try cutting our way out," Kit said.

"Not faster than it can cut its way in," Beq said. "There has to be some way to talk to it. We don't even know what it wants from us."

"It sounded like a Chosen," Kit said. "And since we're two humans and a ghoul-construct, I doubt we'll have much luck. Though you can feel free to throw me out of the boat if you think it will help."

A Chosen. Maya closed her eyes for a moment. *A Chosen left here, on a ship they called their last hope. An empty ship.*

And a nursery...

The world seemed to go still. Maya opened her eyes.

"Beq?" she said carefully. "Do you recognize any of these controls?"

"What?" Beq looked around, flipping lenses rapidly. "A...a few, I guess. Some of the basic flight and navigation stuff. They're not too different from a skyship's, and I studied those at the Forge—"

"How long would it take you to crash the ship?"

"*Crash* it?" Beq said. "Maya, do you have any idea—"

"*How long?*"

"Um, um, a couple of minutes maybe? I could jam the attitude roller and then—"

"Oh, I like where this is going," Kit said, claws pricking as she danced a little jig. "Are you sure you're not a Doomseeker too?"

"Get everything set," Maya said. "*Don't* actually do it unless I tell you."

"Chosen defend. Are you—never mind, no time to argue. Okay." She ran to the control panel and unfolded her tool kit. "Just keep in mind that I don't know what I'm doing and if I kill us all I'm really, really sorry—"

The center of the door began to sag. Maya took position directly in front of it, haken drawn, and waited. It didn't take long. The orange glow had gone to yellow, then to white, unmetal deforming like taffy under the incredible pressure. A gap opened, no wider than a fist, but a waterfall of brilliantly colored motes exploded through it and swirled wildly before re-forming into the towering apparition.

"*You meddle,*" it said, "*with things you cannot possibly understand. Loathsome creatures.*"

"Actually, I think I do understand," Maya said. "You called this the ark. You're its guardian, aren't you? The protector of this ship."

"*I am. And I have grievously erred in my duties. But at least I can destroy you.*"

"Only if you want to fail in your duties completely," Maya said, trying to project all the confidence she didn't feel. "If I give the word, Beq will send us all into the rocks. I doubt it'll be a soft landing."

"*No!*" the apparition shrieked, seeing Beq at the controls. "*Hateful thing! Why would you destroy yourself so?*"

"You're going to destroy us anyway, aren't you?"

"*You do not understand,*" it wailed.

"Then *explain it to me,*" Maya said. "We came here in peace, to ask for help, and you attacked us."

"*But—*"

The thing hesitated. Its shoulders hunched miserably, a gesture that made it seem abruptly very human.

"*If I explain,*" it said, "*will you keep the ship safe?*"

Maya nodded, hope expanding in her chest.

"*Then I will tell you everything. It seems I have little choice.*"

A distant humming ceased, leaving a ringing in Maya's ears. The apparition shrank in on itself, reaching ordinary human proportions. It sharpened, growing details, until what stood in front of them was the glowing white shape of a man. He was ancient, his face creased like worn leather, only a few strands of hair remaining on his bald pate.

"My name is Ular-Min-Fiarag," he said, without the bone-shaking roar. "Guardian of the *Pride in Power*. And I fear you have come here in vain. There is no help left for either of us."

Chapter Fifteen

There was, first of all, a great deal of shouting and explanation.
Tanax shouted at Gyre, which led to Nina shouting at Tanax,
and Kit running in circles happily shouting at everyone. Then Apphia
had run out of strength and sat down heavily on the floor, which led to
another round of shouting and the dispatch of a servant to fetch Elariel
and some other necessities. Gyre had explained where they were to the
sisters, explained who the sisters were to Tanax, then tried to explain to
everyone that they were on the same side now and no one was going to
imprison or kill anyone.

The net result was that Nina and Apphia were taken to a bedroom
with Elariel in tow, while Gyre returned to his own room to sleep. In
deference to Tanax's frantic state, he arranged to be woken after a few
hours, and promised the centarch that he would listen to his explanation of what was happening in Deepfire then.

Thus Gyre was back in one of the Spike's innumerable meeting
rooms, sitting across a table from Tanax, with Kit's spider on his shoulder and exhaustion bearing down on him like a pack full of lead. A

servant arrived, blessedly, with coffee, and Gyre poured himself a cup and drank it like it was the elixir of life.

"First things first," Gyre said. "Kit, is Maya okay?"

"At the moment," Kit said. "It's been a bit crazy, but I'm cautiously optimistic. Your sister's a little mad, you know that?" The observation sounded admiring.

"I'm gathering," Gyre said.

"And you obviously found Apphia, as you hoped," Tanax said. "I take it you encountered some resistance?"

"You might say that," Gyre said, rubbing his eyes. He took another sip of coffee. "What's happening in the city?"

"The tunnelborn are on the verge of revolt, and the Merchant Council is being so harsh it seems like they're egging them on," Tanax said. "Tourmarch Ritabel is openly questioning my authority and half the Auxiliaries are on the verge of desertion."

Plaguefire. Gyre closed his eyes and leaned back in his chair. "Start from the beginning."

"I think it starts with Gemspotter. That's Rikard Gemspotter, a tunnelborn who used to work for one of the mining concerns. There were quite a few leaders trying to organize the workers, but he brought the others to his side or chased them out, and now he's basically in charge."

"What's he telling them?"

"That the Empire is coming," Tanax said. His expression was sour. "Sarah can tell you more."

As though summoned, Sarah opened the door, a bit out of breath and looking as worn-out as Gyre felt. She managed a broad smile.

"Glad to see you brought Apphia and Nina back safe," she said. "Was it awful?"

"Pretty bad," Gyre said. "I'll fill you in later. Tanax was telling me about Gemspotter."

"Yeah." She flopped heavily into a chair. "He's telling anyone who'll listen that when the Empire retakes its old boundaries, they're going to abolish the distinction between citizens and tunnelborn. That the

Emperor has already ordered it, but the merchants and the Auxies are suppressing the news to keep the workers in chains."

Gyre winced. *The plague of it is, he has a point.* The legal discrimination against tunnelborn—who lived outside the city proper, and thus outside the borders of the Republic and without a citizen's rights—was one of the great injustices of Deepfire, and one that Yora and her father, Kaidan Hiddenedge, had both died trying to correct. Much of the support for Yora and Halfmask's rebellion had come from tunnelborn literally left out in the cold at the barely habitable margins of the crater.

But I doubt the Corruptor is going to ride in on a white horse and fix everything. He certainly hadn't shown any tendency to address the grievances of the rebels in Khirkhaz. *More likely he'll starting rendering the lot of them down for parts.*

"Gemspotter organized a big strike at some of the major manufactories," Sarah went on. "The Merchant Council's thugs broke it up and chased them off, and now Rikard's people are staying in the tunnels, with Auxies and Council people glaring at them from across the way. It's practically a siege, and it can't last."

"I've been doing what I can," Tanax said. "But the Council won't listen, and Ritabel is getting suspicious. And obviously anything I say, as a centarch, the tunnelborn find suspect." *Maya would have been upset by that,* Gyre thought. Tanax seemed to accept it as a matter of course. "That's why we were rather urgently hoping you'd return before things got worse."

"Don't expect miracles," Gyre muttered. "Everyone knows Halfmask, but everyone knows he failed, in the end. I'm not sure how much weight the name still carries." Still, it was one of the few cards they had left to play. "Sarah, will you come with me and try to talk to this Rikard?"

Sarah nodded. "Of course."

Gyre turned to Tanax. "Make sure Apphia and her sister are comfortable. They've been through a lot."

"I will," Tanax said. He brushed his haken and sighed ruefully. "Though they don't seem to be very fond of centarchs either."

*   *   *

On the carriage ride to the edge of the city, Gyre filled Sarah in on what had happened in Khirkhaz, the mass arrests and use of prisoners to build the Corruptor's armored plaguespawn.

"Fuck," she said when he'd finished. "*Fuck*. From what Nina told Kit, I thought it would be awful, but…"

"There's no reason to think he'll stop at Khirkhaz, either," Gyre said. "It's clear he doesn't see humans as much more than livestock to be processed into soldiers. If he's building an army of Perfected, he's going to need a *lot* of human meat."

Sarah sat quietly, digesting that. Gyre leaned back against the cushioned seat. Sleep felt close, like a monster dogging his steps, and he desperately wanted to give in. Instead he rubbed his face with his knuckle, hoping to massage some life into it.

Their driver pulled up, somewhat more quickly than Gyre had expected. Sarah sighed.

"We have to walk from here," she said, in answer to his questioning look. "You'll see."

The cool air outside revived Gyre somewhat. This far from the life-giving warmth that flowed from the Pit, the breeze was always biting, though it didn't yet have the killing chill of winter. The last time Gyre had been this way, there had been a bustling market square just at the city border, where the wealthier tunnelborn emerged to shop. Now the square was abandoned, stalls gone and shops boarded up. Only at the far end, by the entrance to the tunnel, was there still a crowd.

The street leading out of the market plunged into the side of the mountain, continuing uninterrupted down a big oval passage lit by torches and glowstones. The sides of the tunnel were lined with wooden buildings: shops, taverns, and restaurants on the bottom floors, lodgings above and behind.

At the mouth of the tunnel was a milling crowd, split in two by sullen-looking Auxies to leave a narrow corridor open for a few people to trudge along. Both the crowd and those coming and going wore the drab brown long coats of tunnelborn, but the people gathered around shouted their anger and scorn at those walking, who scurried by as fast as they could. Closer to Gyre, on the city side of the border, several large stalls were full of food—stacked bags of rice and grain, piles of produce, cuts of meat, and wheels of cheese.

"This is the council's latest idea," Sarah said, scowling at the scene. "After Gemspotter kept the manufactory workers home, they shut down food deliveries to the tunnels and closed all the markets. Then they opened their own stalls, but they only accept scrip they're handing out at the manufactories. So if you don't come to work—"

"—you don't eat," Gyre said. Watching the stalls' customers—those who'd risked their neighbors' ire by crossing the lines to work—he wasn't sure if he should feel anger or pity. The gathered tunnelborn, clearly, had come down on the side of anger. A few rocks pelted one woman, prompting a shout from the Auxies. She hurried past the gauntlet and into the depths of the tunnel. *I see what Tanax meant about the council making this worse.* "That's ugly."

"Yeah. Officially, everyone on the city side is voluntarily going along with it, so the tourmarch says we can't stop them. Unofficially, the council has their people lean on anyone who objects. A lot of the smaller merchants are hurting too."

"So how do we get across?" Gyre said. No one from the city side was going to the tunnel side except for those returning from the stalls.

"Technically, there's no reason we shouldn't be able to just walk through," Sarah said. "In practice…"

"We'll see." Gyre grimaced. "Stay close to me."

He drew himself up from a slouch. He'd dressed for the occasion in something like his old working blacks—dark trousers and a tight shirt, meant for minimal noise and maximum flexibility—along with his scavenger's coat, inset with plates of scrap unmetal. The silver sword hung at his belt, and Halfmask's signature disguise nestled in his front pocket.

Sarah, too, was wearing her old scavenger costume, making no effort to conceal her artificial arm. They attracted some notice as they walked past the council stalls, ignoring the watching thugs, and started for the tunnel. The Auxies craned their heads to look, and the shoppers glanced nervously at them and walked faster.

The crowd, meanwhile, didn't seem to know what to make of them—there were a few shouts of "Fucking bootlickers!" and "Council scum!" but more questioning looks and whispers. Gyre watched a few men and women whose gazes seemed more attentive, and marked how several of them worked their way to the back of the crowd and broke free as he and Sarah passed through the lines and into the tunnel.

"Now what?" Sarah said. "Where do we find Rikard?"

"Just walk slowly," Gyre said. "It'll only be a minute."

A big woman, her shaved head thick with tattoos, stepped in front of them. Another pair of men slipped in behind.

"Hello," he said. "You're the welcome party, I take it?"

"Something like that," the big woman said. She hooked her thumbs in her belt, prominently displaying scarred knuckles. "You two are hard to miss. Sarah Blackarm, isn't it?"

"Hard to deny," Sarah said, rubbing the arm in question.

"Is that what they're calling you now?" Gyre said.

"Better than Sarah Lackarm," she said, only a little nervousness showing in her grin.

"And that makes you Silvereye," the woman said. "Last I heard you'd fucked off to Khirkhaz."

"I answer to that name," Gyre said, reaching into his pocket. "But you probably recognize me better like this."

There was silence for a moment as he fixed the mask in place. He'd drilled a hole through it, which let him see from his silver eye and allowed its faint green glow to shine through. It was, he thought, a rather nice effect.

"Halfmask," the woman said, pronouncing it like a curse.

Gyre bowed. "At your service."

"Everyone thought you were dead, with Yora and the rest."

"It seemed prudent to allow that belief to continue," Gyre said.

"Why come back now?"

"I need to speak to Gemspotter. This seemed the best way to get an audience."

"An audience." Her face twisted into what might have been a smile. "Heh. I like that."

"Can I see him?"

She nodded slowly. "Yeah. I think that can be arranged."

They were led deeper into the cold underworld. Buildings this far down were small and mean, nothing more than wooden boxes to trap the warmth of a precious fire. They went far enough, in fact, that Gyre realized they were taking a purposely circuitous route, one they wouldn't be able to retrace.

"May I ask your name?" he said, pulling his coat tighter to fight off the chill.

"Enta Thickskull," she said, giving him a glare that dared him to comment on the cognomen.

"And you work security for Rikard?"

She laughed. "After a fashion. He's my little brother."

"Ah." Gyre scratched at his mask, an old habit. *The scar doesn't even itch anymore.*

"In here," Enta said. She stepped aside for Gyre and Sarah to pass, the two other men who'd accompanied them waiting a respectful distance behind.

They passed through a curtained-off crack in the rock into a small side cavern. Gyre liked it immediately—large enough for a good-sized group, off the beaten path, and with several exits in case of emergency, exactly the sort of place he'd scouted for Yora's crew. *Someone here knows their business.* Inside, there was a table made from planks laid across a couple of barrels, a firepit, and a few hastily drawn maps.

A man with blue-white hair and a narrow, neatly trimmed beard was explaining something to a couple of others.

"Rikard!" Enta said. "Got someone to talk to you."

"Can it wait?" the man said. "We're a little busy."

"Think this one might be worth a minute." Enta put her hand on Gyre's shoulder. Rikard looked up and paused at the sight of the mask.

"That's all for now," he said, without looking back at the others. They hurried away, and Enta leaned against the wall of the cavern, arms crossed. Rikard tossed a packet of papers on the table and circled around it, still looking at Gyre.

"It's good to meet you," Gyre said uncomfortably.

"You certainly have the right look," Rikard said. "But anyone can pick up a mask. How do I know you're the real thing?"

"I vouch for him," Sarah said. She held up her artificial arm for display. "Everyone knows I lost this arm when Yora's crew was ambushed. This is the Halfmask who ran with us."

"Hmm." Rikard studied her. His eyes were a luminous purple, bright and intelligent. "All right. I accept that you are who you say you are. What do you want?"

Straight to the point, this one. Gyre hesitated. *He's not going to like this.* "I wanted to talk to you about what you're doing here."

"It's not *me* doing it. It's the tunnelborn. I'm just coordinating a little." He gave a slight smile with little humor in it. "No offense to Yora's memory, but that was the problem with her whole approach. Too focused on her personally, not enough on the people she was helping. Trying to become her father without any of the groundwork."

The casual dismissal got Gyre's back up, but he restrained himself. When he trusted his voice, he said, "What the tunnelborn are doing, then. You're aware that, as Silvereye, I recently went to Khirkhaz?"

"I've heard rumors to that effect," Rikard said, crossing his arms.

"The new Empire is already in full control there, and I've seen what that means for the people. If you think they're going to be better than the Republic, you're going to be badly disappointed."

"It's hard to imagine how they could be worse."

"Hard to imagine," Gyre said, "but nonetheless true."

"I see." Rikard's eyes narrowed. "And you raced back *here* from Khirkhaz to warn us out of the goodness of your heart? That's a fast trip, even with relays of swiftbirds."

Plaguefire. He could hardly admit to traveling by Gate. "I had assistance."

"Assistance," Rikard deadpanned. "And, having made this long and arduous journey, you now come to me to suggest...what?"

"We have to keep the Empire out of Deepfire."

Rikard gave a startled laugh. "Out? Keep the *Empire* out? You're madder than a loadbird with feather-rot."

"It's not impossible. Not if we work together—"

"*We*, is it?" Rikard's smile faded away. "Let me tell you what *I* think. You heard the tunnelborn of Deepfire were finally *doing* something, when you and your crew had only talked about getting around to it eventually. That got your cock in a twist, so you march down here with this story and hope that hunk of silver on your face is enough to get us to put you in charge. That about right?"

"That's ridiculous," Sarah said, taking a step forward. "Gyre *has* been to Khirkhaz. If he says—"

Enta's heavy hand landed on her shoulder. "Quiet."

"This isn't about me," Gyre said, with the sinking feeling that nothing he could offer would rescue the situation. "I'm happy to help you however I can. But I promise, if the Empire gets inside the walls, it'll be death for all of us."

"Sounds a lot like what the Merchant Council has been telling us," Rikard said. "That nothing's going to change, and so we'd better get back to work or we're all in trouble when the Empire gets here. I don't buy it. They stink of panic, and the Auxies stink worse. *I* think they know everything's going to be turned upside down, and since they're on top now that means they're going to be down in the shit."

"I'm not saying you have to go back to work. We can break the council, make them agree to concessions. But—"

"But you want us to line the walls and, what, get slaughtered by Legionaries and centarchs?" He snorted. "How about this? We break the council. We take the manufactories. Then we present the Empire with a done deal. Think they'll send in the troops to turf us out, or just go along with the new reality? I know where I'm placing my bets."

They'll crush you and turn you into monsters. But Gyre could see he wasn't getting through. He fell silent.

Rikard shook his head. "Either you're bought, Halfmask, or you're fucking crazy. I don't know which, and I'm not going to bother trying to tell the difference. You want to help, take off the costume and join the lines. Otherwise, get the fuck out of here." He gestured to Enta. "Help them get back to the surface."

"Come on," Enta rumbled. "Let's go."

The return journey was by another wandering, circuitous route. When they'd made it back to the upper tunnels, Enta patted them each on the shoulder and smiled, not totally unfriendly.

"Glad I could meet you, Halfmask," she said. "That's one for the books."

"Your brother's making a mistake."

"Don't bother," she said cheerfully. "He's the smart one, I don't try to tell him what to do. I just hit people who need hitting."

"But—" Sarah said.

Enta chuckled and sauntered away, leaving them alone at the center of the underground street. The few passersby gave them a wide berth.

"Well," Gyre said. "That could have gone better."

"Arrogant bastard," Sarah said. "I know the type. Think everything is a pissing contest."

"Maybe," Gyre said. He felt an odd pang of empathy. "I think he's feeling the weight of what he's started. You put yourself in charge of something, because no one else seems to be doing it, and then suddenly..." He shook his head. "You're *responsible*. You make decisions and other people live or die. It's hard to hold on."

"Either way, he doesn't seem likely to listen."

"No," Gyre agreed. He sighed. "We'll have to find a way around him."

Nina was waiting for him in the corridor outside her room. She was wearing fresh clothes, a noblewoman's dress that didn't suit her, and her pink hair had been washed and brushed out into a wavy cascade that fell past her shoulders. The smile she gave Gyre was almost shy.

"Hey," she said. "They told me you were out in the city. Are you okay?"

"Just tired," Gyre said. "Trying to get a handle on the next crisis. Are they treating you all right?"

"Fine. Too well, actually. Less than a week ago I was hiding in a closet in a burned-out village, praying nobody would find me. Now they're laying out my dresses and bringing me eel-and-onion soup. I'm a little worried this is all a dream."

"If it was a dream, I'd be getting more sleep," Gyre said. He nodded toward the door. "How is she?"

"Hurting." Nina's eyes were haunted. "Elariel helped as much as she could. But watching the people who'd followed her taken, one by one…"

Gyre swallowed. "I understand."

"Talk to her." Nina stepped away from the door. "She'll want to see you. If you get the chance, tell her she needs to eat more."

Gyre gave a slight chuckle. "I'll see what I can do."

The room was a large one, with an elegant table, a large fireplace, and a bed covered in embroidered pillows. Apphia lay on her side, staring into the embers of the dying hearth. Firelight played across the lightning scar that covered the left side of her face and brought out highlights in her purple hair. Gyre shut the door behind him and cleared his throat, but she didn't stir.

"Apphia?" He crossed the room slowly. "Are you awake?"

"Gyre?" Apphia blinked and stirred, focus returning to her eyes. She sat up with a yawn. She wore only a thin silk shift, and Gyre pushed away a brief flare of embarrassment. "Sorry. I've been dozing off a lot."

"Rest is good for us, or so Elariel tells me." Gyre yawned himself. "Haven't been able to put that advice into practice."

"I know that feeling," Apphia said. "After we gathered the Commune, they couldn't go an hour without needing me to make some decision. Now all of a sudden nobody needs me for anything." Something flickered across her face, an emotion she refused to allow to lodge there. "It's...less stressful."

"Nina's worried about you. She asked me to tell you to eat more."

Apphia laughed. "I'm sure she did. The food here is just a bit too much. Someone should tell the kitchens that five different desserts are too many."

"Can I sit?"

Apphia nodded. Gyre settled down across from her on the vast bed, folding his legs underneath him.

"And how are you doing, apart from the food?"

"About as fucked up as you'd expect," Apphia said. "When I get to sleep, I dream about black spiders tearing me apart and building something out of the pieces. Or I'm watching Brennard again, but he's calling for help, and I'm just standing there doing nothing. Or..." Her voice cracked, and she looked at the blankets. "Sometimes it's Nina."

"Nina's okay," Gyre said gently.

"No thanks to me," Apphia said bitterly. "And Brennard isn't. All the others...they died trying to defend the Spire, or afterward in the camp. And for what? We spent most of a decade fighting the Republic, and now it's been replaced by something even worse."

"Just because we lost doesn't mean it wasn't worth trying," Gyre said. "I have to believe that. Chosen know I've lost more than I've won."

"I always thought...I don't know. That what we were doing was *important*." Her hands tightened on the sheets. "Freedom for Khirkhaz. My family name. My father's legacy. Now I wonder, if I'd taken Nina and Brennard and fucked off into the Splinter Kingdoms for good, would everyone have been better off?"

"The Corruptor still would have come. As long as he's at the head of the Empire, none of us are safe, not in Khirkhaz and not in the Splinter Kingdoms."

"You're still at it, then."

"At what?"

"Fighting back. Except now it's not just the biggest nation on the continent, with armies using Elder weapons and knights with flaming swords. Now there's a plaguing *Chosen* with who-knows-what *dhaka* and, also, *he* has a legion of armored plaguespawn on top of everything else." She paused, sucked in a breath. "At what point do you just *give up*? I wanted to get even with Baron Rashtun for betraying my father, and that got the people who believed in me devoured by monsters. Maybe we should take the hint."

"And do what?" Gyre said. "What's the alternative?"

"I don't know. Swear loyalty to the monsters? Jump off a cliff?" She pulled her legs in, wrapping her arms tight around her knees. "It would hurt less."

For a long moment Gyre sat in silence.

It's a fair question. He'd gotten Yora and her crew involved with Kit's scheme, after all, and that had gotten Yora killed. *If I'd stayed home and tended vulpi, would she have been better off?* For that matter, would the Khirkhaz rebels have lived longer if they'd kept bickering ineffectually with one another, rather than being united by Gyre's promise of weapons that could stand up to the centarchs? *But...*

"Losing is hard," Gyre said. "I'm not going to pretend it isn't. But you can't take it all on yourself. The people who were with you in the forest, at the Spire, they made a choice to be there. What you were doing, they believed in it too. Claiming all the guilt takes that away from them."

It isn't coming to Deepfire that I regret. It's not being with Yora when she needed me the most. It was a mistake he was determined not to repeat.

"You're amazing, you know that?" Apphia said after a while. "I don't know if I've met anyone quite so...tough. No matter what happens, you just shake it off and try to figure out what comes next."

"That doesn't make me amazing," Gyre said. "That makes me stubborn, and possibly an idiot."

She laughed softly. "That too."

Another silence. Gyre felt, somehow, as if he should talk about *them*, about the brief moment of passion that had connected them back in the Spire. After everything that had happened, he didn't know where they stood. *Or where I want us to, for that matter.* At the same time, Apphia seemed so desperately fragile that he couldn't bear the thought of putting pressure on her. *Better stick to business. That's going to be hard enough.* He gave an awkward cough.

"Speaking of what comes next..."

"I know. Nina and I can't stay here forever. I don't know what deal you have with this centarch, but—"

"What?" Gyre shook his head. "No, of course not. You can stay with us as long as you need to."

"What about the Empire?" Apphia wiped her eyes with the back of her hand. "When they get here, you're not going to want to have a bunch of wanted rebels living in the palace."

"We're all wanted rebels together, at this point," Gyre said. "And we're hoping to keep the Empire *out*. That's where I need your help."

"*My* help?" Apphia shook her head. "We're a thousand kilometers from Khirkhaz and any friends I might have left."

"Trust me, we need all the help we can get. There'll be more, if this works, but first we need to convince people it's something worth doing. That means letting them know what happens under the Empire. You're the only person in Deepfire who's seen that firsthand."

"You want me to...what, talk to people? Shout at them from a street corner?"

"I'll arrange the meetings. Small groups at first. I just want you to tell them your story."

"I'm not sure why you think that would encourage anyone to stand up to the Empire," Apphia said, looking down. "More like scare them into surrendering."

"Maybe," Gyre admitted. "But are you willing to try?"

Another pause. Slowly, Apphia nodded.

The first step was assembling an audience.

That, at least, was straightforward. People in the tunnels were already going hungry, cut off from their regular markets by the council blockade. Prices for food were rising rapidly, in spite of efforts by Rikard and his people to ensure fair distribution. There was—of course—smuggling, but anyone trying to gouge the tunnelborn risked having their goods seized by an angry mob, with or without "official" sanction.

Giving food away, on the other hand, was likely to attract a crowd in a considerably better mood. With Lynnia's grudging assistance, Gyre and Sarah assembled several cartloads of staples and hired people to drive them. The arcana trade to the Republic, long a mainstay of Deepfire's illicit economy, had stalled out completely while everyone held their breath and waited for the fallout of the new Empire to settle. That meant a lot of scavengers, smugglers, and other criminally inclined types short of work. They were only too happy to help circumvent what was, in the end, just another border.

As the Auxies had long since discovered, it was impossible to guard the tunnels. There were too many of them, too many secret entrances and hidden intersections, and to make it worse, cave-ins and enterprising diggers were always changing the map. By staying away from the major routes, their little convoy was able to circumvent both Rikard's people and the council's thugs, though it meant keeping a constant watch for the plaguespawn that roamed the wilder passages.

"People *live* down here?" Apphia said. She watched, wide-eyed, as the endless tunnel unfolded in the dim light of their glowstones. "Why?"

"Because it's even worse anywhere else," Gyre said. "The Republic won't let them live in the city proper, and aboveground there's only the mountains. If you think it's cold down here, wait for winter in the Peaks. At least the tunnels close to the crater get a bit of warmth from the Pit."

"We got caught in a blizzard in the mountains once," Kit said, poking Gyre's cheek with one of her tiny legs. "Remember? We—"

"I *remember*," Gyre said. "But stay quiet."

"I was telling Maya about that," Kit whispered. "She was intrigued."

"Kit."

"Mind you, she and Beq gave us a run for our money—"

"*Kit.*"

"You'll have to fill me in sometime," Apphia said, smiling.

When they arrived at the spot Gyre had chosen, a disused gathering place several levels below the populated tunnels, some of their people were waiting. The room was large and rough walled, with scraps of wood and other debris scattered amid years of dust. Two scavengers Gyre had hired to keep order waited by one barred door, a tall man in a goggle-eyed helmet and a squat woman with a fearsome-looking club strapped to her back. The cart drivers started hauling sacks and barrels inside.

Apart from himself and Apphia, Sarah and Nina had come along, in addition to the ubiquitous Kit. Tanax reported that the tourmarch and the Auxies were growing ever-more rebellious, and there were increasingly violent demands from the council that the "authorities" do more about the strikers. Elariel was still holed up with Jaedia most of the time, Xalen scarcely left her room and her books, and Varo had yet to reappear. Maya and Beq, of course, were still on the *Pride in Power*, though according to Kit they hoped to return soon.

When they'd moved everything from the carts in through the back door, Gyre nodded to the tall man, who opened up the front entrance. For a moment Gyre felt a tingling of nerves—he *knew* this would work, knew the city and its people well enough to be sure of it, but there were always imponderables. Maybe Rikard's hold over his people was just too strong, or he'd gotten wind of the meeting and sent Enta to scare people off, or—

They were queued up outside the door, as he'd known they'd be. Men, women, and children, whole families dressed in layers of coats and mittens, pushing into the empty cavern and gaping at the bounty laid out in front of them. Gyre's scavengers stood around, not drawing their weapons but prominently displaying them, and that kept a rough kind of order.

Several boxes pushed together formed a stage. Sarah clambered up it, having taken off her coat to show her artificial arm. Murmurs ran through the crowd at the sight of her. Being the center of all eyes clearly made her a little green, but she pushed on.

"Friends!" she said. "You all know me. I ran with Yora's crew, with Halfmask and the others. We stole from the Auxies and spread the profits down here. I know the tunnelborn remember."

An approving murmur. Yora had taken her responsibility to the tunnelborn seriously, whatever Rikard thought. Much of their theft had gone to fund free kitchens and hearths in the colder tunnels, keeping people alive through the worst of winter. Gyre nodded along, staying in the shadows behind the stage. He had the silver mask in his pocket but hoped he wouldn't have to don it. *Save that for when we really need it.*

"Yora's dead," Sarah said, and the room went quiet. Many heads were bowed. "She was my friend, and I miss her. What pains me most, though, is how much of her good work died with her. Hopefully what little we can offer here helps."

"It's free, then?" a woman called from the crowd, pointing at the food. "Really?"

"Really," Sarah said. "Take what you need. All I ask is that you listen to a friend of mine for a few minutes."

"I'd listen to a goat farting all night if I could get a bit of bacon," another tunnelborn shouted, to general laughter. Sarah laughed along with him, then hopped down from the boxes. Apphia climbed up in her place.

They'd taken their time costuming her. She was in scavenger's leathers, of course, rough and ready for a fight, with a sword at her belt and her purple hair tied back, showing the full length of her scar. But Lynnia, choosing her outfit, had picked something with a bit of martial flair, the suggestion of shoulder pads and the clean lines of a soldier's uniform. Unmetal chestplates gleamed iridescent rainbows in the flickering glowstone light. At the sight of her, the crowd's muttering got louder, and Gyre heard "Khirkhaz" on more than one set of lips.

"Greetings, tunnelborn of Deepfire." There was no trace of the hesitation Apphia had shown back in the palace. For her, speaking to people who didn't want to listen had become second nature over years of trying to keep the disparate factions of the Commune together.

"My name is Baron Apphia Kotzed of Khirkhaz. I was—I am—the leader of the group called the Khirkhaz Commune, which fights against the arbitrary tyranny the Republic inflicted on my father, my family, and our people. Though we are separated by a great distance, I have always felt a kinship with the people of Deepfire through our shared struggle."

One major aspect of that "kinship," Gyre knew, had been regular shipments of arcana weapons to the Commune in exchange for much-needed cash. Yora had brokered quite a few such deals. *But better not to clutter things up with details.*

"I hear people talking about the Empire," Apphia went on. "Saying that things will get better once the Empire arrives. I want to tell you what happened when the Empire came for *my* people." She swallowed, voice thick. "There aren't many of us left."

She told the story without embellishment, though it hardly needed any. Gyre's own part in it was mostly brushed aside. The rebellion and the seizure of the Spire, the Republic's failed counterattack. The arrival of the Empire and its Perfected. The march to the camp, the daily disappearances, and finally the revelation of what happened to those who were taken away.

It sounded half-mad, Gyre had to admit, even in Apphia's unadorned words. He watched the faces of the tunnelborn. There was skepticism, horror, worry; tight lips and furrowed brows. *And no wonder.* What they were saying wasn't what anyone wanted to hear. *But it's probably what they expect.* After centuries of Republic exploitation, the tunnelborn were naturally inclined to mistrust.

When Apphia was finished, she hopped down, and Gyre's scavengers stepped aside, letting the tunnelborn past to the food. People grabbed what they could carry, sacks of flour and wheels of cheese, packages of vulpi bacon in waxed paper, rice and vegetables and even nyfa seeds. When their arms were full, they hurried out, both crowd and food rapidly melting away. Within a few minutes there was nothing left of either.

"I didn't tell them what I wanted them to do," Apphia said, joining Gyre by the back wall.

"That can come later," Gyre said. "For now we just want to get your story out. Each of these people will tell a dozen others. If Rikard hears enough of his folk questioning whether the Empire is going to be good for them, maybe he'll be willing to talk to us."

"Or maybe he'll come and try to make us stop."

Gyre sighed. "Probably that too."

The reaction he'd expected came during their third meeting. The crowds had been getting larger each time, and Gyre made sure to bring more carts of food so nobody had to go away empty-handed. His emergency stash of thalers was just about exhausted, but fortunately Lynnia was willing to contribute, and she still had most of the sackful of money Gyre had dropped on her doorstep the last time he'd come through.

"Not that this means I've forgiven you, mind," the alchemist had admonished. "But feeding hungry people is something Yora always believed in."

By the third meeting, though, there were people in the audience who didn't seem to be interested in the food at all. When Apphia finished telling her story, they asked questions—about the Commune, about the Perfected, about what she'd seen in the camp. Some of the inquiries made Gyre wince, touching as they did on the horrors Apphia had been through, but she remained in control of herself. *She really is impressive.*

Nina had taken to mingling with the crowd, talking to people who weren't comfortable speaking in front of everyone. The younger tunnel-born seemed drawn to her. At her own suggestion, she dressed as a Communard, complete with three-cornered hat. She certainly cut a dashing figure. Gyre kept half an eye on her from his position at the back of the room and tried to remember that Nina could look out for herself, young or not.

They changed locations each time, changed routes and rendezvous. Still, Gyre was far from surprised when Enta pushed in, followed by a cluster of leather-coated bruisers. There was no real way to keep the meetings a secret, not if they wanted people to show up—word had been bound to get back to Rikard sometime. *Now we see how far he's willing to push it.*

Nina had already spotted the thugs and extricated herself from the crowd. Gyre skirted the edges, staying close to the wall, and slipped in behind the newcomers as they ambled toward the stage. Apphia had spotted them too, and she trailed off in the middle of one of her answers. Gradually, recognition spread through the crowd, and a clear space opened around Rikard's people.

"There's a lot of you here," Enta said. "My brother wanted me to see what all the fuss was about. Being left out of things makes him sad, you know."

"We're bringing food past the blockade," Apphia said. "Didn't seem wise to call attention to it."

"That's not all you're doing, from what I hear," Enta said. Her eyes narrowed. "You're the one who claims to be Baron Kotzed."

Apphia touched her scar. "It's a pretty hard thing to conceal."

"There's a lot of people with scars in the world," Enta said. "But truth is

I don't care who you are. This is Deepfire, not Khirkhaz. You've got your rebellion, we've got ours. From what I hear, yours isn't doing so well."

Apphia blinked, swaying a little on her feet. She couldn't muster words, but the crowd spoke for her.

"What if she's right?"

"The Republic was bad, doesn't mean the Empire's gonna be better."

"I don't trust any of the plaguepits!"

"No Republic, no Empire!" It had the sound of a slogan, and a few others repeated it. Beside Enta, a big potbellied man raised a well-worn cudgel and moved threateningly toward the crowd, which opened rapidly around him.

That's about far enough. Gyre slipped his mask on and stepped into the clear space around Rikard's enforcers. People in the crowd noticed him first, pointing and whispering.

"Halfmask?"

"He's dead—"

"Has to be fake—"

"Looks the same—"

Enta turned, slowly to show she wasn't frightened. She hooked her thumbs in her belt and glowered.

"You."

"Me," Gyre said.

"Should have known. This is exactly the story you spun my brother."

"I had hoped he would help me tell it to everyone. Since he declined, I had to do it myself."

"So you hired some girl to dress up as a Communard and claim to be Baron Kotzed?"

"That seems a little elaborate, don't you think? If I wanted to fake a witness, there have to be easier ways."

"I never said you were very bright." She frowned. "So now what?"

"That depends on you. You're welcome to stay and listen. Take some food if you like. But your colleague seems inclined to stir up trouble."

"I'll show you trouble, you little fucker," the big man said.

Gyre ignored him and kept looking at Enta. "Are you here to shut us down? When I was with Yora, she told me tunnelborn wouldn't put up with a leader who tried to tell them what to think. Is that not true?"

"You may not have noticed, but we're in a war," Enta said. "Us and the council have knives on one another's balls, and we're waiting to see who starts cutting first. That makes it pretty important that everyone on our side *is* on our side, if you know what I mean."

"I'm not telling anyone to help the council," Gyre said. "It's what comes after that which concerns me."

Enta found his gaze and held it. This wasn't really about freedom to speak, or even the Empire, and they both knew it. It was about a challenge to Rikard's authority, which had to be either met or accepted. *You could listen. We don't* have *to do it this way—*

The big man with the club moved first. He raised the weapon, quick in spite of his bulk, and swung for Gyre's skull with a roar.

Click. The world stretched into shadows.

Gyre left the silver sword in its sheath. *We don't want to kill anyone if we can avoid it.* The ghoul augmentations gave him *speed*, but not strength—even in the shadow-world, trying to go toe-to-toe with the bruisers would probably end poorly. Fortunately, none of them had the training and discipline of Va'aht. His silver eye read them easily, projections sweeping far ahead of the clumsy blows. It was just a matter of finding the right point to apply leverage.

Gyre sidestepped the big man's club, kicked him in the back of the knee, spun around him, and planted a foot on his rump to help him down. The next thug, eyes widening in comical slow motion, got a jab in the throat that left him gasping. The third tried to grab Gyre in a bear hug, only to find his target slipping away and an outstretched boot tangling his legs. The last, pulling a knife, had it wrenched from his fingers and jammed into one meaty thigh.

Time jumped forward, and Gyre stood amid four swearing, groaning men, his hands in his coat pockets, his eyes still fixed on Enta. Her eyebrows went up, and there was an audible gasp from the crowd.

"As I said. You're welcome to stay and listen, but not to cause trouble."

"Hmm." Enta grabbed one of the thugs and hauled him upright. "I'll tell that to Rikard."

"Please do. If he'd like to meet the baron and hear what she has to say, I'm sure that can be arranged."

"I'll tell him that too." She turned her glare on the rest of her men. "Oh, it's just your leg, for plague's sake. You're barely bleeding. Someone help him up."

They followed her out, variously limping and gasping. The crowd was still staring at Gyre, and he gave them a deep bow.

"I didn't want to make this *my* story, when the stage rightfully belongs to Baron Kotzed," he said. "But know that I believe every word of what she says. It won't do us any good to break the Merchant Council if we turn around and welcome the Empire."

That was the third meeting. By the fifth, the room he'd chosen was packed. No more of Rikard's people came to bother them—Gyre saw Enta, once, but she only caught his eye and gave a slight smile and a shrug. *But I'm sure he's not going to give up that easily.*

Nina brought the news as they were cleaning up from the sixth meeting. "Rikard's started talking about a mass march into the city, straight to the square outside the Moorcat Combine."

"He wants to force the issue while he still has the upper hand," Apphia said.

"And he thinks the council won't be able to stop him," Gyre said. He looked at Sarah. "Can they?"

Her brow furrowed. "They don't have the numbers to match the tunnelborn, but their mercenaries are a lot better armed. It depends how far the council is willing to go."

"Rikard obviously thinks they'll back down," Apphia said.

"They won't," Gyre said grimly. "And when he finds that out it's going to be a bloodbath."

Chapter Sixteen

Maya

Maya and Beq followed the ethereal form of Fiarag into the depths of the skyfortress.

At first, Maya had wanted to leave Beq at the controls to make sure Fiarag didn't turn on them. But all the fight had gone out of the ship's self-proclaimed guardian, replaced with an insistence that they hurry.

"No harm will come to you," he murmured. "I was wrong, wrong, so very wrong, and I regret it, but *please*... there is only a little time left..."

Eventually, they decided to leave one of Kit's bodies in the control room. The construct probably didn't have the dexterity to crash the ship, but Fiarag didn't know that. He led them back to the lift, which activated of its own accord and whisked them down past the habitation level.

"You said you'd answer my questions," Maya said, as the walls of the lift blurred around them. "So who are you? *What* are you?"

"A volunteer. The last volunteer. To maintain the *Pride*." Fiarag wrung his hands. "The ship has needs. I supply them."

"Power, you mean? *Deiat* power?"

"Yes, yes. To keep us in the sky, to keep up the barrier storm, a thousand little lights and drains. To hold us out of harm's way."

"For four hundred years?"

"Is that how long it's been?" He bowed his head, his deep-sunk eyes invisible. "A long time. Too long. It was never meant to be like this."

"How?" Beq said. "The Plague killed all the Chosen."

"I was shielded. Safeguarded. So I could do my duty. The last duty."

The lift stopped. After descending for so long, Maya had instinctively expected a dank, poorly lit basement, but of course this was a hallway like any other. Fiarag hurried out, his translucent feet making no sound on the unmetal floor.

"The end was coming," he said, his breathy voice half a whisper. "We knew, oh, we knew. Couldn't stop it. *Plague*. Stone, glass, even unmetal didn't stop it. Found the cracks. Like something alive and hateful. But *Pride* was the newest, the most advanced. New armor. Twisted space. Very strong."

"Flux-stabilized," Beq breathed, as though in the presence of the divine.

"Yes, yes. Tricky, tangled stuff. *It* could stop the Plague."

"Can you translate?" Maya said. *Although it sounds familiar...*

"Flux-stabilized unmetal was invented just before the war," Beq said. "It works by running a *deiat* charge through special *n*-plaited conduits under the surface, which distorts—"

"I said *translate*, not make things worse."

"Sorry." Beq was practically bouncing on her feet. "It's a special kind of armor, even stronger than unmetal. Not even *deiat* weapons can scratch it. But it requires a constant source of power to maintain—if it loses that connection, then it collapses into ordinary unmetal."

"If you were looking at it," Maya said slowly, "it would sort of... twist, right? A kind of pulsing."

"Probably," Beq said. "Everything we know comes from prewar books, for obvious reasons."

Ashok's lab. That's where she'd heard the word and seen that strange pulsing—in her nightmares. *A special armor plating that could keep out even the Plague.*

"*Pride* was selected for our last hope," Fiarag broke in. "Already infected, of course. Infested like the rest. But if a way to cleanse it *could* be found..." He shook his head wildly. "Impossible. But they tried. And they died. One by one. Until I was all that was left."

"What was the cargo?" Beq said. "I understand trying to clean the ship and sealing it against the Plague, but if that didn't work, isn't whatever's aboard ruined?"

"I hoped. Working, somewhere, on an answer. Final answer. Wait, they told me. And I waited. So long. Until it came. The fire of the sun, burning away the shadow. Burning the little monsters wherever they tried to hide. I *felt* it. At last."

"The Purifier," Maya said quietly. She remembered being able to see the whole of the world, and watching the expanding shell of white light scouring it free of the black specks of Plague. It hadn't occurred to her that anyone else could have felt it too.

"It's gone," he continued. "Gone, as though it never was. Wiped away. At last. Free. I thought they had finally succeeded. Surely they would come here, to me. For our last hope. My duty could end. At last."

"But no one came," Maya said. "Until we showed up."

"*Yes.* Inside the mountain, I saw you. Felt your power. I made ready for your arrival. But when you came, when I saw you clearly..." He shook his head violently. "You are *not* Chosen. Strong, but human. Your friend is human. And a ghoul construct..."

"Things have changed out there," Beq said. "As far as we know, there are no other Chosen left."

Except one, Maya thought grimly.

"I hoped," Fiarag mumbled. "But I knew. Doesn't matter. Nothing matters. Except. This." He came to a halt at a door, put his glowing hand against it. "I will show you."

The door opened, rising into the ceiling with a slow gravity that implied considerable weight. Beyond it was a room, veiled in darkness. Lights came on overhead, row by row.

"This is the secure armory," Beq said quietly. "Where they would keep the superweapons. The sort of thing that made the Pit."

Maya nodded and resolved to step carefully. Fiarag didn't seem worried, but she wasn't clear on whether or not he was physically here, or how much sanity remained to him.

When the room was lit, they could see large oval shapes all along the walls, surrounded by arcana displays glittering with crystal. Directly opposite the door was a larger version of the same egg-shaped thing, festooned with conduits and cables that ran from it in thick bundles. On the front of each egg was a round window like a porthole.

"These..." Beq stepped forward, rapidly flicking through her lenses. "I've never seen anything like them. Or even read anything in the pre-war texts we have left. Are they..."

"Secret," Fiarag said. He went to the closest shape and stroked its surface reverently. "Built here. The very latest technique. Never attempted before. Last resort. Last hope."

"They're something like stasis webs, aren't they?" Maya said. The room felt colder than the rest of the ship, though that might have been her imagination.

"Yes. Stasis. Crude technique. Degrades organic matter. These are superior. Need energy. Last forever. *Forever*."

"And what's in them?" Beq said. "Weapons?"

"Not weapons." Maya's suspicion had hardened into certainty. *The little chairs, pushed in around little tables*. "Children."

"Last hope," Fiarag said. His voice was even quieter now. "Dying. All of us. All dying. Too late, even if we stopped the Plague. Children lasted longest. Brought them here, to the *Pride*. Hoped to cleanse it, let them grow up, find a way. Failed. So they stayed in stasis. Last resort. Wait, they told me. Until...until."

Maya walked carefully to the nearest unit and looked in through the window. There was a girl inside, silver-haired and wrapped in a white robe, perhaps seven years old. The next held a boy of nine. The next...

She looked around. There were about thirty of the pods. *Thirty children out of a whole race.*

Thirty Chosen *children*. She didn't know how quickly Chosen gained their *deiat* mastery. But once they were grown, thirty would be more than enough to take on all the rest of humanity.

"Chosen defend," she muttered, then twisted her lip at the irony of the oath.

"What's in the big pod?" Beq said.

Fiarag's head drooped. "Me."

Maya blinked. "But you're—"

"Special stasis. Very, very special. Stasis by *degrees*. Brings me close to reality, then sends me back. Keeps me alive. Not forever. But a long time. Too long."

"A variable stasis chamber," Beq said. "So it would keep him frozen most of the time, then bring him back long enough to recharge the ship's sunsplinters."

"Back and forth," Maya agreed. "For four hundred years."

She stood on tiptoes to look in the window of the big pod. Fiarag's real body looked like his projected image, a wrinkled, bald old man, skin spotted, eyes closed.

"The ship is my body," he said. "I see with its eyes. Hear with its ears. Roam within it. Fight, if I must. To defend it. But hard, so hard. To speak, to fight, I must be close to the surface. Close, and no time left. Desperate. Failing. Body failing. My duty."

"Failing," Maya said. "You're dying?"

"Yes. Heart damaged. Blood too thick. Dying. Might have stretched it longer, decades, but when you came..." He shook his head violently.

"Thought you were the ones I'd waited for. Then angry you weren't. Now no time left. Brought myself up, back into time. Can't return."

Plaguefire. Maya tried to imagine it. Body failing, a heart attack maybe, a few final minutes of life stretched out into years—decades—by a cradle of arcana. Knowing that time was running out.

"You are not. Who I waited for." Fiarag's speech grew more labored. "But you must. Assume my duty. Keep the ship safe. Keep *them* safe. Last hope."

"Wait," Beq said. "If you want Maya to get in that machine—"

"No need. Stasis guards me. From Plague. Plague gone." He grabbed at Maya with immaterial hands. "*Please.* You must."

And then, slowly at first, he began to fade.

"Wait," Maya said. "Wait a minute! *Now?* I have questions—"

"Last. Duty." The Chosen's voice slipped into inaudibility. "Everything...I...have..."

His body lost cohesion, dissolving into motes of rainbow light. They vanished one by one, like popped soap bubbles. Maya stretched again to look into the pod. Nothing about the old man had changed, but nevertheless she felt like something had departed.

"Is he..." Beq said.

"I think so." Maya shivered. "No wonder he was in a hurry. Fighting me must have been the last straw."

"Children," Beq said, looking around at the pods. "A last hope. But not a weapon."

"No." Weariness was abruptly pulling Maya down. "Not something we can use against the Corruptor."

"Not to interrupt the general gloom," Kit said after a moment, "but something has started flashing up here. You should probably come and check whether the ship is about to fall out of the sky."

"It's telling me that the power input has been cut off," Beq said after several tense minutes prodding unfamiliar controls. "Which we knew."

"How much energy does the ship have in reserve?"

"If I'm reading this right, the sunsplinters are about half-full. That gives us a couple of months, I think?" She shook her head. "Unless I'm completely wrong and we have two minutes to live. But I think if that were happening, something would at least beep."

Maya sat in the high-backed chair at the center of the control room. Four centuries ago, some Chosen captain had probably taken this seat, directing one of the most powerful pieces of arcana ever created. *It's honestly not very comfortable.*

But a tinge of excitement was working its way into her mind. *There has to be* something *here we can use.* Whether the Chosen had intended it as an ultimate weapon or not, the *Pride in Power* was still a *skyfortress*, the size of a city and encased in impenetrable armor. *That should be worth something.*

"How much can you control the ship?"

"Uh." Beq looked around the room. "In theory? Completely. Nothing I've found seems to be locked. In practice? It's supposed to have a crew of hundreds of Chosen and I have only the faintest idea what I'm doing."

"Can you move it? Take us out of the storm?"

"I..." Beq looked uncertain for a moment, then set her jaw. "Probably. It won't be very fast. It's set in some kind of minimum-power mode and I'm not sure how to change it."

"*Fuck* yes," Kit said. "Can I fly it?"

"No," Maya and Beq said together.

"Aw. You guys are no fun."

"Slow is fine," Maya said. "I just want to get back to Deepfire to begin with."

"What are you thinking?"

"There has to be something aboard we can use. And without Fiarag, if we leave it here, it'll just crash. Tanax and I can probably provide enough power to keep it afloat."

"Makes sense to me," Beq said. "I'm itching to see if this thing has a library. There's so much we could learn..." She stopped. "What about...you know. The cargo."

"The children," Maya said.

"Yeah." Beq twisted the dials on her spectacles nervously, lenses clicking. "Do we let them out?"

"Not yet. We need to...figure things out first." Maya took a deep breath. "Actually, I don't think we should tell anyone else about them."

"Not that I'm here to spy on you," Kit said, "but if that includes Gyre, I have to say you'd be putting me in a tight spot."

"I'll tell Gyre," Maya said. "But no one else. Half of them would want to destroy the pods, and the other half would wake these kids up and expect them to be saviors. I don't think either is a good idea."

Beq nodded slowly. Kit said, "Not to mention if Refuge found out, the ghouls would probably come after us with everything they have. That's not a fight we need."

"Then we're agreed." Maya drummed her hands on the arms of the chair. "Take us back. As soon as you can."

"Aye, aye, sir!" Beq barked. At Maya's blank look, her face slowly reddened. "Isn't that what they say on ships?"

"I don't know. I've never been on one."

"Neither have I. I just read—in the books, they..." Beq trailed off and bent over the controls. "Never mind."

The endless storm over Mount Shroud was ending at last. It had never been natural, Beq reported, but was generated by some camouflage mechanism aboard the skyfortress. Now that they were underway, Beq had shut it off, and the shell of dark clouds was being slowly torn apart by the wind.

Maya wondered how long it would be before anyone noticed, and what they would think. Whether the rumors would make it back to Deepfire before they did. *Slow* turned out to be an understatement, and *Pride in Power* was drifting back toward the city at little more than a walking pace. It would be two days, at least, before they were hovering over Deepfire's crater.

In the meantime, Beq had discovered a map and found the crew quarters. They'd taken the captain's cabin—*Why not? No one else is around to complain*—and banished Kit, who'd responded with a variety of salacious remarks. In truth, Maya didn't think she had the energy to do anything in the wide, comfortable bed apart from sleep in it. *Maybe tomorrow.* It *would* be nice, for once, to have an actual bed…

In fact, everything about the cabin felt strange, plain in appearance but with capabilities Maya associated with the heights of luxury. Light came from sunstones in ceiling sconces, as it did in the houses of the very wealthy, but the fixtures themselves were simple glass. The bedsheets were beige and unembroidered, but made of Chosen cloth so finely woven Maya couldn't feel the threads. There was a private toilet, with running water; familiar from the Forge, but unthinkable for anyone outside Skyreach's towers. No bath, but a tall box filled with warm rain on command, which Beq said was called a "shower." Maya tried it and decided that it was worth restoring the Chosen Empire, all by itself.

When she emerged, wearing only her spare shirt and toweling her hair, Beq was sitting at the foot of the bed playing with the image projector. It was built into the opposite wall, three prongs enclosing a space about the size of a man's head. Looking at it made Maya think of Ashok's handsome, deceitful face, and she fought down a wave of uneasiness. *It's just a piece of arcana. Of course it has other uses.* Currently, it was displaying a diagram of the skyfortress, which turned in place and changed as Beq touched a small control panel.

"More maps?" Maya said.

"Just trying to figure out what we have on board." She sighed. "There's no weapons, not even the normal complement for a skyfortress. A lot of things were apparently stripped out when they were converting the ship into a survival ark. But there's plenty of food and a water treatment system. Thousands of people could live here for months, if we had enough power."

"Worse comes to worst, maybe we can just run away," Maya said. "You said these ships were designed to cross the oceans, right? Maybe we could leave the Corruptor behind and go...somewhere else."

"Assuming there's somewhere else to go," Beq said. "And that whoever lives there doesn't take issue with us."

"Yeah." Maya flopped on the bed, damp red hair spreading out around her. "And it wouldn't help everyone who got left behind."

Beq turned away from the projector, refocusing her lenses. "Are you all right?"

"Just tired," Maya said. "And...I don't know."

Beq's eyebrows went up, and she waited patiently. Maya stared at the ceiling, trying to order her thoughts.

"First I wanted to get Jaedia," Maya said. "I had this idea that if we could wake her up, she'd save us and fix everything. That was stupid, I *knew* it was stupid..." She swallowed. "Then that didn't happen. But Xalen had made us get these files, and if Prodominus wanted me to have them, they had to be important. And they *were*, but not in a way that helps. So here we are again, back where we started."

"We're not back where we started," Beq said, crawling across the bed. "When we *started* you were dying in a rotten abandoned cabin. Now we're flying home in a skyfortress and Elariel's helping Jaedia."

"Fine," Maya said. "We're back where we started *with respect to* the insane Chosen-ghoul hybrid who wants to take over the world and do something horrible to me, personally, for reasons I still don't understand."

"Yes," Beq said, considering. "That seems accurate."

Maya snorted a laugh. "Very cheering."

"You said it, not me."

"It doesn't bother you?"

"It probably should," Beq said. "But I just discovered the ship *does* have a library, and right now all I can think about is what I'm going to look up first in the morning."

"You're easy to please," Maya said, grinning in spite of herself.

"Sometimes," Beq said, bending over to kiss her.

Zephkiel

Days passed, but Zeph could still hear Nia's screams. Her screams were the easy part, actually. Late at night, lying in bed beside Ashok, she could hear the sounds that had come after, the crunching and squelching. Sleep seemed farther away than Skyreach.

Ashok was playing the loving partner, attentive to her needs, willing to give her space, happy to do anything she asked. Except what she really wanted—to close the lab on the fifth level and burn the monstrosities he'd created—she'd never asked, because she knew in her heart what he would say. Her mind had been connected to his for more than a year, even though in recent days she'd walled herself off as completely as she knew how. She understood him if anyone did. And the work—the work *she* had begun with him—mattered more than anyone's life to Ashok.

During the day, he went down to the lab. His experiments had overflowed their original space, and he'd kicked a number of fourth-level researchers—Zeph's own former colleagues—out of their rooms. He accepted no help now, not even from Zeph. She wondered if black-muscled *things* were lifting his vats and scrubbing his tanks. She wondered if some scrap of Nia was part of them.

More than anything else, Zeph wanted to leave. To *flee*—she could admit that. Run from this place, from *him*, from the monsters in the deep. Get work at some local hospital and never look back. The passion she'd felt for *dhaka* and its possibilities had curdled inside her.

But the brief message she'd gotten from Spinakker had told her to stay put and wait for instructions. So she remained, afraid of Ashok, afraid the intelligence agent wasn't coming, afraid of what would happen when he did. She passed through the halls and the cafeteria like a ghost, shunned by her old friends. *Not that I ever had many of those.*

When the call actually came, she was lying in bed and heavy with exhaustion, though the clock on the wall said it was just after noon. Night and day always blurred in the underground lab, and all the more so when sleep came only in fitful half hours. She jolted up from a doze at the chime of the communicator, blinking to chase away the remnants of dream. Her heart was pounding.

Seeing her name hovering over the image projector, Zeph stumbled over to it. It had to be Spinakker—no one else from the outside would contact her here except Iraph, and she hadn't spoken to her sister in weeks. When she hit the control, however, a woman's face appeared, blandly pretty, her tone carefully neutral.

"Hello," she said, eyes narrowing as she looked at Zeph's image. "This is Spinnie. Is this a good time to talk?"

"It...uh..." Zeph looked over her shoulder. The door to the room was closed, and Ashok was down with his experiments. He wouldn't return for hours. "Yes. I can talk."

"Wait, please." The woman, whoever she was, disappeared and was replaced by Spinakker's craggy features.

"Thank the sun," Zeph said. "I can't stay here any longer. I think I'm going mad."

"I understand," Spinakker said. "You've done very well. Just a little longer, and this will all be over."

Over. She had no idea what that meant. *But what choice do I have?* "What do you want me to do?"

"I'm on my way down. Can you come to the main entrance and meet me without alarming Ashok?"

She nodded. "He's in his private lab. Nobody disturbs him there."

"Perfect. I'll see you soon."

The connection vanished. Zeph sniffled, took a deep breath, and ran her fingers through her hair.

Just a little longer. She went to the bathroom and cleaned herself up, though there was no hiding the sagging bags under her eyes. It took a few moments to gather her courage and open the door of her suite, though of course the corridor outside was empty. Walking through the facility, as she had ten thousand times, suddenly felt like traversing enemy territory.

At the front entrance, its newly installed isolation doors yawning wide, a security guard was on his feet and staring wide-eyed at Spinakker and his companions. The intelligence agent wore the same long gray coat as the last time she'd seen him, but the four men he'd brought with him were in tight-fitting black bodysuits plated with silvery unmetal and laced with circuitry and crystal nodes. They wore wraparound helmets with bulging visors, the slits filled with eerie green light.

When she recognized them, Zeph's breath caught. *Enforcers.* She'd never seen one—practically no one had—but it was the only possibility. It wasn't four *humans* inside the augmented armor suits, but four *Chosen.* Four, when a single one of them could have melted half the facility to slag. And while most Chosen weren't trained for combat with *deiat*—not that it made them less than deadly—the Enforcers were relentlessly focused on a single objective. *Subduing other Chosen.* They were the Directorate's—and the Emperor's—ultimate trump card.

"Spinakker," Zeph said when she got her breath back. "I...I didn't expect..."

"No one does," Spinakker said. "That's the point, really. They"—he gestured casually at the four men with the power to annihilate cities— "are just a precaution. If Ashok surrenders quietly, this will all be over in a moment."

"What do you need from me?"

"Show us where to find him. And, if you can, encourage him not to make trouble."

"I can't." Zeph swallowed. "I can't face him. Not when he'll know that I..."

"We will guarantee your safety," one of the Enforcers said. His voice was as flat and dead as his eyeless gaze.

"I can't." Zeph looked back at Spinakker. "*Please.* I did what you wanted."

Spinakker gave her a bland smile. "We appreciate your continued cooperation."

He gestured at the door. Feeling numb inside, Zeph led the way, the intelligence agent and his deadly escort staying close behind her.

Back in the first-level atrium, other researchers recoiled at the sight of her companions, hurrying out of their way. Spinakker had an official-looking document bearing the seal of Directorate Intelligence, and he waved it in the direction of anyone who stared too long, fixing them with his colorless smile. The few looks anyone spared Zeph were pitying.

Whatever that is, she's mixed up in it, people thought. *Better her than me.* Or maybe, *She deserves it for trying to sleep her way to the top.*

Down the central stairway. First level, second level, third level. More stares, more sudden gasps as someone was abruptly confronted with the iron hand of the Directorate in the flesh. At the top of the fourth-level stair, Zeph paused.

"Something wrong?" Spinakker said.

"I don't know exactly where he is," she said. "His main lab is on level five, but he's taken over parts of four as well."

The intelligence agent glanced briefly at one of the Enforcers. "Show us where he might be on four," he said. "If he's not there, we can work our way downward."

Like flushing out some dangerous predator. Which, from their perspective, was exactly what they were doing. Nia screamed again in Zeph's mind. *I can't even blame them.*

Only a few researchers remained on level four, and they cleared out quickly at the Enforcers' curt orders. Zeph led Spinakker through empty rooms, past her own former lab, where plaintive squeaks still came from bored vulpi yearlings. They quickly encountered Ashok's new security perimeter, windows frosted over and door sealed shut with a *deiat* lock.

"Open it," Spinakker said.

One of the Enforcers stepped forward and held out a hand. There was a smell of burning metal and a wash of heat. The unmetal frame of the lock sagged. He pulled the door open, and his fellows went through, moving low and fast. After a moment, Spinakker followed, gesturing to Zeph to keep up. They went through the next room and the next, Enforcers meticulously clearing each before moving on.

The Chosen soldiers seemed uninterested in the actual contents of the lab, but Spinakker looked around intently. The setups were familiar to Zeph—glass tubes of reflective agent, like thick black syrup, and bigger jars containing the animal experiments. Most were empty, as though Ashok had stopped using this part of the complex. *I thought he needed the space...*

"Contact," one of the Enforcers hissed. He made a series of hand signs, and the four of them spread out to either side of a doorway. The door was closed and the glass was frosted, but Zeph could see something moving on the other side.

"Call to him," Spinakker said, moving close to Zeph's side. "Tell him you want to see him."

If she'd wanted to, she could have warned Ashok at any time, and the intelligence agent would've had no way of knowing. *Either he still doesn't know about our blood-bond, or he trusts me.* Zeph knew which one of *those* she found more likely.

"Ashok?" she said. "It's me."

Zeph? The response came in her mind. *What are you doing here? I thought...*

Spinakker waved for her to keep talking. Zeph swallowed and said, "Someone needs to see you. He says it's important. Can I come in?"

"Of course," Ashok said, his voice muffled by the door. "You just startled me, that's all."

"Stay back," Spinakker said, chopping his hand downward like a falling blade.

One Enforcer yanked the door open and the other three burst through, moving sideways to clear the doorway. Zeph saw Ashok on the far side of the room, dressed in a protective suit of the sort they wore around dangerous samples. Several large vats of reflective agent stood on two big tables, while a large tank contained dark brown liquid. Something shifted inside, gory strands of muscle briefly visible against the tank wall. Past him, another door led back into the central stairwell.

"Nial-Est-Ashok!" Spinakker shouted from the doorway. "The Directorate places you under arrest. Sever your *deiat* connection and allow yourself to be bound!" He grabbed Zeph's arm, painfully tight. "Tell him to give up."

"Ashok!" Zeph said. "Please don't fight! I don't want anyone to get hurt."

She wasn't sure if Spinakker expected her plea to work, or just intended to use her as a hostage. Either way, Ashok turned from the tank, slowly spreading his hands.

Are you all right? he said in her mind. *They haven't hurt you?*

I'm fine, Zeph said. *But I'm scared.* Please. *Just... come along, and we'll talk everything through.*

You— She felt surprise in his mind, and then a spreading tinge of rage. *You did this, didn't you? You called them.*

What was I supposed to do? Nia's dead, *Ashok! That thing took her apart in front of me, and you want to make more like it!*

It was an accident! We can't just give up because of one failure. Progress sometimes means sacrifice.

Will you listen *to yourself—*

I would have saved you. His mental voice was a growl. *Remember that.*

Zeph gasped. "Be careful—"

Ashok closed his hands into fists. White light bloomed around him, a sphere that quickly went mirror smooth, like a metallic soap bubble. The Enforcers stopped advancing, shimmering shields springing up in front of them.

"Drop him!" the one in the doorway shouted. "Subdue subdue subdue."

The air split open with a wrenching *boom*. White beams stabbed from the three leading Enforcers, slamming against the mirror-sphere with fountaining bursts of power. The sphere flickered, then burst apart, curved pieces blowing outward in lethal shards. They broke against the shields of the Enforcers, vanishing in sprays of twinkling dust.

Every piece of glassware in the room shattered. Reflective agent spilled across the tables, a powder so fine that puffs of it wafted into the air. The big tank broke, too, and a wave of brown stuff sloshed across the tile. Left behind in a nest of broken glass was one Ashok's experiments, like a great multiarmed octopus, but with three vulpi heads fused horribly together. It gave a bubbling squeal and reached for the closest Enforcer, while behind it Ashok was running for the door.

"Burn it!" the lead Enforcer shouted. "Follow him!"

Tentacles snatched at the armored Chosen but didn't reach him, crisping into blackened flesh as they brushed the man's shield. He slashed a hand, and white fire stabbed out and obliterated the monstrous creature. Ashok had the door open and was sprinting down the stairs. Two Enforcers ran after him.

"What's downstairs?" Spinakker said, still holding tight to Zeph's arm.

"His private lab," Zeph babbled. "More experiments."

"Anything dangerous?"

"More things like *that*. But the lab is armored. Flux-stabilized unmetal."

"Shit," the lead Enforcer said. He brought up one hand, speaking into a miniaturized communicator. "Stop him before he seals the door. Watch for more hostiles—"

He coughed, tried to continue, and coughed again.

"What's wrong?" the last Enforcer said. "Are you—"

The leader doubled over, fumbling at the straps for his mask. He got it off and flung it away. Black sludge dripped from the mouthpiece, spattering across the floor. The man tried to breathe, but something *bubbled* in his chest. When he coughed again, great globs of black stuff were all that emerged. The other Enforcer backed away.

"Fuck *fuck* possible contamination, report—report status—" He, too, was coughing, struggling to draw breath. The leader was on hands and knees now, vomiting up a continuous stream of black streaked with bits of red viscera.

Zeph stared at the dying men, at the billowing clouds of reflective agent. She yanked her arm free of Spinakker's grip, his nails cutting bloody tracks in her skin.

"Run!" she shouted at him.

"But—" He watched the second Enforcer collapse, uncomprehending. "How—"

"*Run!*" Zeph was halfway across the room and accelerating. Overhead, an alarm began to sound.

"*Move!*" Spinakker shouted, pounding up the stairs past the second level and shouldering a junior researcher aside. "Out of the way!"

Zeph had fallen a few steps behind. The agent had taken a few moments to follow her, but he seemed tireless, while she was already fighting a brutal stitch in her side. Everyone in the facility was out in the halls, drawn by the sound of the alarm, but nobody knew what to do. The automated alert was supposed to be followed by instructions, but those would have come from Ashok.

Everyone will be all right if they just stay calm. The sound of his voice in her head nearly made Zeph trip on the first-floor landing. *The reflective variant only affects Chosen.*

What the fuck *did you do, Ashok?*

I knew they would try to stop me eventually. I couldn't allow it. He seemed calm now, his anger gone. *The alert automatically seals the facility, so the reflective agent won't spread. We'll have to figure out a way to get supplies in and out, I suppose. I'm afraid you and your colleagues are in here for the long haul.*

What the sun-blasted fuck *are you talking about?*

I assume you saw what my modified reflective agent did to the Enforcers.

It'll do the same to any Chosen who tries to interfere. It should keep them out, but by the same token none of us can leave, at least until I figure out an antidote and come to an agreement with my superiors.

What about you?

Oh, I'm quite safe. Even reflective agent can't penetrate flux-stabilized armor.

They'll kill you for this, Zeph said desperately. *You know they will.*

They're welcome to try.

Spinakker turned the corner to the main entrance, and Zeph followed, but she already knew what she would see. The huge isolation doors had swung shut in front of the startled security guard, bolts slamming into place on the far side. A Chosen might have been able to cut through, but nothing they had in the lab would even make a dent.

"*Fuck,*" Spinakker swore. "Is there another way out?"

"They'll all be closed," Zeph said numbly. "The alarm system is designed to isolate the complex completely. It shuts down the Gate and blocks the door here and on the hangar level."

"How do you open them?"

"Only the site administrator has the authority."

"We'll see about that," Spinakker growled. "Where's the nearest communicator?"

"My room." She pointed, but he shoved her forward, and she stumbled into a run.

Ahead of them, researchers were coming around the corner and realizing for the first time they were trapped. Some screamed, while others rushed forward to pound uselessly against the sealed doors. A few recognized Zeph and shouted to her as she shoved past, heading the opposite way. Their meaning was lost under the wall of noise.

I want you to know I understand, Ashok said. *What you did. It hurts me, but I understand. It was your friend who was killed, not mine. I should have been more considerate.*

You're fucking crazy, Ashok.

Now, now. No call for that.

She found her suite, opened the door, and stumbled through. Spinakker closed and locked the door behind her. He ran to the communicator, entering a rapid series of commands she didn't recognize.

A handsome Chosen appeared in the image projector. "Spinakker. What in the name of the sun is going on?"

"Ashok laid a trap, sir," Spinakker said. His bearing had gone straight and formal. "He's sealed the complex. Alpha team is down. I need support."

"Support from *where*?" Zeph said. "The Gate's shut down."

"Skyfortress *Glory in Victory* is already overhead," he snapped.

"Who's this?" the Chosen said, eyes narrowing.

"Local asset, sir. Someone needs to get the door open from the outside, and then we'll need full containment. Everyone inside may need to be processed."

"Everyone?" The Chosen's eyebrows went up.

"Ashok has spread some kind of airborne poison. Fast and lethal. I don't know how long it lasts or how far it will spread."

"It's not a poison," Zeph said. "It's called a reflective agent. It's used to help direct an organism how to self-modify with *dhaka*. Ashok must have tailored it for the Chosen and had it direct them to . . . self-destruct, basically."

The man in the projector had gone pale. "I need to consult with my superiors."

"But—"

The connection broke. Spinakker whirled on Zeph.

"When I need your expertise, I'll ask for it," he snarled. "Do you know how long this 'agent' lasts?"

"No," Zeph said, shrinking away. "I'm sorry. Ashok never told me more than that. I mostly helped him with the animal side."

The communicator chimed. Spinakker swore again and turned back to it, but instead of the Chosen he'd spoken to, it was Ashok's face that appeared.

"Ah, I thought you'd be in my quarters," he said. "May I ask your name?"

"Spinakker. Directorate Intelligence." He growled the words. "Open your lab and cooperate in resolving this situation, and it's possible you'll avoid execution."

"Rather the opposite, I'm afraid," Ashok said. "If I left the lab, I would end up like your friends. In here, on the other hand, I am secure. And if I open the main doors..."

"Blackmail," Spinakker growled.

"I'd prefer to say *incentive to negotiate.* I want nothing more than to serve the Empire. Leave me alone to do my work, and everyone wins."

"They won't stand for it," Spinakker said. "You know they won't."

"They have little choice."

"You don't want to back the Directorate into a corner. Trust me."

But Ashok had cut the connection, his serenely confident smile vanishing. Spinakker barely had time to spit a string of curses before it chimed again, this time with the image of his Chosen superior.

"Agent Spinakker," the man said, still looking pale. "Can you secure the complex? Ensure that no one can open the doors?"

Spinakker looked at Zeph, who shook her head, terrified. He grimaced.

"No, sir. Not without support. We need to seize control of the lab's system."

"I see." The Chosen swallowed. "In that case, I regret very much to inform you that we will be executing the final contingency."

"Sir—"

"Thank you for your service, Agent."

The image disappeared. Spinakker sat heavily in the console chair, shoulders slumping.

"What does that mean?" Zeph said. "What's the final contingency?"

The agent didn't respond. His eyes were closed.

"Spinakker." Zeph put her hand on his shoulder. "*What's happening?*"

"The final contingency," Spinakker pronounced slowly, "is a fucking sunfire bomb."

No. The thought wasn't from Zeph's numbed mind. It was Ashok, pressing in on her. *No, no, no. You have to stop them.*

You did this, Zeph sent him, backing against the wall, eyes squeezing shut against welling tears. *You stupid* fucking *lunatic. You did this and now we're all going to die.*

You have to stop them, *listen to me.* Please, *Zeph, I didn't think they'd be this stupid—*

You think I *can do anything?*

Listen, *it won't* work, *the agent is too dispersed to be destroyed that way, they'll spread it into the stratosphere and then—*

Ashok's mental voice descended into a babble. Spinakker was humming something, off-key. Zeph thought of all the people crowding up against the main doors, hiding throughout the complex, the civilians in the town above them. She gathered her pain and hurled it at Ashok, a raw scream of primal fury, wrapping around his mind like a snake and never letting go—

And there was a soundless moment of light.

Maya

This time, when Maya woke, there was no sense of panic. Just resignation, and sadness, and pain. She sat up, and Beq rolled over beside her, groping for her spectacles.

"You said the ship has a library," Maya said.

Beq sat up beside her, blinking. "Yeah."

"Can you help me find it?"

"Now?"

Maya nodded.

"Sure." Beq yawned wide. "Why? What do you need to find?"

Maya took a long breath. "The truth."

Chapter Seventeen

Allied Imports was a solid concern, well capitalized and with fifty years of history behind its anodyne name. It was housed in a four-story building in the West Central district, only a few blocks from the Spike. The headquarters was gray stone and a slate roof, window niches carved with abstract decorations, the company name on a discreet brass plaque beside the front door. Gyre, dressed in a borrowed gray suit, rang the bellpull and felt out of place.

Sarah, beside him, was if anything more incongruous in a tradesman's cap and dark gloves to cover her artificial arm. She didn't seem bothered, though, and offered the doorman a wide smile when he appeared. Gyre gave a bow and said, "We have an appointment with the import manager."

"Of course," the man said, his own bow somewhat deeper. "Follow me, please."

Inside, the expression of prosperous respectability continued. The hallway was wood paneled, something of an expression of wealth in a place with no trees within hundreds of kilometers. Proper lamps burned overhead instead of blue-green glowstones, and the carpet was thick underfoot. From the name, Gyre had expected a bustling warehouse full of goods, but apparently the actual business of importing wasn't handled here. Instead there were just rows of doors, each with its own brass nameplate. The doorman took them to the second floor and deposited them in front of one such, then stood off to the side, watching in case they were inclined to wander.

"Come in," said Ibb. Gyre glanced at the silent footman and opened the door.

The office was about what he'd expected—warm, well furnished, respectable, without any overt sign of its tenant's adventurous past. Or *almost* no sign, at least. A pair of rapiers hung on the wall, and it would have taken close inspection to see that they were not blunted sport weapons. A rack in the corner held a wool coat and a familiar broad-brimmed hat.

The tenant himself, sitting behind a vast desk polished to a mirror sheen, hadn't changed much. Ibb was in his thirties, with light brown skin and close-cropped platinum hair. He wore a suit, instead of scavenger's leathers, but he still had the faintly amused expression that made it seem like he wasn't taking anything very seriously. He stood up as they entered, grin widening into a real smile, and gave a deep bow.

"Gyre, Sarah. It's been a while, hasn't it?"

"Time does seem to have gotten away from me," Gyre agreed, taking one of the chairs. Sarah took the other, and Ibb came around to sit on the front of the desk. "You're well, I hope? How are Jaken and the kids?"

"All well, thank the Chosen," Ibb said. "He's a senior executive here now. And Pela has just started an apprenticeship."

"Some of my friends couldn't believe you'd gone honest," Sarah said. "I always thought it'd suit you."

"The import trade is many things, but *honest* is not one of them." Ibb's smile turned sharklike. "A pen can destroy a man quite as effectively as a rapier."

"Especially these days, I would imagine," Gyre murmured.

"It's true. Times have been interesting since the new centarchs arrived. With the Gate closed and caravans down to a bare handful, imported goods are quite dear. But that can be its own kind of opportunity."

"I'm sure."

Ibb's smile faded a bit, looking from Gyre to Sarah. He cleared his throat.

"While it's good to see old friends, I have the feeling that you two haven't come here just to reminisce."

"No," Gyre admitted. "You've been following the problems with the tunnelborn?"

"I'd be a poor excuse for a businessman if I hadn't," Ibb said. "We don't own any manufactories, so our business isn't directly affected, but the whole community is on edge."

"Yora would have been excited," Sarah said.

"She would have," Ibb agreed. "But let me tell you up front that I don't intend to get involved, if that's what you've come to talk me into. I always respected Yora, but I worked with her for the money, not the cause."

"She understood that," Gyre said. "And that's not why we're here. I'm hoping that you can arrange a meeting with the Merchant Council."

Ibb raised one eyebrow. "I'm sure I can, but they hold regular open sessions—"

"Not for me," Gyre said quietly. "For Halfmask."

"Ah." Ibb drummed his fingers on the desk. "I see."

"It will have to be secret, obviously," Gyre said. "They certainly can't be seen to meet with the infamous thief. But they have to understand how much better it would be for everyone to make a deal. Rikard Gemspotter is getting ready to march on the Spike—whatever happens, it'll be bad for business. If I can broker a compromise..."

"Logical." Ibb sighed. "I worry, though, that the time for logic has passed. The council members are angry."

"So are the tunnelborn," Sarah said.

"No doubt." Ibb's fingers tapped out a complex rhythm as he pondered. "Yes, I think I see how that could be managed. Let me speak to a few people." He cocked his head. "You understand that I don't promise any kind of success."

"I understand," Gyre said. Frankly, he wasn't sure he expected to get anywhere himself. *But I have to at least try.* His sympathies might be with the tunnelborn, but neither side deserved the Corruptor. "Send a courier to the palace when you have something."

"You've certainly moved up in the world," Ibb said. "Unless they're keeping you in a cell at night."

Gyre chuckled. "Not exactly. But I don't get much sleep."

"You never did, if I recall." He leaned forward. "As a price for my help, I need gossip. Is it true that one of the centarchs is the same woman who burned Raskos' warehouse?"

"She is," Gyre said. "Maya Burningblade."

"I assume she's aware of your presence?"

"It's a long story." Gyre scratched the back of his neck. "She's my sister."

Ibb smiled delightedly. "That *does* sound like a long story. But one I'd be eager to hear."

"I'll fill you in after all this is over." *Assuming any of us are still alive.* "Thanks for your help."

After they'd been escorted from the building, Kit freed herself from Gyre's coat collar and hopped onto his shoulder. The little spider-construct shook itself like a cat.

"He seems to be doing well," she said.

"He left the group before the ambush," Sarah said mildly. "Because he didn't trust *you*, if I recall."

"I can't say he was wrong about that," Kit said. "I wonder if I should have apologized."

"Let's hold off on that for now," Gyre said. He trusted Ibb, but the fewer people who knew about Kit, the better. "Anything from Maya?"

"Nothing specific," Kit said. "We're on our way back. Shouldn't be more than a couple of days."

"Rikard's march is in a couple of days," Gyre said. "I need all the help I can get."

"I'll see if I can get them to speed things up." There was a snigger in her voice that suggested there was something she wasn't telling him. For the moment, Gyre let it slide.

"Have you figured out a meeting place for the next run?" he said to Sarah.

"I think so," Sarah said. "There should be room for a couple of hundred people. Rikard will probably get wind of it, but he hasn't bothered us since you gave Enta that demonstration."

"Hopefully she won't need another." As the groups got larger, there was more and more danger of people getting hurt. *If Rikard sends a mob instead of his sister and a couple of thugs...* "We're not going to get there a couple of hundred people at a time, though. Even with rumor on our side."

"Not if Rikard keeps to his schedule," Sarah agreed. "But what's the alternative?"

"When the tunnelborn march, that'll be a plaguing lot of people in one place," Gyre mused. "It'd be a good time to talk to them."

"Even if we put Apphia somewhere up high, she wouldn't be able to shout loud enough for everyone to hear," Sarah said. "Plus I doubt Rikard's people would just stand there and let it happen."

"Nina and the scavengers can run the next couple of meetings without you, right?"

"I think so," Sarah said carefully. "Why?"

"I have an idea, and I need you to make it work."

Sarah groaned. "Is this like when you needed me to make a remote-activated bomb to break into the palace?"

"It does have a bit of that flavor, yes."

"Oh good," Kit said, capering. "I love that kind of plan."

The last time Gyre had been to the palatial estate owned by the Moorcat Combine, he'd been meeting Kit on the great dome beside the gold-plated statue of Galbio the Moorcat. At the time, he hadn't had the chance to appreciate the Moorcats' gardens, which were extensive and included the obligatory hedge maze as well as endless nooks and crannies stuffed with architectural follies and benches for private rendezvous.

Tonight's meeting was in a large marble pavilion, open-sided and set with heroic statues meant to represent Chosen. Humans the size of children danced innocently around their feet. The gardens stretched out in every direction, to the Pit on one side and the Spike on another. The remaining neighbors were other nobles and merchant houses nearly as rich as the Moorcats. Nearly, but not quite—it was no surprise to find the Moorcats themselves at the heart of the Merchant Council.

Whoever had set up the meeting hadn't done him the courtesy of giving the guards the night off, so Gyre was forced to make his way surreptitiously. A test, of sorts, but not a particularly difficult one. It hadn't been that hard to sneak around the place *before* the ghouls had given him the ability to see in the dark and slow time. When he reached the pavilion, he found two large and well-armed individuals already waiting. Gyre considered tapping them on the shoulder, just to be cheeky, but he guessed they'd react badly. Explaining to the council why he'd killed their guards was not how he wanted to start the meeting. Instead he dropped into one of the pavilion's archways, his mask glowing silver in the moonlight, and gave a polite cough.

The pair were alert, he had to give them that. They both had blaster pistols in hand between breaths, not aimed at him but not far from it. He gave them a bow.

"Halfmask, is it?" one of them grunted.

"Indeed."

"Didn't think you'd show." The man glanced at his companion. "Fetch Their Excellencies."

She slipped into the darkness. Gyre and the big man stared at one another in frigid silence until footsteps announced the council's representatives.

Gyre very nearly laughed out loud. There were three of them, a man and two women, and they were dressed in a penny-opera costumer's idea of what to wear to conduct clandestine business. Hooded black cloaks, so long they dragged over the gravel, with black silk and silver jewelry beneath. All three wore masks—a fox for the man, a warbird for one of the women, and a cat for the other. The one with the warbird didn't seem like she could quite see out of her eyeholes.

"Greetings, Halfmask," the man said in a stage whisper. "I have to admit I'm impressed."

"That I could make it here?" Gyre said in a normal tone. "It wasn't hard. And you don't have to whisper; it defeats the purpose of meeting in the middle of a private estate at midnight. Unless you have other nocturnal guests you're hoping to avoid?"

The man winced but spoke out loud. "As you wish. You may call us Fox, Warbird, and Cat."

"Only fair," Gyre agreed amiably. "You speak for the council?"

"We will hear you on behalf of the full council," Fox said, puffing up a little with self-importance. Gyre got the sense this was a habit—he was a small man who endeavored to carry himself like a large one, with a bald head beneath the hood of his cloak.

"They will, of course, have to review any proposals," Cat said. Her disguise was the most effective of the three, showing little but her pale, fluttering hands. By her voice, she was a young woman.

Warbird, in contrast, was older and somewhat stout, with sensible boots visible beneath the hem of her flowing black cloak. She gave a harrumph that made clear she was not happy with the proceedings.

"Assuming they are worth the council's time," she said. "Which I quite frankly doubt."

"We know what you've been preaching," Fox said. "Some girl dressed up as a Communard, telling everyone how the Empire abused her. Is that about right?"

"She is precisely who she claims to be," Gyre said. "And it isn't her own abuse she's worried about. The Empire arbitrarily arrested large numbers of people in Khirkhaz and used them as raw materials to create plaguespawn soldiers."

"Ridiculous," Fox sneered. "There's so much wrong with that story I don't know where to start. Plaguespawn soldiers! Impossible."

"Not for a *dhakim*."

"*Dhakim* are not unknown in Deepfire," Cat said. "But I have never met one who claimed to be capable of creating obedient humanoid servants."

"Suppose it's not the sort of thing you'd advertise, would you?" Warbird said. "'Oh yes, I'm taking people apart and putting them back together inside out, tell your friends!'"

"But we're talking about the Republic," Fox said. "Not the Splinter Kingdoms or even Deepfire. *Dhakim* aren't tolerated. We certainly don't hand them lawfully arrested criminals!"

"With respect," Gyre said. "It's not the Republic anymore. It's the Empire. And this comes right from the top."

"From the Emperor, you mean." Cat cocked her head. "You're accusing him of being a *dhakim*?"

"Preposterous," Fox said. "He's a *Chosen*."

"All anyone has for that is his word," Gyre said.

"The *Order* has accepted him," Fox snapped. "Did *they* just take his word?"

Gyre smiled thinly. "You may have gathered I don't have a great deal of respect for the Order."

"What, exactly, is your proposition?" Warbird said. "Clearly you have your issues with that loathsome Gemspotter, but why come to us?"

Fox was still sputtering incoherently, but Cat eyed Gyre through her mask with cool interest. Gyre drew himself up and said, "I'm trying to tell the tunnelborn that the Empire won't help them, and my message for you is the same. They're going to be very bad for business."

"Which is exactly why these ungrateful scum must be crushed *now*," Fox said. "If the Empire finds Deepfire in chaos, naturally they'll want to impose a new order. But if we have things in hand before that, no great changes will be necessary. We will be thanked for maintaining the peace."

"Assuming the tunnelborn don't burn the city down around your ears," Gyre snapped.

"Pah. They're nothing more than bottom-feeders. We give them jobs, a semblance of civilization, and this is how they repay us? Show a bit of force and they'll break, depend upon it."

"I may not be as confident as our dear Fox," Warbird said, "but I admit we don't seem to have an alternative. It's all very well to say the Empire is bad, but what exactly would you have us do about it?"

"Resist," Gyre said. "Merchants and tunnelborn together. Deepfire is high in the mountains, well fortified, and the only nearby Gate can be blocked. Working together, we could—"

"Resist!" Fox gave a braying laugh. "Mad. Absolutely stark raving mad. I should have guessed."

"I've been fighting the Republic for years," Gyre said. "The Empire's no different."

"Except they have a Chosen leading them," Cat said mildly.

"And you must admit, dear, that your fight against the Republic has not been notably successful," Warbird said.

"I never had the whole city on my side."

"Plague it," Fox said. "I don't have to stand here and listen to this. You're lucky I'm an honorable man, thief, or I'd call my guards and have you arrested."

"You said you'd take my proposal to the council," Gyre said, keeping his tone neutral. He'd expected this, but he still found his teeth grinding in frustration.

"I was hoping," Warbird said, "that you might be here with an offer from the tunnelborn. I understand Gemspotter would not want to be seen to give in, for the sake of his pride, but this continued defiance serves no one. We would even be willing to grant a few concessions so he could claim a victory."

"Rikard won't give in," Gyre said. "Tomorrow thousands of tunnelborn are going to march on the Spike."

"We're well aware," Fox snapped. "We'll be ready for them. A show of force! Just the thing."

"*Please.* It won't go the way you hope. Start fighting and there'll be a bloodbath."

"So Gemspotter would have us think," sniffed Warbird. "Personally I'm not convinced."

"Even if there is," Fox snarled, "most of the blood will be tunnel-born. Is that what he wants?"

"I'm not privy to his councils," Gyre said. *But this is my third attempt at revolution, and I can recognize a pattern.* "In the name of humanity, I ask you to immediately propose a truce, lift the blockade, and negotiate."

"Never!" Fox said. "Tell *that* to your tunnelborn friends." He spun on one heel, black cloak flaring dramatically. The effect was slightly spoiled when it became stuck in a rosebush.

"Lifting the blockade," Warbird said apologetically, "rather defeats the point of the blockade, I think. Good evening, sir." She bowed and departed as well, with somewhat more dignity than her companion.

"And you?" Gyre said to Cat.

"Oh, I have no authority," she said. "I'm just…intrigued."

"People are going to die."

"Quite likely," she agreed, and bowed. "Good evening, Halfmask. I suspect I'll see you soon."

"There are a plaguing lot of them," Ritabel said. "Thousands. Maybe ten thousand. More every hour."

She had the frozen, eyes-forward look of a person who had told you so, repeatedly, and now that the calamity had come to pass was absolutely determined to avoid any blame. Tanax, sitting across the table from her, rubbed his eyes.

"Do you have any indication of when they plan to march?" he said.

"They're making no secret of it," the tourmarch said. "Sundown."

"Is the council going to try to stop them at the city's edge?" Gyre asked.

"Evidently not," Ritabel said. "Their forces have pulled off the barricade. My people are spread far too thin."

"Bring them back when the tunnelborn come forward," Tanax said. "Regroup here at the Spike. Call in every patrol to man the walls."

"Yes, Centarch," Ritabel said. Her voice had a sliver of well-concealed contempt.

"You may go."

She saluted and stomped out. Tanax glanced at Gyre.

"She thinks we're screwing this up," he said. "And she's not wrong. I don't see a good ending."

"I'm not sure I do either," Gyre admitted. "But I'll do everything I can. Keep the Auxies off the streets. The last thing we need is some overzealous patrol starting a fight."

"The council's mercenaries will probably be worse," Tanax said. "Unless you think they've pulled back as well."

"Possible," Gyre said, "but I wouldn't bet on it. I think they're preparing an ambush."

He leaned forward. A large map of the city was spread out on the table, the Pit slashing through its center like an open wound, with grease-pencil annotations of the tunnelborn's numbers and probable route of march. Gyre laid his finger on a large open area at the edge of the West Central district.

"This is where I would do it, if I were them," Gyre said. "It's the first big square along the route to the Spike. Bottle them up here, and block the surrounding streets."

"And then what? Try to slaughter the lot?" Tanax shook his head. "I don't believe even the Merchant Council would try that."

"They won't *try*." Gyre thought of Fox's bluster. "They'll tell themselves that a few demonstrations and warning shots will send the tunnelborn scurrying back to their holes. But it won't, and by the time they find out, there'll be nothing to be done about it."

"I could go out there and stop the march..." Tanax said hesitantly.

"No. We'd lose any chance of getting the tunnelborn on our side." Gyre shook his head. "I have an idea, if Sarah and Apphia can make it work."

The centarch gave him a searching look, then sighed. "Well. I don't have anything better to offer."

"If worse comes to worst, you and the Auxies can defend the Spike and keep everyone here safe."

Tanax nodded. "If there's anything else you need, let me know."

Gyre's mood was gloomy as he descended the stairs and corridors of the palace. Kit, on his shoulder, shifted out from under his collar.

"Something wrong?" she said.

"How can you tell?"

"You're stomping everywhere. It gives me a headache."

"Really?"

"No. But it would if I still had a head."

"Thank the Chosen for small favors, then." Gyre sighed. "I'm wondering if we're doing the right thing. Maybe we should have fled the city when Tanax first suggested it."

"It's not like that would've stopped any of this," Kit said. "The tunnelborn would still have taken on the merchants."

"That's...surprisingly sensible, coming from you."

"Excuse me. I am *very* sensible."

"Except when you keep telling me to kill people and blow things up."

"That was *before* I lost my body. And a few times after, I guess. I'm getting better!"

"Acquiring morals?"

"Nah. It's a body thing. No adrenaline rush without adrenaline, right?"

"It doesn't seem to have hurt your sex drive."

"Some things transcend the physical," Kit said smugly.

Gyre laughed out loud. "I missed you, after Khirkhaz."

"Ooh, don't tell Apphia! She might get jealous." Kit went quiet a moment. "Sorry. I know you two haven't...I mean, I'm not sure if you're still..."

"Neither am I," Gyre said. "After what she's been through, I'm not going to push it."

"Probably for the best. Not a lot of other prospects, though. Sarah and Elariel seem committed, Maya's your sister and she and Beq are a thing, and Xalen doesn't want anything to do with anything. Tanax or Varo, maybe? I bet Varo would be—"

"Or," Gyre said, "I could concentrate on the task at hand."

"I *guess*."

"Speaking of Maya, though—"

"Oh *ho!*"

"*Kit.*"

"Just teasing."

"Speaking of Maya," Gyre repeated, "how long until she and Beq are back?"

"A few hours, I think? Hard to say exactly."

"There's something you're not telling me."

"Is there?" If the little spider had a face, it would have been looking innocent.

"*Kit.* There are lives at stake."

"But..." She heaved a sigh. "I just wanted to see the look on your face when you saw."

"Saw *what?*"

She told him. And, like a kick had dislodged a stuck piece of grit, the gears began to turn in Gyre's mind.

"Hello?" Gyre said outside the half-open door.

"Gyre?" Elariel said. "Come in. It's just me."

The palace staff had kept Jaedia's little bedroom immaculate, sheets crisp and white, fresh flowers in a bowl on the windowsill. The unconscious centarch looked peaceful, eyes closed, breathing gently under a gray blanket. Elariel sat in a chair at her bedside, a hand on Jaedia's shoulder. She stretched and looked up as Gyre entered.

"How's she doing?" Gyre said.

"As well as can be expected," the ghoul said. "I keep telling Maya, this kind of nerve regrowth isn't dangerous, it's just slow."

"She's not going to wake up anytime soon, then?"

"Not for another few weeks at least."

"I'm not sure whether to be disappointed or relieved," Gyre said, taking a seat on the foot of the bed. "Having to explain everything to her would be a challenge, but having another centarch on our side would certainly be helpful."

"Assuming she *would* be on our side," Elariel said. "Maya thinks she can do no wrong, but who's to say she wouldn't choose the Corruptor? Most of the others have."

"Yeah." Gyre thought of Fox's insistence that the Order had to be right about the new Emperor. "Centarchs aren't any wiser than ordinary people."

"Just a lot more dangerous," Elariel said.

"How about you?" Gyre said. "Are you doing all right?"

"Better," Elariel said. "I still wake up every night with my heart beating out of my chest, but I'm not screaming as much, which is a relief for Sarah."

Gyre winced. "I'm sorry."

"There wasn't much alternative, was there? You saved me from being executed. I couldn't have stayed behind in Deepfire alone. I had to stay with you, and you had to... be who you are."

"I still wish I'd had the chance to take you somewhere safe. After the Spire, you've paid any debt to me twice over."

"There isn't anywhere safe," Elariel said. "Not with the Corruptor out there. That's what I'm trying to tell the Geraia."

"You got in contact with them?"

"Not yet. I send a messenger-construct every couple of days. Some of them must have gotten through, but I haven't heard anything back.

Probably Tyraves is just ignoring them." She shook her head. "And have you had any progress convincing the people of Deepfire to fight?"

"They're going to fight, all right. They're just fighting each other instead of the Corruptor." Gyre frowned. "Tonight we might have a chance to change that. If it works like I hope. If not..." He shook his head. "Tanax should be able to hold the walls of the palace."

"'Should be.' I'll add being torn apart by a bloodthirsty mob to my list of night terrors."

"If it doesn't work, we'll get everyone out of the city by Gate," Gyre said. "Look for somewhere else to hide."

"I thought you needed to find the Corruptor's lab to figure out a way to strike back."

"If the city's tearing itself to pieces, it's not worth the risk. He must be on his way here. If we can't stop him when he arrives, it won't matter anyway."

"Cheery."

"Is it me or are you more sarcastic than usual?"

"It's my influence," Kit said from Gyre's shoulder. "I'm very proud of her progress."

"I didn't need much tutoring. Leaving Refuge has been one long lesson in why I should have stayed home."

Gyre smiled. "What about Sarah?"

"Sarah is..." The ghoul blushed slightly and bit her lip. "She's going with you tonight, isn't she?"

"She's the only one who can make all the arcana work. Why?"

"Just... take care of her." Elariel looked down, abruptly interested in the pattern of the blanket. "Make sure she gets back okay."

"I thought ghouls didn't care about their sexual partners," Kit said.

"We don't care about them *because* they're sexual partners," Elariel said, too quickly. Her blush deepened. "But Sarah is a... a friend, too."

"I'll take care of her," Gyre said.

Elariel gave him a shaky smile. Gyre slipped out, shutting the door quietly behind him.

He *ought* to have headed for his room to get a few hours of sleep. *It's going to be a long night.* Instead he found himself climbing the palace steps, one after another, until he emerged onto a slate-flagged patio adorning the roof. In better times, it would have been a place for guests of the dux to take their breakfast, but at the moment it was unused, elegant wrought-iron furniture concealed under a tarp.

From here, Gyre could see most of the city. The Spike itself, the tall Chosen-built spire, rose behind him like the gnomon of an enormous sundial, the waning sun sending its sharp shadow across the estates of the rich. In the other direction was the Pit, running north to south like a great wound, belching white smoke. Beyond it was the West Central district and its market, where all tonight's preparations were focused, visible as a gap in the sea of roofs.

Gyre's eyes, however, were turned north. And he wasn't the only one. Xalen stood at the iron railing, staring into the darkening clouds. He joined her, and she shot him a sideways glance.

"Can you see it?" she said, without preamble.

Gyre shook his head. "Just clouds. Maya said it generates them itself." He closed his real eye, focusing the silver one on the northern rim of the crater. Were the clouds there darker and thicker than the wispy gray haze that painted the rest of the sky? *Or am I seeing things?* He felt a thrill of nerves. *If Maya and Beq don't get the timing right, things could get very bloody tonight.*

"Any other day," Xalen said, "I would be looking forward to the greatest discovery of my career. Instead all I can think about is—"

"—what use we can put it to," Gyre supplied. "Yeah."

"The joy of discovery for its own sake is a luxury of happier times." Xalen sighed. She looked at Gyre again. "I understand there may be trouble tonight."

"You might say that." *If you were trying for a massive understatement.*

"I apologize for not offering my assistance. I don't have anything to add in these matters of politics." She gestured at the horizon with her one good hand. "My attention has been somewhat occupied."

"If this works, it'll be because of what you and Maya figured out," Gyre said. "No apology needed. In fact"—he shifted awkwardly—"I've been meaning to say I'm sorry to you."

Xalen blinked. "What for?"

"When we first met, in the Forge. I was...unkind. About your father."

"Prodominus." Xalen cocked her head. "You could not have known our relationship. It would be unfair of me to be angry with you."

"Still." They'd barely spoken since. "I wanted to say it."

"Thank you, then," Xalen said, still looking a little baffled.

"You're doing okay?"

"I am not crippled by grief, if that is your meaning. I have spent my time attempting to solve the problem of the Corruptor."

"For your father's sake?"

"In part." She put her hand on the rail. "It may be hard for others to understand, but I was happy in the Forge, among my books and relics. I would have been glad to grow old without ever leaving. The Corruptor took that from me when he commandeered the Order, along with everything else." Her knuckles were white on the iron. "Not the most terrible of sufferings, perhaps. But it is mine."

Gyre felt an urge to put a comforting hand on her shoulder and fought it down, remembering her reaction the last time. Instead he leaned against the railing himself, not sure what to say.

"We all have our own reasons for fighting," he hazarded. "I wouldn't want to compare one to the other."

Xalen nodded. After a moment, her hand relaxed and fell to her side. Together, they watched the clouds drift overhead and wondered what they might hide.

Come on, Maya. Make this work.

When he'd returned to his quarters and tried to sleep, of course, rest had eluded him. For the moment, humming adrenaline masked the exhaustion, but Gyre was certain he'd pay a price before the night was over.

"Check in with everyone," Gyre said, watching the tumult at the edge of the city.

"Yes, sir!" Kit saluted with one of her tiny legs. Gyre rolled his eyes.

The sun was nearly set, slipping behind the mountains at the western rim of the crater. In that direction, where the council had set up their scrip market, a great mass of humanity had emerged from underground carrying torches and glowstones, like a sea of fireflies. With his silver eye, Gyre could zoom in and see the leading tunnelborn pushing through the portable barriers protecting the market, shoving aside abandoned stalls and empty tables. Both the Auxies and the council mercenaries who had manned that line had vanished, leaving an open path into the center of the city.

As I expected. From where Gyre stood, on the roof of the Glysen Vineyards building—one of the tallest in the district, and centrally located—he could see most of the city. A crooked but relatively direct path led down several large avenues from the poorer western districts into the better-off West Central, ending in the broad flagstone square that was the West Central Market. From there, the mob would have to turn north, skirt one end of the Pit, then loop south to reach the forbidding tower of the Spike.

If they get that far. That the market would be an early stop was obvious to anyone who could read a map. The local shopkeepers had boarded up their establishments and cleared out, and all the cafés were closed, leaving the normally bustling square empty. *If they know what's coming, the council certainly must.* There had been activity in the surrounding streets all day.

"Barricades are going up," Kit said. "All around the square, except on the west side. You called it."

"Not much of a stretch," Gyre said. He'd watched the Auxies do riot control, and there was a standard playbook. *Box them in, cut them off, confront them with overwhelming force, arrest whomever you like.* He suspected some ex-soldiers—or possibly current ones—were on the council's payroll. "Sarah's equipment is in place?"

"All set," Kit said. "She's double-checking it now."

Gyre thought of Elariel. "Tell her to make sure to get out of the square before the crowd gets there."

"She says, 'Don't try to teach a warbird how to kick.'"

Gyre chuckled. "Fair. Apphia and Nina are ready?"

"Ready." Kit paused a moment, listening. "Nina says she wants to be closer to the action. Apphia is shouting at her."

"All normal, then. And Maya?"

"She says they're ready. They need about a minute's notice."

Gyre couldn't help glancing to the north. *Not that I don't have faith, but...* Lightning flashed against the darkened horizon, and gloomy clouds blotted out the stars.

"Okay. Then we're ready."

He looked back at the crowd. The marchers were into the city proper now, packing the avenues shoulder to shoulder. Their voices were raised in a rhythmic chant. At this distance, it sounded like a roll of thunder. Watching them come, he could sympathize for a moment with the council and the merchants, their fear of what Gemspotter had unleashed. *Who wouldn't be afraid of something like this?*

Kit kept up a running commentary in his ear. "Sarah's finished her final check. She's out of the square. Council mercs are mounting the barricades—Chosen defend, they're packing a lot of firepower—uh-oh."

"That I don't like the sound of."

"I'm putting some of my bodies on the rooftops, and I'm not alone."

"Lookouts?"

"Snipers with blaster rifles. At least a half dozen of them."

"Plaguing *fuck*." Gyre turned to look toward the market. "That's just what we need. Do you have enough bodies to jump them?"

"I can handle...four," Kit said. "Two of them are together on the big stable roof. I can't get close enough without someone spotting me."

"I'm on my way." Gyre looked at the crowd again. He had minutes at best. "Try not to kill anybody unless you have to."

He concentrated, and his augmentations came on with a *click*. His silver eye drew the world in telescoping shadows, the few birds visible in the twilight becoming long cones of overlapping possible futures. Gyre turned away, running with a long, loping stride like he weighed nothing at all.

He'd chosen his observation post carefully, falling easily into the habits of his Halfmask days. The Glysen building, a six-story structure, was surrounded by other buildings on three sides. To the east was a four-story block of flats, its roof invitingly lower and separated by only a narrow gap. Gyre pushed off the edge of the sloping slate roof, Kit's ecstatic shriek in his ear, and sailed out into the night.

The shock of hitting the next roof shook the tiles underfoot, but his augmented muscles absorbed it with a crouch, and he sprinted to the next building. Another narrow alley passed underneath him, then another. The next roof was the stable, but a larger street gaped between Gyre and his target. He gritted his teeth and accelerated, straining.

"Yesssss," Kit said, "do it do it do it!"

Gyre didn't trouble himself to respond. He reached the very edge of the roof and leapt with all the strength his augmentations could muster, shooting out into the empty space like he was propelled from a crossbow. His hands stretched out, grasping, as though he could *will* the opposite rooftop closer—

His fingers scraped on the wooden shingles, one fingernail tearing as he scrabbled for purchase. A moment later his body swung against the side of the building with a *thump*, knocking the breath out of him. He felt like hanging there for a while, precarious position or no, but he forced himself up and over the edge, broken nail leaving a bloody streak on the wood.

Two dark forms were huddled along the side of the roof, carefully positioned where they wouldn't show a silhouette. Each had a blaster rifle by their side. The first, closer to Gyre, was starting to look up in slow-motion surprise.

Gyre moved, covering the distance between them with preternatural speed. He slammed a fist into the man's gut, doubling him over, and kicked his rifle away. The second sniper, hearing this, also got to his feet, but Gyre was already digging in his pouch for an alchemical. He'd gotten a fresh batch from Lynnia, after a thorough debriefing on the effects of the last satchel-full, and there were a couple of dreamers in among the more common bombs. He hurled one directly in the second sniper's face and it burst in a puff of white gas.

The first man drew a knife, swinging at Gyre in a slow arc behind a line of shadow-images. Gyre sidestepped, grabbed him around the throat, and squeezed, waiting until his opponent went limp in his arms. The other one was also out cold, the gas around him shredding in the light breeze. Gyre grabbed both blaster rifles and chucked them off the back of the roof, then made an easy leap to the neighboring building, where he could get a view of the oncoming crowd.

"Nicely done," Kit said.

"Did you take care of the rest?"

"Of course. How did you ever get anything done before I turned up?"

"With fewer sarcastic asides and dirty jokes?"

"Boringly, you mean."

"Pretty sure that's not a word." Gyre let his silver eye focus down the broad avenue. "Here they come."

The march had reached the square, spilling out from the tightly packed street and spreading out across the flagstones. Among the chaotic mass of shouting tunnelborn, a small group stayed in a tighter formation. Gyre recognized Enta at their head. *That'll be Rikard. Time to get in position.*

He'd put Apphia and Nina in one of the hotels that fronted the square, where they'd have a good view from the window and a quick escape route if something went wrong. He headed in that direction now, jumping across a few more roofs before descending to street level. The hotel was boarded up like the rest of the storefronts, and its main doors were chained shut. In the alley behind it, however, there was a service entrance, and its iron padlock was no match for the edge of Gyre's ghoul blade. He slipped inside, past the kitchens, and found a back stair up to the third floor. Nina opened the door to their suite at his knock and wrapped him in a spontaneous hug.

"Sorry," she said, disentangling herself. "Nervous. I get clingy when I'm nervous."

"Me too," Kit said. "Ask Gyre about the time we got stuck in a closet."

"Later," Gyre said. "Is Sarah here already?"

Nina nodded. "She and Apphia are almost finished."

The suite's sitting room had large windows facing out across the square. Two of Kit's smaller bodies were already here, standing at attention like multilegged hounds. The table and chairs had been dragged away, and a large circular pad occupied the center of the room, surrounded by inward-curving spines like a mouthful of teeth. A boxy piece of arcana sat next to it, covered in colorful lights and connected to the pad with a coil of wire.

"Gyre!" Sarah said. She was standing at the window, hand shading her eyes to get a better view. "You're late."

"Kit and I found some uninvited guests," Gyre said. "We handled them. Is something wrong?"

"Just keeping an eye on the projector," she said. "If someone finds it before we start—"

"Nobody will be poking around broken water towers," Kit said. "Not tonight. And I've got two bodies waiting."

"Still," Sarah said. "We're not going to get another chance at this. *And* I was up three nights building the plaguing thing."

"I'm still amazed you finished in time," Gyre said. "You're a genius."

"Well. We got a lot of the pieces whole in the scavenger markets. But I won't deny it."

"It feels strange to be watching from up here," Apphia said. She'd been sitting on the couch, reading intently from a small notebook. Now she set it aside and came to join them. "We should be down there with them. If something goes wrong…"

"If something goes wrong, we're not going to be able to stop it," Gyre said. "We'd just have to fight our way out, and that means we'd be adding to the bloodshed instead of preventing it. If we're going to make this work, it's going to be by persuading people."

"I know." Apphia shook her head, rubbing her arms as though against a chill. "It still seems...I don't know. Cowardly."

Gyre had to smile at that. Apphia's brand of rebellion, like Yora's, involved placing herself at the front of the charge. *I think they would have gotten along. That, or fought like cats in a sack.*

"There's a scuffle in the avenue on the northern side," Kit said. "I think—yeah, they've found the council barricade. No shooting yet, but they're moving in on the western side."

Gyre could see that for himself. The stream of people pushing into the square had thinned down to a few stragglers, and these were abruptly running in panic. Behind them came a phalanx of armored soldiers, wearing no uniform but heavily armed with blasters, crossbows, spears, and large oval shields in the Auxie pattern. Many wore alchemical masks to guard against vapors, turning them into bug-eyed abominations. They made a line across the avenue, and more men were rolling heavy carts into place behind them.

The tunnelborn were trapped in the square, ringed by heavily armed council mercenaries. Rikard and his personal guard were near the center of the vast crowd, and Gyre didn't see any panic there. The rebel leader could read a map as well as anyone else. *He knew something like this would happen. He's betting that, if push comes to shove, numbers will trump weapons.* He could easily be right—Gyre didn't have much respect for the council's planning if it included people like Fox. *But if it does come to that, we're all in trouble.*

"That's it," Apphia said, stepping up beside Gyre. "Should we turn it on?"

"Not yet." Gyre turned to Sarah. "You can get us sound from out there, right?"

"Yeah, hold on." She went to the arcana box and touched the controls. "This should—"

Noise burst out of it, a vast, incoherent chatter, like being in the midst of a flock of crows. Sarah twisted something, and it quieted slightly but became no more comprehensible. It was a thousand voices at once, ten thousand, overlapping in an endless babble. Chants sometimes broke through, synchronizing and drifting apart like audible tides—

"Fair pay for fair work! Fair pay for fair work!"

"No more two tiers!"

"Citizens out, tunnelborn in!"

"Give us food! Give us food!"

"Someone's on the roof," Kit said. One of her large bodies pointed at the window. "There."

Gyre spotted what she was referring to, though he doubted any of the others could see. His silver eye showed him a small group on a rooftop opposite the hotel, several armed soldiers standing beside a short man holding a conical megaphone. Gyre was pretty sure it was Fox, and became certain when the man put the megaphone to his lips and shouted. His voice emerged from the arcana box.

"People of the tunnels! Neighbors of Deepfire! Hear me!"

Neighbors. Only those living within the city limits were *citizens.* Tunnelborn had none of their rights or freedoms.

"My name is Oslan Thalersworth, of the Meerkat Combine, and I am president of the Merchant Council!" A chorus of rising boos and jeers threatened to drown him out, but he shouted louder, his voice cracking. "This illegal gathering is in violation of the curfew rules established by the council. We ask that everyone remain calm and orderly!"

"You're the one who's blocked the plaguing streets!" Rikard's voice cut through the babble, which gradually fell away. "If you want order, get out of the *fucking* way and let us march!"

"I'm afraid we can't allow that!" Oslan said. "We have an obligation to our members and the community to keep the peace."

"Keep it somewhere far away from us!" someone in the crowd shouted back. Rikard bellowed a laugh, joined by a thousand others.

"Your behavior has given us no choice but to take decisive action," Oslan said. "You will remain calm and throw down any weapons while we search the square. Everyone will be permitted to return home except for the ringleaders." He glared down at Rikard. "If you would surrender yourself immediately, it would save a great deal of trouble."

The crowd roared as one, a barely comprehensible fury.

"*No!*"

"*Never!*"

"*Kill them!*"

"This is my final warning!" Oslan raised his hand high.

What was supposed to happen at that point, Gyre guessed, was a warning shot from the snipers, sending blaster bolts *cracking* across the night sky. *Followed by a volley down at Rikard when the crowd panics.* Instead, for a moment, there was nothing. Then, above a broken-down water tower, a flickering white light appeared in the air. A figure took form, fifteen meters high and glowing at the edges. He wore dark, practical clothes, a well-worn sword, and a silver mask that covered half his face.

Gyre watched his doppelganger stride the heavens like some mythical deity. He was standing inside the ring of teeth, which felt unpleasantly like inviting something to eat him. Every move he made was instantly mirrored by the huge figure out in the square, like a monstrously oversized reflection. Looking at himself, Gyre had to suppress an urge to wave.

People were shouting. Individual voices were impossible to make out, but Gyre could guess the theme. *Halfmask.*

"Hello, Fox," Gyre said, and his voice boomed through the square, Chosen arcana louder than any megaphone. "If you're hoping for blaster fire, I'm afraid you're going to be disappointed."

"You!" Oslan's shout was barely audible over the tumult. "A thief and a traitor! What are you doing?"

"I'd like to know that as well," Rikard said, somewhat more composed. "We're here to take what's ours by right—and what *will* be ours by law, when the Empire comes. Are you with us or against us?"

"Preposterous!" Oslan said. "The Empire will follow the time-honored traditions—"

"The Empire will do neither," Gyre said, his amplified voice rolling over them. Sheer volume was an unearned advantage, rhetorically, but he'd take anything he could get. "The Emperor cares only for himself. He wants all of you—*all* humans—to be his slaves. He has no interest in helping the poor, and no tolerance for competition from the rich. To him we're just *meat*, to be carved to his whim."

"Pre-preposterous!" Oslan said, apparently unable to think of another retort.

"You claim to know the Emperor's plans, then?" Rikard said.

"I've seen them, and so have others. This is Baron Apphia Kotzed." Gyre stepped out of the transmission ring, and Apphia's image replaced his in the sky over the square. The arcana box burbled with the murmurs of the crowd. Apphia took a deep breath.

"I have been fighting the Republic most of my life," she said. "I was there at the founding of the Khirkhaz Commune, after Republic injustice took my father and my home. I have been hunted by centarchs and crossed swords with Legionaries.

"I say this so you understand I have no cause to love them. And I hope you believe me when I say that the Empire, since it arrived in Khirkhaz, has outdone the Republic a thousandfold in cruelty and malice. My best friend and most loyal companion was *disassembled* before my eyes by a vile *dhakim*, his body used to create the Emperor's monstrous new Perfected. And that is far from all."

She'd found her rhythm, settling into the story that was by now familiar. Confident she was on a roll, Gyre went to the window with Sarah and Nina, watching the crowd's response. Thousands of heads were focused on the apparition in the sky, giving it their rapt attention.

It's the best audience we could have hoped for. If anything's going to convince them . . .

Oslan was watching as intently as any of the others. The point of danger would come when Apphia finished. *If the crowd supports us, he could order an assault.* Timing, timing…

Apphia was finishing her story. Gyre turned to Kit.

"Tell Maya now."

"Now? It could cause a panic—"

"*Now!*"

"Got it," Kit said. After a moment's pause, she hopped up and down. "Sixty seconds."

Apphia fell silent, giving a bow reflected by the huge shape outside. At Gyre's gesture, she stepped out of the circle and he stepped in, his mask once again gleaming above the square.

Come on, he urged Rikard. *Come on. Before Oslan gets twitchy.*

"I have nothing but the greatest respect for Khirkhaz and its people," Rikard said, as calm as if he weren't having a conversation with a giant projection in front of thousands. "But is this what you're asking of us? To become a new Commune, turning against the Empire, *inviting* the anger that Baron Kotzed admits has done so much damage?"

"It is," Gyre boomed, counting backward in his head.

"Pre…prepos…posterous," Oslan managed weakly.

"Even if we *wanted* to," Rikard said, "what makes you think we'd have any chance of success?"

Thank you. Gyre's lip curved into a broad grin. He kept up his count, pausing a moment.

"Because," he said, "we have something no rebel has had before."

The air *throbbed*, a vast hum that made Gyre's teeth buzz and the windows rattle. Far over the head of his enormous reflection, black clouds had been gathering, almost unnoticed against the darkness of the early mountain night. Now they bulged, distending and then shredding apart as something descended through them, accompanied by wild crackles of lightning.

Even Gyre, who knew what was coming, found himself gasping. The skyfortress *Pride in Power* hung over Deepfire like a floating mountain, untold tons of polished unmetal hovering a kilometer in the sky, pregnant with understated power. It had no obvious weapons, no visible threat, but the mere fact of its immensity was enough to provoke awe. In daylight, its shadow would have covered half the city.

Rikard was speechless. Oslan had sat down heavily, jaw hanging open. Gyre raised his arms, triumphant, and abruptly the awe and terror of the crowd transmuted into excitement. Screams and cheers went up, so loud that Sarah ran to the arcana box and cut them off.

It was ultimately a cheap trick. The skyfortress wouldn't stop the Corruptor, especially since Maya had reported it was unarmed. But in the street, the balance had tilted, and that was all that mattered.

For now.

Chapter Eighteen

Maya took a flitter from the skyfortress's hangar down to the Spike. There had once been a landing field for exactly such a purpose, but it had long ago been built over by a wing of the palace, so she was forced to bring the little craft down in the middle of one of the vast lawns. Wind whipped fallen leaves away from the descending flitter, and servants stood well back, gaping. Even farther away, but visible during the descent, were mobs of tunnelborn and Deepfire citizens lining the outer walls of the complex, cheering at this new development. Seeing them gave her prickles of discomfort. *We've dragged them into this, and we still don't know what we're doing.*

Beq had stayed aboard the ship, so Maya had to pilot the flitter herself. Fortunately, the descent was nothing like as perilous as the climb from the mountaintop had been, with *Pride's* guardian storm deactivated and the ship hovering peacefully in clear skies. She could see its shadow slashing across Deepfire, like a second Pit at right angles to the first.

By the time she landed, Gyre and Tanax had arrived, waiting by a hedge until Maya opened the cockpit and hopped down. Gyre was grinning widely, and even Tanax looked a little less disgruntled than usual.

"See," Kit said on Maya's shoulder, "wouldn't this have been much more fun as a surprise?"

"I'm sure." Maya hadn't known about Kit's attempted prank until the construct had sulkily divulged it. "But we *do* have other things to worry about."

"Yeah, yeah. Live while you're alive, that's what I say."

"Are you...I mean..."

"No, but that makes it even *more* important!"

"Welcome back," Gyre said with a generous bow. "Apparently there was something to Xalen's files after all."

"Not *exactly* what we were looking for," Maya said.

"I'll take it," Tanax said. "Things have improved considerably since the night before last."

Maya had taken a day to make sure she understood how *Pride*'s power system worked and to be certain the thing wasn't going to fall out of the sky. From Kit's brief reports, Tanax and the others had also been busy.

"Rikard Gemspotter has officially agreed to work with what we're calling the Deepfire Defense Militia," Gyre said. "I suspect he saw the way the wind was blowing. Oslan Thalersworth has gone into hiding, along with a good chunk of the council, but the rest are on our side. They've committed to addressing the tunnelborn's grievances once the crisis is past."

"Which not everyone is happy about," Tanax said. "We're going to have to be careful when the time comes."

He's already starting to think about after. As though it were a foregone conclusion. Maya couldn't fault him, but...

"We're starting to organize the volunteers," Gyre said. "Apphia's taking the lead, obviously. Sarah's helping her round up some of the scavengers, too. They're a little unruly but they're well armed, and with smuggling shut down everyone's at loose ends."

"What about the Auxiliaries?" Maya said.

"I'm folding them in to the new militia," Tanax said. "Tourmarch Ritabel resigned, but otherwise they're taking it well enough."

And just like that, we're running the city. It felt like half a dream. *But who's going to argue with a skyfortress?* Even the revelation that two of the new leaders were centarchs didn't seem to have unduly dampened the excitement.

"We have a great deal to do," Tanax said. "I'm having the city searched for every blaster we can find, and all the sunsplinters, dead or not. Some will be damaged, but you and I can recharge the rest. After that—"

"I'll help however I can," Maya interrupted. "But there's something I need to show Gyre first."

"Ah." Tanax stood back a step. "Of course."

"Not here." Maya pointed skyward. "Up there."

"Now?" Gyre said. "I wanted to talk about possible defenses—"

"Now," Maya said. "It won't take long."

Gyre glanced at Tanax and shrugged. "If you say so. Can you show me how to get in this thing?"

The ride back up was quiet. Gyre had his head pressed to the window, the green light from his silver eye reflecting off the glass, watching the enormous shape grow until it seemed to blot out the rest of the world. The ship's system took over when they were close enough, bringing the flitter in for a neat landing in the vast hangar. A small auto was parked nearby—one of the things Maya and Beq had figured out during their trip was where the transports were kept. Maya fed it their destination with a *deiat* ping and it drove itself, the walls blurring past with a barely audible whine.

"This is . . ." Gyre let out a breath and shook his head. "I'll never understand the Chosen."

"What do you mean?"

"*Look* at this place. The people who built this didn't need *subjects*. But they ruled humanity for centuries anyway."

"*Deiat* has limits," Maya said. "It can't *think*."

"And that justifies enslaving millions of people?"

"It doesn't—" Maya bit back her reply. She didn't want to have this argument, especially now.

Fortunately, Gyre seemed to sense her tension. "Sorry. It's just a little overwhelming."

"Believe me, it took me a while to get used to it," Maya said. She looked at him sidelong. "Was it the same in Refuge?"

"Hard to say. I was half-dead when I got there, so I didn't see much more than a bed for a while." He grimaced. "The thing you have to get used to is the constructs. They're *everywhere*, and they do all the work. The ghouls hardly notice them."

"I feel like I should be offended on behalf of my fellow constructs," Kit said. Maya had half-forgotten she was there.

"Not everyone can be as smart as you," Gyre said.

"Flatterer."

"Sorry."

"I didn't say stop."

Maya couldn't help a chuckle. "You two get along well."

"He knows he can't live without me, so he's learned to behave," Kit said.

"Oh, is that right?" Gyre said.

The auto slowed to a halt in front of a lift. Maya led Gyre inside and showed him the controls. One floor up from the transport tunnels was the ship's core and the secure armory. Maya stopped at the outer door.

"Kit?" she said. "Do you think Gyre and I could have a little time alone?"

Kit heaved a sigh, drooping. "If you must. I expect a full report on anything interesting."

The construct hopped down and scuttled to a corner. Maya opened the doors with another *deiat* command. The lights came on, revealing one row of pods after another. Gyre frowned at them as Maya closed the doors behind them.

"What are these things?" he said.

"Look inside."

Gyre stepped close to one and peered into the porthole. He froze, then very slowly raised his head and took a careful look around.

"All of them?" Gyre said.

Maya nodded. Her chest was tight. "Children."

"*Chosen* children." He stepped away from the pod. "You didn't tell anyone else about this."

"Beq and Kit know. None of the others."

"Good. They shouldn't have to..." Gyre wiped his palms on his shirt. "Plaguing *fuck*." He looked back at her. "You know what we have to do, or you wouldn't have brought me here."

"I do?"

Gyre's breath was coming fast, his face drawn into a rictus. "They have to be destroyed."

Maya had half expected that, but her breath still caught. "You're not serious."

"I'm—" Gyre shook his head. "We can't—"

"They're *children*, Gyre. Chosen or not. We are not going to *kill* half a hundred children, whatever else happens."

"I..." Gyre paused, then seemed to deflate. "You're right. Obviously. I just..." He shook his head. "We'll have to hide them. Bury them. Find a cave in the mountains."

"Gyre!"

"What's the *fucking* alternative?" Gyre shouted. "Wake them all up?"

"Yes. Exactly. Now that the Purifier has destroyed the plague, we wake them up and help them. Isn't that what you're supposed to do if you see a child in danger?"

"They're not in danger, they're just...sleeping. They're probably safer in the tanks—"

"Oh, cut the plaguing bird shit," Maya said.

"Fine." Gyre gritted his teeth. "We can't have the Chosen back. We *can't*. *One* Chosen is bad enough! This many..." He turned around, arm outstretched. "Even if they were all *ever* so grateful, their children would enslave humanity all over again. It's everything I've been fighting against since they first took you away."

"You've been fighting the legacy of the old Empire," Maya said. "I understand that. Things had to change, and now the Corruptor has made that inevitable. But none of *these* Chosen is responsible. You can't blame them for other people's sins."

"They're not responsible for it *yet*. Let them grow up and they'll become tyrants."

Maya snorted. "So tyranny is in their blood?"

"Like it's in yours and every other centarch's. Look what the Order has become since the Plague. The Chosen in miniature."

"That's because—" Maya stopped for breath. "Look. I want to tell you a story."

Gyre looked guarded. "What do you mean?"

"You know I'm blood-bonded with the Corruptor."

"Yeah. Has he been telling you things?"

"Not exactly. But there was...someone else. Someone who was blood-bonded with *him*. And something—an echo of her, maybe—is left in his mind."

"That's..." Gyre hesitated. "Is that even possible?"

"I'm not sure anyone knows what's possible. From what Elariel said, the ghouls only use blood-bonds between couples. I don't know if you're allowed to do it again if one of them dies." She shook her head. "Doesn't matter. It's real, I'm sure of it. The echo—her name is Zephkiel—has been showing me her memories. Memories from when she knew Ashok, before the Plague War."

"Do you know why?"

"I think because she hates him," Maya said thoughtfully. "Or maybe hates what he ultimately became. Whatever he's doing, she doesn't want him to succeed."

"Hmm. Knowing more about the Corruptor might give us some clues, but I don't see—"

"Just listen, would you?"

As briefly as she could, she summarized what she'd seen of Zeph's life. Her job at the Stoneroot laboratory, her love for Ashok, his descent into forbidden experiments and the catastrophic attempt to arrest him. The sunfire bomb, descending into a final inferno.

"There's a library on the ship," she went on, as Gyre lapsed into fascinated silence. "A library *intended for Chosen*. Everything they left us— the *Inheritance*, the Archive, the records at the Forge—it was all meant for *us*. It's been…expurgated. Censored. But here they recorded what really happened. It backs up Zeph's memories."

"Does it say what came after?"

"A little bit. The Chosen turned on the *dhakim* all across the Empire. Most were arrested and executed, or just hunted down like animals. But the Shattered Peaks—not shattered back then, of course—had been the center of *dhaka* research and development, and some of the *dhakim* here fought back. They created constructs by the hundreds of thousands, dug vast new tunnels, went deeper and deeper underground. And the Chosen created the Legions to find and destroy them, humans equipped with *deiat* weapons."

"The Plague War," Gyre said.

"Except it was *already too late*," Maya said. "The Plague wasn't developed by the *dhakim during* the war. The Plague is—was—Ashok's 'reflective agent,' scattered all over the world by the sunfire bomb. It multiplies in any living tissue, but it only turns deadly in someone who can channel more than a certain amount of *deiat*." Maya touched the dead remnant of the Thing. "That's why I got sick when I was little, and why Ashok and Basel put an inhibitor in me. They wanted to keep me alive until I was strong enough to use the Purifier."

"Ashok created the Plague," Gyre said, turning the idea over. "What about the plaguespawn?"

"I think he created them as well," Maya said. "I think he's been seeding them, over and over, letting them spread. For testing, maybe, or just to torment humanity. In the Republic, there were times we'd be certain they were wiped out, but fresh outbreaks would appear out of nowhere. It was the same with *dhakim*. We'd destroy them, but the knowledge would never die out. Somehow it always survived."

"Ashok's black spiders," Gyre said.

Maya nodded. "Until I used the Purifier, he couldn't leave his hideaway without dying of the Plague. So he created those...things, little copies of himself, and sent them out through the Gates to sow chaos."

"Chosen fucking defend," Gyre said. "Four hundred years of misery and it's all his fault. *Why?*"

"To keep us weak," Maya said. "You told me, once, that the Order kept humanity from advancing so that people would always be dependent on us. We didn't—not on purpose—*but Ashok did*. If there are always plaguespawn, then there's always a need for the Order. And as long as the Order is in power—"

"—he can walk in and take over."

"A few promises, a few lies, and he's at the head of a new Empire," Maya said.

"So..." Gyre leaned back against one of the tanks. "Fucking plaguefire. This is important, but what does it have to do with these... Chosen?"

"These children," Maya said firmly. "Listen. The *dhakim* who fled into the mountains weren't a separate race. Zephkiel was human."

"I've seen the ghouls," Gyre said. "They aren't."

"They aren't *now*. But you know what they did to Elariel. All their differences, the fur and the eyes and so on, they must have done that to themselves, to help them survive underground. Zephkiel worked on modifying vulpi to make them better farm animals. *Humans* are modified. We all are."

"Again, what does that have to do—"

Maya gritted her teeth in frustration. It seemed so *obvious*. "*There are no Chosen*. No ghouls. Just *people*. Some have *deiat* power, some don't, just like some are tall or have green hair or whatever. The rest of it is just something we made up!"

"So...what? We're all supposed to join hands in harmony?" Gyre straightened up again, real eye blazing, silver eye glowing green. "The bandit who steals from the farmers is human. The only difference is that he's strong and they're weak. That doesn't mean we shouldn't stop him."

"Does it mean we should kill everyone strong, because they have the potential to be bandits? Burn everyone smart because they might trick us?"

"Of course not—"

"Killing these children won't make *deiat* die out." Maya put her hand on her chest. "I'm proof of that. I was born with more *deiat* potential than the average centarch, so much more that the Plague would have killed me. Now that the Plague is gone, there'll be more like me, and even stronger. Are you going to find them all and kill them? Would you have killed me, if you knew?"

"Maya..." The fight went out of Gyre, his shoulders slumping. "You know I wouldn't. But..."

"But what?" Maya snapped.

"Are we doomed, then?" he said quietly. "The Chosen are inevitable. Tyranny is inevitable. Why even bother?"

"No. At least not anymore." Maya looked at him seriously. "The *Inheritance* tells us that the Plague War was a rebellion, that it proved the ghouls—and *dhaka*—couldn't be trusted. The truth is that it was more like a massacre. Not because *dhaka* couldn't be trusted, but because the Chosen thought it could threaten their power. And they were *right*.

"I haven't seen half of what the ghouls can do, I know, but in a world full of things like your eye and Sarah's arm and *Kit*, having *deiat* potential isn't the only way to be strong. The Chosen were tyrants because they created a world where that was all they *could* be. But we don't live in that world and we don't have to make the same mistakes."

Very slowly, Gyre smiled. "You really believe that?"

"I do." Maya paused, out of breath. "I've been thinking about this a lot."

"You realize how big a project this is," Gyre said. "You want to, what, let these kids out and raise them to work with humans and ghouls instead of ruling them, while simultaneously remaking the world along the same lines?"

"It may take a while," Maya admitted. "I'm not saying we should wake them up now, or all at once. But that's the world we're headed for, no matter what. We need to prepare."

Gyre held up his hands. "All right. There's more to think about, but that can wait." He pursed his lips. "We're going to have to keep it quiet until we're ready, though."

"I know."

"For that matter, why did you tell *me*? Beq would have kept it secret, I'm sure."

"Kit wouldn't," Maya said. "And... I lied to you once, to get you to come to the Purifier. I couldn't see any other way. But I wanted to do things right this time."

"Sometimes I think you've come a long way from the girl who believed whatever the Order told her," Gyre said. "But you haven't, really. It's just the Order didn't measure up."

"Well. For what it's worth, you *have* come a long way from the boy who wanted to activate the Leviathan and watch the world burn."

"Maybe." Gyre scratched his chin and looked embarrassed. "It still leaves us the question of what happens now. The Chosen's last resort wasn't the weapon we thought it was, and we still don't know where to find the Corruptor's lab—"

"Oh," Maya said. "I thought you would have figured that one out."

"Figured what out?"

"Where the lab is. The bottom level of Stoneroot was protected by flux-stabilized armor. It's right where it's been all along. At the bottom of the Pit."

Chapter Nineteen

U m, Halfmask? Sir?”

"You don't have to call me 'sir,'" Gyre said mildly. "Save that for the baron and your commanders."

The girl—she couldn't have been more than sixteen, her brown militia uniform hanging off her like a feed sack—considered this for a moment. "Your...Mask...ness? Or, um—"

"Never mind. What's the message?"

"The—oh, the message! Sorry, sir. I mean, not sir, but—"

"Please just spit it out."

"Right." She took a deep breath. "We've captured a prisoner at the main gate. Possibly an Empire spy."

"How can you tell?"

"He keeps asking for you and Centarch Maya, sir. By name."

Gyre frowned. "Did he tell you who he was?"

"He claims to be called Varo Plagueluck, sir, which if you ask me is suspicious—sir?"

"Bring him to the palace." Gyre shoved his chair back and got to his feet. "And tell Centarch Maya that Varo's here."

"Yes, sir!" She straightened up and saluted. "Um. Which should I do first?"

"Find someone else to do one," Gyre said, fighting an incipient headache, "and then go and do the other."

"Oh! That's clever."

"*Go*, please!"

"Yes, sir!" She saluted again and then, mercifully, went.

Gyre looked over the papers on his desk, decided there was nothing that couldn't wait, and grabbed his coat from the rack. He was still getting used to the idea of *having* a desk, much less an office in the palace. The closest thing he'd ever used was the top of a dresser in his room at Lynnia's. But trying to organize people sprouted paperwork like a wet dung pile sprouted mushrooms, and it had taken practically no time at all for the Deepfire Defense Militia to acquire its own unique procedures.

Apphia had done a fantastic job, all told, in the limited time they'd had. With the Merchant Council compliant, or at least well cowed, the manufactories of the city were at their disposal. Uniforms were not something Gyre would have prioritized, but she was adamant that they promoted group identity and esprit de corps, and so a former manufacturer of fine trousers and leggings was set to making thousands. A leatherworks had been tasked with helmets and boots, and a steelworks with spearheads and knives. Not the most impressive kit, but better than nothing.

Of course, there were plenty of weapons already *in* the city. Sarah had been gathering these, along with people who knew how to use them—scavengers, mostly, with a leavening of keen former Auxies and picked soldiers from the ranks of the volunteers. This elite group layered makeshift unmetal armor over their uniforms and wore blasters, alchemicals, and whatever arcana oddities they could find.

It was going as well as they could have hoped, which didn't mean anything like well enough. *Let's hope Varo has good news.*

The scout, when Gyre found him, did not look like someone bearing good news. He was considerably the worse for wear, in fact, his coat speckled with dried mud and fraying at the hem, his normally bald head fuzzed by days without a razor. He had the same deadpan look, though, with just enough levity around the eyes to convince you it was all a joke at everyone else's expense. Gyre bowed in greeting, and Varo returned it, then started as Maya entered at a run and hugged him.

"You *stupid* plaguepit," she said. "You couldn't have *asked* before running off by yourself?"

"I could have," Varo said, scratching his peach-fuzz head. "But you'd have said no, and then where would I have been?"

"A lot safer," Maya said. She pulled away and wiped her nose. "Chosen defend. I thought you were dead."

"A friend of mine told me that once," Varo said. "I'd gotten lost in the salt marshes, and the rest of the troop was out looking for me. She was reaching down to pull me into her boat, and then *bam*, crocodile. It only got her head, though, and honestly that was never her best feature."

"I'm glad your sense of humor is intact," Gyre said.

"That's exactly what I told her afterward." Varo leaned back against an overstuffed chair. "I *was* a little alarmed to be accused of being a spy, since I *am* a spy, just on the other side. It would be terrible to be executed for a crime you *did* commit, but in the opposite direction."

"It hasn't been long since we started the new militia," Gyre said. "They can still be a bit overenthusiastic."

"What happened?" Maya said. "After you stayed behind. With the Gate closed we've had nothing but rumor."

"Well," Varo said, with a self-satisfied look. "As I suspected, it wasn't hard to blend back in with the other scouts. The new Emperor is very interested in the two of you but doesn't have much to say on the subject of the rest of us. So I had a front-row seat, more or less, when he moved in with us."

"He's staying at the Forge?" Maya said. "Not in Skyreach?"

Varo nodded. "He was, anyway, while he was organizing things.

Called in the old Council of Kyriliarchs, commended them on their good work, and announced he was making some changes. A few of them kept their posts. The others have *retired*, and he's named replacements. They're not a council anymore, just officers in command of the centarchate."

"No one objected?"

"Not in public," Varo said. "Can't say that I blame them. After the old Council just went along with it, opposition seemed unhealthy." He tipped his head. "Your old friend Basel kept his job, incidentally."

"No surprise," Maya muttered. "He's been serving Ashok for years."

"I'd wager that all the new Kyriliarchs have," Gyre said. "We knew his people had infiltrated the Order."

"Anyway," Varo said, "once that was sorted out he started sending centarchs to every big city in the Republic with marching orders for the duxes. Anybody who objected was removed. My guess is not many did. Hard to muster much courage with a haken at your throat, and the Senate is on hand to stamp everything 'okay.' So the Auxiliaries and the Legions are with him."

"Have you seen the Perfected?" Gyre said. "The new soldiers in silver armor."

"Getting to that," Varo said. "With everything locked down, he collects a few centarchs and a force of Legionaries and sends them out through the Gate. I tag along with them—"

"How?" Maya said.

"Disguised myself as a warbird," Varo said, without missing a beat. "Old scout trick."

Gyre snorted a laugh.

"We ended up in the plains near Obstadt. Spent a few days camped there, then started marching north. Rumor said we were heading for Deepfire, that it was in rebellion. I thought it was odd, at first—we didn't have enough soldiers to attack the city—but when we entered the mountains they were waiting for us."

"Perfected?" Gyre said.

Varo gave a grim nod. "Hundreds of them. And that's not all. They had plaguespawn with them, big brutes the size of ponies, and I can't even *guess* how many of those there were. Thousands. Some of the Legionaries were worried, but the centarchs and their officers quieted them down. About that time I decided I'd seen enough, so I stole a swiftbird and rode like plaguefire."

Chosen defend. Gyre had known something like this was coming, expected it, but to hear it confirmed was still a shock. *No wonder it's taken him so long to get here.* With Deepfire cut off by Gate, the Corruptor must have decided to take no chances. He'd brought a hammer big enough to squash the whole city.

"How long?" Maya said.

"Before they get here? A week, two at the longest."

"Fuck." She closed her eyes and shook her head. "*Fuck.* We won't be ready."

"We'll have to be," Gyre said.

Varo coughed. "It sounds like you two have a lot to work on, and I'd really like to hear the story of why you seem to suddenly be in charge here. But right at the moment I have an urgent need to collapse into a bed and sleep for a minimum of thirty hours."

"Of course," Maya said, hugging him again. "You have no idea how much we all owe you for this."

"I have *some* idea," Varo said. "For starters, I'm never paying for my own drinks again."

"I think that can be arranged." Maya took his arm and led him to the door, speaking briefly to the militia soldier waiting outside. When she came back, Gyre was staring into the unlit fireplace.

"I can't believe he did that," Maya said.

"I can't believe he *survived*," Gyre said. "I think he should change his cognomen."

"He likes to say that the bad luck only applies to his friends and not himself."

"Is it true?"

"I haven't been notably unlucky in his company, no."

Gyre's eyebrow rose. "Except for unleashing an insane Chosen *dhakim* who wants to convert all of humanity into plaguespawn slaves?"

"Well, *obviously* except for that," Maya said.

She kept a straight face for a moment, then broke down in giggles. Gyre couldn't help the smile tugging at his own cheeks, which only made Maya laugh harder, and before long they were both bent over and breathless. Maya sat heavily in one of the armchairs, gasping for air, and Gyre took the one opposite.

"We"—she gave another hiccupping giggle, then leaned her head back to stare at the ceiling—"we're *doomed*, right? Completely doomed. A few thousand militia with spears against thousands of plaguespawn and Perfected, not to mention Legionaries and centarchs. If our soldiers don't run for the hills at the first sight of the enemy, we'll be lucky."

"Don't underestimate the tunnelborn," Gyre said. "Or the rest of the people of Deepfire, for that matter. If they were all armed and armored like Legionaries, I'd say we had a good shot."

"But they're not."

"They're not." Gyre closed his eyes. "There are a few tricks we can try. But it's not going to help with the larger problem."

"There's a *larger* problem?" Maya gave another hysterical giggle.

"Larger than this army, I mean. Even if we somehow crush them, the Corruptor can send another, and another. We can either run and turn this into a chase, or stand, fight, and eventually get hammered down. Right now he's still consolidating the resources of the Republic, but before long..." Gyre shook his head. "We have to take the fight to him. Personally."

"He doesn't seem the kind to stick his neck out," Maya said. "He was surprised by Prodominus in the Purifier. Since then he talks to us with projected images, he speaks in my head, but otherwise Varo says that he's stayed in the Forge. I don't want to imagine what kind of protection he has there. We'd never get close to him."

"We have to lure him out," Gyre said. "Somehow."

"I'm open to ideas."

Gyre let out a breath. "His lab. It's the only option."

"You don't know there's anything in there that'll help."

"I don't. But if there isn't..."

"Yeah."

There was a long silence.

"Well." Maya pushed herself out of her chair with false enthusiasm. "Let's see how Beq and Xalen are getting on."

The arcanists had taken over the Smoking Wreckage.

The precariously situated bar had closed its doors the night of the tunnelborn march and had yet to properly reopen. With its clientele largely composed of Auxies—Gyre had painful memories of his last brawl there, deliberately instigated by Kit—no doubt its owners had decided a discreet vacation was in order. The boarded-up doors had been reopened by the militia on Beq's instructions, since the club was ideally positioned over the deepest part of the Pit.

Since then, Gyre hadn't paid much attention, other than to note that Lynnia was complaining Beq had requisitioned an increasing number of the city's alchemists, arcanists, and tinkerers. He found the main room of the Wreckage emptied of tables and littered with big hexagonal plates of unmetal, coils of resilk with ragged ends, and a wild collection of tools, broken arcana, and general detritus. There were people everywhere, from a young boy to a white-haired grandmother cheerfully bashing something on an anvil. Beq, working behind the old bar in the center of the room, looked like the lunatic impresario of some scavenger circus, her spectacles rapidly flicking from lens to lens, her braids fraying in a tangle.

"Now, this I like," Kit said, ensconced once again on Gyre's shoulder. "Reminds me of getting a scavenging expedition ready."

"Maya!" Beq said excitedly. At the name, work and conversation gradually stopped throughout the big room. Beq vaulted the bar and rushed over to them, grabbing Maya and pulling her into a kiss. After a bit too long, she disengaged and gave a belated bow to Gyre.

"You've been busy," Gyre said, covering for a still-blinking Maya. "I didn't realize you'd gotten far enough to start doing...all this." He waved vaguely at whatever process was occurring around them.

"A lot of it is testing," Beq said. "You want to go down to the bottom of the Pit. Okay, fair enough, how? The lab we want to get into is protected by flux-stabilized armor, so obviously we need to make our capsule out of the same stuff. Fortunately we have an essentially unlimited supply hanging in the sky above us. But nobody really understands how flux-stabilized unmetal *works*, so first we get a bunch down here and start banging on it, basically, until—"

"Hey," Maya said, taking Beq by the shoulder. "Slow down a little."

"Right. Sorry." Beq paused long enough to suck in a breath. "Do you know what flux-stabilized unmetal is?"

"Unmetal with, um, stable fluxes?" Gyre guessed. "Or unmetal that's stabilized *against* fluxes, or—"

"Here, look at this." Beq pulled them over to two identically shaped hexagons of unmetal, about a meter across. "This one is regular unmetal. This one is flux-stabilized."

The difference only became apparent after a few seconds of observation. The surface of the flux-stabilized plate *swam* in front of Gyre's eyes, as though it were shifting in regular waves. It was vaguely nauseating to watch.

"Maya," Beq said, "try and cut them with your haken."

The *snap-hiss* of the weapon's ignition still made Gyre flinch, and he took a surreptitious step backward. When Maya pressed the tip of the blazing sword into the center of the ordinary unmetal, it rapidly began to glow, and then to sag, letting the haken punch through into the floorboards beneath. Maya hastily pulled it free and quenched the small fire that had started to smolder.

"Sorry," she said. Beq, looking more excited than ever, gestured for her to try the other one.

Somewhat more hesitantly, Maya pushed her weapon slowly down against the flux-stabilized unmetal. When the tip touched the shifting surface, something strange happened. The haken's blade stopped behaving like a solid object, vanishing as though it were no more substantial than a flame in truth. White-hot energy rippled over the unmetal, like splashes in a pond, quickly fading. Maya pulled her flaming sword back, and the shimmering ripples of power continued for a few moments before vanishing.

"There's a laminar flow of *deiat* energy across the surface that redirects incoming power along its own guideways," Beq said. Seeing incomprehension, she groped for a metaphor. "Like…trying to spit through a waterfall? Only not really—"

"Good enough," Gyre said, and Maya nodded, grinning. "Where did you get this stuff?"

"The whole skin of the *Pride in Power* is made of it," Beq said. "We dismantled a little bit."

"'We' meaning 'me,'" Kit said. "Beq didn't want to walk on the outside of the ship."

"*You* told me it wasn't safe," Beq retorted.

"I told you I gave you fifty-fifty odds of falling off," Kit said. "*I* wouldn't have let that stop me, back when I had a body."

"Well, look where that got you," Beq said.

"*Please* don't fall off the skyfortress," Maya said anxiously.

"So we have an unlimited supply," Gyre said. "Why does that sound too good to be true? Can we make armor out of it?"

"No," Beq said. "Firstly, because we don't have the tools to really *work* unmetal. But secondly, getting it off the skyfortress intact is a pain. Watch."

She lifted the plate. Underneath was a crystalline sunsplinter, glowing with *deiat* charge. Beq grabbed it and pulled it free, and the shimmering effect vanished instantly, leaving the flux-stabilized unmetal identical to its partly molten counterpart.

"Even if I plugged it back in, it wouldn't do any good," Beq said. "It has to be *constantly* powered, or else it collapses. I haven't the faintest idea how it was manufactured in the first place."

"Like the big towers in the Chosen cities," Maya said. "When they lost power, they fell apart."

"Exactly." Beq flicked a dial on her spectacles, retracting all the extra lenses. "With me so far?"

"I think so," Gyre said. "Ashok's lab survived because it was armored in this stuff. We'll build some kind of ship with the same armor to get down to it."

"Calling it a ship is a little grandiose," Beq said. "It's a box on a very long string. The sunfire bomb is a lot weaker than when it was dropped, so a resilk cable should survive, but only flux-stabilized armor can block enough heat that you won't get cooked."

Gyre noted, without particular surprise, the assumption that he and Maya were the ones descending. *It's what I would have suggested, of course, but . . .* He wasn't sure if it was flattering or horrifying to be auto-matically volunteered for the most dangerous assignments.

"So how soon can you be ready?" he said.

"There are still a few problems," Beq said. "Since the lab has flux-stabilized armor, how do we get you inside? If we can do that, how do we keep the heat of the bomb from getting inside as well?"

"Ah." Gyre looked around. The assembled arcanists and alchemists were watching them in silence. "So . . . how long?"

"I want to run more tests," Beq said. "There are some alchemicals that might hold up to the heat, but we need to be careful—"

"How long?"

"Um. A month?" Beq looked from Gyre to Maya, reading tension in their faces. "Three weeks, if I rush—"

"You have three days," Gyre said.

"Three *days*?" Beq spluttered, turning to Maya. "We can't—I'm sorry, it's just not possible. We won't be able to build the capsule in three days, much less test everything we need to—"

"That's what we've got," Maya said. "They're coming for us, and we have to be ready."

"We can give you all the labor you want," Gyre said. "Resources, anything. Name it."

"I need . . ." Beq shook her head, turning away from Maya. "More hands, obviously. And if you can pry Xalen away from her books, I think she knows a lot of theory that will come in handy. But actually building the thing, and a bigger gantry—"

"You need Sarah," Kit said.

"Sarah?" Beq frowned. "I know she tinkers, but—"

"Trust me," Kit said. "Get Sarah down here. I'll bring as many of my bodies as I can get together. We'll get it done."

"I'll talk to Sarah and Xalen," Gyre said.

"I'm sorry to put this on you," Maya said. "You know I wouldn't ask if we had another option."

"I know." Beq swallowed, looking like she wanted to say something more, then bit it back. "I won't let you down."

"You call that a volley? I've seen tighter grouping from a team of load-birds taking a shit! *Again.*"

"Fire!" someone else shouted, followed by a series of *cracks*. The roar of detonating blaster bolts echoed off the hillside.

The cab turned the last switchback, giving Gyre a good view of the practice yard. It was one of several set up at the northern edge of the city. The wall of the crater rose in the middle distance, steep and unbroken, its edge jagged with rocky promontories. With no tunnel entrances nearby, this was lightly trafficked ground, far enough from the warmth of the Pit that the autumn chill made Gyre's breath steam. It was a good place for a gang of tunnelborn recruits who'd never so much as seen a blaster to drill. *The worst they can do is blow themselves up.*

Across the broad, flat space, targets had been set up on the hillside, rocks painted red and now chipped and blackened from stray fire. A line of about forty people, under the nervous supervision of a sergeant from the Auxies, held blaster rifles to their shoulders. An undersized teenage figure paced in front of them.

"What I should have heard was a single *crack*," Nina said, slapping two wooden sticks together for emphasis. She was dressed in one of the militia's new uniforms, her pink hair pinned back in a severe bun. "Instead I heard a sound like a giant eating a cracker. *Galan Lackwit!*"

"Y-yes, sir!" A small man, twice Nina's age, saluted and gulped.

"When your sergeant says *'fire,'* what do you think that means?"

"Um. Fire, sir?"

"When, exactly?"

"Right away, sir!"

"Right away. It doesn't mean, for example, 'maybe fire when you get around to it, no big deal really'?"

"No, sir."

"I see." She paused in front of him, then whirled neatly on one heel. *"Then how do you explain your behavior?"*

"Finger slipped, sir!" Galan said, standing so straight his feet were in danger of leaving the ground.

"Finger slipped. Been eating vulpi bacon? Galan Greasefinger, is it?"

From the round of laughter from the others, Gyre suspected the man had just been given a new cognomen. Nina turned, face twisted in a snarl.

"Why are you laughing? The rest of you think you did so much better?" She shook her head. "Keep trying until your splinters are empty. If you're not doing better by then, I'm going to tell my sister we're better off sending you to shovel bird shit and starting with another lot."

Nina stalked off the field, even the sergeant stepping carefully out of her way. From his shoulder, Kit said, "She's certainly taken to the role."

"You can say that again." Gyre looked down the long practice ground. Other groups of tunnelborn were loading crossbows, forming a line of spears, or practicing close-in swordwork.

"Gyre!" Nina jogged over, light on her feet and wearing a cheery smile. "Come for an inspection?"

"I wouldn't know where to start," Gyre said. "How's it going?"

"Eh." She waggled her hand. "About what you'd expect."

"You've done this a lot?" Gyre said. "You've certainly got the scream-ing down."

"It's my Brennard impression," she said. "He handled new recruits in the Commune. I'm not as loud as he was, though."

"Volume isn't everything," Gyre said. "They seem to be listening."

"Shooting off blasters is a lot of fun," Nina said. "We'll see how com-mitted they are when things get difficult."

"By then it'll be too late to change their minds," Gyre muttered. "I was looking for your sister, if she's here."

"I think she just went back to her command post."

"We have a command post?"

"It's a shack we covered in a tarp, but she says language is impor-tant." Nina pointed. "Over there."

She waved and headed back to her hapless pupils. Gyre walked down the lines, listening to the boom of blaster bolts, the hiss of crossbows, and the occasional shriek of pain from someone who mishandled one or the other. The command post, when he found it, was as humble as Nina had described, a long-abandoned trapper's shack hastily restored. Several swiftbirds pecked contentedly for nyfa seeds outside. Gyre rapped beside the open doorway, knuckles raising a cloud of dust.

"What now?" Apphia snapped.

"It's me," Gyre said.

"Oh. Sorry."

Inside, gritty dirt was still piled up in the corners, and the only fur-nishing was what looked like someone's kitchen table, laid with a map of the city. Apphia stood on one side of it, Rikard Gemspotter on the other, with Enta glowering down from over his shoulder.

"Halfmask," Rikard said with a slight bow. "Or should it be Silvereye?"

"Gyre is fine," Gyre said. "We're all in the open now. What's going on?"

"Rikard was just explaining a few of his concerns to me," Apphia grated.

"Rikard was just bringing you more of his endless complications, you mean," Rikard said with a disarming smile. Now that he wasn't shouting furiously, it was easy to appreciate the man's casual charisma. "I'm sorry to be the bearer of bad news."

"I'm sure you're just doing the job you agreed to," Gyre said, hitting the last few words with special emphasis. "What's the problem?"

"There's been brawls during training," Apphia said. "A couple of people have gotten badly hurt, and it's slowing us down."

"I did warn you about this," Rikard said. "The tunnel communities are proud. You can't just throw East Deep people in with North Fracture and expect everything to stay peaceful."

"What I *expect* is that they all work together to keep us from getting overrun by the Empire," Apphia said. "Is that too much ask?"

"I've spent half my life wondering the same thing," Rikard said.

"And?"

He shrugged. "I decided it's easier just to separate them."

"He thinks we should reorganize the units," Apphia said. "I was about to suggest we bring this to you and Maya. It might take time, but—"

Gyre nodded. "Do it. Rikard, you must have dealt with this when you were organizing the strikes."

"Among other things," Rikard said.

"Pick out some people you trust to be sergeants." Gyre looked up at Enta. "I think you should be in charge of keeping them in line. Can you handle it?"

The siblings exchanged looks, and Rikard smiled again. "I think so," Enta rumbled.

"Good. If you don't mind, though, I need a few moments with the baron."

"Give me your proposed reorganization by the end of the day," Apphia said. Rikard and his sister slipped out, and she slumped forward on the table, hands on her forehead. "This is never going to work, Gyre."

"You don't think they'll fight?" Gyre said.

"They'll fight. They're eager enough." She straightened up with a groan. "Getting them to all march in the same direction is the problem."

"Fortunately, we don't need a mobile force." They hadn't settled on a plan of defense yet—that was more Tanax and Varo's department—but even a military amateur like Gyre could see that the only possible approach was to dig in and wait for the Empire to come to them. "As long as they know which end of the blaster to point at the enemy, that's good enough."

"Provided they're clear on who the enemy are," Apphia muttered. "Some of these groups have feuds going back centuries, apparently."

"I'd have thought you were used to that."

"The banners were never quite *this* bad." Apphia pondered for a moment, brow furrowing. "Well. Maybe they were. But at least a few leaders like Vaela could crack heads and keep order."

"I'm confident you'll get them there." Gyre coughed apologetically. "Speaking of leaders. I need to borrow Sarah."

"That's going to be a problem," Apphia said. "She's been doing good work with the scavengers, and we'll need them."

"I'm sending over someone else with experience in that area. Another old friend of mine." It had been something of a surprise that Ibb had agreed to take the job. His note to Gyre had been surprisingly nonchalant. *Probably angling for government contracts after we win.* "We have a special project that needs the best arcanists and engineers we've got."

"Well. I hope it's worthwhile." Apphia shook her head. "We're going to need *something* to go right. I don't know what the Corruptor is sending after us—"

"I do," Gyre said quietly. He glanced over his shoulder, making sure no one was listening. "Legionaries, centarchs. Hundreds of Perfected, thousands of plaguespawn."

"Chosen fucking defend." Apphia stared at him. "How long do we have?"

"A week at the worst."

"We don't have a chance." She shook her head. "Those things took the Spire without breaking a sweat. *This* lot doesn't have a chance. Fucking plaguefire. I can't..." She backed away from the table.

"Hey." Gyre hurried over to her, pulled her into a close embrace. Apphia buried her scarred face against his collar. "Hey. You're okay."

"It'll happen again," she whispered. "It happened at the Spire and it'll happen again and it'll all be my fault."

"It won't," Gyre said. "Whatever happens, you've done as well as anyone could possibly do. I'm not going to lie and tell you I'm sure it'll all be okay, but if we lose, it's not because of any failure of yours." It didn't sound reassuring, even as he said it, but some of Apphia's tension eased.

"They believe in me," she said. "The great Baron Kotzed of Khirkhaz. Legendary rebel. 'She wouldn't march us into certain death, would she?'" She shifted, looking up at Gyre, eyes heavy with tears. "Would we?"

"No."

"Tell me we have a chance." Her hands tightened on his shirt. "That there's a *chance* we won't all end up like Brennard and the others."

"We have a chance," Gyre said. "And if it works, we'll find the man who killed Brennard, and we'll take *him* apart, piece by piece."

Apphia stared into his eyes for a long moment. He wondered what she saw there. *A lie, or the truth?* He wasn't sure himself.

He wondered if he should kiss her. If she wanted him to. If that would be a lie as well.

"Okay." She breathed out and pushed herself away from him, breaking the moment. She wiped at her eyes with her palms. "Sorry. I just..."

"I understand," Gyre said.

"I know." Apphia looked lost for a moment, staring down at the map. "When this is over..." She set her jaw and raised her head, determined. "No. Never mind. Send your old friend over as soon as you can, and I'll tell Sarah to check in at the palace."

"Actually," Gyre said, "tell her to go straight to the Smoking Wreckage. They'll fill her in from there."

*   *   *

Three days passed, too fast and too slow all at once. Gyre busied himself with the never-ending work of making sure thousands of people got fed, watered, armed, and instructed on what they were supposed to be doing. Kit stopped riding his shoulder, apologetically informing him that the work at the Smoking Wreckage was taking all of her attention. Maya took the flitter back and forth from the skyfortress, ferrying down supplies and fresh sections of repurposed armor plating.

The morning of the third day, Kit's little spider perked up again as Gyre took a cab from the Spike to the Wreckage's island. She yawned and stretched her tiny limbs.

"I thought you didn't sleep," Gyre said.

"I don't. I just need to not think so hard for a while." She tapped the top of her carapace with one leg. "How do I have a headache? I don't even have a brain!"

"Force of habit?"

Kit grumbled something. The carriage pulled to a stop, and a militia-woman opened the door for Gyre. He nodded to her and a half dozen others who were guarding the bridge out to the bar turned experimental facility.

Things had changed quite a bit since his last visit. A twenty-meter pole rose over the building, with a wheeled pulley at the top and several lines descending. Farther on, beside the cliff face, another massive pulley wheel stood on a heavy unmetal gantry.

"Gyre!" Sarah ran out the front door to greet him. Her cheerful attitude couldn't disguise the dark circles under her eyes, which seemed to be replicated on everyone Gyre saw. "Where's Maya?"

"Coming. She was working on supply issues with Tanax." He looked over his shoulder and spotted another cab approaching. Maya got out, and he waved her over. Sarah bowed deep.

"Sorry," Maya said, a bit breathless.

"Anything exploding?" Gyre said.

"No more than usual," Maya said. "You have something to show us?"

"I think so," Sarah said. "We're nearly there."

" 'Nearly' doesn't count for much at the bottom of the Pit."

Sarah made a face. "Believe me, I know. I want to show you—"

She paused, because Gyre had halted in the doorway, eyebrows going up. One whole wall had been deconstructed in a hurry, leaving the room open to the rocky verge. Chunks of timber and wainscotting were piled in one corner, and broken boards still lined the edges of the hole. The pulley and tower Gyre had seen were anchored to the rock just outside where the wall had been. Between them and the old circular bar top sat—

Beq wasn't wrong. It was a box, a cube about three meters to a side, edges ragged where the hexagonal panels interlocked like the corners of a log cabin. It sat on a pallet atop wooden rollers, carefully chocked. A cable led from the big pulley to a bulb on the top of the thing. Together, they made it horribly clear what was supposed to happen—this contraption would be pushed to the cliff and shoved over. *With us inside.*

"Is that it?" Maya said, apparently having similar thoughts.

"That's it," Sarah said. "I know it looks a little rough, but the important stuff works. There's a way to bend the flux field around the corners—ask Beq, I don't understand it—and a hatch we stole from the skyfortress. When it's closed, the whole thing is proof against blaster fire, we've tested it. The cable, too—we tried lowering test payloads to the bottom, and it holds."

"Test payloads, in this case, mostly meaning me," Kit said.

"She *is* very convenient," Sarah confirmed.

"There's definitely something down there," Kit said. "The sunfire bomb is sitting on a surface of this flux-stabilized stuff. Most of the lab is buried in the rock, but there's a clear circle around the bomb."

"You *saw* it?" Gyre said.

"Briefly," Kit said. "We tried strapping a bunch of protective plate on one of my bodies and lowering it in a smaller version of the box."

"How long did it last?" Maya said, fascinated.

"A little under two seconds once I opened the door."

"Which is honestly pretty good!" Sarah said. "The bomb is putting out a *lot* of energy, even after four hundred years."

"Last time I was here," Gyre said, "Beq told me the biggest obstacle was getting into the lab. Have you figured it out?"

"Um. *Partly*," Sarah said. "We actually wanted Maya to test something for us. Come on, let's talk to Beq."

They found her lying on an out-of-place sofa someone had left amid the debris, eyes closed and snoring loudly. If Sarah had bags under her eyes, Beq's were craters beneath her lenses. She looked like she hadn't slept in weeks.

"I hate to wake her," Sarah said. "But..."

"I'll do it." Maya leaned close, whispering something. Beq's eyes flickered blearily, and Maya bent farther and kissed her. It was some time before she straightened up, long enough that Gyre cleared his throat and looked away.

"Hey," Beq said quietly.

"Hey." Maya pressed her forehead against her lover's. "I know you're tired. But we're almost there. After this you can sleep for days."

"I know." Beq sat up with a yawn. She'd given up on her customary braid, her long green hair tied up in a loose knot. "Just...you know. Resting."

"Chosen know she deserves it," Sarah said. There was newfound respect in her sunken eyes.

Beq snorted. "I copied some things from the *Pride*'s libraries and made some lucky guesses."

"Sarah said something about a test," Maya said.

"Right." Beq got up, moving like an old woman. "Over here. I think we've got it, but we wanted to be sure."

She led them to a back corner of the three-walled room, where a hexagon of flux-stabilized unmetal hung shimmering from chains in the ceiling. Beside it was a compact black arcana that looked more ghoul than Chosen, with none of the wires and crystals of *deiat* equipment.

"Okay," Beq said. "Maya, hit this with a flame hot enough to melt ordinary unmetal. As narrow as you can, we don't want to burn the building down."

Maya nodded and touched her haken. A pencil-thin beam stabbed out from her open hand, hitting the hexagon dead center. As at the last test, the *deiat* energy rippled out from the point of impact in shimmering waves, with no effect on the unmetal underneath.

"Here goes," Beq said. She twisted her spectacles, flipping dark lenses into place, then did something to the black arcana. The shimmer of the unmetal abruptly froze in place, bright ripples scorching lines along its surface. The point where Maya's beam touched began to glow. A moment later, *deiat* energy punched through and scorched the opposite wall. Maya hastily waved the flames away.

"My fault," Beq said. "Should have thought of that. It's okay. It works." She patted the black arcana smugly and raised her voice. "It works, Xalen!"

"I told you I thought it had a thirty-five percent probability of working." Xalen came down the big staircase Gyre had once fought his way up. She held a clipboard clamped in the armpit of her withered arm, turning the pages rapidly with her free hand. "That's hardly a reason for shouting. It's not like you've overturned fundamental law."

"I didn't realize you'd been helping here," Maya said.

"There was frustratingly little else for me to do," Xalen said, reaching the bottom of the stairs. "I continued to study the files from Prodominus' safe, but it had become clear to me that the information there, while interesting, would not materially aid our cause. When Sarah asked me to assist Beq, I was glad for the diversion."

"She knows the theory better than either of us," Sarah said. "Even if she's never used a wrench before."

"I consider that a compliment," Xalen said. "My proper place is no more in a workshop than it is on a battlefield."

"And it is?" Gyre prompted.

"In a library, of course," Xalen snapped. "But I have been ... temporarily motivated."

"In any case," Beq said, "it worked. The suppressor knocks the field back far enough that Maya can burn through."

"Is that another device from the skyfortress?" Maya said.

"Quite the opposite," Xalen said.

"It's one of the *deiat* shields the ghouls gave us," Beq said. "Just a few modifications. I don't understand ghoul arcana—the interior looks like it was *grown*—but I tweaked the antenna to project the field in a particular direction. Push it over a piece of flux-stabilized unmetal, and it loses its invulnerability."

"So that's how we get in," Maya said excitedly. "If we use that thing, then I can cut through."

"Exactly," Sarah said. "Which leaves one problem."

"Only one?" Gyre muttered.

"The capsule won't be sealed to the lab's surface," Sarah said. "If you open the hatch, then the heat from the bomb will get in. Um. Broil you."

"The effect would actually be almost instantaneous carbonization," Xalen said, "followed by—"

"Doesn't really matter what it's followed by," Gyre said.

"We have a way to seal the gap," Beq said. "A sort of skirt that will extend the field between the lab and the capsule. But it needs to be fastened down, which you can't do without going outside, which you can't do without getting cooked. Sort of a circular problem."

There was a brief silence.

"Is that all?" Kit said. "That's easy."

"Oh?" Xalen said. "I'm eager to hear your solution."

"Make an armored box on the outside of the capsule. Put one of my bodies in it. Open it when we get to the bottom, I jump out and secure the seal. Easy."

"Except you'll get cooked by the heat," Gyre said.

"Last time I got nearly two seconds. That's long enough."

"We'd have to use four of your bodies," Sarah said. "One on each side. It *ought* to be long enough, but..." She paused, glancing at Beq, who bit her lip.

"There'll be no way to test the seals," Beq said. "If Kit doesn't get it right on the first try, you'll be opening the door into an inferno. And there's no way to tell from inside the box."

Gyre looked at the machine and its exhausted makers, then at Kit's tiny spider, then at Maya. She gave a quick nod.

"Let's do it," he said. "Kit hasn't failed me yet."

"Except for that one time," Kit volunteered, capering.

"Okay. Kit hasn't failed me *since* she stabbed Maya and left us both for dead." He met Beq's and Sarah's blank stares, and shrugged.

Chapter Twenty

I hate this," Beq said.

"Cuddling?" Maya said. "I think it's pretty good, honestly."

"You know what I mean."

Beq curled in on herself a little tighter. Maya, wrapped around her, squeezed a little harder in response. The light coming in through the window of Maya's palace bedroom was already the bright sunshine of midmorning. *Time to go.*

"I'll be fine," Maya said.

"You don't know that."

"I do. You know how?" Maya brushed green hair aside and kissed the back of Beq's neck. "Because it's *your* plan, and *your* machine."

"So when you die, it'll be my fault."

"I'm not going to die," Maya said. "Besides, you can always blame Kit."

"*Maya.* It's not funny."

"Sorry. I just..." Maya rested her forehead against Beq. "It'll work. I know it will."

"I want to go with you."

"We talked about this."

"I *know*. I just thought I was going to be done sending you off and waiting to see if you came back."

"We're getting closer," Maya said. "Remember what I told you. When all this is over—"

"Yeah." Beq swallowed. "We should go."

"Come here."

Maya propped herself up on one arm, her red hair falling amid the green. Beq looked up at her, the shape of her freckled face odd without her spectacles, her beautiful eyes wide and nearly blind. Maya kissed her, and with her free hand traced a line down the hollow of Beq's throat and along her collarbone. She pulled back and brushed away incipient tears at the corners of her lover's eyes.

"It'll work," Maya said, as though repeating it could make it so. Beq gave a tiny nod.

When they finally got out of bed, there wasn't time to do much more than dress and hurry down to meet the cab. On the ride to the Smoking Wreckage, Maya wolfed down a roll and some bacon, while Beq gnawed unenthusiastically on a slice of toast. A night's sleep had considerably improved Beq's complexion, but her eyes were still deep sunken.

Compared to their previous visits, the Wreckage was nearly empty, militia guards at the bridge keeping spectators away. Most of Beq's team was gone, too. There would be nothing for them to do once the descent was underway, and Maya and Gyre had agreed that they wanted to keep the news of what happened—*whatever* happened—as close to the chest as possible. It was a near certainty that the Corruptor had *some* agents in Deepfire.

In place of the extra hands, Kit had brought in all the bodies she could muster. They filled the now-derelict bar, a plague of enormous black spiders, skittering in every direction on business of their own. A dozen of the largest size were out by the box, ready to haul it into position and guide it as it fell.

How exactly the fall was to be accomplished, Maya hadn't quite understood, but Beq assured her it was under control. It had something to do with the big tower and a dozen heavy iron rings around its base, counterweights connected to an elaborate gearing system. Sarah was inspecting it when they arrived, making some last-minute adjustments, which didn't make Maya any more comfortable. *You trust Beq's arcana,* she admonished herself. *Let Sarah do her job too.*

Xalen was there, as well as—to Maya's surprise—Elariel, sitting nervously on the stairs away from any of the others. Gyre stood on the edge of the cliff, looking down into the Pit with a pensive air. Maya went over to him, Beq peeling away for her own final checks.

"Not much to see," Maya commented. A roiling cloud of white fog occupied the Pit only a hundred meters below where they stood.

"No," Gyre said. "But white fog's better than green. The green fog will melt the silver off your buckles."

"Really?"

Gyre nodded sagely. Maya shook her head.

"Why does *anyone* live here?" She held up a hand to forestall comment. "I know. It's amazing what you can learn to put up with."

"At least it offers convenient trash disposal and sewage outflow," Gyre said.

"Are we going to get to the bottom and find it awash in decades of shit?"

"Let's hope not," Gyre said, grinning. "Are you ready?"

"I suppose." Maya checked her haken and her panoply, then smoothed her uniform. "Let's go see what the Corruptor is hiding."

It was warm and quiet in the box.

Somehow—though she'd seen the windowless capsule several times—it hadn't occurred to Maya that there wouldn't be anything for them to *see* during the descent. They'd climbed in through the hatch, along with one of Kit's tiny spiders, and waited while Beq sealed the door. For a moment it was utterly dark, until Gyre shook a dim blue glowstone to life. There was a second hatch, in the underside, which in theory would let them drop straight into the lab. She and Gyre sat on either side of it, legs crossed, and waited.

"Everything looks good," Kit said. "I'm pushing us out."

The flux-stabilized armor blocked *everything* from the outside, even the sound of Kit's claws on the hull. All Maya felt was a lurch in her stomach to indicate they were moving, the box shifting along the log rollers. After a minute, it stopped, and Kit said, "I'm ready to drop us. Sarah says there may be a bit of a jerk. Brace yourselves."

The box tipped, wobbled, and Maya felt an unpleasant shifting in her inner ear. Her guts protested.

"We're, um, spinning a little," Kit said. "It'll damp out, don't worry. Everything else looks good."

"Does the silver eye help with seasickness?" Maya asked Gyre.

"No idea." He tried closing his eyes, first the real and then the artificial. "Neither's pleasant."

"Descending," Kit said. "Down we go."

Maya braced, absurdly. There was nothing to see. *If anything dramatic happens, we'll be dead.* It still felt like an anticlimax, just her and her brother in a tiny room with Kit, the nauseating feeling of the spin gradually fading, a slight lightness telling her they were definitely headed *down*.

"How long to reach the bottom?" Gyre said.

"A quarter of an hour, maybe," Kit said. "Beq says to remember to tug three times on the cord to get pulled up if I get melted."

"I remember," Maya said, smiling. Beq had impressed that on her last night as well.

There was a drawn-out silence.

"Well," Maya said, "now we wait."

"How shall we pass the time?" Gyre said.

"Ooh, gossip!" Kit said. "Did you know Varo has already found a nice boy from the militia? I saw them up on the roof, stargazing, and then he stayed the niiiiight."

"Kit," Gyre said, "what have I told you about spying on our friends?"

"I wasn't *spying*. I'm *supposed* to keep watch. It's not my fault they chose to canoodle near one of my duty posts." The little spider hopped down and skittered across to Maya, jumping on her knee. "What about Tanax, eh? Does he have someone waiting for him back at the Forge?"

"I don't think so. He's never mentioned it," Maya said. "Centarchs aren't really... encouraged."

"Are you supposed to stay *celibate*?" Kit said, aghast. "Honestly, that would explain a *lot*—"

"It's not like that," Maya said. "The only actual *rule* is not to sleep with other centarchs, since it might interfere with your duties. Or anyone under your command, like scouts or servants, obviously. Otherwise..." She frowned. "It's not official. It's just... part of the culture. You sleep where you like, but you don't get *attached*."

"A policy I've always followed myself," Kit said.

"So you and Beq would be frowned on?" Gyre said.

"Probably. Because she's an arcanist, and because I... I love her." Maya shrugged. "I'm not sure what would actually happen. Maybe nothing but dirty looks. It's hard to *make* centarchs do anything."

"I suppose it hardly matters now."

"Because I've committed treason against the Order?" Maya gave a shaky laugh. "I suppose not. If we win—" She thought of the skyfortress, far overhead, and its innocent, dangerous cargo. "We'll have to figure it out as we go along."

"As usual," Gyre said quietly.

"What about you?" Maya said after a moment. "Kit told us you and Apphia were together."

"I remember," Gyre growled. Kit's tiny spider contrived to look innocent.

"Are you still?"

"I don't know. I don't think so. When I left..." Gyre frowned. "I think we both knew we weren't going to be like that."

"You haven't talked to her about it?"

"He hasn't," Kit said. "Because he'd rather ache in stoic silence than get some clarity."

"Because I don't want to make a bad situation worse," Gyre said. "After what happened to her..." He cleared his throat. "Is this really what we're going to talk about? Now?"

"It was Kit's idea."

Another silence.

He's my brother. He'd closed his eyes, breathing calm. *Can't we have a normal conversation? Not some grand debate but just... talk?* Apparently not. *Then again, it's not like either of us has a normal life to speak of. Maybe gossip about bedmates is the closest we can get.*

"Nearly there," Kit said.

"How can you tell?" Gyre said.

"They're measuring the cable up top," Kit said. "We know the right length from our test runs. Should be hitting the lab any second—"

The box jerked, still soundless, and the feeling of descent finally stopped. Maya stood up, though she wasn't quite sure why.

"Next step's up to you, Kit," Gyre said.

"Yeah." The little spider danced from one set of legs to the other. "Okay. Here goes."

Kit's body froze. Maya counted under her breath. *One. Two. Three. Four. Five...*

"Got it," Kit said. "Whew. It is *hot* out there."

"We're a hundred meters from the most devastating weapon ever built," Gyre said. "Even if it is four hundred years old."

"You're sure?" Maya said.

"Of course I am," Kit said. "I had a second or so with each body. Plenty of time."

"One way to find out," Gyre said, looking at the hatch. "You want to do the honors or should I?"

"Let me," Maya said. "With a panoply up, if there's a problem, I *might* be able to close it in time."

"You won't," Kit said cheerfully.

Maya rolled her eyes. She touched her haken and threaded power to her panoply, then stood behind the wheel that opened the hatch. Gyre, sensibly, retreated to a corner of the box.

It'll be fine. Maya took the wheel and gave it a turn. *I trust Beq.* She could almost feel the sunfire bomb out there, still hot enough to melt rock, waves of heat kept from the interior of their little craft by a thin skin of *deiat* and artifice. *I trust Kit.* Odd, to think that, but somehow it had happened.

The wheel stopped turning and the hatch popped inward. There was a brief rush of heat, like the breath of a furnace, and Maya's heart jumped. It subsided after only a moment, though, leaving nothing but a faint scent of sulfur.

"Little bit of air left between the capsule and the lab," Kit said. "Nothing to worry about."

"You could have warned us," Gyre said.

"Didn't think of it," Kit chirped. "Onward!"

Gyre came forward with the modified *deiat* shield. Maya lifted the hatch all the way open, revealing another layer of flux-stabilized unmetal beneath it, smooth and unscarred. When Gyre activated the shield, however, its shimmering surface went dull at once. He stepped back, and Maya ignited her haken. With four long, slow cuts, she chopped out a section of the plating, cooling the glowing edges back to gray with a gesture.

"Be ready," she said. Gyre nodded, Kit's spider back in place on his shoulder. Maya took a deep breath, checked her panoply, and dropped into darkness.

They hadn't planned much past this point. *How could we?* Maya had a vague notion of the layout of the lab, but she had no idea what the Corruptor had done with it since Zeph had last been there. *For that matter, maybe he's still spending his time here, and he'll be waiting for us.*

She hit the floor in a crouch and waited a moment, holding her breath. The blade of her haken threw long, strange shadows on the walls, shifting as the flames swirled. Otherwise there was no movement. Slowly, she straightened up and stepped forward, gesturing for Gyre to follow. He landed a moment later, eye glowing bright green in the semidarkness.

"Safe to make a bit more light?" she whispered.

"Seems quiet," he said.

Maya created a *deiat* light overhead. They were standing between two rows of arcana set on metal tables, each one a large glass jar surrounded by wires and crystals. Maya recognized them after a moment— this was the place where she'd first "awoken" in her and Ashok's shared dream. There the jars had been crackling with lightning; in reality, apparently, they were silent.

"Plaguing *fuck*," Kit said. "Speaking as a scavenger, just setting *foot* in the place gave me about sixteen orgasms."

"You know what these things are?" Gyre said.

"No, but they look fucking valuable."

"I *think* they're some kind of energy storage," Maya said. "Like sunsplinters, but bigger. Empty now."

"What would the Corruptor be doing with so many?"

"There is—was—a whole lab complex above us. This was the bottom level, with a lot of the heavy equipment." Maya parsed carefully through Zephkiel's memories. "It was designed to be self-sufficient for months."

"There's three more," Kit said. "Do you guys have any interest in, you know, stripping the place and living like Splinter Kings?"

"I doubt the Corruptor would let us get away with it," Gyre said. "Plus, don't you already have a whole skyfortress?"

"Maya wouldn't let me take anything," Kit said sulkily.

"You couldn't sell it right now anyway," Maya said. "Come on."

"You know where we're going?" Gyre said.

"I'm making it up as I go along," Maya said. "But if my dreams are any indication, the central chamber is down a corridor, this way."

"You need to get some more exciting dreams," Kit said as they crept forward. "Seriously."

Walking the halls of Stoneroot was a deeply strange experience. In one sense, Maya had never been there before; in another, this was her third visit, after Ashok's vision and Zeph's memories. It felt like her dream had come to life, and she half expected each door to lead to an endless upside-down waterfall or some other nonsensical mindscape. The air smelled exactly as she remembered it, glacially cold and tinged with the tang of metal.

The corridor was lined with archways, and she sent her light forward to reveal the rooms beyond. Most seemed disused, empty or crowded with ancient equipment, heavy with dust. Others bore shelf after shelf of specimen jars, carefully labeled. Maya deliberately avoided looking too closely.

Nothing moved, whichever way she looked. If the Corruptor or his servants *were* here, they were keeping very quiet.

"What should we be looking for?" Gyre said as they passed yet another graveyard of derelict arcana. "There could be anything in here, under the dust."

"If it's dusty, he hasn't been using it," Maya said. "We want what he's been working on recently. We'll search the whole place if we have to, but I'm hoping we can find some notes that will give us somewhere to start. Up here."

The corridor ended in another arch, just as it had in her dream. Beyond, she saw the now-familiar shape of Ashok's large image projector, horns curving upward to enclose a considerable space. Controls—tantalizingly familiar to the ones she'd seen aboard the skyfortress—were arranged on a circular console surrounding it. A ring of other doorways led to other corridors. Behind the console, against the opposite wall, was the delicate white arch of a Gate.

This place is huge. She hadn't really understood that from her dreams—Zeph always seemed to know where to go. *She would come down the main stair...*

Maya looked up. Overhead, the ceiling was dominated by a massive pair of doors, reinforced with enormous crossbars. These were the doors Ashok had closed against the Enforcers after he'd unleashed the Plague against them. *And then he stayed down here for four hundred years.* She'd have thought the confinement would be enough to explain his insanity, but apparently madness had taken hold of him before he'd even begun his long wait.

I need his personal record console. Zeph had had one of those, a piece of arcana that allowed you to keep notes, linked somehow to the lab's communication system. The details were frustratingly vague, since the ancient *dhakim* hadn't thought the device was particularly important. *Even Ashok must have notes, right?* He'd certainly seemed like a meticulous documenter in her dreams.

"At least we won't have to ride back up," Maya said, indicating the Gate. "Which is good, because we haven't figured out how to detach without torching this place. If we get the others down here to help look—"

"We may not have a chance," Gyre said. "We have no idea how long it'll be before he notices someone's been here."

"Searching it ourselves would take—"

"Quiet a moment. I'm trying to see something."

Maya stopped, watching him curiously. He padded forward and hopped up on the control console. His real eye was closed, the green pupil of the other burning bright.

"He doesn't seem like someone who cleans up all that often, right?" Gyre said.

Maya blinked. "The Corruptor? Not really. Back before the war the Chosen had servants for that."

"Look at the dust. That passage, there." He pointed. "Move slow."

Maya waved her *deiat* light closer. The trail in the dust was indistinct, but it was definitely there. *He must use those rooms more than the others.*

"You're right. Well spotted."

"The eye is good for fine detail," Gyre said modestly. He clambered down from the console and walked cautiously around it, trying to disturb the dust as little as possible. "Keep behind me. Kit, stay here and scream if something comes out through the Gate, would you?"

"On it." Kit's little spider hopped to the tip of one of the projector spines. "Be careful."

Maya kept the light overhead as they passed under the arched doorway. The trail in the dust led past the first few doors to one a few meters down the hall. Gyre reached it, pressed himself against the wall, and peeked around the corner. He pulled back at once. Maya stopped, eyebrows raised, and mouthed, "Trouble?"

"I don't think so," Gyre said. "Just...research."

Plaguing fuck. She'd seen what the Corruptor's *research* looked like. *But we have to search it.* Steeling herself, she stepped around the corner.

It was better, in some ways, than what she'd seen at the village on the Forsaken Coast. There people had been still alive when they were pulled apart, screaming until their lungs were ripped from their bodies. Here, the dead flesh was *dead*, very definitely dead, neatly separated and sorted by category. Racks of bones, blobby piles of muscles, slithering heaps of brains. Coiled loops of intestines, organs of every color and description. Stretched sheets of skin.

Not all of it was human, and much of it was unrecognizable, no more resembling a living creature than a piece of vulpi bacon. But here and there were fragments, bits of dissection not yet completed. A head, scalped but still recognizable, features slack in death. The front half of a dog, otherwise intact, as though bisected by an impossibly sharp razor. A woman's torso, obscenely bare-breasted, hanging from one arm with the head and other limbs removed.

Maya fought an intense desire to burn it, to raise her haken and obliterate the nightmare with a wash of cleansing flame. *We need to find what he was doing here.* Her throat worked frantically, guts roiling. *They're dead, it's a butcher shop, no one's in pain.* A male corpse, too small to be an adult, had been opened like a butterfly, its organs set beside it on a central workbench crusted with rusty brown stains. *Fuck fuck* fuck—

"Breathe," Gyre said quietly.

"He must bring people here. His...spiders collect them and haul them through the Gate. Cleanse them of the Plague so he can experiment." She allowed herself to look away long enough to meet Gyre's mismatched eyes. "No wonder he was eager to get out. It makes his work much easier."

"I know," Gyre said. "The spider in Khirkhaz seemed...enthusiastic."

"So did the Eldest," Maya muttered.

"That machine, beside the table. Is that what you're looking for?"

Maya had scarcely noticed it. In the midst of the horror was an arcana device, half the height of a man and topped with a horned image projector. A large number of crystalline controls protruded from the side. Maya recognized it—Zeph had used something similar for her record keeping.

"Yes," she said hoarsely. "That looks like it."

She stepped forward. The floor was sticky underfoot.

A few minutes of fiddling confirmed what she had suspected. The device woke to a *deiat* ping, lines of text filling the space above its projector. Outside scattered words, none of it was comprehensible to Maya. She tried touching a few controls, experimentally, and the text changed but didn't grow any clearer.

"We need to get Xalen to look at this," Maya said. "If anyone can make sense of it, she can."

"See if you can move it," Gyre said. "We're certainly not bringing her down *here*."

Maya nodded grimly and tried shifting the device. It was heavy, but not unmanageably so, and didn't seem to be attached to the floor. She put her arms around it and lifted, walking it carefully back toward the door.

"We'll have to take it together," Maya said, waddling into the corridor. "But I think—"

"*Maya.*"

There was alarm in his voice. Maya dropped the arcana and spun.

Something was moving amid the butchered remains. Long limbs crept out of the organic debris, insectoid but impossibly extended, segment after jointed segment. At first she thought there were a dozen creatures, like great earthworms, but as a stack of fatty tissue collapsed with a wet squelch, she saw a central black mass rising at the intersection of many legs. It was small, a half meter across, little more than a junction for the chitinous tendrils that writhed among the ruins of the dead.

Then, to Maya's enduring horror, it spoke.

"You-outsiders are not I-Master. Not belong here-home."

Gyre had his sword drawn, but he looked to Maya. She leveled her haken.

"I-individual am First-title. I-Master create I-individual *first*. Above all other-inferior I-individual. *Exalted.*" The limbs eeled closer, upsetting piles and stacks. Bones clattered across the floor. "You-outsider gather for I-Master. Please…"

I've heard enough. Maya pulled *deiat* through her haken, unleashing the broad wash of flame she'd been holding in since she first saw the macabre nightmare. It filled the room, rippling off the walls and blasting into the corridor, vanishing when it touched the *deiat* shield Gyre wore. Maya's hair whipped wildly. The *stench* was immediately unbearable, burning flesh and carbonizing hair, fat sizzling and searing.

Something punched through the inferno, three armored limbs twisted together and striking as a single bludgeoning fist. Maya interposed her haken, the blade severing a chunk of chitin, but the strength of the thing picked her up and tossed her into the hall. Her panoply flickered blue. She hit the opposite wall with a pained *oof* and fell to her knees, the chill of *deiat* drain running through her.

Gyre stepped into the doorway, moving with the preternatural speed of his ghoul augmentations. His sword flickered, carving through armored tendrils faster than Maya's eyes could follow, broken segments rattling against the walls or falling underfoot. But the creature's limbs simply jettisoned the ruined portions and came on again, barely diminished. Gyre ducked, spun, danced backward, and grabbed Maya with his free hand, hauling her to her feet.

"Back up!" he said. "Don't let it get behind us!"

Maya had caught her breath. She raised her haken again, giving ground beside Gyre, the two of them standing shoulder to shoulder against a corridor full of whirling, twitching limbs. Gyre's ghoul blade and Maya's flaming one danced, biting deep into chitin whenever the thing came close. Between the two of them, they blocked the hallway, but the weight of the creature's strikes pressed them inexorably backward.

"Plaguing *fuck*!" Gyre's eye blazed. His sword was a blur. "Ideas?"

"It's one of the spiders," Maya gasped out. "Prototype, maybe."

"How do we *kill* it?"

"Main body," she said. "Get close."

"*How?*"

"In here!"

Through a nearby arch, Maya spotted a set of heavy metal shelves. She ducked through, letting Gyre get past her, and threw all her weight into shifting the shelves to block the opening. Gyre grabbed the other side, and between them they manhandled them into position. The improvised barricade jumped and bounced under a barrage of blows, and they both had to put their shoulders to it to keep it in place.

"Where the *fuck* did that thing come from?" Gyre said.

"It was hiding in the . . . mess," Maya said.

"Well, now it's between us and the exit."

Maya hadn't even noticed that nuance. They'd backed away from the central chamber, putting the many-limbed First in their path to the Gate.

"And the Corruptor's notes," she said.

"Less worried about that right now." Gyre winced as a particularly strong blow dented the shelves. "Can you melt it?"

"Too much armor. Maybe up close."

"Great." Another terrific blow jolted the shelves against them. "I might be able to push the tendrils back and buy you a window. A couple of seconds, but afterward I'll be wide open."

"I can make it," Maya said. "You trust me?"

"I wouldn't be here if I didn't." A smile ghosted across Gyre's face. "On three. One. Two. Three—"

They pulled the shelves inward, toppling them with a clatter. Gyre exploded through the doorway, slashing at the closest tendrils. Maya followed him through, haken swinging, but the tentacles had curled inward, surrounding Gyre.

But wherever they struck, he was no longer there. He danced through the melee of clattering chitin, somehow always an instant ahead of the incoming attacks, more and more tentacles swinging close in a wild, writhing frenzy. Maya followed behind, watching Gyre find gaps in the increasingly narrow spaces between the churning limbs. When she thought he couldn't possibly dodge a moment longer, he shouted—

"Maya, *now!*"

Gyre spun in a sudden arc, ghoul blade carving a complicated pattern in the air. Not a wild strike, but precisely directed, aimed not at the pressing tips of the tentacles but closer to their roots. The silver sword slashed cleanly through a half dozen limb segments, and huge swathes of the field of tendrils fell away to lie twitching on the floor. Farther down the corridor, Maya could see the main body of the First, the creature shrieking incoherently with rage and pain. Its remaining limbs contracted, closing into a sphere that wrapped tighter around Gyre.

Maya blew past at a full sprint, flames from her haken streaming behind her, hopping from clear patch to clear patch on a floor covered in still-writhing severed limbs. The First saw her coming, and two tentacles detached from the mass to curve in behind her. Maya ignored them. She leveled her haken like a lance, sharpening its fire to the blue-white heat that carved through unmetal. It passed through the First's carapace without resistance, bubbling black blood gouting outward from the wound. A moment later, the creature cracked in half like a walnut, its exoskeleton unable to contain the pressure of its boiling innards. Tentacles flailed wildly with a tremendous clatter before falling silent.

"*Exalted*," Maya spat at the steaming corpse, wiping vile fluids from her face. "Ask the Eldest how it likes it."

She turned on her heel and ran to the mass of tentacles. A silver blade thrust outward, slicing blindly.

"Gyre?" she said. "Are you okay?"

"Just a bit stuck." Gyre's head thrust up from the gap he'd cut. "Give me a hand?"

Maya sheathed her haken and grabbed his outstretched arm, hauling him free of the bleeding remains. For a moment they silently contemplated the wreckage, the entire hallway littered with bits and pieces of the defunct spider.

"Helloooo?" Kit said from the central chamber. "Nothing came through the Gate; I was watching. Can't blame this one on me."

"No one's blaming you," Maya said, suppressing a chuckle. She pointed to the arcana lying farther up the corridor. "Let's get that thing out of here."

Chapter Twenty-One

Gyre

"The Empire is coming."

The whisper was everywhere, around every corner, carried on the endless fogs and mists of Deepfire. Whenever two people met, they would exchange the latest rumors in furtive tones, the news growing worse with every hour and every retelling. The Empire was coming, an Auxiliary army already marching through the passes. No, they were backed up by Legionaries, or they were *all* Legionaries, the entirety of the Legions coming to subdue the city that had dared to declare itself in opposition to the new order. There were centarchs with them—two, five, a dozen, a hundred, the entire Kyriliarch Council. The Emperor himself was coming, bestriding the battlefield like a golden colossus, fresh from having reduced Splinter Kingdoms like Grace and Meltrock into piles of rubble. He would knock the rebellious skyfortress from the air, scatter the pathetic militia, and turn his wrath on the ants that scurried beneath his feet. Baron Kotzed had been right, and there were thousands of plaguespawn in the vanguard, coming to render them all into meat and offal.

"Is it me," Kit said into Gyre's ear, "or does morale seem low?"

The question was rhetorical. The militia was still training up in the north of the city, and patrols in their new uniforms were a regular sight on the streets, but the other citizens shied away from them as though they were the bringers of a new plague. Food was becoming hard to find, not just in the tunnels but throughout the city, as those who had it squirreled it away in anticipation of disaster.

"A bit," Gyre said quietly. "They're not wrong, you know."

"Oh, I know," Kit said. "I'm the one on the front lines. I *am* the front lines."

This was a stretch, but only a little one. Kit had sent a pack of her smallest bodies down the main road, charting the progress of the enemy force.

"We appreciate your sacrifice," Gyre said.

"You try getting devoured by plaguespawn over and over, see how you like it."

"I think you may be uniquely qualified in that regard."

"And many others." She did her claw-pricking dance on his shoulder.

Militia guards waited at the entrance to the palace, but they recognized Gyre on sight and waved him through. He was returning from a meeting with Lynnia, who refused to come to the Spike when she had a perfectly good parlor. Gyre suspected the old alchemist still harbored mistrust for the seat of the authority. She'd taken the lead on supplying the militia with alchemical munitions, some of which she'd invented specifically for the occasion. In spite of her swearing and complaints, Gyre was certain they'd be ready in time.

But will it be enough?

Kit had taken to describing Xalen, Beq, and Sarah as "the brains of the operation," which Gyre had to admit wasn't entirely wrong. All three of them, plus Maya, were waiting for him in a downstairs office Xalen had taken over for her own use. This meant pushing all the furniture against the walls, stacking books from the palace library on every available surface, and covering several improvised desks with papers. Her ability to manage the mess—one-handed, no less—was almost as impressive as her intellect.

When Gyre entered, she gestured for him to shut the door, her features more animated than he'd ever seen them. Beq, Sarah, and Maya had the slightly stunned looks of people who had been left in the dust some time back. Gyre raised his eyebrows.

"I take it you've found something," he said.

"You have no idea," Xalen said. "Is there anyone outside? This needs to be kept quiet, I assure you."

"I didn't see anyone," Gyre said.

"Good. This—well, the ramifications of the techniques alone will keep us busy for years. It's nothing less than a translation key to a whole world our scholars have never understood, and—"

"Maybe," Beq broke in, "you ought to start from the beginning."

"I— Yes." Xalen cleared her throat, some of her reserve returning. "Sorry. New knowledge can be…exciting."

"I understand," Gyre said. "If you can, try to concentrate on more immediate concerns." *No use in theoretical advances when the Corruptor kills us all.*

"Right. Okay." She glanced down at the notes on her table. "The device you and Maya obtained—which is an amazing piece of arcana in itself, incidentally—has a complete record of approximately four hundred years of the Corruptor's experiments, notes, and theories. It will take a long time to study it fully"—Gyre could see Xalen salivating at the prospect—"but for the sake of, as you say, immediate concerns, I have done a brief overview.

"The important thing, from an academic standpoint, is that these notes represent a study of *dhaka*, which has always been a mystery to us, written in the language and manner of a Chosen, which we can follow quite well. The summary of basic practices *alone* is invaluable, even without the Corruptor's further work—"

"We saw the results of his *work*," Maya said, her features tight. "It's not something I'm eager to reproduce."

"I...ah. Yes. I understand." Xalen looked around. "I'm sorry, again. I'm not accustomed to sharing my findings in person."

"There's a *dhaka* tutorial," Sarah said encouragingly. "In a language we can read."

"That's right," Xalen said.

"Enough that we could make use of it?" Gyre said.

"Eventually, maybe. Not soon. It would take years of study."

"Ah." He wasn't sure if that was a disappointment or a relief. "All right. What else?"

"The Corruptor has pursued many different lines of research over the years," Xalen said. "Which, ah, I will mostly leave to one side for now. One thing that has stayed constant, however, and has consumed all his attention in recent times, is the issue of *adjusting*—it's the term he uses—living tissue at its most basic level, so organisms will pass on the altered traits to their offspring."

"The old Empire knew how to do that," Maya said. "That's what Zephkiel was working on in her memories. They'd changed vulpi and loadbirds and a lot of other things to be more useful."

"Humans, too, according to the notes," Xalen said. "But the Corruptor wanted to take the process much further. He had two major goals. The first was *obedience*."

Gyre snorted. "Like altering people to be more loyal? Turning us into dogs?"

"That sounds like him," Maya said.

"Worse, I think." Xalen tapped one of her scribbled pages. "Artificial organisms, like plaguespawn and ghoul constructs, can be controlled via *dhaka*. It's part of their basic design. The Corruptor wanted to give humans the same property. He tried to tweak a natural organism to have it, but that doesn't seem to have worked. Instead, he focused on trying to build an artificial organism with the abilities of a human."

"The Perfected," Gyre said grimly.

"Those are the silver-armored soldiers we saw in Skyreach?" Sarah said.

Gyre nodded. "Not too different from the ones we fought in the Purifier."

"Or the things the Eldest sent against us on the Forsaken Coast," Beq said. "But they didn't seem smart enough to be humans."

"The notes make it clear that he hasn't managed it yet," Xalen said. "But the Perfected are, as you say, a first step. And his second goal is, if anything, more ambitious. He was investigating the biological basis of the ability to access *deiat*, with the goal of adding *that* trait to his perfect organism."

"Artificial Chosen," Maya breathed. "He's trying to create artificial Chosen?"

"That appears to be the case," Xalen said.

"A new Chosen Empire needs new Chosen," Gyre said.

"But Chosen he can control, this time," Maya said.

"That's..." Sarah looked from Maya to Xalen. "That's impossible, right?"

"I wouldn't presume to say what's possible," Xalen said.

"None of the black spiders have been able to use *deiat*," Maya said. "When Jaedia was under their control, she couldn't use it either."

"I don't believe he's succeeded to date," Xalen said. "Although he does appear to have made some progress. In his notes, he bemoans a lack of samples of sufficient power. His own flesh, tainted by his reflective *dhaka*, is apparently not useful. He has a great interest in acquiring material from the most powerful *deiat* user aside from himself."

"Maya, in other words," Beq said.

For now. Gyre avoided looking at Maya and Beq. *The Chosen children aboard the skyfortress are exactly what he needs.*

"That explains why he wants me so badly," Maya said.

Xalen nodded. "Other powerful *deiat* users will eventually be born, now that the Plague is dispersed, but for the moment you are his best bet."

Beq reached for Maya's hand. Sarah looked down at her feet, troubled. Kit, uncharacteristically silent until now, shifted on Gyre's shoulder and said, "This is all very educational, but is there anything we can use? Knowing *why* he wants Maya doesn't put us any closer to stopping him."

"Is there anything irreplaceable in his lab?" Maya said. "We can get back there through the Gate. Can we slow him down that way?"

"I..." Xalen frowned, shuffling through papers. "Nothing *irreplaceable*, no. But there are experiments in progress, specialized reagents, a few other items. If they were destroyed, it would take him years to rebuild."

"That's something, then," Maya said. "If we destroy them, we can buy time."

"We don't need to buy time," Sarah said. "We need to *stop* him."

"We need to *kill* him," Gyre said. "Let's not talk around it. And I think you're on the right track."

"You want to destroy his experiments?" Kit said.

"I want to use his experiments as bait," Gyre said. "If his lab was threatened, he'd want to move that work somewhere safer, wouldn't he?"

"Probably," Xalen said. "But you've already breached his lab. It's too late."

"He doesn't know that. Not yet. When is the last date in his notes?"

Xalen paged through some more paper. "A few weeks before you went to the Purifier."

"I thought so," Gyre said, excitement rising. "There was a lot of dust in the lab, even in the places where he was working. I don't think he's been back there in some time, maybe not since he left. So he probably hasn't noticed, yet, that we got in. That gives us an opportunity. If he *thinks* we're getting close, he'll go there and we can set an ambush."

"How can we make sure he finds out we're *close* without knowing we're *inside*?" Maya said. "We've been trying to keep his spies away from the capsule..."

"Simple. You tell him."

"I *tell* him? Why would he believe me?"

"Think about it. He probably knows we're trying *something* in the Pit. But he *doesn't* know that we've gotten a supply of flux-stabilized unmetal from the skyfortress. That was added when it was rebuilt as an ark, right?" He looked to Beq, who nodded hesitantly. "Without that, we'd have had a lot more trouble getting in. So if you brag to him we're getting close, he'll still be confident."

"That's . . . plausible," Xalen said. "But hardly assured."

"It's a better chance than we have at the moment," Gyre said. "We're certainly never going to get to him while he's holed up in the Forge behind an army of centarchs and Legionaries."

"I can see another problem," Sarah said. "Even if you're right about how he'll react, he has an easier option than moving all his experiments out of the lab. His army is on the way here already; he can just wait for them to wipe us out."

Shit. Gyre was taken aback for a moment, his enthusiasm wobbling, but he forced a grin. "Then we just have to win."

Tanax was upstairs in the meeting room. He never seemed to leave these days, alternating between the big map of the city on the table and the equally large one covering the surrounding countryside that hung from the wall. He looked as tired now as Beq had before their descent to the Corruptor's lab. Varo, by contrast, had recovered considerably from his ordeal and was nearly his old self again.

"Are the others coming?" Tanax said, without looking up from the report he was reading.

"They're still helping Xalen compile her results," Gyre said.

"Hopefully she has good news," Tanax said, "because I certainly don't."

"How bad is it?" Gyre said.

Tanax gestured to Varo, who pointed to the wall map. Small red pins made a path along the road from the south.

The scout cleared his throat. "These are the approximate spots where Kit encountered—"

"—got eaten by—" Kit interjected.

"—got eaten by, thank you, plaguespawn. They're not moving as quickly as you might expect—they have to carry supplies for the Legionaries—but they're still coming. I give it four days before they reach the city, at least the vanguard."

It was better than the worst case Varo had initially provided, but not by much. "What happens then?"

"A mess," Tanax said flatly. "Deepfire's walls weren't designed to keep out a serious assault, just prevent random plaguespawn from wandering into the city. We've been trying to strengthen them, but we don't have the resources or manpower." He shook his head. "It gets worse. If we keep them out of the city, that makes it a siege, and we don't have the supplies to last long."

"We've been stockpiling, haven't we?" Gyre said.

"What we can." Tanax sighed. "The numbers just don't work out. You can't *grow* food anywhere within a hundred kilometers of here, except maybe mushrooms. Enough comes in by caravan to keep the city fed in good times, but there's not a lot to spare to build up a reserve."

"And we certainly can't hope they starve before we do," Varo said. "Plaguespawn enjoy eating, but they don't have to."

"So it can't come to a siege," Gyre said. "We need them to attack and get bloodied so badly they fall back."

"Easier said than done," Tanax said. "We have too many kilometers of wall and not enough soldiers. There are so many weak spots—here, for example, near the northern tunnels, and here—"

"Forget the wall," Varo said. "It's not going to help us."

"What, then?" Tanax said, frustration evident in his voice. "Fight them in the open? We'd be massacred in minutes. They have the numbers, and we have a bunch of barely trained manufactory workers and scavengers."

"And two centarchs," Gyre put in. "And a skyfortress."

"Which isn't going to help us, apparently," Tanax said bitterly. "It's not enough."

"He's right," Varo said, drifting to the map. "We can't fight them in the open. But I think we can do better than a tumbledown wall." He traced a finger along the imperial line of advance, beside the red pins, and jabbed at something. "We take them here."

"Stonehand Pass?" Tanax read, without comprehension. "What's there?"

Gyre stepped closer to peer at the map. "I came through there with a caravan once. The road switchbacks five or six times up a slope at the end of the valley."

"Exactly," Varo said. "The mountains are steep on either side of the valley. One front to defend, and the switchbacks make a good perch to shoot from. With a little bit of time to dig trenches and build barricades, it'd be better than a fortress."

"It's a day's march from the city," Tanax said. "If they break through, the plaguespawn will run us down before we can get back to the walls."

"You said yourself we can't hold the walls," Gyre said. "I think this is perfect. Either we stop them here, or they back off and spend weeks trying to go around us."

"It's not the worst plan I've ever seen," Tanax admitted.

"We need to start preparing defenses," Varo said. "I volunteer to supervise."

"You're sure you're up to it?" Gyre said. "You just got back."

"Order scouts are trained to do this kind of work in the vanguard of the Legions," Varo said. "Unless you know of someone else who's been studying up—"

Gyre shook his head. "If you want it, the job's yours."

Varo grinned. "A friend of mine once told me that when I volunteered to collect firewood. When I came back—"

"Let me guess," Gyre said. "Crocodiles?"

"It might have been an alligator, actually. It didn't stick around long enough for me to ask."

Even Tanax smiled for a moment, before coughing and restoring his habitual frown. "How many soldiers will you need?"

"A couple of hundred," Varo said promptly. "And some supplies and birds to carry them. I'll make a list."

"Kit, can you send some of your heavy bodies along to help?" Gyre said. "And one of the little ones for communications."

"I'm running a bit short," Kit said, distracted, "but I'll send what I have."

"I should get started," Varo said. "The timing will be tight as it is."

"Go ahead. I'll tell the others." Gyre watched the scout hurry off and tried to ignore the nervous tightening in his chest.

Stonehand Pass. One way or another, they were committed.

Maya

There had been many nights in Maya's life when it had been hard to get to sleep. Nights when she'd been nervous, or unhappy, or had simply drunk too much coffee. The night before her duel with Tanax, or after she'd first seen Ashok through the resonator.

But trying to get to sleep with the intention of contacting the Corruptor in her dreams had to top the list. Beq had wisely found somewhere else to rest for the evening, so she was spared Maya's endless tossing and turning on the strange, slick sheets of the Chosen-made bed. It had been Maya's idea to set up their quarters in the skyfortress—there were endless identical bedrooms to choose from, and it gave Maya easy access to add more power to the giant ship's reserve. But now, staring at the darkened ceiling, she could feel the countless minute flows of *deiat* around her. She imagined being trapped in an endless spiderweb, suspended high above the world.

She must have dozed, eventually, though she didn't remember drifting off. When she found herself standing in Ashok's lab—the clean, well-lit version of their shared dream, rather than the dusty, blood-spattered reality—she gave a sigh of relief.

I wasn't sure that would work. Living Zephkiel's memories had given her a *feeling* for how to make the blood-bond's mental link function, but the tie between her and Ashok was weaker than the connection he'd shared with his lover. *Which is why we can only talk in dreams, I guess.*

Ashok was waiting for her, as always, golden-haired and handsome. The smile he turned on her had a touch of pity around the edges and no humor at all.

"Hello, *sha'deia*," he said. "It's been some time."

"I've been a bit busy," Maya said. "Did you miss me?"

"Terribly. But I won't for long." His smile widened, sharklike. "Some friends of mine are coming to see you."

"So I hear. We're getting ready to receive them."

"Wonderful. The Perfected have been so bored lately." He chuckled. "Though that will change, too. The lands that have the arrogance to declare themselves outside the universal Empire need . . . a reminder."

Maya could imagine it all too easily. The Legions marching across every border of the old Republic, thousands of Perfected at their head, laying waste to Grace and Meltrock and the rest of the Splinter Kingdoms. In their wake would come black spiders, and *experiments*.

She kept her expression calm, walking around him as though the prospect wasn't interesting enough to hold her attention. Her eyes wandered over the controls and the image projector.

"I wondered from the beginning about this place," Maya said, trying to keep her tone casual. "If it was real, or just something you'd invented for my benefit."

"It's real enough," Ashok said. He leaned closer. "Come to me, *sha'deia*, and I'll show you. We don't need to be at odds like this. I can afford to be magnanimous. Take your place at my side."

"As a puppet," Maya snapped, letting her anger bleed through.

"As a partner."

"You don't have partners."

"You don't know me," Ashok said. "Have you been hunting old

stories? It's an odd feeling, listening to my own mythology. I scarcely recognize myself."

"I like to stick closer to the truth," Maya said. "This place, for example. I know it's real, because I found it." She forced a smile. "Down at the bottom of a hole."

"Did you, now?" Ashok's expression shifted, his grin fading. His eyes were hard. "And you think this wins you something?"

"Once we break in, we'll have all your secrets," Maya said. She felt a faint pang at the lie, even here, even to *him*. *It's technically correct. The timing is just a little off...* "I'll find a way to destroy you if I have to smash every bubbling vat and tube."

"Barbarian," Ashok said cheerfully. "Why not burn down the art museums while you're at it? No one appreciates a true genius." He shrugged. "Fortunate, then, that you won't have the chance. Rattle the doors all you like. You'll still be out in the cold when the Perfected come for you."

"You're very certain of yourself."

"I have the benefit of long experience. When I was young, I didn't think that mattered." His smile returned. "After four centuries, it's safe to say my opinion has changed." He cocked his head, studying her. "Oh dear, *sha'deia*. Was *that* your trump card? Have I ruined your little speech by not being properly appreciative?"

"We'll see," Maya snarled at him, frustration not at all feigned. She willed herself out of the dream, his voice fading away.

"We will indeed..."

She woke with her head hanging off the foot of the bed, all the sheets kicked into a pile on the floor, her eyes scratchy and raw. She sat up with a yawn and fumbled at the controls to open the door. One of Kit's small bodies waited outside.

"Do you always thump around so much?" Kit said. She skittered across the floor and hopped up beside her. "I feel bad for Beq."

"Only when I'm trying to lay a trap for the Emperor," Maya said.

"It worked, then?"

"I gave him the message. Whether he bought it, I have no idea."

"I have a body waiting in the lab. If he shows up there early, I'll let you know."

"That's something." Maya flopped back into bed. "Now all we need to worry about is thousands of hungry plaguespawn..."

Gyre

Deepfire had grown very quiet by night.

To Gyre, a connoisseur of the city's moods, this one felt particularly strange. Ordinarily, only the depths of winter would shut down Deepfire's raucous nightlife, fueled by caravaneers blowing off steam after their trip from the south and scavengers eager to spend their ill-gotten gains. But it had been weeks since a caravan arrived, with the main southern road blocked by the approaching imperials, and scavenging had been shut down even longer. There had been a burst of excitement when the militia had first been organized, tunnelborn testing their new freedom to wander the upper city, but the prospect of action had dampened everyone's spirits. Tonight, the streets were mostly empty.

It served his purposes, for the moment. Gyre walked beside Elariel and Kit—both her tiny body on his shoulder and a larger one flanking the ghoul, in case of emergency. He wore his sword beneath his cloak, and a full energy bottle on the opposite hip. Gyre didn't *expect* trouble, but you never really knew, with ghouls.

"They have to listen," Elariel said. "I sent another messenger-construct with everything we've learned about the Corruptor. They'll see he's not some mythological monster. Just a mad Chosen who needs to be stopped. Right?"

"It's not me you need to convince," Gyre said. "I'm just grateful you sent to them at all."

"Yeah." Elariel looked at the ground. "Well. I know I was a bit... negative, at first."

"Believe me, I understand. I wouldn't be here if I thought there was another way out."

"That's just the thing. There isn't another way, is there? Even for Refuge. If we fail, he'll find the city eventually, and that'll be the end of my people."

"Refuge condemned you to death," Gyre said. "Some people might not be inclined to fight for them."

"I can't blame them for that. What Naumoriel did—what I helped him to do..." She shook her head. "It's strange, right? I know it was wrong. And Refuge punished me because it was wrong. But I doubt we'd agree on *why*."

"Perspective is a funny thing," Gyre said. "Here we are."

They stopped in front of an empty lot. There had been a building here, bits of its brickwork clinging to its neighbors like scabs, but a fire had demolished most of it and exposure to the elements had done the rest. In the tight-packed streets of Deepfire, it stuck out like a broken tooth in a smile. The salvageable pieces had long since been hauled away by a city perennially desperate for building material, so all that remained were rotten floorboards and piles of scorched, shattered bricks.

Something squatted among them, a low, multilegged shape not too different from Kit's bodies. It was a ghoul-construct, black muscle over iron, with an arcana device embedded in its back. It lacked the characteristic horns of a Chosen image projector, but Gyre recognized it as the same sort of thing—Naumoriel had used one to speak to him from Elariel's safehouse, when he'd first encountered the ghouls.

The construct shifted as they approached, turning to face them. Elariel said something in her own language, and the thing settled back on its haunches. Above it, the air glowed blue, faintly at first but quickly brightening into a translucent image of a ghoul woman—big-eyed, with long, twitching ears and brown-and-white fur. Gyre recognized the piercing at the base of one ear, and in any case there was only one ghoul who was likely to speak with them: Tyraves, Minister of the

Exterior, in charge of handling all contact between Refuge and the outside world.

"Elariel. We were surprised to receive your message." She stayed in the human tongue for Gyre's benefit. She was fluent but had the formal air of too much study and not enough conversation. "You understand the terms of your exile prohibit any attempt to interfere with Refuge, even indirectly."

"Elariel sent that message at my request," Gyre said smoothly. "It seemed the most expeditious route to contact you."

"We make contact difficult for a reason, Silvereye," Tyraves said. "I must admit I did not expect to see you again. Your quest to destroy the Republic seemed quixotic."

"You supported me," Gyre said.

"A matter of expediency. You helped remove a bone of contention among the Geraia. A few crates of weapons were a small price to pay for consensus."

"I'm glad to be of service," Gyre said. "But, as Elariel's message informed you, the situation has changed."

"For you, perhaps," Tyraves said.

"Nial-Est-Ashok—the Corruptor—has taken control of the Republic and proclaimed a new Chosen Empire. I'd say that changes things for everyone."

"I think you misunderstand our position, Silvereye," Tyraves said. "Refuge has remained hidden from humanity, because to us there is no difference between your Republic and the Chosen Empire that preceded it. However it manifests, the power of the surface world is a threat to us only if we are discovered."

"The Corruptor's empire is not like the Republic," Gyre said. "He's mastered *dhaka*. That gives him a self-replicating army of plaguespawn that doesn't get bored or cold or hungry. If he sets them to searching, he'll find you."

"All the more reason to keep him ignorant of our existence," Tyraves said.

"You can't hide forever."

"We've managed for four hundred years."

"Only because there were no Chosen left to look, and humanity thought you were extinct. Ashok knows the truth of the Plague War."

"So Elariel said." Tyraves raised her eyebrows. "I admit I'm not convinced. You have only the word of a centarch."

"I believe her," Elariel said. "And I saw Ashok myself at the Purifier."

Tyraves shrugged. "Either way, it matters little."

"I think it matters a lot," Elariel said. Her voice shook at first, but gradually strengthened. "Gyre's right. If Ashok isn't stopped, Refuge is in terrible danger. We have a chance to head that off, here and now."

"So you say," Tyraves snapped. "I have yet to hear how you intend to defeat this Corruptor. But suppose I believed you—what then? Send a construct army to the surface to fight at your side?"

"Yes," Gyre said eagerly. "You wouldn't have to risk a single ghoul—"

"We would risk *everything*," Tyraves said. "Our defenses would be stripped bare. And more importantly, we would *reveal ourselves*. A few weapons or constructs can be explained as plunder from ruins, but a force sufficient to assist you would be as good as telling everyone we exist."

"But we can stop him—"

"How?"

Gyre stiffened. "I have a plan."

"I have seen what comes of your *plans*. But *either way*, we would be exposed. If you lose, the Corruptor will find us, as you so confidently assure me. If you *win*, then every human in the mountains will come looking for the ghouls, as you once did. You are just as tireless and ravenous as plaguespawn. At best, it will mean constant war. At worst, destruction for Refuge, as you once destroyed the rest of my people."

"We wouldn't allow it," Gyre said. "After we win, we can come to an agreement."

"Really. You speak for all humans, then?" Tyraves snorted. "No."

"You don't understand," Elariel said. "If they lose, it'll be the end of *everything*. I've seen Ashok's research. It's *sick*."

"I understand that we were right to banish you," Tyraves said. "And to give you that appearance. You think more like a human than one of us."

"All I want to do is *help* you," Elariel said. But Tyraves' image had already vanished. The viewer-construct made a rapid popping sound, like the bursting of an alchemical, and its body began to shake and bubble. In a few seconds, it had melted into a puddle of noxious black fluid and scrap iron.

"Hey, I wonder if I can do that," Kit said into the silence that followed. "Definitely makes for a cool exit."

"She wouldn't listen," Elariel said, looking down at her clenched hands.

"Are you surprised?" Gyre said.

"No." Elariel breathed out. "Before I left Refuge, I would have said the same. It's easy to see only the monstrous part of humanity. You are so cruel, so careless of one another. But... not always. And you do not have our advantages."

"Like constructs to do all the actual work," Kit said.

Elariel nodded jerkily. "Even so," she said. "This is the *Corruptor*. I thought she might understand."

"As far as she's concerned, he's a childhood bogeyman," Gyre said. "Either he's not real, in which case there's nothing to worry about, or he's half a god, in which case hiding under the bed is the best answer."

"You were right," Elariel said abruptly. "When you spoke to the Geraia. You said humanity would find Refuge eventually. At the time, I thought that a bluff, but having seen more of you..." She shook her head. "You were right. We cannot hide forever. The Corruptor is just advancing the schedule."

"Unfortunately, I don't think we're ever going to get Tyraves to believe that."

"I suppose not." Elariel's fists clenched again. "I wish I could do more to help."

"I had a thought along those lines," Kit said. "Back in Refuge, you were a construct expert, right?"

Elariel nodded. "It was my specialization, yes."

"Can you afford to leave Jaedia alone for a while?"

"Oh yes. The process is well underway. Her recovery is mostly in the hands of her own body now."

"Then why don't you come visit me in Leviathan's Womb?" Kit did a little wiggling dance of excitement. "There are pieces of the Leviathan's manufacturing system I still don't understand. If you can help me increase production, then we might be able to get an army of constructs after all."

"Would you be able to get there in time?" Gyre said.

"If she rides one of my heavy constructs, we can be there in less than a day," Kit said. "I don't need to stop for rest, and I know some shortcuts. Might get a bit bumpy, though."

"It seems worth a try," Gyre said. He looked to Elariel. "Only if you're willing, of course."

"I'll go," Elariel said immediately. "Trying to do something is better than simply waiting."

"How soon can you be ready?" Kit said.

"I need to collect my things," Elariel said. "And...speak to Sarah." Her face fell; Gyre could almost see the drooping ears.

"You'll see her again once we're finished," he said.

"Only if we both survive," Elariel said, squeezing her eyes shut. "But I appreciate the thought."

"Can you give us some privacy?" Gyre said.

"Oooooh," Kit said. "Getting laid at the last minute?"

"Kit—" Gyre took a breath. "Just wait here, all right."

"Fine." The little spider scuttled down from his shoulder and hopped to the wainscotting. "But I expect gossip."

Gyre rolled his eyes and left her behind. Apphia's door was guarded by a young militiaman, who saluted nervously at the sight of Gyre.

"Is she in?" he said.

"Yes, but she's resting," the boy said. "If you could—"

"It's all right," Apphia said from inside. "Let him in."

The boy saluted, and Gyre opened the door, looking a little embarrassed. "I can come back later. It's not urgent."

"Don't worry about it." Apphia emerged from the suite's bathroom dressed in a fluffy palace bathrobe, her hair still wet. "Has something happened?"

"No, nothing like that. I just wanted to talk before...everything starts."

He hadn't talked to her, Kit had said, "*because he'd rather ache in stoic silence than get some clarity*." And maybe it was true. *But I owe her this much.*

How much Apphia could guess from his face, he didn't know, but her expression went still. She nodded and beckoned him to the sofa. They sat side by side.

"What's on your mind?" she said.

"When we march, tomorrow..." He hesitated. "You don't have to come along, if you don't want to."

"Excuse me?" Apphia said, sitting up straighter.

"I asked you to tell your story, and you did. And somehow that turned into *this*. You've done wonders. I just don't want to force you into anything you don't want to do."

"It's a bit late for that, Gyre," Apphia said. Her expression softened a little. "You're serious."

"I—"

"Look." She leaned closer and lowered her voice. "You saved my life. Twice, at least. And I'll always be grateful for your help in retaking the Spire, even with...what happened after. But none of that makes you *responsible* for me. Neither does fucking a few times, if that's what you're thinking. If I hadn't wanted to do this, believe me, I wouldn't have."

"What about Nina?"

"That goes for Nina too. You think she and I haven't talked about it? It goes for *everyone*. They got into it because you're *right*, not just because you told them to. The Corruptor has to be stopped. That's why we're all here."

"All right." Gyre held up his hands. "Sorry. Maybe it was a silly thing to ask."

"It was," Apphia said, "but believe me, I understand. I've been where you're sitting. You know what has to be done, but then you realize— I'm going to give the order, and all these people are going to *obey*. And some of them are going to die."

"Yeah." Gyre looked down at his hands.

"Remind yourself why we're doing it. And if that doesn't convince you, then you should call the whole thing off." Apphia smiled, the lightning scar tugging at her lip. "That's the extent of my words of wisdom. I hope you didn't need any others."

"I'll manage," Gyre said, fighting a smile himself. "But there was one other thing."

"You and me?" Apphia guessed.

Gyre nodded. She sat back against the cushions with a sigh.

"I thought it might get complicated," she said.

"Maybe it doesn't have to," Gyre said. "I didn't want to leave it unsaid."

"Yeah." Apphia scratched the back of her neck. "What we had was... a moment, right?"

"A moment," Gyre agreed.

"If things had stayed as they were, if we'd kept fighting in Khirkhaz together, who knows? But now..." She shook her head. "When this is over, if we survive, I'm going to go home and mourn and try to build something better. And you'll do...Chosen-know-what, but it won't be that."

"Probably not," Gyre admitted. In all honesty, he had no idea. *Thinking past the next day seems like a luxury I can't afford.*

"It's probably better that it stay just a moment, then." She leaned forward and touched his cheek. "I'm sorry."

"You don't have to be sorry." Gyre took her hand gently. He let out a breath, past a thickness in his throat. "I had thought...along similar lines."

"Good," Apphia said, lowering her hand. "I didn't want to think I was breaking your heart."

"I'd hate to have to get the ghouls to replace it," Gyre said.

"Well?" Kit said, when he let her scuttle back to his shoulder.

"Well, what?"

"Well, what happened? You barely look out of breath."

"We just talked, Kit. Like you told me to, back in the box."

"Oh." For once, there was hesitation in Kit's voice. "And?"

"Circumstances have changed. For both of us."

"I hate it when that happens," Kit said. Gyre thought she sounded relieved.

He found himself at the end of a hall and opened a pair of glass doors onto a small balcony overlooking the grounds. Beds of flowers went untended, their gardeners recruited for more important tasks. Small green shoots were already poking up between them.

"Have you thought about what you're going to do after?" Gyre said. "If we win."

"I'm not exactly equipped for celebrating anymore," Kit said mournfully. "Can't drink, can't eat, can't fuck. I guess I could dance, if I could find a partner with six legs. Maybe I'll learn to dance with myself."

"I don't mean the party. I mean *after*."

The little spider shifted uncertainly. "How should I know? It's not like my life has been going according to plan."

"Nor mine."

"Why, what are *you* going to do?"

"No idea. I want to stay close to Maya. I'm not going to lose her again."

"What if she wants to go back to the Order?"

"We'll work it out." He thought of the Chosen children, still and silent aboard the skyfortress. "We'll need to work out a lot of things."

"I can help out. I make a pretty good courier service."

Gyre laughed. "You're pretty good at a lot of things."

"Aw. I'd blush if I still had skin."

"Seriously, Kit." Gyre looked at the tiny construct. "Ever since Leviathan's Womb, you've been right at my side. You don't need me. You don't need *anyone*, really. I don't want you to think I don't appreciate it."

"Well." From her tone, Gyre got the sense that now Kit really *would* be blushing. "I've had a lot of time to think. It's all I really *can* do, to be honest. And there are some things I did, before, that...I probably shouldn't have done. I was scared and dumb and ready to die and you helped me anyway. So I thought I could do worse than sticking by you."

"Thanks," Gyre said. "I missed you, after Khirkhaz."

"I...have more fun when you're around, too." The spider danced a tiny jig. "Seriously, I was *so bored*. I was playing solitaire with rocks, that's how bored I was. You have no idea. I was sneaking in people's windows at night, you know, when they were getting ready to fuck, and just as they were getting going I'd make a noise like an angry loadbird—*ka-squawk*—and watch them freak out—"

Gyre grinned, and turned toward his own chambers.

Maya

Maya opened her eyes, very slowly. Her mouth felt like it was full of sand.

"Hey," Beq said.

"Hey," Maya croaked. "Urgh. What time is it?"

"About seven in the evening," Beq said cheerfully.

Maya sat up, too quickly. Her head pounded. "Why didn't you wake me?"

"You looked like you needed the rest," Beq said. "And I've been busy in the archives. Do you want something to eat?"

Maya realized that she very much did. It was easy to lose track of time in the bowels of the skyfortress, where the rooms had softly glowing panels instead of windows. Beq, thankfully, had anticipated this, and had dinner—*breakfast?*—ready. *Pride in Power* had nothing edible aboard after four centuries, so food had to be brought up from the city by flitter. Maya touched her haken and sent a wave of warmth through her sausages, pleased with her ability to do so without any of them exploding. *Jaedia always said I needed to practice my fine control.*

"Did you find anything useful?" Maya said between bites. "For our trump card?"

That was the trap they were laying for the Corruptor, the final move in the plan. It felt like hubris to plan so far ahead, with the battle still to fight. *But if we win, it has to be ready, or all this is meaningless.* The thought spiked Maya's nerves. *So much has to go right...*

"Yeah. I think I've got something. It'll be ready by the time we need it." She shook her head. "I haven't had as much luck figuring out how *Pride* can help in the battle. There's no end of weapons in the Chosen archives, but they all require arcana we don't have."

"We could crash it into them. Like the one at Grace." Maya waggled her eyebrows to indicate this wasn't a serious option. *For starters, we can't move the Chosen children...* "Can we mount blasters somehow?"

"Even if we could, what does that really achieve? They need all the blasters they can get on the ground." Beq pressed her lips together. "I keep trying to come up with a way to use power from the reserve directly, channel it through some system or other, but nothing's practical. The ship is designed to *prevent* that."

"Yeah." Maya finished the last of the sausage. "Maybe we're overthinking this. Talk to Sarah. I feel like a scavenger would have better ideas."

"I'll see if she has time. She's taken on a lot since Elariel left." Beq sighed. "I can't blame her. If I was stuck here without you, I'd try to drown myself in work too."

Maya took Beq's hand and interlaced their fingers. "I'm not going anywhere."

"I know," Beq said. "I just…"

She trailed off, and before she could speak again, there was a scratching at the door. Beq jumped up and opened it to find Kit hopping from one set of legs to the other in excitement.

"It's starting," she said. "Varo and the advance team just fought off a wave of plaguespawn."

"Is he okay?" Maya said, climbing out of bed.

"He's fine. Just scouts, we think. But Gyre and Tanax put out the order to march. They want the first of the militia in position by morning. Maya, he wants you to come down as soon as you can."

"That's it, then," Maya said, turning to Beq. "Are you ready?"

"I'll have to be, won't I?" Beq fiddled with her spectacles for a moment, then leaned forward for a kiss. For once Kit refrained from comment. "I'll start getting the ship ready."

"Good luck," Maya said.

"You too." Beq's smile was only a little shaky. "I'll be there when you need me."

Chapter Twenty-Two

Stonehand Pass was everything Varo had promised. Standing at its highest point, Gyre contemplated the view. The road ran east to west here, before curving north to Deepfire in the valley behind him. Ahead, backed by the just-risen sun, was the valley of the Voss, a stretch of mostly flat ground slowly descending out of the mountains. It was about two kilometers across at its widest point, with the Voss a thin ribbon meandering its way along the valley floor in great loops and bows. Trees lined its banks, but much of the rest of the valley was too dry for anything but patchy grass and occasional shrubs. The flanks of the valley climbed to rocky cliffs along most of its length, with gaps leading off into other vales and canyons.

Between the two valleys, the ground rose into a high, bald ridge, a saddle running between two imposing peaks to the north and south. The main southward road climbed it in a series of long, painful switchbacks, winding back and forth up the rising ground like a tightly coiled snake. There were no trees on the slope, but plenty of rocks, from small stones to enormous boulders.

There were also, courtesy of a few days of hard effort by Varo's advance party, the rudiments of fortifications. The east-facing verge of the road, looking down the slope into the valley, had been lined with obstacles. Varo had incorporated the rocks where they stood and improvised the rest with sandbags and timbers. He'd also dug trenches, as much as the stony soil would allow. The result was a series of breastworks, where soldiers could stand and fire with only their head and arms exposed. Gyre counted five levels, each able to shoot over the heads of the last.

In between the positions, and in a great arc stretching downward from the bottom, the scout had erected all the obstacles he could think of. There were fields of wooden spikes, driven deep into the turf and clustered in knots to break up incoming cavalry or hordes of plaguespawn. Between them were chunks of scrap unmetal, their ends sharpened. Strings of tightly twisted resilk, thick as wire, were woven around posts, the webs of unbreakable fabric forming low fences like spiderwebs. Here and there these had already caught some prey—the deliquescing corpses of a dozen plaguespawn were still tangled up in them.

Militia soldiers were marching past, if not precisely in formation then at least in organized groups, filing down to their positions in obedience to the cries of their officers. Gyre saw Nina screaming several squads into position and smiled. When he turned around, Apphia was approaching, walking beside the densest knot of soldiers and shouting to make herself heard over the racket of marchers.

"Yes, send those three wagons down to the lowest level," she was saying to a worried-looking officer in a broad, floppy hat. "Rikard's down there, he'll know what to do with them. Tell him I want everything unloaded and the birds back up here as soon as possible." The young man nodded vigorously, a dumbfounded expression on his face, and Apphia heroically restrained herself from slapping him. "That means *go*. Now, please."

He started, saluted, and hurried off. Apphia stopped beside Gyre, watching the column continue past, plagued by a thousand small disasters and miscommunications.

"The joys of command," Gyre said.

"You know, every time I plan an operation like this, I think, *this* time I'll get it right. This time every order will be clear, and nobody will misread something or wake up late or generally fuck everything up. And somehow it never works out."

Gyre laughed. "That sounds like...well, humans, really."

"I wonder if the Chosen had these problems."

"I imagine they did. Being able to crush mountains with *deiat* doesn't help when somebody tripped over his shoelaces or forgot to get his papers countersigned."

It was Apphia's turn to chuckle. "You're probably right, but it's a horrifying thought."

"I know." Gyre nodded at the men and women walking past. "How are they holding up?"

"Tired. The night march didn't help anybody. But they're glad to finally be doing something."

"You think they'll hold out?"

"At least for a while." She gestured approvingly at the fortified position. "It's good ground. Almost too good. You really think they'll attack here?"

"They'll attack," Gyre said. "The Corruptor doesn't care about casualties, and the plaguespawn certainly don't."

"Yeah." Apphia frowned. "Whatever else happens, we'll certainly take a lot of them with us."

"We'll beat them," Gyre said. "I'm sure of it."

"You may be the only one." At the look on his face, she laughed out loud. "Just being realistic."

"There's such a thing as too much realism," Gyre said.

Apphia snorted skeptically. Up ahead, a snarl in the column caught her attention, and she broke away from him and ran toward it, waving. "That's not where those go; be *careful*—"

Another figure came up over the ridge, wearing a broad-brimmed hat at a rakish angle. Behind him were a motley collection of people with mismatched armor, long leather coats, and a startling variety of weapons. The scavengers of Deepfire might lack discipline, but most of them were veterans of years in the tunnels, fighting plaguespawn, bandits, and one another. Ibb, at their head, stopped beside Gyre and doffed his hat, using it to wave his charges on down the hill.

"Don't say it," Ibb warned.

"Say what?"

"Some line about how you were always certain I'd come out to help. We both know it isn't true. I meant what I said back in the office."

"And yet," Gyre said with a grin, "here you are."

"Here I am." Ibb sighed and put his hat back on. "Your Baron Kotzed there has a lot to do with it."

"She's not *mine*, by any stretch of the imagination."

"Whoever's she is, she paints a dire picture. I don't want those things coming anywhere near Jaken and the girls."

"Also, I hear Lynnia offered you a stack of thalers."

"Well, there's that as well. I'm not made of stone."

Gyre snorted. "Any problems with the scavengers?"

"Nothing I couldn't handle. They don't like taking orders, but they *do* like shooting things."

"We have a confluence of interests, then. I wish them the best." Gyre turned back to the plain. "You be careful, though. I don't want to explain things to Jaken."

"You can say that again. He'd send you home in a sack. But fear not—I know how to look out for myself."

"Good luck."

Ibb waved his hat again, following his troops down the hill.

The day wore on. Maya and Tanax arrived with the last of the militia, herding stragglers forward. By an hour before noon, everyone was in position. *And what a laugh it will be if the Corruptor calls the whole thing off...*

He hadn't. The first evidence of the oncoming army was a swarm of black dots coming up the valley in a roiling mass. From the vantage of the hilltop, they looked like a carpet of ants. Looking closer with his silver eye, Gyre could see they were plaguespawn, nightmare constructions of twisted flesh and bone. No two were alike, but all were man-sized, moving low and fast like a pack of wolves.

Behind them, slower-moving, were the humanoid soldiers. Legionaries, marching in a tight column, flowed up the valley like a river in reverse. When they came within sight of the defenses, the dense formation blossomed outward, squads splitting off with perfect timing to take up positions in a looser skirmish line. Farther to the rear, another line of silver-armored soldiers caught the sunlight. *Perfected.*

One of Kit's tiny spiders hurried over, crossing the dusty ground and grabbing onto Gyre's trouser leg. It scuttled up to his shoulder, claws pricking, and settled in.

"Everything ready?" he said.

"Yup!" she said cheerfully. "I've got bodies with Apphia, Ibb, and Varo down on the front lines, and one up with Beq. Spreading myself a bit thin these days!"

"And our reinforcements?"

"Coming." Kit danced a little. "Elariel's been *very* helpful. But we need more time."

"We'll do our best," Gyre said.

Tanax pointed. "Here they come."

The plaguespawn surged forward. Distance and perspective made them seem slow at first, but as they approached their speed was evident. Galloping on four legs or six or a hundred, they covered ground faster than a charging warbird. The swarm grew denser as the valley narrowed, gathering like a great dark wave about to crest. Gyre saw a few crossbow bolts fly, falling far short, and heard nervous officers shouting for discipline.

Judging range was tricky business, but some of Ibb's scavengers were spread throughout the first two tiers, and they were experts—in the mountains, hitting a rabbit at fifty meters might be the difference between life and death. As the great wave came close, they were the first to shoot, a couple of dozen quarrels arcing skyward and then plunging down to tear through flesh. A few seconds later, the whole of the first two tiers opened fire.

The volley blackened the sky like a horde of locusts. When it descended, the whole leading edge of the plaguespawn swarm came apart, the creatures tumbling and dropping to form great steaming piles of still-struggling flesh. The mounds of dead were visible for only a moment before the swarm washed on, plaguespawn jumping their comrades or scrambling over them, taking mouthfuls of flesh as they went.

A second volley of quarrels slammed out, trajectory flatter than before, scything great gaps in the oncoming horde. Commands were given on the upper tiers of the slope, and blaster rifles joined in. The arcana weapons were longer ranged than a crossbow, so Apphia had deployed them high on the hill, maximizing fire in the killing zone.

The effect was terrific. Gyre had never seen so many blasters firing at once—a rapid series of *cracks* grew into a snapping, popping chorus that went on and on. The bolts detonated with a bass roar, sending sprays of dirt and chunks of flesh in all directions. While the crossbows shredded the front ranks, the blasters blew them apart, their concentrated fire creating a curtain of detonations that walked closer and closer as the plaguespawn came on.

Gyre couldn't imagine any mortal creature walking into the fire. But plaguespawn, of course, had no fear. They pressed forward, leaping the stakes and obstacles, shredding themselves on densely packed unmetal spikes, blocking them with their quivering bodies so their comrades could use them as stepping-stones. Crossbows were firing flat now, choosing their targets, a half-dozen bolts immediately picking off any twisted creature that made it through the curtain of fire. In spite of everything, the monsters came on, mangled and dripping gore. The front of the wave was boiling nearer, moment by moment.

"Tell Ibb *now*," Gyre said to Kit.

A second later a hundred alchemicals were in the air. Deepfire's alchemists had worked day and night to equip the militia with their finest tools of destruction. As Gyre had arranged with Ibb, the first volley was all burners, the explosives detonating with an eye-searing *whoomp* of flames that grew into a towering inferno covering the entire front. Hundreds of plaguespawn were incinerated in the initial burst, and hundreds more tried to force their way through, only to find that alchemical fire burned so fast and hot they were little more than charred meat when they came out the other side. A few, still burning, stumbled toward the line and were brought down by crossbows.

"They're breaking off," Tanax said. "Look."

Gyre could see for himself. The rear of the great swarm, now compacted into a solid black mass, was flowing in reverse, running just as quickly in the opposite direction. Crossbow fire chased them, but Gyre was glad to see no blaster bolts did. He'd told the officers to stress that blaster charges were too important to waste on any target that wasn't immediately threatening. A distant cheer rose from the lowest tier of the defenses, getting louder as it swept up the hill.

"Didn't expect to see plaguespawn running away," Maya said.

"They aren't wild," Gyre said. "Someone doesn't want to waste them to no purpose."

"It was a test," Tanax said grimly. "To see if we'd break at the first pressure. Now they'll push in earnest."

Indeed, before the plaguespawn had finished pouring out of the way, the line of Legionaries began its advance, officers waving their men forward. For the moment, Gyre was glad to see, the Perfected stayed in the rear, as though waiting for something. Maya was looking skyward, where a front of roiling cloud was approaching from the west.

"Kit?" Gyre said. "It'd be nice to take them in the flank, if you're close enough."

"Still coming," Kit said. "Sorry. Mountains are slow going."

"Your bodies here are ready?"

"On your command." She capered excitedly.

When the Legionaries reached blaster-rifle range, they broke off their orderly walk and came forward in a series of rushes, taking what little cover the valley floor offered. Their squads worked in pairs, one group firing while the other moved. Blaster bolts detonated among the lowest tiers of defenders, sprays of dirt and showers of flaming splinters from the breastworks. Protected by the fortifications, the crossbowmen loaded and fired in turns, their silent quarrels almost invisible against the barrage of glowing blaster bolts. Here and there a Legionary fell to a lucky hit, but most of the missiles stuck harmlessly in the earth or glanced off unmetal armor.

The disciplined soldiers of the Empire kept coming, reaching the piles of dead plaguespawn and using them for cover. They had to thread their way through the belt of obstacles, choked with misshapen corpses, and the higher tiers of defenders now opened fire as well. Blaster bolts *cracked* down, exploding among their lines in a continuous barrage of smoke and flame. The first tier threw another wave of alchemicals, and burners bloomed like brilliant flowers, while bombs detonated with huge *thumps* that threw great clouds of burning earth skyward.

None of it was enough. Legionary armor wasn't impenetrable, but only a direct hit from a blaster could really do critical damage. The armored soldiers came on, firing their own weapons at close range. The lower face of the hill was pockmarked with craters, as though it had suffered from some disease, and the wood-and-stone breastworks were collapsed in several places. More alchemicals detonated, right along the line, flames spattering attackers and defenders alike.

Then the Legionaries were over the first wall, and slaughter and panic began. It was one thing to watch a soldier approach, firing as he came, but it was quite another to stand up to him in the confines of a trench. The tunnelborn, sensibly, streamed backward. A few stood their ground, maddened by the fight, and died on Legionary blades. The breach in the line spread rapidly as more and more Legionaries pulled themselves over the breastworks.

"Kit, tell Varo to get everybody up the hill," Gyre said.

"He's already doing it," Kit said cheerfully.

"Perfect. Give Beq a sixty-second count. And Ibb needs to be ready."

Maya was looking at the clouds again. Tanax had his hand on his haken, fingers clenched as people fought and died below.

"Wait," Gyre said.

And let's hope this works...

Above the battlefield the front of dark clouds broke apart, shredding as the vast prow of the *Pride in Power* pushed through. The skyfortress was flying low, only a thousand meters above the valley, and for a moment Gyre wondered if it would scrape the surrounding peaks.

Just the sight of it gave the Legionaries pause, and no wonder. *If the thing was fully equipped, the battle would already be over.* But whoever was commanding the Corruptor's forces had clearly been warned in advance about the rebels' new toy, and knew that the *Pride*'s weapons had been stripped when it had been converted into an ark for its final, desperate mission. As its shadow slid across the battlefield, the Legionaries looked up only briefly before continuing their push forward, driving the first line of defenders up the slope to the second tier.

This left them with a difficult problem, however. Varo's trenches were cleverly designed with protected fronts but open rears, so the upper tiers could shoot into the lower without obstruction. Blaster fire began bursting among the Legionaries as soon as the defenders had scrambled out of the way, and there was no cover to be found. The white-armored soldiers tried to keep climbing, but there were only a few paths leading between the tiers, and alchemicals blocked them with clinging fire. The hillside between these routes was steep and cluttered with rocks, making for an arduous climb with defenders blasting away at the top.

Still, Gyre wouldn't have laid odds against the Legionaries. More and more of them were reaching the bottom trench, pushing through the spikes and obstacles now littered with human corpses in addition to plaguespawn. They formed in small groups, taking the hill at a rush. The situation was still critical when the first stone fell from the sky.

It wasn't a stone, really, but a chunk of masonry the size of a horse. It landed across a pair of Legionaries and crushed them into the earth of the trench like insects. More rocks followed, large and small, like the world's most dangerous hailstorm.

Up on the *Pride*, beyond the limits of anyone's vision but Gyre's, teams of men and women sweated and strained to push the stones over the lip of the landing bays. It had been Sarah, apparently, who'd come up with this "weapon" everyone else had overlooked. *Sometimes having the high ground is all the advantage you need. Just a pity we didn't come up with it earlier.* The flitters had been able to ferry only a limited number of stones up to the skyfortress.

Under the killing rain, the Legionaries' resolve shattered. There was no protection from the missiles that fell in a steady torrent, crushing bodies beneath them. Unbreakable armor did little to protect against the brutal, bludgeoning impacts. Soldiers began to fall back, scrambling through the fields of corpses, desperate to get out of the zone of destruction. A few fired upward, but the bolts burst harmlessly against the skyfortress' flux-stabilized armor.

"That's enough," Gyre told Kit. "Tell Ibb to go forward."

The command, relayed to Beq and then to the teams in *Pride*'s belly, brought the shower of stones to an abrupt end. Just as the battered Legionaries were raising their heads, a wild cheer went up from the second-tier trenches, and hundreds of whopping scavengers came down the hill preceded by a volley of alchemical grenades. Unmetal blades came out, and blaster pistols raised smoking explosions all along the Legionary line. The tunnelborn recruits might be reluctant to tangle with armored Legionaries, but it was old hat to the scavengers, who'd made their living flouting the laws of the Republic.

An intact line of Legionaries might have held, exploiting their opponents' indiscipline. But the remaining imperial troops were battered and confused and had lost all cohesion. In the face of this new threat, they broke, huge groups of them scrambling back over the breastworks and heading for the safety of the valley. Those officers still in effective command called for a retreat, firing as they went to cover their companions. Within a minute, the scavengers were in control of the devastated first trench, its floor littered with bodies and chunks of stone.

"Nicely done," Tanax murmured, his white-knuckled grip on his haken relaxing.

"We're not finished yet," Gyre said.

The cheers of the scavengers and tunnelborn were gradually dying away. Down in the valley, the mass of silver-armored Perfected lurched into motion. And, behind them, three bars of brilliant energy appeared—the blades of haken, visible even through the dust of the battle.

Chapter Twenty-Three

Maya

Gyre had described his fight with the Perfected in Khirkhaz, and Maya had thought she'd understood. She'd faced something like them on the Forsaken Coast, after all. Humanoid plaguespawn, faster and stronger than any ordinary soldier. Armored like Legionaries as they were, she'd expected them to be formidable.

The Perfected were more than that. The Eldest's creations paled in comparison to its master's. They *bounded* forward in long leaps, scrambling on all fours where the ground was cratered by stones or blaster fire. The obstacles at the base of the hill didn't even slow them. Spikes scraped off their armor, and where the way was blocked they shouldered aside wood and stacked corpses with brute strength.

At Gyre's urgent call, the skyfortress began dumping its load of stones again, rocks crashing down across the devastated zone at the bottom of the hill. A few crossbowmen sent quarrels arcing downward, joined by volleys of brilliant blaster bolts that burst in a furious crossfire. Scavengers added more alchemicals to the maelstrom, bursts of flame and splintering explosives ripping the air apart.

The Perfected kept coming. Stronger and tougher than the plaguespawn, with none of the Legionaries' human weakness, they barely seemed to notice the defenders' efforts. Silver-armored figures kept moving with huge smoking wounds in their chests, or impaled by unmetal spikes, or shredded by alchemicals and dripping black blood. They didn't stop to fire back or take cover. For every one that finally went down, a half dozen more bounded over the corpse, leaping the first breastwork in a storm of silver and black.

Once they were there, they went through the defenders like a reaper's scythe through hay, barely even slowing their advance. Their clawed gauntlets sent spatters of gore over the battered fortifications, not even seeming to notice the men and women they cut down. The first wave was past the trench in seconds, swarming up the rough ground toward the second tier without difficulty. They were met by massed blaster fire at point-blank range, blowing the leading Perfected apart; the next line leapt the smoldering wreckage and landed in the trench, and the slaughter began anew.

"Plaguing *fuck*," Maya heard herself say. The world seemed distant, unreal. "We have to help them."

To her surprise Gyre nodded. "If we can't stop them, that's the end. Kit, we could really use some assistance."

"Coming as fast as I can," Kit said.

"So are they," Gyre snarled. "Sorry. I know. Send everything you have in. I'm going in too."

Maya ignited her haken, the familiar *snap-hiss* bringing her a step closer to reality. There was a cheer from the closest soldiers when they saw the blade. *Tunnelborn cheering a centarch.* The world had turned in strange ways. Beside her, Tanax ignited his own blade, its twisted geometry flickering with uncanny light.

"I'll take the middle," she said. Without waiting for agreement, she charged.

There were narrow paths leading from tier to tier on the rocky hillside. Maya sprinted down the top tier, leapt to the breastwork, and took the next at a run, only barely avoiding a tumble into the ditch. On both sides of her, tunnelborn soldiers were firing, the *cracks* of their blaster rifles merged into a continuous thunder of bolts and explosions. The Perfected had overrun the second tier and were climbing toward the third, bolts smashing them to pieces or tossing them down the hill, more silver-armored monsters taking their place.

Another scramble brought Maya into the third trench, where most of the militia were already fleeing upward. *Can't blame them.* In fact it was helpful, because it gave her a clear field of fire. She hopped up onto the parapet to find two Perfected coming directly at her, shoulder to shoulder. Maya raised her free hand, fingers spread, and let loose a blast of concentrated *deiat* fire so hot that pools of blood bubbled in the trench beside her. White-hot plasma swept across both creatures, outlining them for a moment in glowing red as their armor softened and sagged. When she closed her hand, the superheated plates dropped to the ground with a *clunk*, filled with nothing but ashes. A scar ran straight as an arrow down the hill and out into the valley.

That may *have been overkill.* But it certainly got the attention of the armored monsters. Until now, they'd barely strayed from their path, as though eviscerating the defenders was an irritating chore. Now a whole swathe of them turned and came at her, scrambling through the trench, leaping into the air, sprinting up the hillside with claws spread wide.

Maya welcomed them with a ballet of flame. The power inside her was still unfolding, like a tree grown in a pot finally moved to an open field. The Thing in her chest, the good-luck charm that had been her unknowing prison, was dead and silent. Wild tornados of flame spiraled away from her outstretched hand, picking up the Perfected and hurling them skyward as they burned, corpses descending in chunks of blackened armor and gently drifting ashes. Those that rose before her she cut down, her haken's brilliant blue-white blade punching through unmetal armor and searing unnatural flesh. Her panoply sparked and popped, its energy keeping their claws from her skin.

Distantly, she could see other knots of monsters, hear the strange crackle of Tanax's twisted space and watch Gyre's blinding speed. Tunnelborn above her fired into the melee, explosions blooming like red-and-white blossoms. But in the middle of it all, Maya felt alone—not lonely, but *complete.* This was the life of a centarch she'd been promised, standing against the nightmare creatures of the world, shredding them with fire and sword.

Her only warning that a new player had joined the game was a crackle in the air and a warning shiver through *deiat.* She swept her hand upward, a dome of fire springing from the battered earth. Crystalline missiles swept down, detonating where they met her barrier in a great burst of mist and steam that momentarily obscured the battlefield. As the sudden fog shredded in the hot wind, Maya saw a lone figure carefully picking his way through the ruined trench and blasted corpses, a long staff in hand.

"Hello, Basel," Maya said. She stepped off the third-tier wall, descending toward him through the field of charred flesh and bone. "I had hoped you'd come to your senses."

"I have been hoping for something similar," the old centarch said. "I am glad to see you still alive, Maya. I hope you understand that."

"Nice of you to bring an army all this way to try and kill me, then."

"Killing you is the last thing the Emperor wants. You're valuable to him."

"Oh yes. His *sha'deia.*" Her lip curled into a snarl. "Such a successful experiment you helped him carry out. You *used* me."

"Was I so cruel to you? Was Jaedia?"

"Leave Jaedia out of this," Maya snapped. "*She* wouldn't have gone along, if she'd known. You had to send her into a trap for one of the Corruptor's black spiders to take her."

"When I implanted the regulator that saved your life, she was there. She approved."

"Because you *lied* to her. You weren't doing it out of the goodness of your heart. Your *Emperor* needed someone with my strength to activate the Purifier." She shook her head. "I wish I'd incinerated his plaguing *resonator* the first time I laid eyes on it."

"It wouldn't have made a difference," Basel said. "If it hadn't been you, it would have been another. He is nothing if not patient."

"All this"—Maya waved a hand at the battle—"seems pretty impatient to me."

"This barely qualifies as a sideshow," Basel said. "He wants to show you what it means to oppose him. You can't win, Maya, you must know that. Scour the valley clean, and the next army he sends will be ten times larger. Turn the skyfortress against him and he'll build his own. He is *Chosen*, with all of their power and knowledge. We humans cannot oppose him."

"Listen to yourself," Maya said. "You're volunteering to be enslaved by a monster."

"Better a monster than chaos," Basel said. "Better slavery than extinction."

"No. It's not worth the price."

"That is *not your decision to make*, you foolish child." Basel drew himself up straighter, leaning on his staff. "Have you even thought on the damage you've done? The lives you've wasted?"

"Of course I have." Maya fought down a wave of guilt. "But everyone here decided the fight was worth having."

Basel sighed. "I am only trying to help you."

"Then take your fucking monsters and go."

"Alas." He tapped his staff on the ground, three times, and with each blow glowing motes of blue-white energy sprang into being around him. "One day, you will thank me."

"I doubt that."

They both struck at once. Maya sent a beam of brilliant fire scything across the cratered hillside, aimed directly at Basel's chest. A disc of solid ice blocked it, sizzling and steaming. At the same time, the ghost-lights fell inward, whipping toward Maya in looping, curving paths, trailing clouds of freezing mist. Maya lashed out with her haken, intercepting the missiles and detonating them in clouds of boiling steam. Spikes of ice *crunched* up from the broken ground, and Maya shattered them and sent a wall of flame rolling down the hillside.

Basel's attacks were precise, with a lifetime of skill behind them. He was too old for swordplay, but it hardly mattered—if she tried to close with him, her concentration would falter. *But I have the edge in power.* Maya gripped her haken tighter. *It has to be a contest of strength.*

She concentrated her energy, readying a monstrous beam of killing fire. *Let's see him block* this. Before she could unleash it, though, there was a sudden movement in the roiling fog on her right, and Maya barely brought her haken around in time to meet the new attacker. Her flaming blade hissed and spat against a line of humming white energy.

"Stonecutter," Maya said.

"Burningblade." Evinda inclined her head, her purple hair tucked away under an unmetal helmet. "I am seizing you in the name of the Twilight Order for the crime of high treason."

"Treason against a monster," Maya spat.

She shoved Evinda away and jumped backward, scrambling for footing on the broken ground. The other centarch advanced calmly, her blade licking out in lightning-fast strikes that darted around Maya's suddenly clumsy haken. Hits on her panoply sent waves of chill through Maya once, twice, three times, draining her reserves. With a shout, Maya threw up a wall of flames, pushing Evinda back.

"The Kyriliarch Council has decided to support the Emperor," the centarch said. "You are subject to the Council's orders."

"There's more to being a centarch than following the Council," Maya said. "The Order has to *stand* for something. If it doesn't, what's the point of any of it?"

She gave ground again, conjuring bolts of flame all around her. But Basel chose that moment to resume his attack, and Maya desperately threw her power into a defense. Evinda charged through the clouds of freezing mist, slashing and thrusting.

I can't fight them both. Her power outstripped that of either centarch, but Evinda's swordplay was on another level. *Plaguefire*—

"What the Order stands for is for the Council to decide," Evinda said, not even short of breath. "All a centarch needs to do is *obey*."

"I used to think that was enough." Space shimmered and bent around Evinda, her panoply flaring as it was suddenly attacked from all sides. She spun away, haken raised, as Tanax's weird, twisted blade emerged from the fog. "Maya taught me otherwise."

"Brokenedge," Evinda said. "You can consider yourself under arrest as well."

Tanax sprang forward, haken spinning, space itself folding around him. Evinda stood her ground, and lines of humming white energy came up to meet him. Maya tore her gaze away and concentrated on Basel. *Just buy me a minute*—

She let her pent-up power explode outward, a blast of flame so hot it punched a hole in the swirling vapor, drawing a sudden clear corridor between herself and her mentor. He raised his staff, barriers of ice springing up in front of him, but as fast as they arose they were shattered and shoved aside. There was no subtlety here, no finesse. *Jaedia would* not *approve. But sometimes, if all you've got is a sledgehammer…*

In desperation, Basel interposed his staff, ice thickening around it into a shield. His long beard streamed in the wind as he braced his feet, pitting his strength against his erstwhile protégée's. His mouth opened in a scream.

"Mayaaaaaaaa—"

The shield shattered. His panoply flared a brilliant blue as the blast of flame knocked him sprawling down the hillside, rolling over and over until he fetched up against a boulder in a heap. The flicker of blue around him spat fitfully, then vanished.

Maya let her energy fade, breathing hard, but there was no time for rest. *Tanax.* Somewhere nearby, *deiat* hissed and popped, and she headed for the sound through the swirling mists and weird ripples in the air. She arrived just in time—Tanax had his back to the broken trench wall, fighting a desperate defense against Evinda's hammering blows. The relief in his face alerted his opponent, who spun to parry Maya's downward strike. For a moment they stood pressed close, blades locked.

"Sorry I'm late," Maya gasped out.

Tanax pushed himself back to his feet. "I had it under control."

Evinda's calm demeanor cracked, very slightly. "How can you stand against Baselanthus? After everything he's done for you, in spite of all the rules of the Order—"

"Because he's wrong," Maya said, pulling away and bringing her blade back to a guard. "In spite of everything, in spite of the rules of the Order. What he's doing is wrong."

"That is not your decision to make."

"It is," Tanax said from behind her. "It always is. That's the point."

Evinda snarled and threw herself forward, hammering at Maya's parries. When Tanax approached, she spun away, but not before he slashed a line of blue from her panoply. The two of them went at her together, forcing her to back away or be surrounded, keeping her on the defensive. Maya closed her off hand, and a wall of boiling flames sprung up behind Evinda, boxing her in.

"You will destroy us," Evinda said. "Destroy the Order. And you offer nothing in return but chaos."

"Sometimes," Maya said, "chaos is better than the alternative."

Together, they closed in.

Gyre

One Perfected had been bad enough. Its speed and strength had nearly gotten the better of him, augmentations or not. Now there were hundreds, and Gyre had no illusions about being able to take them head-on. Fortunately, he wasn't alone.

"Ready?" Kit said.

"Ready!"

Every body she had on the battlefield was gathered at the top of the hill. A phalanx of the largest, each the size of a pony, formed the center, with the medium-sized bodies on the flanks and the smallest behind. Gyre rode atop the frontmost construct, his ghoul sword drawn. He slashed it downward.

"Go!"

They started to move, slowly at first but gathering speed like a tumbling boulder. The constructs leapt from stone to log to muddy ground, clearing the trenches in a single bound. Tunnelborn soldiers threw themselves flat to get out of the way and raised a sudden cheer in the wake of their passage. On the second tier, the Perfected were emerging from the slaughter they'd wreaked in the trench, and they sprinted forward to meet the descending swarm.

"Don't stop!" Gyre shouted.

The two lines of constructs met. Kit's bodies were not truly designed for war, not armored in unmetal, and didn't have the Perfected's claws or absurd speed. But they *did* have momentum, like a squadron of charging warbirds, and their impact was terrific.

Gyre's augmentations came on with a *click*, and time slowed. The Perfected were still fast, but even they couldn't do much in midair, bowled over by the weight and power of the Leviathan's horde. He slashed and cut as they went, targets floating lazily by in his altered perception, giving him plenty of time to find the gaps in their armor. Claws scraped and tore at Kit's constructs, leaving deep gashes and severing limbs, but they barreled on regardless, impervious to pain and fear. Behind the first wave, the smaller bodies pounced on the damaged Perfected, working in teams to tear them literally limb from limb.

Off to his right, light flashed and glared. *Maya.* The line of Perfected wavered, shifting in her direction. *I hope she knows what she's doing—*

His construct mount jerked, then abruptly collapsed, throwing Gyre free. He hit the ground feetfirst, skidding to a halt in the blood-soaked earth.

"Fuck!" Kit said from his shoulder. The body he'd been riding had been chopped neatly in half. "Should I—"

"Keep the Perfected off me," Gyre said. "I'll handle him."

Va'aht Thousandcuts wore his white unmetal armor, but he hadn't bothered with a helmet, and his purple-black hair looked ragged. He held his haken in front of him, its blade a brilliant blue-white. His thin lips were curled back in a savage smile.

"We meet again, Silvereye," he said.

"Can't say I've been looking forward to it," Gyre said.

"*I* have," Va'aht said. "Very much."

"I would've thought you'd get tired of losing," Gyre said. "Did the Corruptor punish you after you let me get away last time?"

"On the contrary," Va'aht said. "He has given me the opportunity to serve him more…directly."

Something shifted, an insectoid limb curling down to Va'aht's shoulder. A black spider—bloated and tiny-legged, more like a tick—clung to the centarch's neck.

"I see." Gyre cocked his head. "Then I'm not talking to Va'aht at all, am I?"

"Fool. I am myself, only *greater*."

He raised his haken, still alight with deiat, and reached out his other hand toward the nearest Legionary corpse. White armor writhed in a hideous parody of life, flesh squeezing out through every chink and crevice, flowing like liquid through the air to wrap the centarch's free hand in ribbons of muscle. A second blade formed there, its edge gleaming white bone.

"I am remade in his image," Va'aht said. "Like him, *all* powers are mine to command."

"That's nice," Gyre said. "Did he give you enough brains not to fall for the same trick twice?"

Gyre reached into his satchel of alchemicals. Va'aht flinched, just for an instant, then roared and charged. This time, however, Gyre was fully stocked, and he hurled a stunner in the centarch's face. It burst with a colossal *bang* and a brilliant flash, leaving Gyre's ears ringing but his silver eye none the worse for wear. Va'aht staggered, swiping wildly, and Gyre popped up beside him with an upward slash that took the centarch's arm off below the shoulder. His haken sputtered out as it bounced free of nerveless fingers.

With a scream, Va'aht fell back, landing in the trench. Blood spurted from the wound in great gouts, spraying across soiled white armor and slack faces. Gyre stalked after him, whipping his blade clean.

"Your problem," he said, "is that you don't learn."

Va'aht's shrieks trailed off. He panted for breath as Gyre approached. Then, all at once, his smile returned.

"And *yours*," he said hoarsely, "is that you take me too lightly."

The floor of the trench heaved. It was thick with bodies, Legionaries from the first assault and tunnelborn shredded by the charge of the Perfected. Flesh and bone, muscle and blood, now shifting together in the grip of Va'aht's borrowed *dhaka*. His own body unwrapped itself around his mangled shoulder, then rewove a new form from long strings of meat that moved like snakes. Three arms grew in place of one, each ending in an overlarge clawed hand. Other limbs stretched up from the ground, grabbing the centarch and setting him on his feet like a puppet before falling away into deliquescing goo.

"The trouble with, you Gyre Lackeye, is that you don't know your place. You never have."

He lashed out with his new arms, bones unfolding horribly as they telescoped to twice their former length. Gyre ducked, slashing, and part of a hand fell to the ground, but it re-formed itself before he'd finished rolling away. Va'aht's sword arm lengthened and softened, tightening into something like a whip.

"You've been like this from the very beginning," the centarch went on. His body drifted behind his *dhaka*-powered limbs, as though being dragged unwillingly along. "A bad seed from the start. If only you'd been able to leave well enough alone, none of this would have happened."

"You came to take my sister."

"We had a *right* to her," Va'aht snarled. Whip and claws slashed, and Gyre parried desperately. "The Order is the heir of the Chosen. It is our right to rule humanity, for its own protection. Your sister was destined to be part of that. You had no choice in the matter."

Another tentacle rose from the writhing mat of flesh, bringing Va'aht's lost haken. The centarch concentrated, and his whip-arm split down the middle, trailing stringy gobbets of flesh. One of the new limbs coiled around the weapon, which blazed to life. Thus armed, he began a furious assault, the shadows of his attacks filling Gyre's vision. He'd lost the precision he'd shown the last time they'd fought, but even so it was all Gyre could do to defend himself.

"And what did you accomplish, in the end?" Va'aht said. "You hurt yourself. Little Maya came with me all the same. Into Basel's care, just as the Emperor intended." He leaned forward, impassive as his arms struck and spun. "Have you really accomplished anything? Or would everyone have been better off if you'd just accepted the inevitable?"

Once, those words would have driven Gyre into a killing frenzy. Va'aht had destroyed his family at a stroke, taken not just his eye but his home. All that came after—his life on the road, his parents' death, Deepfire and Yora and the Tomb—they all came back to that day. It had built a fire in him, an anger that couldn't be quenched.

But it had been tempered, somehow, bit by bit. By what he'd found in Leviathan's Womb. By everything that had happened on the way to Khirkhaz, by Apphia and Nina and the fractious Communards. And, most of all, by Maya.

Once he'd been ready to burn the world. Now he was ready to build a new one, and he knew nothing could be built from ashes.

And yet...

Underneath everything, the anger still burned, in a place beyond politics or grand ideals. The anger of an eight-year-old boy at the man who'd torn his family apart and brought him more pain than he'd ever known existed. Gyre reached down for it, let it fill him.

I don't have to burn it all. Va'aht's haken slashed and Gyre parried, blades grinding against one another. *But I can burn* you.

He reached out, snake-fast, and grabbed the tendril just behind the head. It squirmed in his grip, slippery and strong, but he held it fast long enough to swing around and chop the haken free. As the tendril recoiled, Gyre yanked three burners from his pouch and hurled one at the fallen weapon, wreathing it in sticky flames.

"Insolent *boy.*" Va'aht's limbs unfolded like the bars of a cage, reaching out to close all around Gyre. But Gyre had abandoned the defensive. He pressed forward, dodging the shadow-images of the centarch's strikes. He hurled one burner, then the other, two sprays of flame spreading around Va'aht's feet. Flesh rose from nearby bodies, still ablaze, blackening before it could be shaped to strike.

"Why?!" Va'aht's voice rose in frustration, blades and claws stabbing inward. Gyre parried and struck, carving flesh away faster than it could regrow, surrounded by a lake of flames. "Why won't you just *die*? I have the *right*—the blood of the Chosen—"

A whole limb spun away, then another. Va'aht tripped, falling backward, flames licking at him. Gyre put one foot on his chest, carving another arm off. His face was as rigid a mask as the silver one had ever been.

"You ruined my life, you fucking plaguepit," he said.

"And I'd do it again." Va'aht, suddenly calm, gave him a beatific smile. "Just to spite you."

Gyre thrust. The blade passed through the centarch's neck and into the black spider behind it, pinning both to the ground.

"Some people," Gyre said quietly, "*deserve* to burn."

"Kit, you still there?"

He felt pinpricks on his arm, then his shoulder. Her tiny spider appeared, limbs waving triumphantly. "Had to jump clear for a minute, but I'm back! What'd I miss?"

"Revenge," he said.

"Aw. I *love* revenge."

The Perfected were retreating, loping back over the ground they'd soaked in blood, chased by desultory blaster fire from high on the hill. Gyre looked around until he spotted Maya, standing with Tanax in the second trench over the fallen body of another centarch. He jogged over. Maya looked past him at first, then her eyes snapped back to him, alarmed.

"Gyre!" she said. "Are you all right? You're—"

"Covered in gore?" Kit suggested.

"I'm fine," Gyre said. "There was a black spider, but I've dealt with it."

She raised her eyebrows. "Tanax and I handled the other two centarchs."

"I see that. Will she live?"

Maya nodded. "Panoply shock. She'll be out for a while."

"That's good, because we're not finished."

Gyre's silver eye cut through the smoke, looking down the valley. The imperial forces were still there, reduced in numbers but re-forming their ranks. Legionaries reassembled into disciplined lines. The bestial plaguespawn gathered in a single horde. And the Perfected, still numbering in the hundreds, made a tight wedge of silver.

"Are you sure we're not finished?" Tanax said dully.

Maya looked up the slope. Only the top two trenches were still inhabited by defenders, and fewer of those than before.

"They won't stand another charge, Gyre," she said. "They just won't. They've already been braver than we could have possibly hoped for. And *I* don't have much left."

"We have to retreat," Tanax said. "Or we'll all die here."

"We can't," Gyre said. "You know as well as I do that there's nowhere else to make a stand before the city walls. And if they get that far—"

They'll overrun everything, we'll lose the chance to threaten the Corruptor's lab, and all of this will be for nothing. He fought the urge to wipe his eyes with his filthy hands. *There has to be something—*

"We don't have to retreat," Kit said.

"Why?" Gyre said. "Are your extra bodies finally here? How many are there? It might not be enough, but we can slow them down—"

"You guys held them up and got rid of the centarchs," Kit said. "I can handle the rest. Don't worry about it."

"Kit," Maya said hesitantly, "I'm not sure—"

Gyre waved her off. "This isn't the time for games, Kit. People are going to die. If you can help, tell us how."

"I *said* I could handle the rest."

"*Where are you?*"

"Down in the valley," Kit said sulkily. "On the north side, about halfway along. See the little canyon?"

Gyre found the spot and magnified it in his silver eye. A wide, deep ravine ran into the valley, off on the imperials' right flank. Nothing seemed to move.

"You're not close enough," Tanax said urgently. "They'll just wheel and surround you once you come out in the open. If you wait until they engage us to their front, then you might—"

"Chosen defend, none of you trust me, do you?" Kit said. Her little spider hopped up and down on Gyre's shoulder. "Just *watch*, all right?"

Something moved in Gyre's magnified vision. Rocks, tumbling from the ravine walls. Tiny landslides were suddenly everywhere, as though the earth itself were shaking.

"Kit," Gyre said quietly. "How *many* bodies did you bring?"

"All of 'em!" Kit said.

Something swung into view, enormous and dark. A leg the size of a building, plated in black metal armor.

Gyre swallowed. "I thought...the bomb..."

"Elariel helped me fix it," Kit said. "The constructs have a lot of built-in repair capacity. That's part of their primary function, you know."

Another leg swung past, then another, the ground shaking with every footfall. Then the head, the pillared space where Gyre had fought Naumoriel, and the impossibly broad expanse of the first set of shoulders.

Step by unhurried step, the Leviathan entered the valley.

From this distance, it resembled nothing so much as a beetle, with a fat oval body supported on six thick legs. Its head, lined with two rows of pillars like bristling antennae, had two additional limbs tucked underneath. Its surface was armored all over, with interlocking scales across the joints.

Its size was hard to comprehend. It was only barely shorter than the walls of the valley it had emerged from, moving with a feeling of vast weight, a sense of massive energies barely contained. While the sky-fortress floated overhead so effortlessly it hardly seemed real, Gyre *felt* every thunderous *thump* of the Leviathan's feet, the colossal structure of its legs supporting countless tons of flesh and steel.

There were screams from the trenches. Some soldiers started to flee. Others hunkered down, their depleted blasters ready, expecting the worst. Gyre didn't bother to shout reassurance; no one was listening. *And it doesn't matter. Kit's right. She can handle it.*

The imperials were turning toward this new threat. Gyre had no idea if anyone was still in command down there, or if all three parts of the enemy army were acting on instinct. The bestial plaguespawn and their Perfected brethren turned toward the monstrous construct, while the Legionaries spread out, blaster bolts exploding in volleys against the Leviathan's armor.

"Ooh," Kit said. "That tickles."

The limbs under the construct's head unfolded, long and dexterous. They divided at each joint, two arms becoming four, eight, sixteen, ending in fine manipulators. These sublimbs could move quickly, and they reached out for the plaguespawn as they began to arrive, scooping them off the ground and ignoring their frenzied thrashing. Some of them Kit simply crushed to paste, while others she turned into impromptu missiles, hurling them hundreds of meters toward the line of firing Legionaries.

The Perfected, however, were harder to catch. Gyre started to worry as they reached the great construct's feet and started swarming upward, claws digging in to the metal exoskeleton.

"Look at them climbing all over me," Kit said. "Rude, that's what I call it."

Hatches slammed open along the Leviathan's flank. Constructs poured out, like Kit's ordinary bodies but adapted for war, spiders bearing vicious claws, blades, and spears. The Perfected were stronger and faster, but the Leviathan's swarm outnumbered them dozens to one, large bodies grabbing them and holding them fast while smaller ones darted in to perform gruesome dissection.

"They're running," Maya said, almost disbelieving. "The Legionaries."

It was true. The line of white was dissolving in panic. Even the elite soldiers of the new Empire, it seemed, had limits to their courage. The Perfected, of course, had none, but they were rapidly disappearing under a sea of constructs, clinging to the sides and limbs of their mother while they cleansed her of invaders.

"You don't think," Gyre said after a while, "that you could have told us about this *earlier*?"

"I didn't want to distract you," Kit said. "I wasn't sure if I would get here in time."

Gyre gave her an unconvinced stare. "*And?*"

"*And* I wanted to see the look on your face," Kit admitted. Gyre could imagine her beaming smile. "It was everything I hoped for."

Chapter Twenty-Four

They rode back to Deepfire as fast as swiftbirds would carry them.
In a sane world, Maya felt, they'd have a little more time to
rejoice in their victory. Not to mention rest—her mind was dull with
adrenaline backwash, her limbs ached, and her connection to *deiat*
shivered and jumped with the strain she'd put on it. Gyre looked like
he was in much the same shape, even after he'd sacrificed a clean cloth
to wipe off the worst of the gore. He rode hunched over his saddle, as
though trying hard not to fall.

But there was no time, and there was no one else. They had no
idea how long it would take the Corruptor to hear of the defeat, but it
couldn't be long. *He'll have resonators with the army. We have to get to
the lab before he does.*

They'd stayed only long enough to check in on Varo and Apphia—
both were alive, though Varo had had to cram in under a boulder with
a few other men to hide from the Perfected when they went through.
Rikard and Enta were rallying the tunnelborn to return to the field
and collect the wounded, aided by Lynnia and her fellow alchemists.

Even so, there were a great many who were beyond help. For some there wasn't even anything left to bury.

It felt like a betrayal to leave so quickly, but Tanax and Apphia had been adamant they had things under control. Once they descended from the ridge, it was a flat, easy road, and the swiftbirds lived up to their name as they paced down it with long, loping strides. They didn't stop at the gatehouse—the news had beaten them home, thanks to one of Kit's bodies left in the city, and the few guards had the doors open and the road cleared. The streets were still empty, word of the victory not having spread to the populace, and they clattered through empty markets and squares to the looming bulk of the Spike.

Beq was waiting for them, wrapping Maya in a hug as soon as she swung wearily off her bird. Maya squeezed her fiercely, delighting in the warm physicality of her, the fast, strong beat of her heart.

"I got in the flitter as soon as I saw the Leviathan," Beq said. "Everything's ready for you. Do you think it'll work?"

"No time to worry," Maya said. "If we're going, it has to be now."

Beq gave a tight nod and pulled away, leading them into the palace. The handful of remaining guards stood hastily aside, offering inexpert salutes. Maya could only wave as she went by. Reaching the private staircase, they began to descend, down and down, to the underground chamber where the Gate waited.

Xalen was waiting as well, sitting against the wall and scribbling in a notebook. She jumped to her feet as they came in.

"I take it we won," she said, calm as ever.

"We did," Maya said.

"Kit," Gyre said dourly, "had a few extra cards in the hole."

"Oh sure, blame the hero of the day for having a little fun, grouchy," Kit said.

"We need to move," Maya said. "If he beats us there, it's all for nothing."

"Right." Xalen snapped her notebook closed. "You remember the procedure?"

Maya nodded.

"And you remember the code?" Beq said anxiously. "We set the trap last night. I double-checked, it's in just the right spot."

"I remember," Maya said. She looked to Gyre. "Are you ready?"

"Not really." He was affixing a fresh energy bottle to his hip, tossing the old one aside. "But I'm not likely to get time for a bath and a nap, now, am I?"

"Afterward," Maya said.

"Afterward," he agreed, and let out a long breath. "Let's do it."

"I'm ready too," Kit said. "Not that anyone asked."

"We trust you," Gyre said.

She brightened. "Really?"

Maya turned to the Gate. It was still filled with a black curtain, locking out incoming connections. She cleared it with a mental command, then sent it a thread of *deiat* and a set of coordinates they'd carefully reverse engineered. The delicate archway filled with mist, connecting to its twin several thousand meters down.

Four of Kit's cat-sized spiders, all that was left of the bodies she'd had in Deepfire, waited in the shadows around the Gate. They skittered forward, zipping through the fog one by one. For a tense moment, Maya waited.

"Looks clear," Kit said. "If the Corruptor's here, he's hiding."

The knot around Maya's stomach loosened, just a little. *We're still in time. Assuming he's coming at all. Assuming a lot of things.*

"We're heading through," Gyre said.

Maya grabbed Beq's hand and squeezed it tight.

The lab was as they'd left it, dark and silent, the shadows obscuring the damage their fight against the First had caused. Maya looked around the control room, with its console ring and central image projector, then glanced upward. All she could see was the dusty ceiling, but...

"Yeah," Gyre said. He shook his head and dug into his pouch. "Help me with these."

Maya took a handful of alchemicals and followed Gyre's lead, laying them in an arc around the front of the Gate. Gyre went back over the explosives with a roll of fine wire. Once the trap was set, he looked between the doorways leading off the central chamber, frowning.

"Where's the best place to hide?" he said.

"There." Maya pointed to the corridor where they'd found the Corruptor's gruesome experiments. "If he's worried about damaging his research, maybe he'll hold back."

Gyre nodded and moved slowly in that direction, winding out more wire behind him. He settled in around the edge of the doorway, out of sight of the Gate. Maya sat down beside him.

"Kit?" Gyre said.

"Watching the Gate," her tiny spider said. "The rest of my bodies are in the other halls."

"Thanks." Gyre picked up the small construct with two fingers and transferred it to Maya's shoulder. "You'd better ride here, in case Maya needs to talk to Beq."

Kit snuggled in beside Maya's collar, her tiny claws pricking slightly. Maya closed her eyes and leaned back against the wall. She felt exhaustion dragging at her. *Waiting to ambush the most powerful being in the world, and it's all I can do not to fall asleep.*

For a while, there was only silence.

Gyre coughed. "It would be a lot simpler if we just destroyed the Gate after he came through."

"We'd die," Maya pointed out.

"We'll probably die anyway."

"True." Beq's face, trying so hard to look brave, flashed in Maya's memory. Her heart twisted. "But it wouldn't work. He already survived the detonation of a Gate back at the Purifier. We need something bigger."

"Even if it didn't kill him, he'd be stuck here."

"We came down. He could get up."

Gyre grunted agreement and lapsed into silence again. Time passed, excruciatingly slowly.

"You really think we'll probably die?" Maya said.

"I think you and Beq came up with a good plan," Gyre said. "But..."

"Yeah." Maya shivered.

"I'd do it without you if I could."

"Likewise." Maya swallowed. "There's...something I should tell you. I'm not sure I ever said it out loud."

Gyre frowned at her. "What?"

"It's not *important*. I mean, it *is*, but it's not *new*. I just..." Maya's cheeks were warming, and she hurried through the rest. "I just wanted to say I was sorry. About your eye. And...and everything else. You got hurt trying to help me."

"You're..." Gyre stared at her. "Is this *really* the time?"

"With what you were saying, I might not get another chance."

"You can be very strange, you know that?"

"Fine!" Maya blew out a breath. "I just wanted you to know."

Another silence, broken only by Gyre's faint chuckle.

"Thank you," he said. "And...I'm sorry too."

"For what?"

Gyre sighed. "Quite a lot of things, actually."

"I'm not sorry for anything," Kit said. When they both turned to stare at her, the little spider shifted uneasily. "What? I don't like being left out."

"You said you were sorry for stabbing me," Maya said.

"Okay, maybe for *that*, but those were special circumstances—"

"Or leaving me to die?" Gyre said.

"*Also* special circ— *Oh hey*, the Gate is activating!"

Maya clamped her lips closed, swallowing her laughter. Gyre leaned back against the wall, eyes closed, listening.

There was a heavy footfall, then another, then several at once. Maya thought of the Corruptor's multilimbed, misshapen lower body, and her throat tightened.

"Tell me when he's through," Gyre whispered.

"Almost," Kit said. "Almost... *now*."

Gyre flicked his alchemical firestarter. The wire caught instantly, flame racing along it like a small animal scurrying to its burrow. He put his hands over his ears, and Maya followed suit. The detonation of the alchemicals came as a series of dull thuds. Light painted the shadow of the doorway on the opposite wall, and a wave of heat and noxious gas rushed past them. Maya's ears popped.

Gyre sprang to his feet as soon as the blast wave passed, sword in one hand and another alchemical in the other. Maya followed him, running hunched over, trying to keep the control console between her and the Corruptor.

The bombs had made a mess of the control room. The walls and floors were unmetal, impervious, but the consoles themselves had shattered crystals and torn wire across their faces. The Gate was blackened, though undamaged, and its arch was empty. In front of it stood the Corruptor, Nial-Est-Ashok, returning to his prison of four centuries.

In the projections, and in Zephkiel's memories, Ashok looked like a man in his thirties, devastatingly handsome like all Chosen, his hair gleaming with the luster of true gold. The real Ashok looked the same, from the waist up. Below that, his brown skin ended in a tattered fringe, like a skirt trailing over a trunk of striated black muscle and thick, pulsing tubes. His lower body was as big as a pony, with a dozen mismatched legs, flesh stretched tight over black iron bones. Fluids gurgled and gushed in translucent sacs, and tentacular limbs coiled and stretched. More tubes ran from the guts of the thing up behind his human form, plugging in at intervals along his spine.

Gyre's bombs had wreaked havoc, shredding handsome golden flesh and horrific monstrosity alike, leaving crunchy sections of burned meat and huge rents spurting vile ichor. Yet even as Maya watched, the Corruptor's body rebuilt itself, his wounds knitting closed with horrifying speed. Burned flesh simply sloughed away, falling off in blackened, mucus-flecked chunks, new skin growing outward to replace it. His face, as it rebuilt itself, wore an irritated expression.

"That must be Silvereye," he said. "Charming."

Another alchemical sailed from a doorway, bursting against the Corruptor's chest. Ribs and lungs were visible for a moment before a wave of regenerating flesh closed over them.

"You know it doesn't work," Ashok said. "So what, exactly, are you trying to accomplish?"

"Just getting your attention." Gyre stepped into the doorway, another bomb in hand. "I want to offer you a deal."

Maya stole forward, circling around the consoles until she was close to the Gate. She touched her haken and sent it a thread of power, locking it as she had the one in the palace. She left the thread in place—as long as she was alive and conscious, the lock couldn't be lifted.

"A deal?" the Corruptor said. "Why would I *possibly* make a deal with you?"

"Because there's a hundred bombs just like that one spread through the rooms behind me," Gyre said. "The ones full of all your research. Your notes. Your specimens. Everything."

Maya closed her eyes and focused her power, reaching outward. She felt Beq's device, cobbled together from ancient parts, and sent it a *deiat* ping with a carefully memorized code. It clicked on, drawing power from her, enough to leave her chilled and breathless. Somewhere, a timer was counting down.

"Five minutes," she whispered to Kit. That was how long she thought it would take. How long, at minimum, she had to stay alive. Maya felt the device finish charging and pulled her thread of *deiat* free. "Set."

"I'm counting," Kit said. Maya kept crawling around the console, slipping past the Gate and working her way closer to Ashok.

"Interesting," the Corruptor drawled, his attention still on Gyre. "And your offer is?"

"Just this," Gyre said. "Leave us in peace."

"The coward's way out, in other words," Ashok said. "Saving yourselves at the expense of everyone else you've convinced to follow you." He snorted. "I think not. You're stalling."

"You think it's a bluff?" Gyre raised the alchemical.

Ashok shrugged. "You might have the bombs. But the deal makes no sense. Once you leave here, I'd have no reason to keep my word, and you certainly have no reason to trust me. Besides, Maya would never agree. No, I strongly suspect that your goal here is to capture my attention—"

He spun, impossibly fast for such a large creature, and was abruptly almost face-to-face with Maya. His smile widened.

"—while someone sneaks up on me from behind." Ashok licked his perfect lips, tentacles unfolding. "Hello, *sha'deia*."

Maya's haken ignited with a *snap-hiss*, and she swung the blade in an upward arc intended to slice that smile in two. But Ashok's hands were instantly sheathed in their own swordlike auras of hard white light, crossed in front of him to parry. For a moment they stood straining, *deiat* flaring against *deiat*, and then Ashok shoved hard enough to send Maya skidding away.

"Was that the plan?" he said. "Stab me in the back? Did you really think that would work?"

"I thought I'd give it a shot," Maya said. She held out her free hand, gathering energy. Flames grew around her, and her hair whipped madly in the updraft. "But we can do this the hard way if we have to."

"Really, don't you think you're getting a bit big for your boots, *sha'deia*?" Ashok extended one hand, palm out. "You are, after all, only human. I am *Chosen*."

White light speared out, a concentrated beam of solid fire. Maya brought her haken around to intercept, and the power struck her like a physical blow, her boots scraping backward across the unmetal floor. The pressure was immense, her muscles screaming. She threw all her power into defense, but it wasn't nearly enough. The white beam fractured against her blade, spraying fragments of gleaming light all around her, burning streaks into the walls and tearing chunks out of the control console.

In that moment, exerting every fiber to ward off obliteration, she felt like she finally understood her brother. What it was to be an ordinary person in the presence of a centarch, someone who's merest whim could annihilate you and your village in an instant. Ashok spent his power casually, wastefully, with none of Basel's skill or Jaedia's artistry. And yet, even so, he was farther above her than she'd dared dream.

An alchemical exploded against the Chosen, wrapping him in clinging fire. Ashok closed his hand, cutting off the beam, and Maya fell gasping to the floor. The monster turned in place, legs moving precisely even as his skin blackened and charred. Tentacles whipped around, grabbing for Gyre as he leapt forward, ghoul blade raised. Gyre, as usual, was faster than he had any right to be, dancing around the squirming limbs with preternatural grace. He sank his sword deep, right where the human body met the twisted plaguespawn.

"Ow," Ashok said. His face was a blackened ruin, the eyes empty sockets, fire still alight in his hair. When he spoke, flesh cracked and fell away. "All right, well done, one point to you."

One of his larger tentacles swept around. Gyre tried to yank his sword free and jump away, but the rent flesh of Ashok's midsection reshaped itself, tightening around the blade and holding it long enough for the tendril to connect with a *thump*. The impact tore Gyre's grip from the sword and sent him flying across the room, slamming hard into the unmetal wall and sliding down a half meter to the floor.

"And if Maya is too full of herself, I don't even know what to say about *you*." More carbonized flesh flaked away from Ashok's face, revealing grimy but perfect skin underneath. A tentacle pulled the ghoul blade free and tossed it aside with a clatter. The rent it left behind sealed over immediately. "You just won't recognize when you're outclassed. It's like watching an ant planning to take on a loadbird."

"Kit," Maya gasped out. "Help him."

The Corruptor stalked toward Gyre, but a small shape, moving so fast its legs were a blur, darted from one of the doorways and leapt into his underbelly. Another alchemical went off, shredding the Corruptor's guts. Long tubes uncoiled and flopped to the floor, leaking fluids in a range of hideous colors.

Another small construct ran at the monster, but this time Ashok saw it coming. His tentacles snapped out, grabbing Kit's little body and lifting it into the air. The Corruptor turned Kit over and over, like a boy contemplating an insect he was about to dismember.

"*You* merit study," he said.

"I'm honored," Kit shot back.

"When we're done here, I'm going to find your brain and take it apart," Ashok said. "It should be an interesting project. For the moment, though—" He whipped the construct against the wall. The alchemical Kit had been carrying broke with a *whoosh*, covering the unmetal in fire. "Now, where was I?"

He turned back toward Gyre, only to find him several meters across the floor, crawling doggedly toward his dropped sword. Ashok's tentacles reached down and scooped him up, holding him aloft by the wrists. Beneath the Corruptor's body, his innards were reassembling themselves, tubes reeled back in and knit together.

"I'm not one to bear grudges," Ashok said. "But I'm afraid that tearing you limb from limb will make *just* the right impression on your sister. The good news is that I can make sure you don't lose consciousness until the very end!" He cocked his head and barked an ugly laugh. "Maybe that's not good news, from your point of view."

"You..." Maya tried to shout but managed only a hacking cough. She fought to steady her voice, but the air was full of clinging smoke and the stench of burned flesh. *Gyre—you can't—*

And then, in a sudden rush, she threw her mind into the connection she'd thus far felt only in dreams, the *thrum* of shared blood that connected her to the twisted creature Ashok had become.

Zephkiel was right. His head snapped around as the words rang in his mind. Maya slowly struggled to her feet. *You* are *a monster.*

How do you know her name? Ashok tossed Gyre aside and turned back toward Maya, gliding forward on his multiple legs. *Have you been keeping secrets from me,* sha'deia?

She hated you, Maya sent back. *At the end. She hated you so much that she burrowed into your mind, pushed her memories inside you, in the hope that someday she would be able to bring you down.*

Did she? Ashok stopped across from Maya, who defiantly raised her haken. *Well, now. Well, well, well. That poor, stupid, brilliant girl. I loved her, you know.*

She didn't love you, Maya said. *Not really. And after what you did—*

Bombs and deiat *have failed you, so now you're going to try and hurt my feelings, is that it?* Ashok snorted in disgust. *I've had a long time to come to terms with what happened to Zeph. I did what I had to do to protect myself and my work. I wish she'd shared my vision.*

You could have listened to her, Maya said. *It didn't have to be like this.*

I once thought you really might understand. Ashok raised his hands, white light crackling around them. *Pity.*

Maya took a deep breath, spun, and ran for it.

It wasn't a *great* plan, she'd be the first to admit, but it was all she could think of.

I have to keep the Corruptor away from Gyre. Which meant taunting him. *I have to keep him from escaping.* Which meant staying alive herself. *Not that he seems much interested in escape.* But power was building, up above them, and sooner or later he'd sense it. *Which means I just need to stay out of his grip.*

Easier said than done. She ducked through a doorway into one of the corridors, then abruptly threw herself flat at a surge in *deiat* from behind her. A lance of white light slashed sideways, cutting through unmetal walls, doors, equipment, and everything else in its path, stopping only when it splashed against the flux-stabilized armor of the outer shell. When the beam snapped off with a thunderclap of superheated air, debris clattered down, machines falling to pieces, jars exploding against the floor.

In hindsight, the Corruptor said, as he stalked toward the ruined corridor, *I should have expected your failure, as I should have expected Zephkiel's. I have come to know, over the years, that my understanding of the universe is a singular one. I am always hoping for more from lesser minds, and I am always disappointed.*

Maya rolled onto her stomach, gripping her haken, and spread her fingers. Streaks of flame raced across the floor, snaking toward the Corruptor and then detonating into spumes of volcanic fire. At the same moment, she surged to her feet, running down the corridor and choosing a doorway at random. It was a dusty room that had once held tables and jars, now spread on the floor in a mass of cauterized debris. She threw herself into the corner and waited.

Another beam stabbed out, scything through the rooms on the other side of the hall. Something detonated in a burst of steam. The Corruptor stepped delicately into the corridor, his legs picking their way through the mess.

Fortunately, he said, *in the future, in* my *future, people will not have need of understanding.*

That's right, Maya. *All they'll need to do is bow.*

Is that not the natural order of things? The Corruptor stepped forward, hands raised, peering into each doorway as he passed.

The natural order is that people hate being slaves, Maya sent. She dropped to her knees, crawling along the wall, hoping to get around behind him and back into the corridor. Glass *clinked* as she brushed it, and the Corruptor stopped dead, turning toward her.

Not my people, he said. *They will love me. They will not even know they are slaves, because they will not be able to conceive of another condition. Obedience will be written into their very flesh.*

I'd rather live free in a messy world than be a slave in a neat one, Maya said.

A smile spread across Ashok's handsome features. *Fortunately, you do not get a choice.*

He pointed at Maya, energy crackling around his fingers, ready to lance through her like a pin skewering a bug to a board. Maya had no illusions that her panoply would protect her, not against *that*. Her breath came fast, and her heart hammered. *Beq. I'm sorry.*

Kit's voice was soft in her ear. "Thirty seconds. I've got a body behind him."

Maya nodded just a fraction.

One of Kit's little bomb-carrying constructs leapt from among the shattered wreckage of the furniture, clawing its way up Ashok's back legs and along his spine. Tentacles unwrapped to grab it, but Kit was already hugging the twisted black flesh tight. The alchemical went off, spattering bits of gore against the walls of the corridor, and something structural in the Corruptor's body broke with a *crunch*. His back half sagged, leaving his front half trailing a dead weight.

Maya ran, pushing every bit of power she had left into a defensive wall. Ashok's beam brushed by, and even a glancing hit was enough to stagger her. She tucked her head and kept running, jumping over his broken hindquarters. She gestured wildly, filling the space behind her with fire and smoke.

"I am getting *tired* of this," Ashok snarled. He was pulling himself around by his forelimbs as his body filled in the massive wound, losing precious seconds scrabbling inelegantly across the unmetal and leaving a massive slick of gore behind him. "You *stupid* girl. What is the *point*?"

Maya darted back out into the control chamber, lungs burning, legs trembling, looking for Gyre. She found him half-conscious on his hands and knees, trying to rise. She grabbed him and hauled him up, and together they limped toward the Gate.

"Ten seconds," Kit said. "Go go go."

"*Sha'deia!*" Ashok screeched. He was in the doorway, getting back to his feet. "You can't run forever."

I don't have to. Maya sent a *deiat* thread to the Gate, reconnecting it to the basement of the Spike. She and Gyre stumbled forward toward the curtain of mist.

The Corruptor raised his hand, and another beam of brilliant light stabbed out. Maya squeezed her eyes shut, kept running, and hoped.

The beam hit the edge of Gyre's *deiat* shield, a bubble that—barely—included Maya. The energy splashed away, the backwash destroying what was left of the control console. The crackling shield flickered and shuddered wildly. Maya had overwhelmed it, back in the Purifier. It wouldn't hold against the Corruptor for more than a couple of seconds.

But a couple of seconds was all she needed. Maya threw herself through the Gate, dragging Gyre behind her.

"You think this will stop me?" Ashok screamed. Maya severed the connection, locking the Gate, but his voice rang in her mind. *There is nowhere you can go that I cannot follow—*

In the depths of the Pit, Beq's device finished its cycle.

It was a strange machine, cobbled together from half a dozen different sources. Ghoul arcana and Chosen, mixed in ways their creators had never intended. A stack of sunsplinters, storing a vast hoard of *deiat* power, and the modified *deiat* shield capable of breaking flux-shielded armor. Circuits to connect and activate it all, and an armored box to lower it to the bottom of the ancient wound.

Xalen had found, in the *Pride in Power*'s archive, a description of the weapons of the old Empire and the principles on which they operated. Nobody else understood it, but she and Beq had worked together. Some chain reactions, once begun, would go on until the energy that sustained them wound down. And even then, like a stopped clock, they waited only for a fresh wave of power to start them up again.

The *deiat* shield flared, hammering the outer shell of the lab into ordinary unmetal. At the same time, the other half of the device sent out a wave of power, reaching out *just so* to prod and press and *squeeze—*

And the sunfire bomb resting on the roof of Ashok's lab came to life.

The colossal heat that had kept Deepfire warm for centuries was an aftershock, a leftover. This was the *true* fire of the sun, a tiny piece of celestial brilliance brought to earth. The lab had withstood it once before, but the patch of broken armor the device had created—impossibly tough by human standards—evaporated in an instant in the face of the wave of raw power.

Maya imagined energy filling the lab, a brilliant radiance that spread to its every nook and cranny, purifying the Corruptor's vile experiments with plasma fire. Walls and floors, jars and arcana, all evaporating in a fraction of a second. And Ashok himself, without time to even blink.

The voice in her head was gone as though it had never been. The palace was shaking, dust sifting down from the ceiling, cracks running through the plaster. No one had thought this far ahead. For a moment, Maya pictured the entire city falling into the gullet of the Pit, people and buildings sliding into that gaping maw and vanishing in the blaze of light at the bottom...

"Maya!" Beq's voice. The shaking was starting to subside. Beq grabbed her, pulled her close, saying her name over and over. "Maya, Maya—"

"Outside," Maya said, her voice ragged. "Please. I need to see."

She let Beq guide her up the stairs, saw Elariel rush past to help Gyre. After an interminable interval, they reached a landing and stepped out onto a broad balcony—

—and into the light.

The Pit had widened, its edges crumbling. Even as Maya watched, the island supporting the Smoking Wreckage gave way, the bridge snapping as the precarious inn finally surrendered to the void. A vast breath of ash and dust had exploded out of the fissure, rising far above the city in a bulbous cloud.

As it cleared, the radiance from the Pit brightened. Maya felt warm air on her face, and as it emerged from the depths of the earth, she saw the brilliant light of the sun.

Epilogue

Maya

"We should go," Beq said into Maya's ear. Her breath was soft and warm.

The room aboard the skyfortress was always comfortably cool, but Maya was nonetheless sheathed in sweat. Beq, curled naked on the bed beside her, was no better off, her breathing still ragged, her braid half-undone.

"Should we?" Maya said.

Beq propped herself up on one elbow and fumbled her spectacles on. "If you don't want to keep Elariel waiting."

"I shouldn't." Maya groaned and pulled the pillow over her head.

"What's wrong?"

Maya's voice was muffled. "You'll think I'm stupid."

"I won't." Beq lifted the pillow aside.

"What if..." Maya looked away. "What if I can't think of anything to say?"

"Then don't say anything." Beq bent forward and kissed her. "It works with me, doesn't it?"

Maya kissed her back, hungrily, but Beq pulled away before they could get entangled again. She rolled out of bed and went to the washroom, and Maya heard the still-unfamiliar hiss of the shower. She sighed and sat up, resigning herself to the inevitable.

Half an hour later, washed and dressed in fresh clothes, she was in the flitter beside Beq. They dropped away from the vast bulk of the skyfortress toward the city below. They'd moved *Pride in Power* a kilometer or so to keep its shadow from obscuring Deepfire for most of the day. Not that the inhabitants saw much of the sun in any case—wisps of steam rose from the rocks all around the crater, climbing into a layer of hazy cloud.

The reactivation of the sunfire bomb had done more than just widen the Pit. Its initial brilliant illumination had faded—Xalen theorized it was covered in a layer of boiling rock—but it was emitting more heat, and the rising air had forced open fresh channels. There was still a constant breath of warmth from the Pit, but dozens of smaller vents had opened up on the flanks of the mountain and throughout the tunnels. The glaciers that had surrounded Deepfire for centuries were shrinking, snow and ice melting to fill streambeds with unseasonable runoff.

The flanks of the Pit had once been the property of wealthy nobles. Now, where they hadn't toppled into the chasm, they'd gone beyond pleasant warmth into uncomfortable heat. Even the Spike had lost a chunk of its gardens, and it was practically balmy in the palace. It was an inconvenience to the nobles, but a blessing for the rest of the city, especially the tunnelborn huddled at what had once been the edge of livability. Deepfire, Maya suspected, was going to grow quite a bit larger.

"Another procession," Beq said. "Look."

She dipped the flitter, and Maya spotted a double line of Legionaries winding through the street, escorting a carriage adorned with whipping flags. She tried to make out the colors and shrugged.

"Another dux," she said. "I can't tell which."

They'd started arriving in the weeks after the Corruptor's destruction. Maya had kept the Gate closed, fearing retaliation, so the notables of the Republic turned Empire made the trek overland, bringing their guards and retinues with them. She was certain there were centarchs, too, though they were understandably keeping a low profile.

"They know something's happening here, even if they don't know what," Beq said. Her eyes flicked upward to the looming skyfortress, which was proof enough of that.

"*I* don't know what," Maya said. "No one does. That's the problem."

"You'll figure it out."

"It's not my decision."

Beq smiled. "You'll figure it out anyway."

There were, in truth, a great many things to be decided. The Emperor had wreaked havoc on the administrative apparatus of the Republic. Now he was dead—no one apart from Maya and Gyre knew precisely how—and what happened next was a mystery. The duxes and other local authorities had taken the reins, for the moment, but it wouldn't last.

The flitter landed in the palace gardens. Tanax and Varo were waiting for them, along with a militia honor guard. Maya had sent the tunnelborn soldiers home after the battle, but a surprising number had volunteered to stay on, providing order and protection for the city under Tanax's watchful eye. There was talk of setting up some kind of governing council. Xalen, as conversant with the details of long-dead governments as she was in *deiat* esoterica, had taken a stack of books from the skyfortress to ransack for examples.

"Anything exploding today?" Maya said, as Tanax gestured them inside. It was hot enough in the gardens that she wished for short sleeves.

"No more than usual. Another dux turned up."

"Pretty soon we'll have the full set," Varo said.

Maya grinned. "We saw. Did he say what he wanted?"

"Not exactly," Tanax said. "His message said he would be 'open to discussions regarding a path forward.'"

"We're going to have to say something officially," Beq said.

"*Officially* we're still wanted criminals, right?" Varo said.

"Who have a skyfortress," Maya said.

"And with a friend who's a city-sized war construct," Beq said.

"That doesn't mean anyone else recognizes our authority," Tanax said. "They may want to work things out among themselves."

"But they don't know the half of it. Not yet." Maya halted in a long corridor, glancing around to be certain they were alone. She'd taken the others into her confidence regarding the skyfortress's cargo, but it still wasn't general knowledge. "It not just a question of what happens to the Republic. One way or another, we're going to wake those children up."

"Some people won't want to," Varo said. "They don't want things to change."

"Things are changing, whether they like it or not." Maya slipped her hand into Beq's, felt her momentary squeeze. "Sooner or later, new Chosen will be born, now that the Plague isn't culling them. And without the Corruptor to replenish them, the plaguespawn will eventually be wiped out. There's no going back to the old world. But we have a chance to build something better. If we can get it right *now*, then we won't have another tyranny, another war."

"No pressure," Varo said.

Tanax was smiling. "You sound almost like Gyre."

"He may have rubbed off on me a little," Maya admitted. "And I think I've rubbed off on him, too." She coughed. "Now, if you'll excuse me, I have an appointment."

"I'll stay," Beq said. "I have some things to go over with Tanax."

So Maya walked alone down the last few halls. Windows were broken all over the palace, and she could feel drafts of warmth and the smells of the gardens when she passed them. Eventually she stopped in front of a small bedroom on the second floor and—after a moment of hesitation—knocked.

"Come in," Elariel said.

Jaedia lay in the bed, just as she had for so many months. The ghoul sat beside her, one hand on Jaedia's forehead. The centarch's color looked a little better than it had the last time Maya had seen her. *Or is that my imagination?*

"Hello, Maya." Elariel got up. "Here. Sit."

"I..." Maya shifted uneasily. "Are you sure she's ready?"

"I'm sure. I've been keeping her under the last few days, just to be certain."

"Okay." Maya took a deep breath, sat down, and blew it out. "Now what?"

Elariel laid a finger on Jaedia's forehead, just for a moment, then stepped away.

"I'll leave you for a bit," she said.

"Wait," Maya said.

Elariel raised her eyebrows. "Something wrong?"

"No. Just... thank you. For this. For everything."

Elariel grinned. "It's a good first step. We've got a lot of work to do."

Maya nodded. Convincing humanity the ghouls weren't as bad as everyone had been taught they were—and vice versa—was a tall order, but it had to be done. *One chance. To stop the next war before it starts.*

No pressure.

Elariel closed the door softly behind her. Maya sat beside her mentor, taking her hand, the skin grown translucent and delicate. She waited. Jaedia's features shifted, her eyes moving under her eyelids.

Then, finally, she woke up.

"Where..." Jaedia turned her head, struggling to focus. "M... Maya?"

"I'm here." Maya squeezed her mentor's hand, blinking away tears. "I have so much to tell you."

Gyre

However eager they might be to embrace the new world, ghouls were still ghouls. They preferred to have a stone roof over their head, ideally one the size of a mountain. Gyre and Elariel left their carriage behind near the northern edge of the crater and made their way on foot into the tunnels.

There were no buildings here, none of the dense habitation of the tunnel entrances on the eastern and western flanks of the city. Before the reignition of the sunfire bomb, these sites, farther from the warmth of the Pit, had been cold even at midsummer. This particular tunnel hadn't been used for *anything* in quite a while, Gyre judged, although that might change soon—the new warmth had already pervaded it, and the walls were slick with runoff from melting ice.

"You could ask them to change you back, couldn't you?" Gyre said as they disembarked.

"I thought about it." Elariel looked down at herself, blushing a little. "I may, someday. But...you remember what that was like for me."

"Painful," Gyre said.

"That does not *begin* to describe it," Elariel said.

"Plus Sarah might have something to say about it," Kit said from Gyre's shoulder. "Although, who knows, being covered in fur might help keep things interesting in bed."

Elariel's blush deepened. "Sarah said I should do whatever makes me feel like *me*. And...I don't know. My life before seems more like a dream."

"I know the feeling," Gyre said. "Take your time, obviously. I was just curious."

"I might have them fix my ears." She touched her ears, frowning. "Human ears just feel so dead. I can't even wiggle them."

"I can!" Kit said. "Or I could, back when I had any. Funny story, actually, when I was getting the Leviathan running again, I found what was left of my old body still sitting up there! It looked better than I expected. I've always had a very attractive skeleton, if we're being honest, and it was nice to see it on full display."

"That's more horrifying than funny," Gyre said.

"What'd you do with it?" Elariel said.

"Chucked it in the recycler," Kit said promptly. "No point in being sentimental."

After a short walk, they came to a section of tunnel closed off with wooden walls into something like proper rooms. A construct, human-oid and sleeker than one of Kit's, waited outside the front door. It bowed and opened the way at the sight of Gyre, who couldn't help bowing back.

Inside, the space was a strange mix of human and ghoul furnishings. The furniture Gyre had acquired in Deepfire, but the inhabitants had altered it to their own specifications, lowering the chairs and disassem-bling the beds to turn into floor-level nests. A wooden table supported several weird, multiarmed arcana, with multijointed limbs and inter-locking lenses. An analytica, a cubic mesh of minuscule shifting rods, sat among them.

Warasiel was waiting for them, his huge eyes bright, tabby-pattern fur rippling. He gave Gyre a deep bow, ears twitching.

"Welcome," he said. "We are honored by your visit."

"I've told you it's not that great an honor," Gyre said. "Don't make me out to be so important."

Warasiel clearly didn't believe a lick of this. Stories of what had hap-pened to the Corruptor and Gyre's part in it had been circulating inside Refuge, thanks to a plan that Elariel and Kit had cooked up. Through patient trial and error, Kit had discovered a path through the shifting maze of tunnels that surrounded the ghoul city. Her constructs had slipped inside, unnoticed. They'd contacted certain ghouls of Elariel's acquaintance, delivering notes and stories from the outside.

Tyraves and the Geraia, it turned out, had kept the rest of the popu-lation completely ignorant of what was happening. There were quite a few, especially among the younger ghouls, who were more than eager to have a connection with the rest of the world. Gyre had arranged to host a small but growing group of them near Deepfire, hiding them from the city until he and Maya thought both sides were ready. In the meantime, the ghouls were enthralled with human culture, learning the language with staggering ease and devouring the books he and Elariel brought them. An unfortunate side effect, from Gyre's point of view, was that the young ghouls treated him like some kind of king, or at least an honored elder.

"We had another new arrival," the ghoul said. "Miphania. She disobeyed her elder's wishes"—a grave crime, for a ghoul—"and traveled alone for weeks. She is most anxious to meet some humans."

"Hopefully I won't disappoint her," Gyre said.

"Of course not—"

"It was a joke," Gyre said. "I'd be happy to see her. But first there was that... other thing. Is it ready?"

"Yes, as we promised!" Warasiel said. "This way."

"What's this?" Kit said. "Nobody told me about a new project."

"Hush," Gyre said. "I'll show you."

"Don't tell me to hush," she fumed, hopping up and down on his shoulder. "Are you keeping secrets now?"

"It's a surprise," Gyre said. "I thought you liked surprises."

Kit fell silent as they moved through the little complex. Other ghouls were at work, pausing whatever they were doing to bow to Gyre, while around them dozens of constructs of every size and shape imaginable scurried about. Every time Gyre saw the place, his mind lit up with the possibilities. *If we can get people past their prejudice, no one would need to do a dangerous job again.* Constructs could dig the mines and plow the fields. *The world would never be the same.*

That was for the future, though. They stopped in front of another door.

"It's in here," Warasiel said. "Shall I... ah... activate it? Or would you like to?"

"I think it's better if it's just the three of us," Gyre said. "Elariel can do it."

"Of course." Warasiel handed a lumpy part to Elariel, then bowed again and withdrew.

Gyre opened the door. The room was small, with a low bed on one side and not much else. Something was sitting on the bed, draped in a long white sheet that brushed the floor.

"Okay," Kit said. "That's enough patience. *What* is going on here?"

"It's . . . Well. A bit embarrassing." Gyre grinned. "I wanted to thank you."

"To *thank* me?" Kit's little spider hopped from limb to limb. "Why? For what?"

"I'm not sure I can even make a list." Gyre blew out a breath. "I feel like the rest of us take you for granted, to be honest. I've lost count of the number of times you've saved my life now. You pitched our tents, relayed our messages, fought for us, *died* for us, over and over. When I sat down to think about it, it's extraordinary."

"Okay, now *I'm* blushing again," Kit said. "Except no face, et cetera."

"Sorry," Gyre said.

"I didn't say *stop*," Kit said. "Can we build a statue of me? Not too big, don't want to be tasteless, but it should be solid gold. Maybe one of those that has one leg on each side of a street, right, and when you go underneath I'm not wearing any—"

"You'd have to ask Maya about a statue," Gyre said with a smile. "Elariel and I had something else in mind."

"While I was working with you on the Leviathan, I found some interesting things," Elariel said. "After the battle, I reverse engineered the technique that keeps your bodies connected to the Core Analytica. It's actually not complicated—there's a resonant liquid, and the bodies contain a small sample— Well." She held up the part Warasiel had given her. "What it comes down to is with one of these and the right analytica, we can make any construct part of the swarm."

"That's great," Kit said. "Can I have one of those big war-beds like Naumoriel's?"

"Probably," Gyre said. "But we've got something else for you."

He nodded to Elariel, who went over to the sheet-covered thing. She lifted up one corner of the shroud and placed the little resonator inside, touching it for a moment to seal it in place with *dhaka*.

"*Whoa*," Kit said. "That...feels weird. *Really* weird. Are you...did you..."

"Try moving it," Gyre said.

Under the sheet, something shifted. Slowly, with a great deal of wobbling, the construct stood up. Its covering slid away.

"I...how?"

"I found your original body, too," Elariel admitted. "I stole a couple of bones, just little ones. I was hoping you wouldn't be mad at me. Did you know that every piece of your flesh contains the blueprint for the whole thing? Warasiel and the others helped, but it wasn't that different from some of our standard techniques. And..."

The likeness, Gyre thought, was almost perfect. The construct was still nearly bald, with only a peach fuzz of Kit's teal hair, but the rest of her body looked as he remembered it—lithe and short, with an indefinable energy, as though always ready to explode into emotion. Her features, and the wild look in her huge blue eyes, were instantly recognizable.

They'd dressed the construct in a light shirt and loose trousers. Kit moved slowly, fascinated by the fabric sliding over her skin. Then, eyes widening in delight, she pulled out the front of the pants and looked inside.

"It may not be perfect," Gyre said. "Warasiel tells me that interfacing some of the sensoria with the analytica may take some fine-tuning—"

Kit threw herself across the room, grabbing Gyre by the shoulders and wrapping her legs around his waist. Gyre staggered back a step under her weight, coming to rest against the wall. She kissed him with a hot and desperate need, but only for a moment. Then she broke away. Her nose was running, and there were tears at the corners of her eyes. She looked abruptly uncertain, almost scared.

"Do you still...I mean...are we...?"

"Partners," Gyre said.

"Who spend time naked together?" Kit said.

Gyre leaned forward and kissed her.

Eventually Elariel coughed and left the room.

Acknowledgments

I'll never quite get used to finishing series. I plan them out, but it always seems like too big a project to imagine that one day I'll just be *done*. And yet, one day at a time, here we are, and it's time to put this down and work on the next thing.

See *Ashes of the Sun* for the origins and inspirations that led me to this point. For this book in particular, I want to thank the usual suspects:

Brit Hvide, my editor, whose insight and support has been invaluable. Also everyone else at Orbit: Natassja Haught, Ellen Wright, Angela Man, Paola Crespo, Alex Lencicki, Stephanie A. Hess, Lauren Panepinto, Bryn A. McDonald, Rachel Hairston, and Tim Holman.

Seth Fishman, my agent, who makes all this happen, and his team at the Gernert Company: Jack Gernert, Rebecca Gardner, Will Roberts, Nora Gonzalez, and Ellen Goodson Coughtrey.

My wife, Casey Blair, who in addition to her excellent contributions helping me work out plots and characters, has been the best pandemic companion one could ask for. She helped keep me sane, and hopefully vice versa.

And, most of all: Zeralyn Max, born 3/19/22. Thank you for joining us, and someday you will get to read about my gooey monsters.

Glossary

agathios (pl. agathia)—a person in training to be a **centarch**. The **Twilight Order** searches out children with the ability to touch *deiat* and trains them as agathia from a young age. Agathia become full centarchs on being granted their **cognomen**.

alchemy—the process of refining and recombining ghoul **arcana**. Even broken, rotten remnants of the ghouls' organic "machines" can be rendered down into useful by-products, from which an alchemist can create **quickheal** and other medicines, bombs, powerful acids, and a variety of other tools depending on the materials available. The **Twilight Order** forbids alchemy and considers its products *dhak*, so the practice is more common in the **Splinter Kingdoms** than in the **Dawn Republic**. A few alchemicals, like quickheal, are so useful that the Order considers them legal, **sanctioned arcana**, provided they are made by a few carefully controlled suppliers.

arcana—any tool or implement of **Elder** origin, from rare and powerful weapons like **haken** or **blasters** to **alchemical** creations like **quickheal**. Common people generally have little understanding of the differences between types of arcana.

auto—a **Chosen** ground vehicle. Oval-shaped with a curved bottom, it floats half a meter above the ground and has seats for four to eight passengers. It requires a **sunsplinter** to power itself, and it can only function on a **repulsion grid**. In the present day, they are used only in **Skyreach**.

Auxiliaries—one of the two major branches of the armed forces of the **Dawn Republic**, along with the **Legions**. The Auxiliaries are by far the larger force but, unlike the Legions, carry no **arcana** weapons and armor, relying on ordinary human-made swords, spears, and bows. They are responsible for policing, keeping order, and local defense against bandits and plaguespawn, under the command of the local **dux**. Sometimes called by the derogatory nickname "Auxies," especially by criminals.

banners—the subgroups of the **Khirkhaz Commune**, rebels against the **Dawn Republic**. Named for their use of the Commune's flag in colors other than the main group's red: Whites, Greens, and Blacks. Famously fractious and prone to rivalry.

bird—Ordinary birds are common, but the term often refers to the large, flightless varieties used as beasts of burden. See **loadbird**, **swiftbird**, and **warbird**.

"black spider"—Maya's name for the creature—construct or plaguespawn—that controlled first Hollis Plaguetouch and then Jaedia. Resembling a fat-bodied spider or tick, the creature attaches to the back of a human's neck and is apparently able to control their actions and use *dhaka*, though not make use of *deiat*. The host retains consciousness and some autonomy, and Jaedia was able to resist temporarily under extreme conditions. When removed, it leaves behind poison that kills the host, though Maya was able to prevent this in Jaedia's case. Maya destroyed the spider, but it is not known if it was the only one of its kind.

blaster—an **arcana** weapon that uses *deiat* in a crude fashion, firing bolts of pure energy that explode on impact. Like any arcana making use of *deiat* on its own, blasters are powered by energy stored in **sunsplinters** and are useless once the energy is expended. The **Legions** use blasters as their standard ranged weapon. Pistol and rifle variants both exist, with the latter having greater range. Since charged sunsplinters can only be acquired from the **Twilight Order** or occasionally scavenged from ruins, functioning blasters are very expensive and a mark of status.

centarch—one of the elite warriors of the **Twilight Order**, capable of wielding *deiat* through a **haken**, unlike all other **humans**.

Chosen—one of the **Elder** races, along with the **ghouls**. All Chosen could use *deiat*, without the aid of tools like **haken**, and this power made them unchallenged rulers of a continent-spanning empire for centuries, with **humans** serving them. They were wiped out by the **Plague**, but in their final years, they founded the **Dawn Republic** and the **Twilight Order** to help humanity survive in their absence.

cognomen—**Humans** in the former **Chosen** Empire have either only a given name or a given name and a family name for city dwellers and elites. In addition, some people have a cognomen, a third name that describes some aspect of their history, character, or appearance. Cognomen are granted by general acclamation, not chosen, and trying to pick one's own cognomen is the height of arrogance and opens one to mockery. Cognomen are not always complimentary but can be very hard to shake once applied. They are often two-word compounds: Rottentooth, Boldstep, Halfmask.

For **centarchs**, cognomen have a greater significance. They are granted, not by the centarch's peers, but by the **Kyriarch** Council when an **agathios** reaches the status of a full centarch. The cognomen matches the way the centarch manifests *deiat*, and the Council often chooses names held by past centarchs, with the oldest names conveying the most favor and honor.

Commune—The **Khirkhaz** Commune is a rebel organization trying to free Khirkhaz from the political control of the **Dawn Republic**. It was created by Apphia Kotzed, who convinced several independent rebel movements to come together and declare a single purpose. The individual groups retain a great deal of independence, and central control is often nominal.

construct—a semiorganic autonomous servant created by the **ghouls** using *dhaka*. Constructs come in a huge variety of shapes and sizes, but many are roughly humanoid, with specialized construction for their particular role, such as armor, weapons, or extra limbs. They are typically built of artificial muscle layered over a metal skeleton, and resemble **plaguespawn**, although the latter are much more chaotic and strange. A device called an analytica provides the construct's ability to understand instructions and make decisions, but only the ghouls understand how these function.

Dawn Republic—a nominally democratic state created by the **Chosen** as their numbers dwindled during the **Plague**. Originally, the Republic encompassed all the land that had been part of the Chosen Empire, but in the four hundred years since the Plague, much of the territory has broken away, forming smaller polities collectively known as the **Splinter Kingdoms**. Even so, the Republic remains the most powerful nation in the known world, with its capital at the old Chosen city of Skyreach.

The Republic has a sometimes uneasy relationship with the **Twilight Order** and its **centarchs**. The Order was charged by the Chosen to defend the Republic and humanity, but not to rule it, and so normally stands apart from the daily running of Republican politics. However, the centarchs collectively wield unmatched power, and the Republic's elite military forces, the **Legions**, rely on Chosen-built weapons and armor that only the Twilight Order can maintain. The upshot is that the wishes and suggestions of the Order carry considerable weight with the Republic government, and centarchs are legally empowered to dispense justice and commandeer any necessary resources in pursuit of their missions.

The Republic is ruled by a Senate, which is theoretically elected, but the franchise is restricted to the wealthy, and senators almost always come from a small group of powerful families. The Senate elects two consuls every year to serve as chief executives. The Senate appoints a dux as military commander and chief magistrate to the various regions of the Republic, typically one per major city. The **duxes** command the **Auxiliaries**, who handle policing and local defense, with the Legions retained under the consuls' direct control or seconded in small detachments as needed.

Deepfire—a city deep in the Shattered Peak mountains. Deepfire is an exclave, considered **Dawn Republic** territory in spite of being far outside the Republic's borders, connected by a **Gate** under the **Chosen** fortress known as the Spike.

Originally, the mountain that stood where Deepfire is now hosted a major **ghoul** city—perhaps the ghoul capital, though stories are conflicted. The Chosen deployed a weapon of unparalleled destructive power against it. While the nature of the weapon is unknown, it blasted the mountain into a kilometers-wide crater and left a giant fissure in the rock known as the Pit. Immediately afterward, the Chosen forces began a systematic purge of the surviving ghoul tunnels.

As the Chosen died out, the **Twilight Order** continued the purges. Humans from the surrounding areas flocked to the crater, since heat from the Chosen weapon—still burning at the bottom of the Pit—kept it warm in the depths of winter, and the Order and **Legion** presence provided protection from **plaguespawn**. Scavenging in the tunnels eventually became a major industry, and the Order maintained their presence to manage it.

Modern Deepfire is a divided city. The crater has long since been filled with buildings, and the edge of it marks the formal boundary of the Republic. Beyond that, the mountain is riddled with tunnels, and the people who live in them are called tunnelborn. Tunnelborn are not Republic citizens, and manufactories set up to exploit their cheap labor have become the city's second primary industry. Tension between the tunnelborn and the Republic citizens living aboveground is common, exacerbated by the plentiful opportunities for smuggling and corruption available to Republic officials.

deiat—the power of creation, the fire of the sun. The **Chosen** could draw *deiat* energy to accomplish a wide range of spectacular feats, from destructive manifestations like balls of flame or bursts of raw force to defensive barriers and more. It could also be used to create unnatural substances, like the indestructible **unmetal**. More advanced uses of *deiat* required specialized tools, now called **arcana**. These devices, when powered by a *deiat* wielder, could accomplish wonders—the **Gates** that wove the Empire together and the skyships and skyfortresses that hovered overhead are notable examples, in addition to more mundane tools like **blasters**, watch charms, water treatment facilities, and so on.

Deiat does have limits. It manipulates physical objects and properties—force, temperature, and so on—and does not interact with biological systems at any level except the crudely destructive. *Deiat* tools also require a continuous flow of power, either from a wielder or a storage device like a **sunsplinter**, and cannot operate without the will of the wielder. In particular, the autonomous **constructs** used by the **ghouls** are impossible to create with *deiat*.

With the Chosen wiped out by the **Plague**, the only wielders of *deiat* remaining are the **centarchs** of the **Twilight Order**, who can use their **haken**—themselves a *deiat*-created tool—to draw *deiat* power, though more weakly than the Chosen could. Why some **humans** have the ability to wield *deiat* and others do not is unknown. Centarchs are typically limited to a particular class of effects—fire, ice, force, and so on—although all can use *deiat* to power arcana such as Gates and **panoply** belts. Only the most primitive of construction techniques are still practiced, but existing unmetal can be reforged and reshaped, allowing the creation of the armor of the centarchs and the **Legions**.

dhak—Originally, this term referred only to **ghoul arcana** produced using *dhaka*. In the centuries since the **Plague War**, its meaning has expanded, and it is now synonymous with unsanctioned arcana—arcana not in the very narrow categories approved for safe use by the **Twilight Order**. Possession of *dhak* is illegal in the **Dawn Republic** and grounds for immediate imprisonment or even execution, at the discretion of the arresting official.

dhaka—a form of supernatural power, distinct from *deiat*, originally wielded by the **ghouls**. *Dhaka* allows a wielder to influence biological systems and processes, to accelerate, change, or even give a semblance of life to nonliving things. It can heal wounds and alter living creatures and was used by the ghouls to create a great variety of living and semi-living tools—light sources, weapons, even vehicles. The most noteworthy were **constructs**, automata that could accept orders and act independently, a type of creation impossible even for the **Chosen**.

Any **human** can learn to wield *dhaka*, though the practice can be very dangerous and much knowledge has been lost. After the **Plague War**, the dying Chosen created the **Twilight Order**, and one of its central commandments was to stamp out the knowledge and practice of *dhaka* forever. This has proven difficult, and the Order pursues *dhakim* down to the present day.

dhakim—a human wielder of *dhaka*. Illegal under penalty of death in the **Dawn Republic**, and even in the **Splinter Kingdoms**, often shunned and likely to be hunted down by **centarchs**. *Dhakim* are widely seen as mad, conducting gruesome experiments and creating horrible diseases. Adding to this perception is the fact that *dhakim* can exert influence over **plaguespawn**, bringing the mindless creatures under their command. Very occasionally, a *dhakim* will establish a reputation as a healer and come to be accepted by their community.

dux—a military governor appointed by the Senate of the **Dawn Republic**, in charge of a major city and its surrounding region. Commands the **Legion** and **Auxiliary** forces within their area of authority. Sometimes an outsider to the region, sometimes drawn from local elites, depending on political requirements.

Ehrenvare—a **Splinter Kingdom** to the west of the **Dawn Republic**, ruled by a king and a military aristocracy, who fight as **warbird**-riding lancers.

Elder—something of the time before the **Plague War**, approximately four hundred years ago, when the **Chosen** ruled an empire and the **ghouls** lived underground. As most common people are hazy on the distinction between various types of **arcana** and ruins, Chosen and ghoul remnants alike are often referred to generically as Elder.

flitter—a small, relatively inexpensive flying vehicle of the **Chosen**. It resembles a small boat with a curved bottom and typically carries four to six passengers. Powered by a **sunsplinter**, it requires far less *deiat* energy to operate than a true **skyship**, but it can only function over a **repulsion grid**. In the present day, they are used only in **Skyreach**.

Forge—the headquarters of the **Twilight Order**, a mountain fortress not far from **Skyreach**. Built with the help of the **Chosen** at the Order's founding, it is a colossal complex, large enough to accommodate the entire Twilight Order even at its height. As the numbers of **centarchs** have shrunk over the centuries, the Forge is now largely empty. It has three **Gates**, the only location to house more than one. The Order's training, storage, and support facilities are located here, as well as the seat of the Council.

Gate—a **Chosen arcana** that allows instantaneous transport from one location to another. A Gate looks like a freestanding **unmetal** arch big enough to admit a wagon. When activated and powered with *deiat*, it fills with a silvery curtain and connects to a target Gate, allowing free passage between the two simply by stepping through.

Because Gates require *deiat* to power them and set their destination, only a **centarch** can activate one, and the Gate network is exclusively used by the **Twilight Order**. Many Gate locations are kept deliberately obscure to prevent enemies of the Order from setting ambushes. In times of extreme danger to the **Dawn Republic**, the Order has used the Gates to transport the **Legions**, giving the Republic military unmatched strategic mobility.

Geraia—the ruling council of the **ghouls** of **Refuge**. Theoretically chosen by acclamation, but in practice a gerontocracy, with the eldest ghouls presiding. Prone to long-winded debates, and famously slow to action, and especially reluctant to do anything that poses the smallest risk of the city being discovered.

ghouls—one of the **Elder** races, along with the **Chosen**. They are basically humanoid in form but fully covered in fur, with wide big-pupiled eyes adapted for very low light and long pointed ears that express their emotional state. They are masters of *dhaka* and produce many **constructs** and biological **arcana**. With the advanced medicine made possible by *dhaka*, ghouls can live for more than four hundred years.

Once spread throughout the Chosen Empire, ghouls were mostly wiped out during the **Plague War**, and **humans** believe them to be extinct. All surviving ghouls live in the city of **Refuge** (known as **the Tomb** to humans), a carefully concealed underground safe haven beneath the Shattered Peak mountains. Ghoul society is almost completely self-contained and egalitarian, with manual labor performed entirely by constructs. Leadership is provided by the gerontocratic **Geraia**, but most decisions are made by slow consensus.

The Chosen taught, and most humans believe, that ghouls began the Plague War with their rebellion, then created the **Plague** and the **plaguespawn** during the conflict. Most ghouls deny this, though the truth of what happened is kept secret even among themselves.

glowstone—an inexpensive light source resembling a glassy stone, producing a dim blue light when shaken hard. An **alchemical** creation and generally **sanctioned arcana**.

Grace—a **Splinter Kingdom** to the north of the **Dawn Republic** and also the capital city of that kingdom, ruled by a monarch known as the Red Queen. The city is built under the canted wreck of the **skyfortress** *Grace in Execution*. **Alchemy** and other ***dhak*** are legal in Grace, and the **Twilight Order** is forbidden. Smuggling *dhak* into the Republic is a major industry.

haken (pl. haken)—the most powerful **Chosen arcana** and the signature weapon of the **centarchs**. Haken resemble bladeless swords, usually adorned with crystals. In the hands of a **human** with the right potential, they allow access to ***deiat***. The wielder can generate a blade of pure energy, shaped according to the manifestation of their talent—fire, wind, force, and so on—and draw power to create a variety of effects or activate other Chosen arcana.

The haken were created by the Chosen in their final days to arm the **Twilight Order** and allow human civilization some access to *deiat*, and the secret of their construction has been long since lost. Fortunately, the centarchs have an instinctive ability to sense haken in general and their own in particular, so when they are lost the Order can generally recover them.

hardshell—a tortoise-like creature used as a beast of burden. Hardshells resemble common tortoises, but on a massive scale, standing nearly two meters tall at the shoulder and three meters at the top of the shell. They are rare and expensive and have to be trained from the egg to be responsive to their handlers' commands. Though slow, they can pull enormous loads and are capable of subsisting on little water and poor forage. They are mostly used in deserts and other badlands where fodder is difficult to find.

human—Humans have always formed a vast majority of the population, both in the former **Chosen** Empire and beyond. After the **Plague War** and the extinction of the Chosen, humans are all that remain, apart from the hidden **ghouls** of **Refuge**.

In the lands formerly ruled by the Chosen, the human inhabitants display some differences from baseline humans in the rest of the world. They display a much wider range of hair, eye, and skin tones, are highly resistant to disease, and heal quickly. Women have control over their fertility and must consciously invoke it in order to conceive.

A tiny minority of humans have the ability to wield *deiat* with the assistance of a **haken**, and these are sought out as children by the **Twilight Order** to be trained into **centarchs**. Humans are capable of learning *dhaka*, though the Order works to suppress this as much as it can.

Inheritance, **the**—the founding text of the **Twilight Order**, written by the **Chosen** to provide guidance after their extinction. It gives a brief history of the Chosen, the **Plague War**, and the destruction of the **ghouls**, lays out the ideals and precepts of the Order, and establishes its basic structure and laws.

Khirkhaz—a region in the southwestern part of the **Dawn Republic**, between the Worldspine Mountains and the coast. While not a **Splinter Kingdom**, it has a traditional local independence under the **Lightning Barons** and the local aristocracy, and it often proves troublesome for the Senate to manage. Currently the home of the **Commune**, a group of rebels against the Republic.

Kyriliarch—one of the twelve members of the Council that leads the **Twilight Order**.

Legions—one of the two branches of the **Dawn Republic** military, along with the **Auxiliaries**. The Legions are small in number but highly trained and equipped with **arcana** weapons and armor. They use **blaster** rifles and distinctive white **unmetal** armor, giving them power that no conventionally armed force can match.

Though they form the core of the Republic's military and can be concentrated against notable threats, the majority of the Legions at any given time are dispersed, sweeping for plaguespawn. The much more numerous Auxiliaries handle local defense, policing, and other duties.

Since only the **Twilight Order** has the ability to recharge **sunsplinters**, reshape unmetal armor, and perform other maintenance, the Legions are ultimately dependent on the Order's **centarchs** to sustain themselves. This makes the Republic as a whole reliant on the Order, which has sometimes rankled Republic leadership. Legionaries are often seconded to the Order for duty combating **plaguespawn** and *dhakim* when the centarchs are spread too thin.

Leviathan—a massive war-construct built by the **ghouls** in the last stages of the **Plague War**. It was intended to be a land-based equivalent to the **Chosen skyfortresses**, and an enormous underground facility dubbed Leviathan's Womb was created to build it, but it remained unfinished at the war's end. Naumoriel assembled the remaining parts to activate it, especially the Core Analytica that serves as its "brain."

Too complex to be controlled by a traditional construct intelligence, the Leviathan had a facility to transfer the mind of a living being into its analytica, for whom it would then serve as a body. In addition to the gargantuan Leviathan itself, it has a swarm of smaller semiautonomous constructs linked to the same controlling intelligence, intended to serve as gatherers for organic material to fuel the Leviathan. Though the Leviathan was crippled by Gyre, Kit's mind was transferred from her dying body to the analytica, and its construct swarm is under her control.

Lightning Baron—one of seven nobles who traditionally rule **Khirkhaz** from the seven **Spires**. Named for the lightning storms of their fortress-homes. There are currently only six Lightning Barons, with the Kotzed family declared traitors to the Republic and their Spire taken by the rest.

loadbird—The most common beast of burden in the former **Chosen** Empire, loadbirds are large flightless birds capable of pulling plows or wheeled vehicles. They look something like emus, standing roughly four feet tall at the shoulder, with a long neck that raises their undersized head much higher. Their legs are overdeveloped and heavily muscled, and their wings are small and vestigial.

Like their cousins **warbirds** and **swiftbirds**, loadbirds are controlled by a combination of reins, whistle commands, and tongue clicks; the better trained and more amicable a bird is, the more likely it can be directed by whistles and clicks alone. Loadbirds can be ridden but are slow and uncomfortable. Bred for strength, they can pull heavy weights alone or in teams.

   Loadbirds eat mostly seeds and insects. They dislike **thickheads**, and clashes between the two species are notorious for causing problems.

nyfa seed—The ubiquitous nyfa bush is a hardy shrub, capable of growing under just about any conditions. It produces acorn-sized oily seeds continuously throughout its growing season. While the seeds are not edible by humans, **loadbirds** and **swiftbirds** love them and can subsist on them indefinitely. **Warbirds** will eat them as well but require insects or rodents to stay healthy.

Order—the **Twilight Order**.

panoply—a type of **Chosen arcana** that creates a defensive barrier, called a panoply field, around the user, absorbing incoming attacks. A panoply needs a constant supply of *deiat* to operate and so is not useful to anyone other than **centarchs**. It will deflect any energy blast or fast-moving object, drawing *deiat* energy from the user in the process.

   A centarch using a panoply is impervious to normal weaponry, and the field will even stop **blaster** bolts or the blade of a **haken**. However, the energy drain to maintain the field in the face of a sustained attack will quickly exhaust the centarch's capacity to draw on *deiat*. Drawing too much power in too short a time will render a centarch unconscious and leave them unable to access *deiat* for several hours. Duels between centarchs are typically fought wearing panoplies, with the loser being the first to be knocked out in this manner.

   Physically, the most common form of panoply is a broad belt of thin silver fabric, worn around the midsection, but other varieties exist with the same function.

Plague—a virulent illness that affected the **Chosen** during the **Plague War**. It was supposedly released by the **ghouls** in their rebellion against Chosen rule, and in spite of enormous efforts at combating it, ultimately proved completely fatal to the Chosen, although it had no effect on humans. It is commonly associated with **plaguespawn**, who appeared around the same time, but the connection is not understood.

plaguespawn—unnatural creatures created with *dhaka* that have afflicted the former **Chosen** Empire since the **Plague War**. It is commonly believed they were originally created by the **ghouls** as living weapons during the conflict, though the surviving ghouls deny this.

Plaguespawn have almost infinitely variable forms. They appear as an assembly of organic parts in a vaguely animal-like shape, mostly muscle and bone, from a variety of mismatched sources. They can be as small as mice or as large as elephants, and there are stories of even bigger monsters. In spite of their hodgepodge, ramshackle appearance, they are universally vicious, fast, and deadly.

While they use animal matter in their bodies, plaguespawn are not biological creatures in the normal sense, and they are powered by *dhaka*. They do not eat, excrete, or reproduce as true animals do. Instead, their sole drive is to find and kill animals, the larger the better, and humans above all others. After killing its prey, the plaguespawn disassembles the corpses using *dhaka* and incorporates them into itself, sometimes completely altering its own form in the process. Plaguespawn thus grow larger the more they kill, though there may be an ultimate upper limit on this process.

It's not well understood how new plaguespawn come into existence. Small plaguespawn have been observed to "bud" from larger ones, and areas infested with plaguespawn tend to become more infested over time. On the other hand, areas swept clean for years can suddenly be subject to plaguespawn outbreaks. One theory is that the **Plague** itself is still present in the atmosphere and periodically causes plaguespawn to form spontaneously. The **Twilight Order** maintains that plaguespawn outbreaks are caused by *dhak* and *dhakim*, and hunts them relentlessly.

Dhakim do have a connection to plaguespawn through *dhaka*, and can exert control over them. Absent this control, the monsters are nearly mindless, driven only to hunt and kill. The more powerful the *dhakim*, the more and larger plaguespawn they can control.

The threat of plaguespawn is ubiquitous throughout the former Chosen Empire. In the **Dawn Republic**, a large part of the **Legions** at any given time are engaged in plaguespawn sweeps, repeated at multiyear intervals throughout Republic territory. Along the borders, the **Auxiliaries** keep constant watch for incursions. This keeps Republic territory reasonably safe from plaguespawn attack, though the effort involved is enormous and periodic outbreaks still occur. In the **Splinter Kingdoms**, with their lesser resources, such sweeps are impossible and plaguespawn attacks are a fact of life. Towns and villages are walled, houses are fortified, and travelers go well armed. Fortunately, the mindlessness of plaguespawn means they are usually no match for the well prepared.

Plague War—the conflict that brought about the destruction of the **Elder** races and the fall of the **Chosen** Empire. The specific events of the war have largely been lost in the chaos of the times, but an outline is preserved in the histories of the **Twilight Order**. The **ghouls** rebelled against the rule of the Chosen, and when their rebellion was suppressed they unleashed the **Plague**, which eventually wiped out the Chosen completely. The dwindling Chosen, however, were able to exterminate the ghouls in turn, and then founded the **Twilight Order** and the **Dawn Republic** to help their human former subjects survive in the wreckage of their empire.

The surviving **ghouls** of **Refuge** contest this version of events, but the truth is a well-guarded secret even from their own people.

pony—a small equine sometimes used as a mount or beast of burden. More expensive and less capable than **loadbirds**, **thickheads**, or **hardshells**, ponies are relatively rare, and primarily used as status symbols by the wealthy.

quickheal—an **alchemical** creation that functions as an anesthetic, prevents infection, and promotes rapid healing. It can be made either in a liquid form or as waxy, chewable tablets. **Sanctioned arcana** when produced by an **Order**-approved alchemist.

Refuge—the last **ghoul** city, buried deep under the Shattered Peak mountains. Ruled by the **Geraia** and protected by an army of constructs, its inhabitants are determined to avoid contact with the outside world.

Republic—the **Dawn Republic**.

repulsion grid—a **Chosen arcana** that allows for relatively cheap and easy flight within the grid's boundaries. **Autos** and **flitters** don't require the full power of a **skyship** to stay aloft, but "push" against the buried grid. The only known functioning repulsion grid is beneath the city of **Skyreach**.

sanctioned arcana—**arcana** or **alchemical** products approved by the **Twilight Order** for general use, including **quickheal**, **glowstones**, and other staples. All other arcana and alchemical products are considered *dhak* by the Order. Sanctioned arcana is always expensive and in limited supply, which creates constant problems with smugglers selling *dhak*.

skyfortress—the largest class of **skyship** created by the **Chosen** Empire. Only eight of these massive vessels were ever built. During the **Plague War**, they were used to deliver the most devastating of the Chosen's weapons against the **ghouls**. Of the eight, three were lost over the sea in a last-ditch attempt by the Chosen to find land outside their continent-wide empire, in the hopes of escaping the **Plague**. The other five were either grounded and eventually destroyed, or crashed due to mishap or ghoul attack. One, the skyfortress *Grace in Execution*, overhangs the city of Grace and was the original reason for its settlement.

Skyreach—the capital of the **Dawn Republic** and former capital of the **Chosen** Empire. The heart of Republic wealth and power, and the home of its Senate and ruling class. The huge Chosen buildings that form the heart of Skyreach would be impossible to inhabit, and indeed unstable, without a continuous supply of **sunsplinters** charged with *deiat*. Only here, with the cooperation of the **Twilight Order**, is something like the Chosen's old standard of living maintained. Living in such a tower is a mark of extremely high status, only available to the hugely wealthy and powerful.

skyship—any of the wide variety of flying vessels used by the **Chosen**. These ranged from small one-man skiffs to the massive **skyfortresses**, generally taking the form of flattened teardrops, with the pointed end being the bow. They were some of the most advanced and complex **arcana** the Chosen created. Many were destroyed in the **Plague War**, and while the **Twilight Order** maintained a few during the first few decades of its existence, they quickly broke down beyond human capacity to repair. No operational skyships are currently known to exist, though there are always rumors among scavengers.

Spire—one of seven **Chosen** structures in **Khirkhaz**, each a single tall tower with a surrounding wall. The towers are topped by hundreds of long rods, giving them a bristling appearance. Every day at dawn and dusk, violent lightning storms hit the Spires, with many bolts earthing themselves on the protruding rods. No one is certain of the Spires' original purpose, but they are now the seats of the **Lightning Barons** who rule Khirkhaz for the **Republic**.

Splinter Kingdoms—portions of the former **Chosen** Empire that have broken away from the **Dawn Republic**. After the **Plague War**, the Republic asserted authority over the entirety of the old Chosen Empire, but maintaining control over such a vast area proved impossible in the face of rebellions and **plaguespawn** attacks. Some regions were abandoned as the **Legions** retreated to a perimeter they could keep clear of plaguespawn, while other cities declared themselves independent under local rulers or ambitious warlords. The Republic crushed some of these rebellions, but strained resources meant others had to be accepted.

Life in the Splinter Kingdoms is generally more dangerous than in the Republic, without the **arcana**-armed Legions to keep order and suppress plaguespawn. However, this varies greatly from polity to polity. In spite of their name, not all the breakaway states are monarchies—there are free cities, republics, and other political experiments, sometimes changing rapidly as they war with one another. As a general rule, the farther from the Republic they are, the smaller and less stable they become, with larger kingdoms like **Grace**, Meltrock, and Drail stabilized by trade with the Republic.

While *dhak* is illegal in the Republic, its status in the Splinter Kingdoms varies. Some attempt to maintain the Republic's ban, while others, like Grace, embrace *dhak* and encourage its creation and sale. Smuggling across the Republic border is a major business. The **Twilight Order** asserts that its centarchs have the right to go anywhere in the old Chosen Empire to hunt *dhak* and *dhakim*, but as a practical matter some Splinter Kingdoms are openly hostile to Order agents, and they must move secretly there.

sunsplinter—an **arcana** device that serves as a *deiat* battery, storing power for future use by other arcana. Most notably used by **blasters** as a power source. Only someone with a connection to *deiat* can refill one, so fully charged sunsplinters are rare and expensive.

sunstone—an **arcana** light source, powered by *deiat*, which produces bright white light. Controlled by *deiat* and requiring periodic infusions of power to keep operating, so used only by the **Twilight Order** or Republic elites.

swiftbird—a cousin of the **loadbird** and the **warbird**, specialized for riding. Generally resembles a loadbird, but with longer, leaner legs. Contrary to its name, the swiftbird specializes not in speed but in endurance. A warbird might outrun one over the course of a short charge, but a swiftbird can keep up a rapid pace for ten to twelve hours a day with sufficient food and water, allowing riders to cover long distances.

thickhead—a large reptilian creature used as a beast of burden. Thickheads resemble giant lizards, with short tails, tough, scaly skin, and bony protrusions around their skulls. They are tremendously strong and can pull very heavy loads, although their fastest pace is not much more than a walk. They are also very sure-footed and can traverse almost any terrain. Slow and expensive to maintain compared to **loadbirds**, they're used for particularly heavy burdens or as pack animals over bad roads.

Though thickheads look fierce, with their beaks and spiked skulls, they are pure vegetarians and display almost no aggressive behavior. Their smell tends to rile loadbirds, who sometimes snap at them or shy away. When threatened, a thickhead lowers itself to the ground and puts its forepaws over its face, protecting its vulnerable eyes and belly and relying on its tough hide to repel an attacker. Once hunkered down, they are notoriously difficult to get moving again.

"Thing, the"—Maya's name for the small **arcana** implanted in her flesh above her breastbone. Baselanthus put it there when she was a little girl, telling her it would prevent the regular illnesses that threatened her health. He and Jaedia taught her to keep it secret, since it could be viewed as *dhak*. During her emotional fight with Gyre in Deepfire, Maya found the Thing growing hot enough to sear her skin, and not long afterward, she was sick with a violent fever.

Tomb, the—human name for the legendary last city of the **ghouls**, assumed to be extinct, which is full of fantastic treasure. See **Refuge**.

Twilight Order—an organization created by the dying **Chosen**, in the last days of the **Plague War**, to give humans the ability to use *deiat* and sustain civilization after their extinction. Key to this purpose are the **haken**, Chosen **arcana** that allow the few humans capable of drawing on *deiat* to wield its power.

The purposes of the Twilight Order are to defend humanity as a whole, especially from plaguespawn and ghouls; to suppress knowledge of *dhaka* and destroy *dhakim*, as part of that defense; and to make sure the power of *deiat* is wielded for the common good. These themes are laid out in a book called the **Inheritance**, which details the history of the Chosen and the Plague War and explains the goals of the Order.

The core of the Order are the **centarchs**. Every **human** capable of wielding *deiat* that the Order can locate is brought to the **Forge** to become an **agathios**, a centarch trainee under an experienced teacher. When they are deemed ready by their master, usually by their early twenties, they receive their **cognomen** and are declared a full centarch. Apart from the **Kyriliarchs**, all centarchs are theoretically peers, and free to choose their own path, though in practice a great deal of deference is paid to seniority. Centarchs, wielding *deiat* through their haken, travel throughout the **Dawn Republic** and beyond, fighting plaguespawn and hunting *dhak* and *dhakim*.

The governing body of the Order is the Council of twelve **Kyriliarchs**. Generally senior centarchs, these members are nominated by the other centarchs, approved by the Council, and serve for life. Only a majority of the Council can issue directions that centarchs are bound by the laws of the Order to accept. The Council sets broad policy for the Order, directs centarchs to particular areas of trouble, and rules on intra-Order disputes and transgressions.

In addition to the centarchs, the Order includes support staff of several sorts. The Forge is maintained by hereditary families of servants, who do manual labor in the fortress. An extensive logistics service handles supplies and tracks the vast storehouse of arcana the Order maintains, and a courier service uses the **Gates** to provide rapid delivery of information. Arcanists help maintain equipment and work with centarchs in the field to research arcana. Another group, euphemistically called scouts rather than spies, supports the centarchs directly on missions and maintains outposts and intelligence-gathering operations throughout the Republic and the **Splinter Kingdoms**, working undercover where the Order is not welcome.

While the Order is not in charge of the Republic, nor subject to the instructions of the Republic Senate, the two groups maintain an uneasy but close relationship. The *Inheritance* instructs the Order to stay out of mundane politics, to preserve its independence and reduce the temptation to corruption. But the Order has traditionally been willing to intervene when the Republic is threatened, and the power of the centarchs is the ultimate guarantor of the Republic's continued status as the most powerful nation in the remains of the Chosen Empire.

unmetal—a material used by the **Chosen** for a wide variety of purposes. Unmetal is lighter than steel but enormously stronger, essentially indestructible except against *deiat*. Even *deiat* takes significant time and effort to damage it. It can have a variety of colors and finishes but is usually identifiable by its iridescent sheen.

With the fall of the Chosen, the means of creating unmetal has been lost, but large amounts remain from various Chosen ruins. Modifying and repurposing them is obviously a challenge, however. The **Twilight Order** retains a limited capacity to reforge unmetal, which it uses to create equipment for its members and the **Legions**.

vulpi (pl. vulpi)—a livestock animal raised for meat, with a unique life cycle. They are omnivores and will eat nearly anything, but can thrive on grasses and weeds. Vulpi are born small and helpless, but rapidly grow into boisterous, playful creatures resembling both pigs and weasels. This yearling phase lasts for approximately their first year or two. Toward the end of it, they mate repeatedly, and females store enough sperm to last for the rest of their lives. They then mature into breeders, nearly doubling in size and becoming squatter and ill-tempered. For the following year or more, the females will give birth to litters of pups every eight to ten weeks.

Finally, the mature vulpi enter their final stage of life, during which they are called terminals. They become sessile, increase enormously in size (up to tenfold if provided with plenty of feed), and their legs atrophy and are eventually lost in the vast bulk of their bodies. In this phase they are extremely efficient eaters and produce little waste. On their own, terminals simply die of starvation, but properly tended and eventually slaughtered they produce large amounts of high-quality, pork-like meat. Vulpi is a staple throughout the **Dawn Republic** and the **Splinter Kingdoms**. Culled at the yearling or breeder stage, they can also provide useful leather and other by-products.

warbird—A rarer cousin of **loadbirds** and **swiftbirds**, warbirds are large, flightless birds bred for combat. They resemble loadbirds but retain larger wings, which they flap for stability while kicking. Unlike their more docile cousins, warbirds have long talons on their toes and a sickle-like claw on the back of their foot, and are capable of tearing an unarmored human to shreds.

In battle, warbirds are typically equipped with armor and have blades affixed to their beaks, while carrying an armored rider who fights with a lance or spear. Outside the **Republic** (where the **Legions** with their **arcana** weapons remain the dominant force) warbird-riding cavalry is often the preeminent military arm.

Warbirds are more difficult to train than their cousins, and more expensive to keep, eating mostly large insects and rodents. They are therefore expensive, and owning one is usually a mark of status.

About the author

DJANGO WEXLER is the author of the Shadow Campaigns novels. He graduated from Carnegie Mellon University in Pittsburgh with degrees in creative writing and computer science, and worked for the university in artificial intelligence research. He is also the author of a series of middle-grade fantasy novels, *The Forbidden Library*, *The Mad Apprentice*, and *The Palace of Glass*.